# Shopping for a Billionaire's Wife

## JULIA KENT

# Shopping for a Billionaire's Wife

SHOPPING FOR A BILLIONAIRE
BOOK FOUR

JULIA KENT

# Shopping for a Billionaire's Wife

*by Julia Kent*

**Who needs a SWAT team to escape from their own wedding? Me.**

My Momzilla turned us into hostages at our own ceremony, so Declan and I are getting married the good old-fashioned way, just like everybody else.

By calling in his private security team, stealing away before the ceremony by helicopter, connecting to his corporate jet and heading for Las Vegas.

The Boston wedding of the year is about to become a trashy Elvis drive-thru ceremony.

Until the best man spills the beans and Mom, Dad, my sisters, his brothers, my maid of honor, my friend Josh, and even my cat, Chuckles, all come along for the ride.

I can't win, can I?

Oh. Yeah. I already did.

Love conquers all.

Even my crazy family.

* * *

*Shopping for a Billionaire's Wife* is the next book in the *New York Times* and *USA Today* bestselling Shopping for a Billionaire series. After Declan convinces Shannon to escape from their own wedding minutes before the ceremony begins, the madcap adventures are just getting started. When the mother of the bride pries their location out of the tortured best man, the whole crazy crew follows the bride and groom to Las Vegas in this romantic comedy from Julia Kent.

# Acknowledgments

To my reader group, <u>Laugh Your Way to Love</u>, I thank you for your encouragement, your wackiness, and your support. You folks are fabulous, and a joy to interact with on a daily basis.

To my amazing husband, thank you for sending me off to Vegas with threats if I didn't indulge myself ;) .

To Daisy, who recommended the tapas bar at the resort next to mine, thus inspiring one of the scenes in this book.

To Sean, who helped with accuracy in my baccarat scenes.

To my kids. I always say "after this book I'll slow down" and you always understand. Guess what, guys? This time, it's for real. <3

# Chapter One

"They look like ants," I shout to Declan as the helicopter lifts me away from the crazy chaos of my mother's insane wedding. I do not speak in error. That wedding? That's not *my* wedding. It's not *Declan's* wedding.

It's *my mom's* wedding, and the relief mixed with terror that pumps through my bloodstream right now confirms that I'm doing the right thing.

My inertia, combined with my future father-in-law's huge error in giving her a bottomless wallet to spend on the wedding, turned my mother into a Momzilla.

A tiny speck of a screaming, frothing Momzilla.

Is it my fault the grin that spreads across my face makes me feel like Dr. Evil? No.

It's *her* fault.

Declan's arm is around my shoulders. He's bent forward, our seat belts firmly on but our bodies leaning so we can look out the window. We can't hear a thing, but my mother is jumping in the air like a trained poodle leaping for a snack.

Except poodles don't look that murderous.

The crowd moves like one entity, the edges coalescing and flowing forward, toward Mom, as people realize something's gone wrong.

*We've* gone wrong. Me and Declan. The bride and groom have escaped from their own wedding.

Oh, God.

Did I make the right choice? Doubt pours over me like hot fudge on salted caramel ice cream. You know. Like it's a requirement.

The little purse around Declan's waist, called a sporran, buzzes and jolts like it's filled with Mexican jumping beans, leaping and slapping against his crotch.

"You answering that?" I ask. Clearly, this is Declan's phone going nuts with texts and calls.

"No." He shakes his head and settles back into his seat, closing his eyes and letting out a long, extended sigh that stretches back in time about, oh, a year. Back to his proposal.

I've heard that sigh before.

It's the sound of exorcising my Momzilla.

*Bzzzz.*

"Your sporran looks like it's having more sex with you than I've had this week," I note. I have no idea what I was thinking when I imposed a three day pre-wedding abstinence rule on my poor fiancé. When you're apart as much as we are because of his crazy travel schedule, the times we *are* together involve making up for lost time. Lots of making up.

Like, two or three times a day of making up.

Three days without, when we're in the same city, is like twenty years. I would imagine having anything vibrate that close to balls so blue I might as well start calling him Papa Smurf would—

Declan's mouth is on mine before I can continue that thought. The warm press of giddiness tinged with authority makes me melt into him, body twisted to take in his heat. We're ascending amid chaos and noise, the helicopter pilot trusted with our welfare, his job clear:

Get us away from that jumping poodle on the lawn.

Er, my mother.

Declan's tongue pulls me to him, his hands cupping my jaw, his strength guiding me closer and closer to him, until our kiss is all raw energy and desperate need. We've just thrust a giant middle finger at all the people who helped put the gala of the decade together, and even though my fiancé—he's still just my fiancé—is doing his damnedest to get me to think more about Papa Smurf than about Momzilla, I can't.

I break the kiss, breathing hard. Am I panting from panic, desire, or...both?

"We abandoned everyone!" I shout. Panic wins. "Is Amanda okay? She nearly drowned! I'm leaving my bestie in crisis! And my dad—oh, Daddy, I feel so bad."

"Jason's down there absorbing the wrath of Marie, I'm sure," Declan says in a soothing voice. Well, as soothing as you can be when you're shouting above the *pftt-pftt-pftt* of helicopter blades cutting through the air a few feet above us. "And he'll understand. Jason's fine. They all will. And Amanda and Andrew seemed fine, too. It'll all be fine," he soothes.

I scowl. There were a few too many "fines" in there. I'm suspicious. "How can you be so sure?"

"Because I don't give a rat's ass what they think or feel." He gives me a thumbs-up and a big grin.

My turn for that long, exorcising sigh.

"You, on the other hand," he shouts, one hand sliding up my calf and going for the garter, "*you,* I would like to feel very much."

I slap his hand away. He snatches it back like I used a taser on him, his eyes wide and just a little feral. I give him a good, thorough look. God, he's gorgeous. The cut of his dark jacket, short at the waist to show off the kilt that rests like a woman's fingers against his mid-thigh, makes me pause. That McCormick tartan picks up a color that matches those eyes, which are currently looking at me with a mixture of *I want to be in you* and—

Actually, and *nothing*. There is nothing *else* those eyes are saying right now.

"Seriously, Dec? We just fled a thousand-person wedding in our honor and all you can think about is getting above the garter?"

His confusion just increases. "Yes," he answers honestly.

I throw my hands in the air, whacking some sort of strap that stretches behind my shoulder. It begins to flap in the wind as we race toward whatever landing strip we'll use to disembark. As it *fut-fut-futs* against my veil, I realize the wind isn't whipping the long, white lace behind me. When we crawled into the helicopter and Declan put on my harness, he tucked my veil in.

I love him so much.

Yet *someone* has to be the target for my guilt. My confusion. My regret. My joy. My...all of it.

And while we aren't husband and wife just yet, he's got a big red emotional bull's-eye on him right now.

"How can you think about sex at a time like this?" I chirp. We're in a half-open helicopter with a guy who looks like Mad Max piloting this black bird of doom.

"It's my wedding day and I have a case of blue balls so bad that these puppies could be weather balloons right now."

Add in this unmarked helicopter and we're pretty much turning into an episode of *The X-Files*.

"And besides," he adds, "when do I *not* think about sex?"

"When you're sleeping."

He points at me, winks, and then uses the pointer finger to run a slow, sensual line along my neckline. I inhale sharply through my nose and fight the tingle that spreads across my skin.

I don't fight hard, mind you, but I *do* fight.

A little. I try. I try about as hard as Kim Davis trying to issue a gay marriage license.

I fail.

"Even then," he says in a low voice, so quiet I shouldn't be able to hear him above the fracas of the machinery, and yet I can. "Even in my slumber, I dream of you."

As I pull Declan in for a kiss and let my hands say a few vows for me, substituting for the words I was supposed to say right about, oh, *now*, a buzzing begins in a place between us that feels a little too good.

"I didn't know you could make *that* vibrate," I marvel as I snuggle in even closer.

"That's my phone," he says bitterly, pulling the sporran out from between us.

"Oh."

"Don't look so disappointed." He shuts it off completely, then taps the pilot on the shoulder. The two exchange words, and as the sentences fly back and forth I realize I can't understand them. Not because of the noise, but because they're speaking in Russian.

We have a Russian pilot? In an unmarked black helicopter?

I look nervously at Declan and realize how little I really *do* know about him.

Declan frowns at his screen.

"That bad?"

His eyebrows shoot up in amusement. "You think it's anything *but* bad? Shannon, we just ditched our own wedding. There were seven camera crews from various news and entertainment programs covering the damn event. Andrew is being waterboarded by Marie right now to get our destination out of him."

"How tough is he? Will he crack?"

Declan affixes me with a dark look. "You're fluffy and klutzy on the outside, but underneath you're hard core."

My turn to give him a thumbs-up and a grin.

Suddenly, my mouth is occupied by other actions. He tastes so good. Like freedom and promise, like peppermint and wind, like the absence of the desperate clawing sensation that tickled my chest for the past year as this wedding turned into something that separated us, rather than bringing us together.

This escape isn't an act of immaturity. Quite the opposite. It is the only reasonable option in a sea of unreasonableness called Mom.

Yet my conscience just won't stop.

The tears run down my cheeks as the kiss slows, his lips warm and tender against mine, his palm moving across my face with the gentle motion of a man who realizes I'm crying.

And I can't stop.

"It's okay," he says, pulling me in for an awkward embrace. The seatbelt harnesses make any act of intimacy nearly impossible, but Declan's determined. "Go ahead," he murmurs against my face, pulling one earphone off. "Feel what you feel."

And I do, in his arms, racing away from the cacophony of a thousand people who fade as we do exactly what we're supposed to do as husband and wife.

Turn two into one.

As Declan holds me, he grabs his phone and looks at the flood of messages. Is this as bad as it seems?

"Four hundred messages?" he shouts. "I normally have hundreds of text messages a day. I have *four hundred* from the past thirty minutes."

It's *that* bad.

"Um, I'm sure it's not as bad as it seems," I shout, trying to reassure him, even though panic is spreading through me faster than Mark Zuckerberg's fortune giveaway rumors on Facebook.

"An hour ago all I could think about was making sure I said my vows without making a fool of myself. Now I'm wondering if Marie is assembling tactical drones to take us out. And charging the bill to my dad!" Declan says in a firm, clipped voice.

I wince and say nothing, keeping my eyes closed, burrowing into him as he thumbs, and thumbs, and thumbs his way through all those messages, making deep grunts of discontent that alternate between sounding like a Star Wars Wookiee and a Highlander with a chest cold.

Then he lets go of me and types rapidly, pauses, types, pauses —a cycle that becomes maddening as his biceps keep boxing my ear.

I finally pluck the phone from him and read the messages myself. Most of them are back-and-forth missives between Declan and Grace, his longtime admin. But then:

*Answer your damn phone*, Andrew's text says.

*Can't*, Declan has texted back.

*You ass*, he replies. Andrew isn't the most delicate person when it comes to making a point.

*K*, Declan answered.

*K? K? What are you, 13?* Andrew replied. *You owe me big. So big.*

*I know. How about I make you CEO? Oh. Wait*, Declan typed back.

Andrew replied with an emoticon that is too vulgar to describe.

I give up. We escaped. The sight of all one-thousand wedding guests assembled below us like a refugee airlift, only with Champagne and really good cake, lingers in my mind as I begin to softly cry against the leather strap of Declan's sporran. He shifts. I feel his erection, and he clears his throat meaningfully. The sound is so subtle, but I detect it even above the helicopter rotor's auditory domination.

He is wondering whether my crying means he's not getting sex today.

"Stop it," I yell, handing him back his phone.

"Stop what?"

"Wondering if I'll sleep with you today."

"How do you do that?" he bellows, moving his hips just so, taking the pressure off me.

Because I'm right, he can't argue. I thumb through my own phone. Most of the messages are from Grace, Jessica Coffin, various news stations, Mom, Mom, Mom and more Mom in there. She is on the attack, the messages varying wildly from nasty incrimination to desperate pleading, back to the nasties again.

It's like reading a string of text messages during my fights with my ex-boyfriend, Steve, only Mom's language is way more colorful. I think I see Dad in there, too, but after a while it's all a blur. The buzz of the helicopter as we continue makes it hard to concentrate. Hell, the last ninety minutes makes it impossible to concentrate.

What did we just do?

I select one from my sister, Carol, figuring that should be safe.

*Thanks for replacing my Worst Wedding Ever. Mom and I are bonding over this*, she wrote. *Please get married by a Liberace impersonator in Vegas. Mom hates Elvis, but she hates Liberace even more.*

"DECLAN!" I shout, pointing to my phone in horror. "THEY KNOW ABOUT VEGAS!"

Side note: I'm so glad to perform an important emotional function for my sister. Huh.

Dec grunts, the sound full of angry chagrin, and stares out the window, thinking.

Our secret lasted a whopping thirty minutes. It's a record.

I grit my teeth and move on to one from Josh.

*Can I have all your centerpieces?* he wrote.

Delete.

Greg's text says, *Hey! Heard you're going to Vegas. We have some mystery shopping clients there and if you happen to—*

DELETE. How in the hell did they find out?

Amanda. Amanda's my bestie. Her messages will be a supportive balm that will get me through this time of crisis. Plus, she'll tell me who told Mom. I'll bet Andrew cracked. I open the most recent text from her.

*Jessica Coffin is here at your abandoned wedding reception telling three different cable channels all about #poopwatch,* Amanda texted. *Your wedding hashtags are now #smartgroomwhew #poopwatchbride and #runawaybillionaire*

Text messages are so overrated.

Vegas. I'm numb. Mom knows we're going to Vegas.

"Shannon," Declan says, pulling the headphone off my left ear, whispering in a husky voice. "Until ninety minutes ago, my day was pretty simple. Wake up. Take care of business in the shower so I don't turn into Two-Minute Husband on our wedding night—"

"What?"

"Never mind. It's not important." He frowns. "Scratch that. It *is* important, but that's not what I want to talk about now." He shakes his head quickly, then resumes his list, ticking off each item with a finger. "Shave. Go to Farmington Country Club. Wiggle like a space worm being poked by harpoons to get into the damn kilt. Remove underwear. Put on socks and shoes with laces. Add man purse and tux jacket. Grit teeth while Andrew laughs at me. Wait for Andrew to stop laughing. Gently punch Andrew's arm when he won't stop pointing and laughing."

He runs out of fingers and starts over.

"*Really* punch Andrew's arm. Kick Andrew out of the wedding party room with a snarl and a glare. Find you. Find you screaming at Marie. Insert self between you and Marie. Listen to your escape fantasy—"

"That is *not* how the day went—" I protest, but he cuts me off.

"Make the escape happen." His words have such an anguished finality to them. "Here I am. I did it. I succeeded. Victory is mine. Then why do I feel so hollow?"

"Oh, Dec."

The earpiece crackles as the helicopter pilot says a series of disjointed syllables that sound like someone with heated marbles in their mouth trying to sing *The Star Spangled Banner*.

"She's *what*?" Declan says, holding his earpiece tight against his ear. He looks down at me and mutters, "Your mom called the FAA and tried to report this aircraft as a hijack."

"You understood that?"

"You didn't?"

"No." Declan's words sink in. "My mom did *what*?"

"Tried to ground us and have me arrested."

"Arrested? For *hijacking*?"

The pilot says more mumbo jumbo.

"And kidnapping."

"Kidnapping? Is she insane?"

"She was insane long before she tried to have the FAA down this copter."

I grunt, the sound decidedly unfeminine, and whack him in the chest. So much for romance.

"You're hitting me because I'm telling the truth about your mother?" he asks, incredulity flowing like melted butter at an all-night Vegas lobster buffet.

"Yes."

"Maybe the insanity is genetic."

I reach under the kilt, knowing what I'll find, and grab something. He sits up so fast, and so straight, that he bangs his head on the helicopter ceiling. I have a death grip on his joystick.

"That's um, quite a hold you have on—"

"This can go two ways. That is the wonder of our world. We're yin and yang. Good and evil. Black and white," I shout above the noise. "Pain and pleasure." I squeeze, giving him a taste of both. "Love and hate. I know you hate my mother right now. A part of me does, too. But the constant negative comments about her are getting old." I give him an icy glare. He gives me a smoldering look.

I may be breathing hard against his lapels, and my hand may cover his throbbing manhood, heat pouring off it like a glowing fireplace poker, but emotionally, I feel like the San Andreas fault just cracked open between us.

Divided by my mother.

The chopper dips suddenly and I roll into Declan, my seat belt harness tangling with the arm that's under his kilt, the pull of my kinetic readjustment making him yelp.

He takes the opportunity to reach under the tartan and clench my hand, which is not going anywhere.

"Shannon," he says in a voice of warning. I can't tell whether he's turned on or in pain.

Maybe both?

"My mother shouldn't be calling the FAA, and certainly shouldn't sic the bloodhounds on you—"

"Reporting a lie to a federal agency is a bit more than that!"

Our first Christmas as husband and wife is going to really suck if Declan's in federal prison. The man has a point. Mom shouldn't have done that.

I take a deep breath through my nose, and as I'm about to speak, the air becomes a swirling mess, our descent imminent. My veil goes in my mouth, a piece hitting the back of my throat, and I gag, so overcome I let go of Declan's joystick.

The helicopter rights itself. It's almost like I was flying the damn bird when I was holding him.

"Don't ever do that again," he says coldly.

"Do what?" I know he means grab his, um, central processing unit, but...

"Grab me like that when you don't intend to do anything about it."

"Can't do anything about it here!" I insist.

He stares me down. "Remember our second date?"

"You want me to stab you with an EpiPen?"

He flinches, clears his throat, and clarifies. "*Third* date."

I scan my memory. Sex in a limo. Something extra in the helicopter. Ah. Yes.

That clears up my earlier confusion. He's *aroused*.

All four chambers of my heart feel like they're full of concrete.

"I'm sorry." My hand goes to his knee. "I'll make it up to you later." One of the most endearing qualities in Declan is his bluntness. He has no emotional attachment to how others perceive his words. For some people, that would be a source of distress, but for Declan it's how he functions. When he wants an emotional attachment, he seeks it out. Cultivates it. Makes it a part of his soul.

The rest of the world, though?

Meh.

I don't want to be *meh* to him. I stroke the soft inner thigh, the skin responding to my fingers, heavy muscles tensing.

"I'm really sorry," I whisper.

"Shannon," he says, his voice low and suggestive. "You don't have to apologize for groping me. Ever."

As he starts to say more, the pilot cuts in. Sprinkled in between unintelligible words I hear enough. The FAA has been called off. Mom's report has been verified to be untrue.

I pat his leg, feeling him swell underneath.

As we land, I realize this adventure has only just begun.

# Chapter Two

We are at a private airport I've never seen before. The sky is that glorious shade of blue that seems to deepen as you look up, with a smattering of clouds that draw the eye to them. It's a perfect, idyllic July day in Massachusetts.

A great day for an outdoor wedding.

Declan and the helicopter pilot, whose name I never caught, exchange a few words in Russian before I rib my soon-to-be husband and whisper, "Would you please speak in English?"

"Why?"

"*Why?*"

He just stares at me with that intimidatingly blank face.

"That doesn't work, you know," I tell him with a pointed sneer. Or, at least, I try to sneer. I'm not so good at the sneering thing. That's more Jessica Coffin's area of expertise.

He doesn't twitch a muscle. For whatever reason, he doesn't want me to know what he and the pilot are talking about. Fine. Fine!

But this alpha-male dominant crap—you know, the stuff I fell in love with him for—is getting on my nerves.

"Declan, please," I concede.

No change.

The exasperated hiss that comes out of me makes my body flush with fury. "It's our wedding day. I am supposed to be kissing you at the altar right now while the minister pronounces us husband and wife. Instead, I listened to *you* and went along with this crazy scheme to run off to Las Vegas and leave everyone —everyone!—behind."

Side note: I know that's not true. The decision to ditch my mother was mutual. But right now, I have zero leverage, and he's giving me that granite look like he's an Easter Island statue, so I have to find some kind of vulnerability in him.

I'm saving sex for the nuclear option.

His lips purse, jaw grinding, as he finally opens his mouth and says, "No one forced you into the helicopter."

The words feel like knife blades against my heart, scraping lightly rather than plunging straight in. He's right. His eyes fill with a kind of measured kindness, as if he understands I'm falling apart in stages.

I am. The Russian thing isn't helping.

"Why won't you tell me what you're talking about with the pilot?"

"Because it's a surprise."

"Not a surprise that involves swallowing, I hope?"

His sharp intake of air makes me realize what I've, um, hinted at.

"I meant swallowing a *ring*," I clarify, clearing my throat.

Emotion finally flickers in his face.

It's disappointment.

He can play this immutable look game for as long as he wants. Two years ago, it worked. I've lived with this man for nearly a year. I know him intimately now. He knows me thoroughly (though, perhaps, not as intimately as his mother's engagement ring knows me, but let's not go there...).

I leave.

Turning away from him and bumbling out of the helicopter in my tartan-and-white monstrosity of a gown isn't easy, but I accomplish the near-impossible and disembark without assistance. I'm a good twenty feet toward a metal-sided building at this tiny airport before he grips my elbow.

"Shannon, stop."

I keep walking.

"Shannon, I said *stop*." His voice is an emotionless growl. He sounds like a CIA agent barking orders.

The catcalls continue, the voices more numerous.

"Why?" I continue, giving him a taste of his own medicine. I can be cool and composed. I can show no more emotion than a cucumber. I can be neutral and blank, slack and granite, a sophisticated ice queen who gives nothing away.

He stands behind me, a wall of heat pressing against my back, hands on my elbows and stopping me from proceeding. Declan leans down over my shoulder, his lips brushing against my ear, and says:

"Because part of the back of your dress is tucked into your tartan thong."

Oh, crap.

Someone in the distance shouts a single word in Russian. I hear hoots and hollers.

Declan tenses, his fingers finding the piece of offending material that twists in my garters and G-string. Unexpectedly, he makes no suggestive moves, his fingertips nimble and purposeful, focused only on getting me into a state of full dress again.

More Russian is shouted. Shrill whistles and come-ons.

Declan practically pulses with white-hot anger.

Maybe his fluency isn't so great to possess all the time. Especially when a bunch of Russian pilots are ogling your not-quite-wife.

"You're not going to punch the pilot this time, are you?" I demand as I turn around, fluffing out my skirts. My legs do feel really warm suddenly. I wonder just how much skin everyone got to see.

"When have I ever punched a pilot?" he asks, his voice filled with incredulity.

Hah. Gotcha. Made him *feel*.

"You punched the scamming photographer at the mall when you played Santa. The Russian mobster guy."

"He tried to pull a gun on me!"

I have to give him that.

"What did the helicopter pilot *say*?" I ask.

Declan gives me a dark look, his hands on my hips, encircling my waist as if doing a quality assurance check rather than displaying affection.

"You don't want to know."

I burst into tears.

"Oh, crap," he mutters, pulling me to him.

"That's my line," I choke out.

His crotch buzzes again.

"This is not going as planned," he murmurs in my ear.

"You had a *plan* for this? We just invented the idea on the fly." I sniff against his chest, the wool making me itchy, but I don't care. His arms muffle the sounds of the world and I want to stay here forever, pretending we didn't just create a massive mess back at the Farmington Country Club that will chase us for decades.

*Bzzzz.*

Declan's fingers shove between us, the heel of his hand digging into a spot on me that is far more sensitive than I'd have imagined it could get. I make an involuntary sound that gives him pause.

"The plane with the private bedroom better be the one that's here," he grouses, his breath coming out of him with a sort of angry huff that I associate with his primal possession of me. I've only seen it in glimpses, micro-slices of dominance that flicker when he feels a need to protect me.

I've never seen Declan act like this without that trigger, though. Mostly, he behaved like this very early in our relationship, when my ex-boyfriend, Steve, was still a part of my life.

I'm musing through this as I watch him, not really paying attention to his words until they hit me. "A plane with a *bedroom*?"

He shrugs. "You want one with a jacuzzi tub? I keep trying to convince Andrew it's worth it, especially now that—"

"Declan!" I squeal. "I've been on private jets with Anterdec before," I try to explain. We're standing on the tarmac, a gust of wind blowing my veil into my face as a small, single-engine plane takes off. "But never one with a private bedroom."

"We never needed one," he says gently, pulling the lace away from my face and kissing me. Oh, his lips are so warm and soft. As his arms wrap around me, my hands splay against the fine cloth of his tuxedo jacket, palms taking in the wool weave as I move up, my fingers finding the nape of his neck and pulling him closer to me.

The whoosh of a larger jet flying over us cracks the air in two, but we ignore it. Our inner world trumps everything else, his mouth grounding me, hands calm and in control. I don't even have to question his love. Two years together have given me more than a glimpse into Declan's heart and soul. From the moment we met, I knew what I felt was more than a horny-porny reaction to a hot guy in a suit.

Not that there's anything wrong with that.

*Bzzzz.*

"I'm ready to throw my phone into a running jet engine," Declan says against my mouth, the vibration of his deep voice making me shiver.

"Better than throwing in my mother," I joke.

His silence makes me stomach clench.

"Declan!" I say with a nudge.

He laughs, the chuckle a tactile sensation I feel through his chest. My hands are still on his neck and back, and he's pressing his forehead against mine.

"Let's not talk about Marie right now," he says.

"Agreed."

Without effort, we pivot and return to the path toward the terminal. My wedding dress has a long train, covered in silk, tartan, tulle and what feels like chain mail. Declan seems to anticipate any potential mishap I may experience, expertly shoving various pieces of fabric out of the way so I can move with freedom and grace. Who on earth thought this monstrosity of a wedding dress was a good idea for a July ceremony in Massachusetts?

Oh. Right.

She Who Must Not Be Named.

I love my mom. I do. But I don't love what the wedding made her become.

We enter the private airport lounge, where a large, thin-screen television is bolted to the ceiling in one corner. When I was a little girl, Dad liked to bring me, Carol and Amy to the local small airport. The place had a diner in it, and we'd order French fries and strawberry milkshakes, spending an hour or two watching the planes land and take off. If we were lucky, a helicopter would come along.

Once, a really friendly pilot let us climb in his plane.

The place is nothing like *that* little airport. This is where millionaires and billionaires go to avoid the TSA.

The rich really do live different lives than the rest of us.

This lounge is all clean glass and smoky brown leather. If you told me that the same interior designer who decorated James McCormick's office at Anterdec had done this job, I'd believe you.

It looks like Teddy Roosevelt came back from the dead and demanded his own airport.

The small bar chairs, dark brown and creased with the kind of patina and age that looks shabby on cheaper leather, but chic and old-world sophisticated among the wealthy, are filled with a smattering of men and women, most in their fifties on up.

All of the servers and bartenders are in their twenties, and not a single one has an extra ounce of fat on them. It's like Crossfit decided to hold a bartender school.

As we walk into the lounge, every single pair of eyes swivels to take us in.

"Why are they staring at us?" I ask Declan, clutching his arm.

"Because you're wearing a wedding dress and I look like something out of a BBC documentary?" he answers smoothly.

I look down at myself. Look over at him. Take in the kilt, the socks covering his calves, the laces on his special Scottish shoes.

"Oh."

One of the patrons, a man who is sitting next to a woman

who looks like an adventurous traveler and not a mannequin on a rich man's arm, points to the television, then back to us.

"You two on the run?"

Declan frowns and pulls me closer to the television.

Where someone is interviewing my *mother*.

# Chapter Three

"And the president just took my daughter and son-in-law away. We're not sure why!" Mom says, eyes wild, her hairdo like something out of *The Hunger Games*. "Maybe it's because Declan speaks Russian. Maybe he's actually a double agent or something," she mutters as Dad pulls her away from the camera, shaking his head.

In the background I see Jeffrey put his fingers in his mouth, stretch it into a grimace, and stick his tongue out, crossing his eyes. Tyler is reaching for the first layer of the nine-layer cake, eating it by the handful, a slow and steady behavior that is mesmerizing to watch, much like those videos of sloths eating that you find all over YouTube.

One of the dogs Amanda rescued from the pool is licking up every crumb Tyler misses. Then the dog starts licking Tyler's hand, which makes him scream. Carol appears, her back turned to the camera, her butt covered with frosting.

"Shannon! I'm coming to find you!" Mom screams into the camera as poor, helpless Daddy tries to pull her away. "I'm never going to give you up!"

I stare in stunned silence at the television. No. No way. She didn't just—

"Did your mother just *rickroll* you on national television?" Declan asks.

She did.

The announcer's voice cuts in as Mom disappears from the screen. "You heard it here first, folks. The Boston wedding of the decade has become a presidential scandal as reports are pouring in from the bride's family that the President of the United States himself landed and absconded with—"

The young reporter, who looks like he should be selling "fries with that" at a fast food counter rather than standing in front of a camera, reaches for his earpiece, frowns, blushes, and looks like he just peed his pants.

"Uh, this just in. Reports confirm that there has been no White House involvement in this wedding whatsoever. Repeat: the White House and United States federal government have played *no role* in any way, shape, or form." The poor reporter's eyes shift left and right, as if he thinks the Men in Black are about to drag him off.

"But the president stole my daughter!" Mom screams in the background, a disembodied voice. "We're coming to rescue you in Vegas, honey!"

She really does know. Great.

The screen cuts instantly to four people back in the studio, all gaping at the viewing audience. They look like every single person in this airport lounge, except these people right here are gaping at *us*.

"Thanks, Obama," I mumble.

I look to Declan, but Declan is alternating his attention between his smartphone and a quiet guy in one corner, who keeps looking at us, then his phone.

"We need to get out of here. Now," Declan barks. He grabs my hand and pulls me through the lounge, toward a set of double doors that leads to the hangar. "She knows we're going to Vegas. How in the hell did she figure that one out?"

"Where are we going?" I ask. He pushes the doors open and stops, craning his neck slightly to take one final look at the quiet guy inside.

"Andrew says the jet's ready. They're fueling now." Declan's frowning. "I wonder if Amanda told Marie." His eyes shift back and forth between the tarmac and that guy.

"Why are you staring at that guy?"

"Because I know him. He's friends with Jessica." Declan narrows his eyes and looks around the asphalt-covered area surrounding the outside of the building, then puts his hand on the small of my back. "I couldn't name him, but I've seen him at plenty of charity events, hanging on her like a leech."

A mushroom cloud worthy of Los Alamos testing goes off in my chest.

"He *what*?"

"Whatever he's seeing right now, he's probably live-tweeting. And I don't want your mother finding us—"

"Forget about my mother finding us. Jessibitch Coughsalot is being fed information from that guy back there?" I spin on my heel and start to go back into the building, ready to rip the guy's head off.

All the day's guilt, all my worry and regret and general confusion, the sum total of all the overwhelm and fury that my mother triggered in me coalesces into a thing of horrible beauty.

And that guy in there is about to experience every ounce of wrath I have in me.

"No." Declan's arms encircle my waist, and not in a gentle, loving way. I feel like a seven-year-old being held back from her nineteenth time down the bouncy slide at the town fair by a parent who has run out of tickets.

In fact, I think I'm having a flashback to a time Dad had to do exactly that...

"Let me go!"

"No." His arms are bands of steel. His tone is even and while I can hear him breathing hard, he's back to showing no emotion. The inflection that normal humans use in their voices is absent.

I have narrowly escaped marrying a cyborg.

A Russian-speaking cyborg.

"If that asshole in there is documenting everything we do and feeding it to Jessica, then...then...I just escaped my own wedding for *nothing*!"

The arms around me loosen like Declan's been teleported. Poof! Instantly free. I've been struggling against him and pulling so hard that the sudden lack of resistance makes me pitch forward, falling on my face, tipped over by the weight of my stupid dress.

Instead of turning over, I just rest my cheek against the pebbly ground.

"I give up," I whisper.

In an instant, I'm in the air, my face pitched toward the sky, the blue expanse bouncing slightly as Declan picks me up off the ground and carries me away from the building.

People in the distance clap. I don't even struggle, because at this point I've gone pretty primal. It's been a little more than an hour since we got on that helicopter. A little more than that since Amanda jumped into the pool to rescue the dog and Chuckles—and Andrew came speeding out of his hiding place behind the glass and rescued her right back. An hour and a half since I learned Mom invited Jessica Twatter...I mean, Twitterhead Coffin to come to my wedding.

And Steve!

"My mom invited my ex to my own wedding," I groan into Declan's pec. It doesn't answer.

See? Cyborg.

Three hours ago I was putting on makeup and drinking giant lattes and trying not to throw up from a case of nerves so big they make my ass look small.

And now I am being carried away from the fanciest airport I've ever seen, a crowd behind us clapping and cheering.

I twist in Declan's arms and see the plane he's aimed for. I start to breathe rapidly, a deep hum inside me turning up volume, a sound only I can hear. Except, I can't actually hear it. I *feel* it. It's warm and burning, and as Declan's thighs push up against my butt, I realize he's walking up a set of stairs. A wall of white-painted steel flashes before me. Carpeting. Fabric. The muted silence of stepping out of a loud environment into a cocoon.

I'm dumped, unceremoniously, on a soft surface, Dec's body stretched out over mine like he has one job.

*One job.*

And he's going to do it very well.

*Bzzz.*

Declan reaches between us, plucks his phone out of his sporran, and tosses it out the open plane door. As his mouth takes mine I hear shattering glass, then the murmur and shout of workers outside.

I reach under his kilt and he groans, the sound full of more *thank yous* than an Oscar acceptance speech. He might be shut down on the outside, rational and commanding, laser-focused and intimidating, but on the inside he's falling apart in his own way.

And this bed? This bed will go a long way toward some much-needed centering. One part of him is centered over one part of me as he slides my layered skirts up, and *snap!*—there goes the tartan thong.

Soon my moan joins his groan and the *thank yous* passed between us are multiple. Wet and wild, welcome and frenzied, so hot and quick, our coupling is like doing a fireball shot. Declan bites my earlobe and plants an open-mouthed kiss on my neck as he slows, my own release so welcome. The few minutes of focusing on our bodies, on the rush of release and connection, feels like the best set of vows we could ever write.

"I'm sorry," he whispers, stroking my hair.

"For what?"

"That was...quick. And not befitting our wedding night."

"That was *hot*. It's not about how long something is. It's about how good the shortness is."

He smiles against my neck.

"Er, I mean—"

"You can quit while you're ahead, Shannon. Let's just leave it at 'That was hot.'"

"And this isn't our wedding night," I add, trying desperately to make up for...something. "I'll forgive the quickness if you make it up to me later," I say, stroking his back, my fingers crawling under his jacket and shirt, finding skin. As my palm flattens against the coiled strength in the back muscles along his spine, I relax. Finally. I melt into the coverlet on what I now realize is a king-size bed on this airplane.

*Private* airplane.

"That's right," he says, shifting just enough to be on his side. I curl and turn to face him, my lips twitching with amusement as his green eyes glitter in the light. Too many emotions swirl in those misty irises. What was barren by choice moments ago is now a storm, cloudy and with purpose.

But he's there. The Declan I know is there.

"What's right?"

"We're not married yet." He picks up my ring finger and fondles the three-carat diamond set in platinum that he gave me nearly a year ago. His mother's engagement ring. The one that could double as the camera on a colonoscope. "And you didn't escape the wedding for nothing, like you said earlier. You walked away from a situation where you weren't being respected."

The afterglow fades quickly as his words sink in.

"This isn't over."

"Not by a long shot."

I groan. It's not a sound of passion. "I thought fleeing the wedding would solve our problems!"

Hot skin rubs against my shivering form as my blood reacts to the reality, Declan's long, muscled body enveloping mine. The enormity of the situation sends ice water through me. The abyss of nuptial dysfunction that my mother has created is a cataclysmic Armageddon. It's all too much.

"I think escaping the wedding did solve one problem, but..." His voice trails off into skepticism.

"But what?"

"I think we've underestimated Marie."

I sit up. "What?" That almost sounds complimentary, coming from Declan.

"She's tenacious."

"Ya *think*?"

He shrugs, one shoulder lifting, face impassive. A flicker of contemplation shines in his eyes. His jaw shifts slightly, muscles working hard as he becomes progressively tenser. "She's really not going to give up."

"And I'm never going to let you down, Declan," I say, struggling to stay deadpan.

# Chapter Four

His eyes dart to me, and suddenly I'm being tickled, Declan on top of me, pinned between his knees as he hisses, "Your mother can get away with rickrolling you, but you do it to me, and I'll punish you."

Between gasps of laughter and the sensitive, almost-pukey feeling I get when tickled, I say, "Punish? *Obey* is bad enough and I won't say it in the vows. But *punish*?"

"You look like a woman who could use a good spanking."

"What about a *bad* spanking?" I rasp, one hand sliding up his thigh.

His eyes go dark. "I'm so glad we have another fifty or so years to get to know each other."

"Only fifty?"

"Your mother is shortening my life. Stress will do that."

"You feel stress?"

He gives me a look.

"You'd never guess. Your idea of stress seems to be going thirty-six hours without sex."

"That is, most firmly, my idea of stress, Shannon."

I seek out something else that's most firm, Declan's eyes smoldering, his hands working the buckle of his kilt.

"We had quick. Time for slow."

"Slow and bad?" I ask, perking up.

"Slow and very, very good."

An intercom squawks. "Mr. McCormick? Your brother is trying to contact you. He says you need to answer your phone. Takeoff is in five minutes." The woman's voice is like smooth jazz and a perfect White Russian all rolled into one scent you savor.

Declan's nuzzling my neck now, frozen on top of me. He groans, the vibration digging deep into my hips. "Damn it," he mutters, climbing off me, leaving me in a puddle of torn petticoats and tartan. He walks to the small bedroom door, then looks down, realizing he is pantless. Kiltless.

Half naked.

"That would be quite an entrance," I say with a giggle.

"My plane. My body. My rules."

I flick my wrist at him. "I know, I know, Mr. Nude Model. Whatever. If you want to couch your exhibitionism under some macho alpha-male billionaire posturing, go for it."

His shoulders hunch and one hand reaches up to pinch the bridge of his nose. Declan's back is turned to me, but I still know that's what he's doing.

"I'm *so* punishing you when I come back," he mutters under his breath as he snatches his kilt from the floor and twists the cloth in the barest of coverings, storming out of the bedroom, slamming the door behind him.

It's a playful slam.

*Bzzzz.*

Declan's phone is outside, currently melting into the asphalt, so that must be me. It buzzes five times before I finally locate it, realizing it's been buried in my bouquet, which has—yes, oh yes, it does—a special case for holding the bride's smartphone.

Why? I dunno. I guess in case you want to order dinner on your Chipotle app? Mom ordered the bouquets with these ridiculous features. For once, I'm grateful.

The screen says it's Amanda.

"Hello?"

"OMIGOD SHANNON HELP US MARIE IS MAKING ANDREW FLY EVERYONE TO LAS VEGAS INCLUDING JOSH AND GREG AND I THINK SHE'S BRINGING HER

YOGA CLASS AND THAT ELEPHANT WE TALKED HER OUT OF."

Huh. I was wrong. It's not Amanda. It's the sound of shattered glass come to life.

*Click.*

If I pretend that didn't just happen, it didn't happen. Right?

My heart hammers in my chest as the phone rings again. Once. Twice. I sigh, and answer it again, bracing myself for the onslaught of Amanda's screech.

"Shannon? This is Andrew."

"Andrew! So nice to hear from you. How are you?" I put the call on speakerphone and reach for a chocolate-covered strawberry the size of one of the dogs Amanda saved earlier today at the pool.

Silence.

"Shannon, you realize we just saw you ninety minutes ago, when you fled the wedding in the chopper Declan appropriated from Anterdec without my permission and left a thousand confused guests here to be terrorized by your mother?"

"Has it only been ninety minutes?" I say, juice dribbling down my chin. "Feels like years."

Declan walks back into the room. "They had Andrew on the line but lost him. Said he's pissed and insists on talking to me before we take off. I told them he can go to hell and we'll talk after we're in Las Vegas."

I look at my phone and flap my hands at him, pointing to the phone.

He pivots out of the layers of tartan wool he's tied around his waist like a pashmina filled with pipe cleaners, and jumps me.

"AAAIIIIIEEEEE!" I scream, howling with laughter, my arm and face covered in strawberry juice, still trying to tell him about the call.

Declan sucks on my face and says, "You taste so sweet. I've been waiting to lick you like this." He runs his tongue along a line of strawberry juice from my wrist to my elbow. "Now it's time to punish you and give you that spanking you've been asking for."

"Ahem." Andrew's disembodied voice sounds about as horri-fied as you'd imagine.

"Who the hell is that?" Declan bellows, scrambling off me, grabbing the first thing he can find and holding it above his head like a baseball bat.

"It's just me. Over here. In hell, where you put me."

"Andrew?" Declan's exceptional composure crumbles, his eyes wild and frantic as he protects me from the predators of the world with a one-liter green glass bottle of sparkling water that cost more than my last pair of shoes.

He's such a caveman.

"Where the hell are you?" Declan demands.

I point to my phone.

"You had your phone this entire time?" He looks at my boobs. "Where?"

"In the bouquet."

"SHANNON! YOUR MOM IS GIVING JESSICA EXCLUSIVE PHOTOS AND INTERVIEWS IN EXCHANGE FOR SOME GUY FOLLOWING YOU AT THE AIRPORT," Amanda screeches.

Apparently, my mother's wedding voice volume has trans-ferred to my best friend, like a parasite that wiggled out of Mom's ear and invaded Amanda's brain.

"Your bouquet had a *smartphone* holder?" Declan asks.

"I know, right? Stupid feature."

"Actually, no. That's a great feature, and perfect for the weddings at Anterdec's hotel chains. I need to get ahold of our director for events and—"

"DECLAN!" Andrew shouts into the phone. "I am in hell here. I have your mother-in-law demanding that I ground your jet and have you arrested."

"Arrested for what?" Declan's voice cracks like a teen boy in puberty on the last word.

"Kidnapping."

"Again? I am here willingly!" I shout at the phone. "She already tried to ground the helicopter. What the hell is she think-ing? I'm here of my own free will!"

"I know that. You know that. Marie damn well knows that. But she's all over cable news claiming that you stole Shannon."

"We saw her being interviewed," I explain. "She doesn't blame Declan. She blames the president."

"You saw her being *what*?" Andrew barks. Declan and I share a confused look.

Amanda's voice comes through, clearly.

"OH MY GOD, ANDREW, THE COURTYARD IS FULL OF NEWS PEOPLE. MARIE IS BEING INTERVIEWED BY —" Muffled sounds come through the receiver as Andrew returns.

"Who's interviewing her?" Declan asks. The jet engine begins a low hum, and a knock on the door interrupts us. Declan scrambles to pull on his kilt, which now looks like a jawa that went through a wind tunnel in the rain, and opens the door just as Andrew answers.

"Geraldo Rivera."

The flight attendant gawks at the phone. Declan pivots back, tight jaw now loose and practically on the floor.

"Mr. McCormick? You and Mrs. McCormick need to fasten your seat belts."

"In *bed*?" I eye the mattress with a new sense of respect.

"No, Mrs. McCormick." *Mrs. McCormick.* A chill runs thorough me. She points to two upholstered chairs next to a lovely oak table. "Those are the takeoff and landing seats."

"GERALDO RIVERA?" Declan shouts, the *non sequitur* confusing the poor attendant.

I give her a gentle nudge out the door and assure her we'll be fine. The hum of the engines is revving up and I tug on Dec's hand, leading him to the seats. He grabs my phone and takes it off speakerphone.

"Listen," he snaps. "We know that Marie knows we're going to Vegas. How in the hell did that happen?"

*Mumble mumble mumble mumble.*

"She *looked* at Amanda and figured it out?" Declan says with a derisive snort.

I knew it. Amanda *is* the weakest link after all.

Declan looks at me. "Should we reroute?"

"Reroute? What?"

"Go somewhere else to get married. Not Vegas. They know we're headed there."

My hand brushes against a black remote control and I look up, seeing a small screen attached to the wall. Pushing the power button on, an action I will deeply regret in a moment, I flip to the news stations.

My mother's giant head fills the screen.

"Have Andrew lie. He can tell her we're going to Atlantic City instead."

Declan's face brightens and he mutters into the phone as I take my seat. A few exchanges later and he hands me my phone, settling into his own seat for takeoff.

"She's not stupid," he muses, thinking this through. "She'll figure it out soon. And Anterdec has a great property in Vegas." He puffs up like a silverback gorilla protecting a harem. "The finest resort on the Strip. We can hide there."

"Daddy will try to talk some reason into her. Besides, it's not like she and my father have piles of money to come chasing after us," I say, giggling with the absurdity of all this. "They will run out of funds faster than Anterdec will."

Declan blinks. "Andrew's letting her use the other jet."

"What? I thought it was in Central America on a humanitarian mission!"

"It happened to finish early. Landing in Boston in about three hours."

"Then assign it to another mission!"

"That's not how this works."

"Make it work that way! Lord knows there's always another natural disaster somewhere that needs your plane to deliver supplies, and if there isn't, *create* one."

"I can't create a natural disaster, Shannon."

"Sure you can! Corporations do it all the time! Conglomerates are more powerful than governments! Mom can't have access to an entire corporate jet, so do whatever it takes."

"She can when she's driving Andrew nuts. He'll say anything to get her to leave him and Amanda alone."

"What does Amanda have to do with this?"

His answer is eaten by the roar of the plane engines as we lift off, the rumble of the plane's effort to stay steady and adjust to the cross-winds turning my already-jangled nerves into a ball of nausea. So much of the day has turned into a circus. A farce. An abomination and distortion of everything I know, and as the plane takes off the ugly tears hit me, driving hard through my body, sending me into a wretched, breath-holding sob that feels like I'm dying.

Declan's face, etched with alarm as he watches me, breaks my heart, because I've never seen him so helpless.

He comforts me the only way you can when you're on a private corporate jet, escaping your own wedding.

In bed.

Bedrooms on planes should be a requirement. Like landing gear, seat cushions as flotation devices, and microscopic packets of peanuts, bedrooms need to be on every plane.

"I'm officially a member of the Mile-High Club," I crow, snuggled next to Declan, both of us naked under the sheets. If I smoked, I'd totally be sucking off a Camel right now.

Okay. That sounds *so* wrong. Let me rephrase that...

"Round Two was decidedly longer," he says. That's it? That's all the man is going to say?

"You're still fixated on being Mr. Two-Minute Man when we got on the plane?"

He bristles.

"That was your fault."

"How was it *my* fault?"

"You primed the pump, so to speak, back in the helicopter."

Trying to fix my *faux pas* with a well-timed kiss, I melt into the connection of our mouths, the rumble of the jet plane making it hard to truly relax. Even a smooth flight like this one, aboard a skillfully-flown private jet, isn't the same as being on the ground and in a bed that isn't moving at a rate of six hundred miles per hour.

At least, um, most of the time we're in it.

"You can't just kiss me every time you say something objectionable and think I'll let you get away with it," Declan says with a condescending sniff.

"Since when?" I ask, agog.

He frowns. "Huh. Good point." His cheek grazes against my bare breast, face skimming my nude body until I'm giggling, then gasping, and finally moaning his name again.

And again.

"One hour to arrival time, sir," says the attendant outside the door. Declan sighs. We've been in a bubble for the past four hours, dozing off, making love, and trying to ignore my smartphone, which has been buzzing so much it might as well be a vibrator.

"In an hour we'll land and take the limo to the resort," Declan says, watching me dress, face tense but a smirk tickling his lips.

"Resort?"

"Anterdec owns two of them on the Strip in Las Vegas. But one is so much better." There's that smug smile again.

"Which ones? I know about Litraeon." Which sounds like a citrus car. Every time someone at Anterdec mentions it I think of a giant lemon on wheels. "What's the other one?"

He snorts. "A total dive at the bad end of town called Louie's Stiff One."

"Is it a brothel?" I shimmy back into my wedding dress. We don't have anything else to wear. Neither of us expected to escape the wedding, so we packed no bags. I'm lucky to have my phone and wallet, and Declan's sporran has his basic ID and credit cards, I assume.

Wherever we're going, we'll have to go like *this*.

"Not a brothel. Even Dad won't let us own whorehouses."

"'Whorehouse'? What is this, 1984? Are you Burt Reynolds?"

He looks at my half-clothed bosom. "If that means you're Dolly Parton, I sure am."

I throw a loose chair pillow at his head and miss. Green, mischievous eyes laugh at me.

"That's what Dad calls them!" he protests, tossing the pillow back, but in a playful manner. This is my Declan. I haven't seen this side of him in ages. The wedding has taken every spare bit of oxygen from our relationship and left it spasming, choking and gasping for air.

Now we can *breathe*.

"James isn't exactly the epitome of pop culture knowledge." The man still refers to his "briefcase phone" at times and drinks Tab.

"We're not going into the sex trade, so it doesn't matter what term we use."

"You own those O spas," I remind him. "Those are super-close to being in the sex trade, if what Mom and Amanda reported is true."

"The guy strippers don't actually have sex with the women. It's different."

Before we can continue this scintillating discussion about the finer points that differentiate male strippers from female prostitutes, Declan jumps out of bed and starts dressing.

"Once we're at the resort, I'll order a shopper to bring you a proper wardrobe," he says, pulling up his socks.

"I have a proper wardrobe."

"Back home, sure. But not here."

"I can find a Target or a T.J. Maxx and get a few things," I counter. "I just need some basics." I perk up. "What about thrift shops? Are they any good in Vegas?"

"No," he says slowly, giving me a long-suffering look. "The resort has one of the best retail sites in the world attached to it. You can get what you need at Prada, Chanel, or Armani."

"Why would I buy anything there? We're not going to a fancy ball, are we?"

"No. But you deserve some nice clothes for our wedding. And honeymoon, wherever we end up." A few seconds pass as he eyes me. "Hell, any clothes at this point. That dress is close to rags, and I can't have you running around Vegas naked." His hand goes to his mouth, eyes narrowing. "As appealing as that might be."

The enormity of what we're doing catches up with me. I

don't have a stitch of clothing that wasn't picked out by my mother, including the plaid butt floss masquerading as underwear. Speaking of which, the tartan thong is hanging off the handle of the fire extinguisher.

"I can buy my own clothes."

"A professional shopper will deal with all that," he says with a wrist twist. "It's what they do. They'll make you look stylish." The instant the words are out of his mouth he winces, realizing what he's said.

"I see." You could use my voice during physical therapy sessions to ice a hundred knees.

"I meant—"

"A long time ago, Declan, you told me you always mean what you say."

"I do! It's just—"

I stomp across the bedroom, fling open the door, storm out and slam it. The air pressure on the plane makes the door close with an anemic *pffft*.

That was so unsatisfying. If you're going to storm out in a huff, do it with better props.

I charge out into the cabin and realize I have about sixteen paces before I reach the cockpit. Damn. He follows me, his heavy sigh a clear sign that this is an argument he's not going to stop having. The fight between us over money is so irrational I can't quite find words for it.

Oh, yeah. I can.

He's a *billionaire*. Officially, even. His stock options matured enough recently, along with trust holdings, for Declan to call himself one. It's real. I'm about to become a billionaire's wife.

On the surface, that's great, right? You're doing a crazy football cheerleader routine complete with pools filled with fifty-dollar bills and Tiffany necklaces as lamp chains at the idea of being engaged to a wealthy man, but halt right there. I'm just a girl from Mendon, who grew up in a tiny Cape Cod dormer house, who shared a one-bedroom garage apartment with her sister until two years ago.

My last car looked like the Iron Giant dropped trou after a

double-double and pooped on it. And the car before that started by shoving a big-blade screwdriver in the hole and turning until the engine groaned.

*You* try shoving a long, tapered instrument in a dark hole and getting something to turn on.

Um. I mean....

"Is this about the money?" Declan's words slice through my thoughts. We've had the same argument for two years. He wants to indulge me. I feel uncomfortable. He argues I'm not letting myself enjoy and it's a reflection of low self-esteem. I assure him my sense of self-worth has nothing to do with not wanting a two-hundred-dollar hot stone massage or a $2,500 pair of shoes, thanks, and maybe he should check his own privilege at the door and see if his need to be a big spender is compensating for something.

That last bit kind of ticks him off.

"It's about wanting to wear what I want to wear. Not what some professional shopper picks out for me. The last time we did this she dressed me like a porny version of Hello Kitty."

"Pink leather is in."

"I looked like a walking labia, Declan. With glitter."

"Maybe that's a thing?"

"Maybe you *wish* it were a thing."

"Maybe if you'd just accept a gift from me, I wouldn't feel like you're holding back trust."

Whoa. What?

"You really believe that?"

He has the decency to look uncomfortable. "No. But it was worth a try."

"Declan," I groan. I hate this conversation. And yet I have a disquieting feeling it's rearing its ugly head now because this is a cornerstone of our relationship. The clash between our backgrounds took a backseat to all the similarities between us, and the complementary ways we fit into each other's lives. Now, under conflict, we're finding the fissures.

"Beginning our descent," the pilot announces. "Please take your seats, Mr. and Mrs. McCormick."

The unearned title makes me smile, a bashful grin that twists the corner of my mouth up, the other held in place by my teeth as I bite the inside of my lip. The tension between us eases as we strap in, a bottle of chilled sparkling water in a silver bucket on ice on a table next to him, the bucket's twin next to me, filled with a bottle of bubbly.

Without asking, because he knows me so well, Declan opens the sparkling water and pours me a glass. I'll sip it during the descent to pop my ears over and over. His fingers brush against mine and I give him a soft smile.

"I love you," he says, as if he feels I need to hear it. I don't. I know.

"I love you, too."

"And you were a smoking hot Hello Kitty," he adds with a wolf whistle as the plane's nose turns downward, taking us to the next step in our hare-brained escape plan.

# Chapter Six

Vegas is big and bright. Duh, right? But I mean BIG. And BRIGHT. It's like Times Square on steroids sprinkled on top of a big dose of Molly with a case of Red Bull thrown in for fun.

I crane my neck, plastering my face against the limo window, looking up.

"I can't believe you've never been to Vegas," Declan says for the fourth time in ten minutes.

"C'mon. Not everyone has the means to travel like your family."

"You never took family vacations?"

"We did. Camping. To the beach. I don't think dragging three girls to a place where toplessness is legal and Santa Claus carries an LED sign on a backpack with crotch shots really quali- fies as a family destination site."

He frowns. "Anterdec's resort is trying to do just that."

I look out the window and see what appears to be Chewbacca from Star Wars receiving oral sex from Elmo.

"You have your work cut out for you," I reply, pointing to the scene.

"May the Force be with you," he mutters.

The limo halts at a red light. Famous performers whose names I've heard growing up have their faces plastered all over the sides of skyscrapers, the buildings jutting up like towers of Babel in the desert. I've seen movies about Vegas. Watched a few documentaries. Even had friends come here and return home with wild stories of gambling and reckless sex.

Until you're driving down a palm-tree-lined boulevard with wide streets, broad sidewalks, and outdoor escalators leading to catwalks that span the road every block as far as the eye can see, with choreographed water fountains, beggars, old ladies wearing stripper-joint t-shirts that say Girls, Girls, Girls and handing out free passes to nudie bars, you don't really get a sense of the electrified chaos and the extraordinary overstimulation of it all.

I'm beginning to think that coming here was a bad, bad idea.

As if he reads my mind, Declan scoots me by my ass across the seat, where he nestles me in his warm arms. He smells like sweat and sex, like remnants of his morning shower's soap, like my deodorant and the sweet grapes we ate on the plane before dashing to this limo. I'm so used to having Gerald or Lance at the helm. Geordi is our driver, and he looks just enough like Harrison Ford with purple streaked hair under his hat to make me wonder if this isn't one big movie set and Declan's playing an elaborate practical joke on me.

"Hey. It's not all like this."

"What isn't?"

"Vegas. This is all for show. For the masses. We'll drive into the underground garage and take the private elevator to our room. You won't have to see a thing."

"See *what* thing?"

He laughs. I elbow him.

"I meant the casino floor. The indoor gardens. The shops you clearly don't want to patronize," he adds with a touch of saccharine. "The craziness."

I twist in his arms and look at him. In the neon glow of nonstop blink and change from signs like Tokyo, he looks well worn. Tired. His guard is down, and a piece of me loves him a little more for it. My mouth stretches open with a noisy yawn and he laughs, then yawns as well.

"It's contagious," I whisper. The familiar sound of Michael Jackson music is muted outside. I turn to find an impersonator on the granite sidewalk, dancing with sharp moves, tipping his hat to the audience as dark ringlets bounce with his steps. The song ends just as the light cycle changes and we creep, slowly, into the parking garage.

We climb out of the limo, attendants everywhere, dressed in burgundy jackets, black pants, and most of them wearing earbuds. Soft, modern pop music floats through the air as Declan climbs out, offering his hand to me. I make it to a standing position and wobble. The day has been long. I purposely didn't drink on the flight, afraid to make a crazy, nerve-jangling day even worse, but now that we're here—really here—I just want a long soak in a big, hot tub and a bottle of Champagne for my greedy little self.

Then about twelve hours of spooning sleep with Declan.

"Mr. McCormick," says the attendant who opens the door to the building, handing Declan a set of key cards. He whispers in Declan's ear. Whatever he tells him, Declan's face folds into a mixture of reactions. I don't ask. I'm too tired to ask.

We walk into a plushly-carpeted hallway, face a set of elevator doors, and a new attendant nods.

"Mr. McCormick, good to see you." Declan's curt nod is all he gives. We enter the elevator and Declan lets out a long, slow exhale.

"They all know you?"

"I called ahead to let them know we were coming."

"How do they *all* know you?'

He cocks an eyebrow. "Because Anterdec owns the place. I interned here in college. I've spent more time here than I should have."

"What's that mean?"

He washes his jaw with one hand. "Let's just say I like the roulette wheel a little too much."

"You *gamble*?"

"Baccarat now. High stakes only. More controlled variables."

"What else don't I know about you?"

The elevator doors ding and he pivots me to the right. "Isn't that why we're getting married? So you can get to know me better?" We stop at a set of double doors. The hallways are done in a mix of beige marble shades and burgundies, ornate color patterns designed to convey richness. Old world. A kind of nouveau decoration scheme that says, *You've made it* with a mix of *Hey, modern plumbing*.

"You don't gamble huge amounts of money, do you?"

"Why gamble otherwise? The thrill is in the risk. Not in actually winning."

"That doesn't make any sense."

"Only a non-gambler would say that, Shannon."

"I thought you play to win?"

"Always."

"Then isn't winning the goal?"

"Sure. But the bigger challenge comes from taking the biggest risk possible and seeing it pay off. Sometimes you have to tolerate some losses along the path to reaching that ultimate achievement."

"And losing giant piles of money is an acceptable way to learn?"

He shrugs. "It's the only way."

"Did you ever lose a lot of money?"

He's immediately uncomfortable. There's my answer.

Declan finds one of the keys the parking attendant gave him and waves it in front of a wood panel, which opens magically. This should impress me, but it doesn't. I've seen almost every form of hospitality technology you can imagine in my work with Anterdec.

The suite is splendid, with a breathtaking view of the enormous fountain below. Gold is the dominant color, that rich shade of oak trees turning to foliage in a New England fall. Dark, stained wood and tasteful bronze accents round out the room, with abstract art that focuses on burgundies and texture, each framed oil painting signed.

Original art. This ain't no fifty-nine-buck-a-night motor lodge.

Two years ago I would have been gobsmacked. Living with a man who walks through life in a cloud of money has changed me, though, even if I'm loath to admit it. The suite is beautiful. It smells like piped-in vanilla. The minibar is well stocked and Declan casually opens the tiny refrigerator, pulls out a soda, and cracks it open.

*Five bucks*, I think. *That's a five-buck soda.*

I tuck the thought away, because why linger over it? I don't live my old life anymore. I have to get used to this new reality. And I have. Slowly.

One luxury at a time.

One area where I have no problem living large is transportation. Not having to worry about driving, or parking, or fighting through airport security turns off the little piece of self-doubt that reminds me of five-dollar sodas. Am I a hypocrite? Yep.

That's the price I pay for not having to worry about my underwire bra setting off the metal detectors.

He opens the minibar again and points to it. "Here. Grab something. You must be parched."

I walk over to him, pluck an empty glass off the counter and walk into the bathroom to fill it with tap water. His eyes follow me and he knows exactly what I'm about to do. While I'm in there, I take a minute to drink, pee, and freshen up, which is loosely defined as taking the "Self-Care Kit" and running a comb through my destroyed hair.

When I come back out into the living room, the table behind the couch is covered in soda pop cans, candy bars, mini wine bottles, small wheels of brie, and three berry bowls.

"What is this?"

He smirks. "I emptied the minibar. Now you have to eat it."

"What?"

"I know what you're doing, and it needs to stop. Shannon, just take whatever you want."

I sip my water. "I'm fine." But man, I'm eyeing that stack of Butterfinger bars like I'm on death row and this is my last meal.

"Eat. Drink." He cracks open a tiny little bottle of wine and drinks it in three long gulps.

There must be two hundred dollars worth of snacks here. That the hotel will charge eight hundred for.

"It's my company's hotel," he says, reading my mind.

"I work for Anterdec, too!"

"It's *your* company's hotel," he intones. "Act like it. Enjoy."

"This isn't business," I say primly.

"What do you mean?"

"We're not on a business trip, so I can't treat this like a deduction."

"I don't understand."

"Life isn't one big business trip."

Blank stare.

"Quit acting like you don't get what I'm saying."

"I'm not acting. Life is business. The time I spend with you is what I squeeze in between work."

Stunned into silence, I listen to the sound of my breath. The fizz of his drink in the can. The noise of candy wrappers as I lower myself to sit on the bed, a few stray delights from the minibar strewn on the bed like bedtime decorations. A ventilation unit goes off. A woman's throaty laugh is muted out in the hall.

He looks at me, brow darkening with increasing concern, as I let his world circumnavigate my mind a few hundred times.

"Will it always be that way?" I ask.

His turn to be stunned. He's blinking harder than an owl in a sandstorm.

"That sounded really bad, didn't it?' he says as his frown deepens, his fingers going to his chin, his eyes troubled.

"Yep."

"I didn't—that's not—" He stops and starts a few times, finally taking a long, slow breath and saying, "Can I have a do-over?"

"A do-over."

"Right."

"Like a reboot?"

"Exactly."

Declan's so self-assured, so precise and confident in pretty much every way possible, that this is interesting to watch. I am not at all above the schadenfreude that comes from observing his verbal klutziness right now.

"No."

"No?"

"You don't get a reboot," I say, my words regal and pompous. "Say what you mean and mean what you say."

He pinches the bridge of his nose, because that is one of his favorite sayings.

"If you like work more than me, Declan—"

"That is not what I said, and you know it, Shannon. I said that life is what I fit in around work. We were talking about a soda or a bag of chips from the minibar and now it's devolved into an argument about work-life balance."

"What's that?"

"Work-life balance?"

"Right."

"It's where you juggle the two to make them evenly important."

"How can you claim to even try if life is what you squeeze in around work? That's not balance. That's gap-filling. I'm nothing but a full caulk gun to you."

"I was using that as a way of defending against your ridiculous contention that you needed to deprive yourself of a Butterfinger because we're not on a business trip!"

"Ohh, low blow, Dec!"

"What?"

"Now you're using my love of Butterfingers to win this argument!" Some lines can't be crossed in relationships.

He picks up one of the offending confections and tosses it to me.

"Dirty fighter."

"Oh, I'm way dirtier than that," he says in a voice that rumbles.

"Sex. Again." I sigh and shake my head. I also crouch and pick up the candy bar, because *hey*. Butterfinger.

"Is that an observation or a...request?"

Considering that question carefully, I fume, and yet, in great anger there is great opportunity. What if I just throw myself at him and end this ridiculous argument? We've been bickering since we got on the plane, and this is not our norm. Other couples may fight in tiny little ways with micro-insults that are all about keeping score in some fifty-years war where the victor—what? Lives?

But I don't want that kind of life.

If sex will heal this rift, then maybe I need to call him on his cute little bluff. Maybe that was just a sweet little joke. A poke.

Maybe I can't tell, because it looks too much like a sharp stick he's poking at me for me to know it's really an olive branch.

"Which do you want it to be?" I peel open the candy bar and wrap my lips around the tip of the long, chocolate-coated piece of layered processed pretend peanutty *whatever* that some lab rat in a candy factory created with chemicals for the perfect consistency and addictive taste.

If this whole marketing-director thing doesn't work out, I think I'll become a chemical taster for candy companies.

"I want it to be whatever gets us to stop fighting. I hate this, Shannon. I hate not feeling connected to you."

This is why I want to marry this man. *This*. Not the thousand guests, the tartan thongs, the cat as flower girl, or the forty-one bagpipe players. Not Mom's Farmington Country Club dream, and not for the lavish gifts people brought.

Him.

Only him.

"Maybe I *should* have sex with you," I challenge, eyes on his, giving him the side-eye like I'm evaluating a rival before a boxing match. Except instead of hitting each other, we're going to play an elaborate game of Battleship.

He's the red peg and I'm G14.

Or pretty much any G spot on the board.

"Maybe?"

"Would it stop all this crazy talk about five-dollar sodas and personal shoppers and the clash between two socioeconomic systems that each make sense in-culture but that create nothing but conflict and inefficiencies when we argue?"

"You're so sexy when you speak like a social economist. Please," he says, licking his lips suggestively. "Do it again."

"Russian cultural resilience in natural disaster resource allocation."

He breathes heavily. I stick the candy bar in my mouth suggestively, making him grunt.

My mind races through sophomore-year classes. "Gunnar Myrdal," I say. "Homo economicus. Prospect theory."

"I'm not sure which is sexier. The way you're mouthing that candy bar, or how you sound when you say 'resource allocation.' How about you allocate some resources my way?" he adds.

I throw a Butterfinger at him. Sure, it's a waste, but in a pinch, you make sacrifices for a greater good.

He tackles me around the waist like an experienced Greco-Roman wrestler and I'm on the bed, wrists pinned, his knee between my legs as it looks like we're about to make up.

"Why are we fighting about money?" I ask him before his mouth lands on mine, the kiss aggressive and demanding, the unraveling ends of our nerves trying to find some sense of order in the flesh.

"We never fight about money," he croons, letting go of one wrist so his hands can go on a peace-seeking mission.

"We do *so* fight about money!"

"Are we now fighting about whether or *not* we fight about money?" He collapses on me as if he's just plain given up.

It's like Declan can't *even*.

"We've gone meta," I whisper.

"Is that like going emo?" His voice is muffled in my hair.

"Worse."

He shudders, then rolls off to the side, propping his head in one hand, elbow on the bed. His tuxedo jacket is open, one button lost somewhere between Boston and here. His shirt is horribly stained, and he smells like a sweaty man at the end of a long day, mixed in with the nose-tickling scent of Coke. Those green eyes are sagging, tired beyond his years, and as he grunts again in frustration I realize how stupid we're being.

"Stupid," I whisper. "Stupid, stupid, stupid."

"I am. I know." It's plain from his tone that he doesn't believe a word of that.

"You are." He tenses. "So am I." He relaxes. "Why are we fighting? Is it because we're exhausted? It's not from lack of sex!"

"That *is* our usual source of conflict," he agrees.

"Then what?"

All the heat he's generating disappears, leaving my body chilled as he walks away. The sound of rushing water from the bathroom indicates a tub or a shower's been started. He comes back into the large living room, searching drawers efficiently. Near the fireplace, he finds what he seeks, and disappears into the bathroom.

Two minutes go by. I close my eyes and count the nerve endings that are jangling like bells in the hands of Salvation Army bell volunteers at the red buckets at Christmastime.

"C'mere," he says from a distance.

I roll on my side, nearly fall off the bed, catch myself, and walk into the bathroom.

Which he has transformed into a glowing fairyland.

"Oh, Dec," I sigh. It's a good sigh. A *great* sigh.

The bathtub, which could seat twelve but *hell to the no* on that right now, is mostly full, covered in frothy delight in the form of lavender bubble bath. It's the perfect size for two.

One is already in there, buried to the neck in bubbles, his hand reaching out for me. I giggle at the sight. Masculine and demanding, authoritative and fierce, Declan's normal countenance is quite compromised by the sight of him swimming in bubbles, glowing in candlelight, ensconced in lavender—

And drinking wine out of a tiny plastic bottle from the minibar.

As my eyes adjust and I strip off my dress, I realize he's taken a bunch of the minibar snacks and alcoholic drinks and put them at intervals around the edge of the giant tub.

"Mmmmm. Pinot Grigio is simply enhanced by the mouthfeel of the threads of the plastic screw cap," he says, finishing off the wine and tossing the empty into the trash can on the other side of this bathroom, which is bigger than my childhood bedroom.

Of course—*of course*—he nails it, the bottle a slam dunk.

"Get in." Declan unscrews another plastic bottle of white wine, muttering something about upgrades and quality, then opens yet another just as I'm dipping my toe in the hot water.

"Two at a time?" I ask, laughing. *Ahhhhhhh*. The hot water feels like entering a different world, as if all the chaos and uncertainty has stepped back five hundred feet and is still causing mayhem, but it's doing it over *there*.

"One is for you." He hands it to me, closes his eyes, leans his head against the stuffed neck pillow attached to the edge of the bath, and just sighs, the end of the long exhale turning into a sound that has become the song of my people.

"I can drink to that," I say, and I do, downing the wine in a few gulps.

"We are stupid," he says slowly, his arm coming up out of the water, dripping as he reaches for the other open bottle of wine. "Me, especially."

Declan is not the self-effacing type. Ever. I say nothing. Even if I knew what to say, I would say nothing.

"I pride myself on being calm in the middle of nearly any storm," he explains, reaching up to pitch the now-empty plastic wine bottle into the trash can. He misses. Hah!

"No one's perfect," I reply, meaning his miss.

"It's not about perfection. It's about being grounded. People throw you off your game if you're not centered. No one wants to be in reaction mode all the time."

"I don't even have a framework for what that means."

"Case in point. You're always reactive. With a mom like Marie, I can understand why. I try to be as grounded as possible."

"And with a dad like James, I understand why."

His eyes are closed, but his mouth twists with a grin. "We're going to have so much fun figuring out the terrain of our respective families."

I slide all the way down, the heat spiking my skin, like

burying myself in hot, steaming velvet. "Fun isn't the word I would use, but okay…"

He unscrews yet another Lilliputian wine bottle, chugs it, tosses the dead soldier in the trash, and hands me another.

"Relaxing?"

"Finally."

Declan's not much of a drinker, but it isn't every day you go through—ah, hell, I can't even remember everything we've been through in less than twenty-four hours. Joining him, I polish off two wines before sinking all the way in to my neck, my toes finding a lovely, soft footrest.

"Hey! I'm attached to that," he protests, reaching down to stop my foot. His thumbs dig into my arch and I think I orgasm. I'm not sure. I'm so tired.

"In more ways than one."

"Mmmmm. Later. Hot bath first. Hot Shannon next."

"Priorities."

"Indeed."

"We're still not married, Declan."

Opening one eyelid, he peers at me like an assassin taking aim.

"No, we're not. But we will be. Soon."

"What if Mom catches up to us?"

"When. Not if."

"When, then. What about—"

His own foot creeps up my belly, tentative, then bold, toes tickling one nipple. "I do not want to talk about *what ifs*. I certainly do not want to talk about, or think about, your mother or my father. I have plenty of wine in me, my body is hot and loose and enjoys this bath, and in about ten minutes I plan to have our naked bodies on that very large bed out there, with you in positions that require an advanced degree in yoga."

He moves over to my other breast. I grab his foot and massage it, digging my thumbs in deep. He groans and leans back. I look up and make a noise of excitement. I point.

"There's a huge television mounted right there!"

He laughs. "Yes. Want to turn it to the fireplace channel?"

"The what?"

"The fireplace channel. The resort has a cable channel that is 24/7 nothing but a video of a fireplace."

"Couldn't spring for a real fireplace in the suite?" I joke.

His face goes serious. "Those are the presidential suites. They're all taken right now. We picked the same week as eight enormous conventions to be here. I couldn't even bump anyone on short notice, but if you really want a fireplace in the bathroom, I'll make sure we move tomorrow—"

A laugh of incredulity pours out of me. "Are you crazy? This is great. Perfect."

His wet hand snakes over to a wall remote I hadn't noticed. Once the television is on, he flips a few channels, and—

A giant, very familiar auburn head fills the wall.

"AUGH!" Dec screams.

"MOM!" I shout.

He starts to change the channel but I stop him. Instead, he reaches for three tiny bottles of wine.

I don't stop *that*.

Some reporter I've never seen before is interviewing my mother, still at the Farmington Country Club. They're inside, guests are milling about, and the cake's been relocated to a table where it rests like the Leaning Tower of Pisa, if the Leaning Tower of Pisa were mauled by hungry tigers named Jeffrey and Tyler.

Mom is still livid.

"Where's Geraldo Rivera? I was told I'd be interviewed by Geraldo Rivera! This is more important than even him."

The poor reporter tries to calm Mom down. I snort. Good luck, buddy.

Mom's on a tear. "What about Oprah! When a woman's daughter is kidnapped by a billionaire and the President of the United States, her story deserves Oprah Freaking Winfrey! What? She's not available, either? What about that nice blonde lesbian who does that funny talk show. What's her name—Elizabeth Hasselbeck?"

*Click.*

We stare at the now-black television, Declan's hand on the remote.

"I don't need the fake fireplace," I say weakly.

Declan's not listening, because he's chugging back yet more wine. He finishes a bottle, tosses the empty into the toilet with an evocative *kerplunk* that makes me nostalgic for how we met two years ago, and gives me a plaintive, but determined, look.

"Shannon?"

"Yes, honey?"

"Would you do me the great honor of *not* being my wife tonight?"

"What?"

"I have a very short window of time as a single man, and I'd like to spend it having sex with the most gorgeous woman in the world before I'm tied down by a nagging ball and chain."

"God, you sound like your father."

He's fooled me, his sloth-like exterior a sham. Standing up like Godzilla emerging from the waters outside of Tokyo, he dips down, pulls me, dripping, out of the tub, and manages to stay sure-footed to the bed, where we become an entangled mess of wet, slippery skin.

"Declan!" I squeal, pink-skinned and soaked, shivering and flushed, his palms lubricated by the soapy, watery mess he's created.

He covers me completely with his hot body, mouth finding parts of me that take my racing thoughts and spin them faster, until everything is a blur and the only thing I can hold onto for the ride is my pleasure.

By the time we're done we're under soggy sheets, wet heads on wet pillows, the sound of Declan's rare snore guiding me to my own slumber, our day complete in its calamity, with so many questions unanswered.

And so many more not yet asked.

## Chapter Seven

I can feel her presence here in Vegas before the phone even rings. They say that evil has its own vibration, a low frequency that masquerades as normal in order to hide among us, a chameleon of extraordinary power, with the gift of destruction.

If it had a name, it would be Marie Jacoby.

Sigh. Not really. But for goodness' sake, she's evil personified when it comes to being a Momzilla.

Someone fetched us a basic care package of underwear and sweats, and also brought Declan a replacement phone last night, a shiny bauble plugged in and charging on the bedside table. Instead of buzzing, it glows, like ET's heartlight, and it's creepy. *Really* creepy. I pick it up like it's a live heart and toss it at him.

He startles, snatching it up and smashing it to his ear out of muscle memory, years of middle-of-the-night calls from Asian properties embedded into him.

" 'lo?" he says, eyes closed and slothlike, his body curled up against my body, except I'm not there. He's spooning *air*. His hair has dried in the night and is smashed against his sleeping side, the crown poking straight up. He looks like a cartoon character. I reach up for my own hair and hit snarls within seconds.

His eyes fly wide open as I hear the *mwah mwah mwah* of the person on the other end of the call. "WHAT?"

See? Knew it. Evil.

"She's where? Already? And did the staff let her in? They did. In the lobby? Who's with her? A television camera crew?" Declan doesn't *do* disheveled and frantic, so I'm enjoying the show.

His patented Crazy Mother-in-Law Sigh comes out as he reasserts control. "Kick the camera crew out. *Out.* I don't care what they say. This is private property. No. I said *no*. Did it sound like I said yes? Absolutely not. You heard me. Let them. They can go to hell if they think they can dictate what I can and cannot do with my company's private property."

*Click.*

My tummy starts to tingle. And...he's back. I love when he becomes a controlling, authoritative asshole who protects me and makes things happen. His domineering side isn't so great when it's projected directly at me, but it's great popcorn-eating fun to watch him in action with others.

Especially Momzillas.

His eyes are bloodshot, the green irises glowing even brighter as the sun hits them, the pupils pinpointing. "That was a call about your—"

"I figured. She's here. Along with a camera crew?"

Khaleesi's here on her dragon, only surprise!—instead it's Mom and Geraldo Rivera.

Oh, God. He wasn't *really* with her, was he?

"The camera crew's not here anymore. I had the news people removed." I don't ask about Geraldo Rivera, because my brain cells are currently occupied in their imitation of a tuning fork being hammered against a table saw.

He stands up and stretches, on tiptoes, his fingertips touching the ceiling. It is a riveting display of sinew and bone, of skin and muscle stretched with coordinated symphony across the same basic parts we all have.

Only his taste better.

"I ordered security to kick out the cable channel. Marie gets a hotel room as far away from us as possible, and under no circumstances is she to know our exact room number."

I snort. "She'll find us within two hours. You know how

bloodhounds can track escaped convicts?" I don't even have to finish that thought.

"Like hell she will!" Emphatic and pissed, he turns away, the view of his carved ass making up for the giant pain in my temples. I hear him in the bathroom, then a flush, then running water. He comes out wearing boxer briefs and a frown that makes him look like Chuckles, my cat.

*Tap tap tap.*

"She's here!" I scream, ducking behind a Morris chair upholstered in a Picasso print, cowering like Elphaba is here to steal my soul.

She already stole my *wedding,* so my concern is not that far out of bounds.

"She is *not* here," he says, answering the door in his underwear. He does that. I don't get it. The man has a body that matches up against David Beckham or David Gandy or any other hot underwear model (are they all named David? Is that a requirement to be paid to parade around at photo shoots wearing tightie whities)?

But the way he casually walks around his apartment or hotel rooms unclothed in front of staff is a quirk I haven't gotten used to quite yet.

In walks a man who is so sophisticated he smells like Italy. I have never been to Italy, but I imagine that if I ever go there, it will smell just like the man who wheels in an entire rack of clothing consisting of nothing but men's suits, dress shirts, and five pairs of wingtip shoes.

Followed by another man who smells like Italy and Old Spice, wheeling in a set of clothing so colorful it could be a box of jelly beans.

"Fabulous." Declan frowns. "It looks like there are no women's shoes here."

Marcello scowls at his assistant, rapid-fire Italian sounding like Star Wars sound effects.

He turns to Declan and gives a stiff bow. "We will be back momentarily with a delightful array of choices for Mrs. McCormick."

"Thank you, Marcello." Declan's voice is friendly and amused.

Marcello bows to me and leaves, taking his assistant with him.

"You ordered clothes?" I snap. The role of Captain Obvious will now transfer from Declan's brother, Andrew, to me, by virtue of osmosis. And bloodhounds.

"You don't have to like them. Would it help if I lied and said I had my staff go to a church rummage sale and buy them, and that the rummage sale proceeds will go to buy goats for remote villages in Africa?"

"You would actually do that?"

"No. But would it help?"

I flip through the clothes on the rack. I vaguely remember Mom nattering on about how bright colors are popular this year. I see a lot of clothing with Chanel labels. The underwear is familiar: La Perla, of course. Victoria's Secret would be more my style, but...

"You sent Marcello to La Perla?"

"He was quite pleased with that task."

"He's straight?"

"How would I know, and why would you ask that?"

"Because he's Italian and he works in fashion. I'm surprised he's—"

"Shannon." There's a tone of disappointment and warning in his voice. "That borders on stereotyping. You sound like Marie."

Ouch.

My expression must be pretty bad, because he crosses the room and apologizes immediately. "I'm sorry. That was low."

"Yes. It was."

"How about we start over?"

*Tap tap tap.*

"Khaleesi!" I scream.

His Crazy Mother-in-Law Sigh comes out. I'm starting to think it's not just for Mom.

A room service waiter, complete with a white jacket and bow

tie, wheels a cart loaded with covered dishes and the Golden Snitch into the suite.

Er, I mean, a coffee pot. Thank God.

Before the poor waiter can even adjust the table to turn it into a full circle and open the wings, I grab the coffee pot, a cup, and the pitcher of cream and am mainlining like we're in the caffeinated version of *Boogie Nights*.

A quick glance at Mr. Walks Around in His Underwear in Front of Staff and maybe we are.

Declan signs something and the discreet waiter retreats, leaving us with a white-tablecloth-topped round cart covered with platters of bacon, mixed berry bowls, handmade whipped cream, coffee, and my undying love.

I fling the silver cover off the bacon and chow down. Bacon in one hand, coffee in the other.

Breakfast of Champions. Wheaties can suck it.

Declan grabs a bowl of berries and the little pitcher that is stuffed with whipped cream. Using his fork to scoop the cream, he spears a combo of strawberries and blueberries and digs in. We eat in silence, both of us starving. Ten minutes later, I've eaten four pieces of maple-smoked bacon, half a bowl of berries, an entire dish of whipped cream, two cups of coffee, and just as I think maybe—just maybe—I can relax and we can figure out our next step, we hear:

*Tap tap tap.*

I laugh at Declan, who frowns slightly, and jump up to answer it. "Must be my shoes, right?" I ask, sated by the lovely breakfast, comforted by the rack of clothes. I have the basics. And we successfully escaped. "Did you order me the four-inch heels or the five-inch heels?" I joke as I open the door.

And come face to face with Satan.

Only this time, I don't have Chuckles to throw at her.

But I do slam the door.

"It's her," I hiss, heart racing and flailing at the same time.

"Khaleesi?" he jokes.

"Worse. Mom."

"Same thing." He arches one eyebrow. "I'll handle this."

Declan doesn't give me a choice, pointing to the bed where I walk over and sit obediently, waiting for his next move.

He sits down at the room service tray and grabs a fork, digging in to the final bowl of berries.

There might as well be a Muzak soundtrack behind him.

"What are you doing?" If my hiss goes any higher it will initiate first contact with alien life.

"Performing psychological torture."

"On who? Mom, or me?"

*Tap tap tap.*

Her knock is surprisingly moderate, neither timid nor demanding. Maybe I was mistaken when I opened the door. Perhaps that's not actually my mother out there, but is just a fashion assistant who *looks* like my mother. I close my eyes and bring forth the image.

Nope. Fashion assistants don't have red, glowing eyes.

Hmmm. Maybe that was actually Chuckles out there.

*Tap tap tap.*

"I know you're in there, Shannon and Declan."

I look at Declan, who might as well be humming "The Girl from Ipanema" and putting on sandals over his black calf socks—he's moving *that* slowly.

"Why aren't you *doing* anything?" I beg him.

"I am."

"Eating your daily allotment of fiber and vitamin C does not count as doing something about the massive crisis with my mother!"

"Ah, but it does. This is the fine art of negotiation, Shannon."

"What the hell do organic blueberries in New Zealand fresh cream have to do with negotiation?"

"Is she in our suite?"

I frown. "No."

"Is Geraldo Rivera covering this on national television from the hallway?"

"No."

"Have I been arrested by a federal agency for kidnapping you?"

"No."

"Then we're winning." He takes a bite of black raspberry and munches, peacefully, as if Mom isn't tapping again on the door.

"You're killing me."

"You're making yourself suffer. I am eating a lovely, healthy breakfast."

"Great. You're loaded up with anti-oxidants and I have enough cortisol floating through my bloodstream to kill a pig."

"And that's the difference between us, honey. As far as I'm concerned, emotion has nothing to do with your mother being on the other side of that door. This is all about tactics and strategy. We have a conflict. She thinks she's going to get us to do what she wants. She will fail. It's that simple."

I'm about to marry a cyborg. Or the billionaire version of Sheldon Cooper from *Big Bang Theory*.

"How can you divorce emotion from, from—" Mom is knocking again on the door—"this?!?"

"How can you not? All my emotion is saved for you." With that, he wipes his mouth on his cloth napkin, plants a kiss on the top of my head, and in only his boxer briefs—which are molded to his body like a latex suit—strides across the room and opens the door with a gesture of magnanimity and welcome that makes me shatter.

Mom is standing in the hall, eyes crazy, hair a combed-out half-mess. She's wearing her mother-of-the-bride dress, the tartan sash crooked and filthy, and she's alone.

"Marie! So good to see you!" Declan leans forward and gives her a peck on the cheek, as if there's nothing bizarre about her having chased us down from Massachusetts, and as if he always stands on the threshold of a Las Vegas luxury hotel suite in his underwear and gives her a kiss.

"What?" Mom's gasp makes all the tiny pieces of myself that are sprinkled around the edges of the known universe start to quiver.

"Have you had breakfast? Would you like to join us? The chef's crop of wild Maine blueberries is particularly fine this morning."

"What?" Mom bleats. Declan steps back and sweeps his arm aside, welcoming her in like he's showing her a prize on *Wheel of Fortune* and she could win it.

If she gets the answer just right.

"How's Jason? He enjoying Vegas?" Declan's words are so calm and casual that I begin to shake, the dissonance too much. I know what he's doing. I've seen him do it before, and worse— I've been at the receiving end of this. It's brilliant, really. Disarm your opponent with a neutrality, a banality that makes their own crazy come to a halt, like they've slammed into a stone wall and are coming to in a daze.

I hate being the target of it.

Normally, though, I love watching it in action.

This is too raw. Too painful. Too hard. Unlike Dec, I can't divorce how I feel about a situation from how I act on it. I wish I could. Oh, how much easier life would be if I could. Limitations abound in all of us, and in this exact moment my emotions are overriding my logic, and I start to cry.

And rush across the room into my mother's arms.

She clings to me like I'm that broken door on the *Titanic* and she's Rose.

"Shannon," she gasps.

"Mom," I sob.

"It's okay, honey," she says, her body shaking as she cries, my own tears making my chest hitch and heave. I look over her shoulder to find Declan standing next to the room service cart, absentmindedly picking berries out of the bowl and shoveling them into his mouth, eyes rolling but a smile twitching in one corner of his mouth.

"I know," Mom says as I nudge my nose against her shoulder, the tears pouring off me. She's rubbing my back the same way she used to when I was little and hurt myself. "Let it all out. I know you're sorry."

I freeze.

Declan shoots me a look that says, *I had this. You blew it.*

"I am *not* sorry," I say in a voice that can only be heard by playing a vinyl record at half speed.

"Of course you are," she says. "I raised you right. You, on the other hand," she adds, pointing to Declan, who is currently eating smoked maple bacon like it's an Olympic sport, "were raised by a sociopath who drinks the blood of virgin llamas for fun."

"Am I supposed to be offended by that characterization of my dad? Because I'm not. It's disturbingly close to the truth," Declan replies.

Mom reddens. "I can't believe that you stole my daughter from her own wedding!"

"He didn't steal me—"

"It was my wedding, too—"

Palms with one-inch manicured tartan gel tips go up, facing us both. "I don't care, frankly, what either of you has to say! You're lucky I'm even speaking to you!" I look down at my own hands and see matching tartan.

My own anger goes up a notch.

Declan takes a slow, steady sip of his coffee and looks at Mom with eyes as calm as the Dalai Lama's.

"Speaking to *us?*" I scream, my own nuclear detonation imminent, compounded by Declan's infuriatingly non-reactive status. If he doesn't show emotion, then I'm going to end up channeling everything I feel and everything I imagine *he* feels into one big reactivity laser that will blast us all into the next galaxy.

*Tap tap tap.*

"Perfect timing for the shoes," Declan says with a smile, making Mom do a double take. Walking across the room with a pinpoint perfection in his slow gait, Dec answers the door to find my father standing there, holding a tray of lattes, wearing his kilt tuxedo from yesterday and a weary smile.

"Mocha latte, anyone?"

"*I* am not speaking to *you!*" I inform Mom, marching across the room to give Dad a peck on the cheek and grabbing a latte. "You turned into a wretched, pretentious, emotionally-manipulative, depraved version of my mother. You took over my wedding and turned it into some warped version of your own. You invited hundreds of people I've never met, bought five thousand dollars worth of ribbon, invited my nemesis and my ex-boyfriend, and worst of all—you rickrolled me on national television!"

Mom's mouth is open and she's ready to jump right in, but her eyebrows go down. "Rickroll?" She and Dad share a confused look.

"Never mind," Declan says, taking the tray from Dad. "Jason, want some blueberries and cream? Fresh from Maine and New Zealand."

Dad sits at the room service tray table and kicks off his shoes, a sigh escaping him like a slashed tire. "I don't care if it comes from the corner Seven-Eleven here in Vegas. Just give me something to eat."

The two men start spooning berries and cream into their mouths as Mom and I unite in our open evaluation of this turn of events.

"What are they doing?" Mom hisses through the side of her mouth.

"They're Declanning."

"Declanning?"

"Pretending to be calm so they rattle us."

Mom snorts. "They always think that works."

"I know." Giving her the side-eye, I realize I'm being nice to her. How can this be? We're re-aligned again, on the same side, and someone must pay for taking the wind out of my sails.

My stomach growls like it's shifting into a bear. Just as Declan takes the last spoonful of berries, I realize they've managed to eat all the fruit.

"That was my breakfast!" I declare.

Declan looks at Dad and they share a smile. "I'll call for more."

Mom gives me a look. "You two need to stop it."

"Stop what?" Dad and Declan say in unison.

"Not you!" Mom snaps, drinking half her mocha latte, then pointing the top of it at Dad. "These two!" She flails the drink in my and Declan's general direction.

"Stop what?" Dec and I ask.

"Stop acting like you didn't cause a major media circus and make poor Jessica Coffin have a nervous breakdown."

"Jessica?" I screech. "Who cares about Jessica?"

"And James is furious! You've wasted all this Anterdec money on a selfish whim!" She gives Declan a condescending look that probably scares preschool boys but just makes Declan burst into braying laughter.

He begins humming Alanis Morrissette's "Ironic."

*Tap tap tap.*

"THAT BETTER BE THE SHOES!" I bellow, roaring across the room to whip open the door.

To find myself face-to-face with Amanda and Andrew making out so hard he might as well surgically implant his tongue in her duodenum and be done with it.

"Do all the men in your family have tongues like that?" Dad asks, tilting his head like we're watching Animal Planet.

"Yes," Mom and I sigh in unison.

"MARIE!" Dad snaps, giving her a look. Sometimes, I forget that Mom and Declan's father dated for a brief time.

"You asked, Jason!" Mom squeaks.

"Someone get me a spray bottle," Declan grouses, neatly folding his cloth napkin on the table and crossing the room, grabbing Andrew's shoulder and peeling him off Amanda. Does the man have suction cups on his—

"Hi!" Amanda chirps, breathless. Unlike the rest of us, she and Andrew are wearing street clothes. They have showered, and both wear the same pink-cheeked, slightly dazed look of two people who have spent the last twelve hours embedded in each other's mucosal glands.

Or something like that.

"Hi!" Declan chirps back, glaring at his brother.

Andrew's arm goes around Amanda's shoulders, her fingers peeking out at his waist.

They are freaking adorable.

"You two!" Mom roars, storming up to Andrew, her finger in his face. "You knew they were in this room all along and didn't tell me!"

Declan's pinched expression softens. "You didn't?" he asks Andrew.

Andrew's jaw tightens, his face going hard. I see the resemblance to James, and why these McCormick men can pull off tough negotiations. "Of course I didn't. Marie got the company jet, but nothing more from me."

"Then how did you two know which room we're in?" I ask Amanda.

"Because the cable news crew you kicked out of the hotel got their revenge," Mom explains, picking out a black raspberry from Dad's bowl and munching on it. "Their high school intern hacked into the hotel database and found you."

"What?" Declan groans.

"He said it was easier than hacking a Minecraft server, whatever that means. Called your computer network security 'a joke.'" Mom uses finger quotes to dig it in. Declan's finally showing emotion. Finally.

Over network security protocols.

Or lack thereof.

Andrew's kissing Amanda again, her back pinned against the door frame, his hands working through a geometry problem where the goal is to find the point of intersection where two legs bisect.

People would like math so much more if it involved real life like that.

"SHOES!" Amanda's squeal halts their kiss, poor Andrew standing there open-mouthed and alone, as the tailor's assistant finally arrives with a shipping container's worth of new shoes for me.

Mom scans the scores of boxes. "All these for you?" she asks me. The assistant brings in the shoes, whispers something to Declan, and leaves quickly.

Amanda bends down and pulls out a strappy little pair of turquoise leather shoes with a red heel.

"Ooooooo," she and Mom gush in unison.

I drink the rest of my lukewarm mocha and try to figure out who to glare at.

Declan catches my eye. *You okay?* he mouths.

I just do my best Grumpy Cat imitation in response.

"Here," Amanda says, distracted by all the shinies in my room. She hands me a shopping bag. I peer in.

My purse from home. My ID! My favorite hoodie and jeans. My own underwear. Slip-on loafers. I grab my purse and clutch it to my chest like it's a lost kitten.

I am *real* again.

Amanda and Mom open shoeboxes like they're Charlie and they're searching for the Golden Ticket. Andrew turns to Declan and the two start hissing about computer security issues and international competitors. Dad looks at the suite like he's a peasant who has entered a palace and is taking it all in.

I realize I'm in a bathrobe, Declan's arguing with his brother in his underwear, and damn it, she did it again.

My mother made this all about her.

"OUT!" I scream.

Mom and Amanda ignore me. Dad gives me a look that says, *About time, kid*, and reaches to tap Mom on the shoulder.

She stands up, holding an Aperlai high heel, her face flushed like she just had a quickie in a department store changing room.

"Everyone out," I say again. Amanda shoots me a sympathetic look and makes a gesture that says, *Call me*. Andrew is muttering words like "non-reversible encryption" while Declan's clearly not listening to him, eyes on me, taking in my attempt to re-assert authority.

I fail.

Amanda tugs on Andrew's shoulder. He ignores her until she stands on tiptoes and whispers something so porny in his ear that the man turns a furious shade of pink and breaks off eye contact with everyone, grabbing her hand and departing.

And then there were two.

"We need to help outfit Shannon!" Mom announces, as if she's gutting a bathroom down to studs and starting over.

"Shannon can dress herself," Dad says.

Mom's giggles remind me of Jeffrey when he watches a television show called *Wipeout*. Or when Declan tries to tell me my mother can be controlled.

"Shannon can't tell the difference between eyeliner and lipliner, Jason. You expect her to color coordinate a—"

"We have a professional shopper for that, Marie. You can go now." Declan's hands are on Mom's shoulders. "Shannon wants you to leave."

"Shannon *thinks* she wants me to leave," Mom insists.

Dad replaces Declan, hands on Mom's shoulders from behind, pushing her like a stubborn mule being coaxed to cross a small stream.

"Shannon wants you to leave," I answer. See? I'm referring to myself in the third person.

My mother has turned me into my nephew, Tyler.

"We're staying," Mom says firmly. "We have too much to talk about for me to leave. First of all, you two pulled that horrible stunt with the helicopter! And Declan, your father spent a small fortune on the wedding. Do you have any idea how livid he is right now? More than a thousand people were left—"

SLAM!

Whoever designed this hotel knew how to pick the right doors. Much better than the one on the airplane.

The doorknob rattles.

"Shannon! Shannon! But Jason, I have one of her shoes!" Mom's voice trails off in a thin stream of chatter, the sound even more muffled as Declan's warm, bare skin envelops me, biceps covering my ears, my face burrowing in his hot, hard chest.

I sigh.

"Thank God they're gone," I mumble, my lips rubbing against a sprinkling of dark hair at his breastbone. On impulse, I lick the skin right there. He laughs, the rumbling comforting. He tastes like salt and spice, like adrenaline spiked with power, his own sigh mingling with another one of mine.

"It'll all be fine," he adds.

*Tap tap tap.*

"GO AWAY!" we shout together. Who cares about the shoe Mom's clutching?

"I own this place. You can't make me go away," says an imperial voice on the other side of the door.

Oh, no.

Declan mutters an expletive, then adds, "That's my dad."

Mom's statement about James' anger makes my blood start to race.

*Tap tap tap.*

I look up at Dec and see the storm in his eyes. I'm sure mine is just a mirror, reflecting back a hurricane of overwhelming chaos. We both close our eyes, like little kids who think if we can't see the monster, he can't see us. Not that James is a monster. He's not.

The *world* is the monster.

"Open up, kids. We need to talk."

With a deep sigh, Declan reaches for the doorknob, his chest expanding as his inhale goes on forever, my arms around him adjusting to the changing space his body inhabits as he just breathes in forever and ever, as if eternity masks what we need to face.

The door opens and there stands The Silver Fox. My soon-to-be father-in-law. The man who just spent nearly three-quarters of a million dollars on a thousand-person wedding we subverted by commandeering corporate helicopters and jets.

To escape.

I keep one arm around Declan's waist, feeling him go tense and rigid, as if preparing for the verbal onslaught he expects.

James, though, is grinning madly.

"Brilliant!" he exclaims, pulling Declan away from me, embracing my fiancé in a man's hug, the quick smash of chests and claps of flat palms against shoulder blades that gets the social nicety over with and expresses masculinity without affection.

"Brilliant?" Declan rasps, clearing his throat.

"Your departure from the wedding. Oh—Shannon!" James comes in for a second, gentler hug, this one fatherly and...sweet? James is about as sweet and sensitive as ISIS.

"Hi, James." I give Declan a look that says, *WTF?* and he gives it right back in double time.

"Was this your idea?" James whispers in my ear. His breath smells like coffee and whisky, his breakfast of choice.

"My idea?"

"The whole mess with the helicopter and the press!"

I am walking a tightrope here. If I say *yes*, will I be screamed at, the target of ire?

"Ummm...."

"Whichever one of you came up with it, you're a genius," James adds.

"It was me," Declan and I declare in unison.

Now we *really* give each other *WTF?* looks.

"That's a power couple," James says with a guffaw. He pulls out his smartphone, a phablet he doesn't really know how to use. "Go find CNN, son," he tells Declan, who takes the phone, finds the browser, and squints at whatever web page he's reading.

"Huh," Dec grunts.

"Our public relations specialists say Anterdec is getting *wicked good* free press here!"

James' carefully-cultured sophistication is falling apart as his South Boston accent emerges in the excitement. He's kind of like Pam, who does the same thing.

Hmmm.

"Every news site and gossip blog is talking about you two—and best of all, they're mentioning Declan's role as VP of Anterdec in the process, which means we're trending."

"Trending?" I ask, knowing exactly what he means, but trying to reconcile his happiness with the horror of wasting all that money on a wedding that didn't happen.

"Our PR department tracks Anterdec press mentions and ranks them for positive, negative, and neutral qualities. You're in marketing—you know the drill."

"Of course." James can be pedantic when he talks about business. I don't push back, because hey—I'm a genius, right?

Or, maybe, half genius. I'll share the title with Declan. We can go halfsies on it.

"And PR works with marketing to find paid promotional spots to generate positive press mentions. At the rate your shenanigans are generating positive and neutral press for the corporation, your wedding will have paid for itself."

"Huh?" Dec and I are in stereo on that one.

James beams. "You two orchestrated one of the most brilliant pieces of free positive PR for Anterdec that I've ever seen. We'll get the resort in the press, too, now that they know you're hiding here at Litraeon."

"Dad," Declan asks, his voice going low. "How does the press know we're at Litraeon?"

"I told them."

"You *what*?"

James shrugs. "I told them. PR said mentions were dropping, so it seemed prudent to keep the story in the headlines. Sending Marie here was easy, so—"

"I thought a high school intern hacked into the resort records and found us!"

"That was the cover story I fed Marie." James waves his hand and takes a deep breath. "Good to know she's following orders."

"Hold on. Hold *on*. You told Marie our exact location—*and* told the press—in an effort to keep the free PR gravy train going and turn our wedding escape into a media storm?" Declan asks, his voice calm and deadly.

"Yes."

Declan says nothing, the only sound in the suite his ragged breaths, as he types on James' giant phone and looks at a series of graphs.

*Here it comes*, I think. The emotional bomb is about to detonate. Vesuvius is about to erupt. The tsunami is hitting land.

John Cusack's jet is about to leave the planet.

And Declan says:

"Look at that spike!" He holds out the phone, showing me the data, eyes lit up by conquest.

Our escape from my Momzilla has been distilled into a graph some intern made from an Excel spreadsheet.

My emotional landscape is nothing but color-coded mentions of Anterdec on news feeds.

Blink.

"I've never seen anything like this," Declan hisses, his voice filled with awe.

"That's why you two are geniuses for doing it! I can't believe I never thought to use my kids as PR pawns to generate more free press for the company!"

"JAMES!" I gasp.

"He's got a point," Declan says, wincing.

Men.

Just....men.

"We're not pawns! And we didn't plan a damn thing. Escaping from the wedding was all about my mother."

"Your mother?"

"My mom. Marie. The Momzilla? The one who made me wear a tartan thong. Who dressed a cat up as the flower girl. The one who sabotaged my bachelorette party and who made the guys go commando in their kilts and use Fresh Balls lotion and—"

James frowns. "I thought that was for tennis balls. No wonder my game was off this morning."

"AND!" I shout over him. "AND, the one who invited Jessica Coffin and my ex to my own wedding, all so she could—"

The realization hits me between the eyes.

"So she could get free press and gain status and make people pay attention to her creation," I say pointedly.

Declan's attention cuts from me to his dad to the phablet. His gaze lingers longingly on the phablet, those numbers enchanting him, a data-driven mistress I can't quite compete with.

"Surely you're not comparing Anterdec's trending prominence with your mother's petty need for a mention in *Boston Magazine*'s society page?" James asks with a smirk.

"I am. You are being just like my mother."

James and Declan inhale sharply together, like I just stabbed them both between the ribs and punctured a lung.

Declan and James exchange a look. "That was low, Shannon," my future husband says.

"She really does have claws," James says with a whistle, giving

Declan a look that tells me they've discussed this, and that James is only now believing something Declan told him. "No spray bottle though, right?" The corner of his mouth curls up with a confidence only a sixty-something, self-made billionaire can possess.

"If the shoe fits..." The dawning realization that I'm still in the hotel-provided bathrobe hits me as I pick up the discarded mate to the high heel my Mom took. Tightening my sash, I walk away, grabbing the coffee pot and a pitcher of cream and going to the one place where I can have some peace.

The bathroom.

Muted, heated discussion takes place outside the closed, and locked, bathroom door before I turn on the bathtub faucet and drown out those testosterone-pumped vocal cords. Just as I turn up the water, I hear James say, "Jesus, Declan. You always ran around the house naked as a little kid, so the underwear is an upgrade, but put on a robe for decency's sake."

I snort.

A wave of emotion starts below my navel, tightening like a wire being pulled taut between two fists. Paradoxically, I bend, curling inward, my body twisting. The world makes it unable to remain straight and upright. This involuntary muscular reaction carries a weight to it that seizes me, highlighting all my senses. The rushing water becomes millions of individual drops pinging against ceramic and marble. The bubble bath that froths in the water becomes a field of fresh lavender. The lights in the bathroom glare like searchlights on a helicopter searching for a fugitive.

*Fugitive.*

I am an emotional fugitive.

My throat clamps shut and I can't breathe. All I am is one enormous, rigid body, the air trapped in my lungs, my mind nothing more than a tornado filled with emotional debris, whirling and traveling at breakneck speed without anyone driving the funnel.

And then I break.

Giving myself permission to cry, I let it come, ignoring the arguing men outside the door, forsaking my robe, dropping it to the ground and perching on the marble edge of the luxurious tub, the room all glitter and sparkles and opulence. The keening sob that bubbles up is the sound of my self. It's the sound of choosing *me*.

It's the sound of grief.

I am grieving the loss of the Shannon who would have just taken what Mom dished out, and done so with a tight smile. Until Declan, that's exactly how I operated. I told myself my mother meant well. I convinced myself that she acted from a good heart, from a mother's core within that wants the best for me.

And that's true.

My ugly cry continues, my face a mask of red streaks and tears in a mirror that's meant to reflect back cultivated beauty, in a city designed to make people feel special as a direct result of their possession of money.

Mom means well.

But that doesn't mean she's right.

Leaving my own wedding was my idea. I own it. Declan made it happen, but I asked for it. I did.

*Me.*

I'm a different person now, and that choice to subvert my mother's will has consequences.

Consequences that are leaking out of my body at an alarming rate, through tears and spasms and visceral sensations that remind me, yet again, that I am human. So much of my life involves thought and analysis, process and procedure. The body, though, demands space. Time. Attention.

And it remembers everything.

*Tap tap tap.*

"Shannon? Honey? Dad's gone. You can come out now. No one's here. We're alone again."

I open my mouth to speak but all the words are trapped in an airlock between my heart and my throat. My skin crawls with heat, the steam from the tub filling the room, brushing against my flushed, naked body like butterflies landing in staccato beats.

*Bang bang bang.*

"Shannon?" Declan's louder voice is tinged with worry. "Are you okay? Say something."

I can't.

But the body knows what it needs.

Shaking, I stand and walk three steps to the door, unlocking it. Before I can twist the doorknob, Declan's pushing against the door, opening it gently, his concerned eyes meeting mine.

"Oh," he says, one syllable that carries the weight of our entire relationship in it. I'm in his arms, Declan bending one knee to reach down and turn off the bathtub water, the layer of joyful, relaxing foam so close to the edge it's about to erupt in a massive spillover that will cause unremitting chaos and mess.

Just like me.

"Shhhhhh," he whispers into my hair, his hands following the well-worn paths across my back, down to my hips, his fingers like a brush in the hands of an artist who uses love, not paint, to make a picture of how the world should be. In his embrace I can let it go, sob and keen, seethe and quiver, invoking my own ire and outrage at a world I can disrupt, but can't steer.

*I* did this.

I did *all* of this.

My power turns out to be so much more than anyone ever let me know.

Except for Declan.

He knew.

He *knows*.

"She—she—thinks I'm supposed to feel s-s-s-orry?" I finally choke out, the words garbled as my lips press against his shoulder, my tears viscous against his skin. "Like this was my fault?"

"She's wrong."

The room is so warm, like a soft cloud inside a cocoon. The only sound is my sniffles.

"I know that! But she thinks it's okay to tell me I'm expected to *apologize* to her!"

"You can't control what she thinks or says. Only how you respond to her."

"Maybe you can be that way, Declan, but I can't! She shouldn't be this way."

He stays silent.

We just breathe.

"Did I—was I—did we—are we in the wrong? We left all those people in the lurch. Your dad's happy because we're a trending story on all the major news outlets and getting all this free, positive press for Anterdec," I say, laughing in spite of myself, giggling against Declan's bare chest, my arms tightening around his waist. "And my dad didn't say anything bad, but that's Daddy. He just goes along with whatever Mom says. He's her lapdog."

A decidedly male sound emerges from Declan's throat. "I wouldn't quite say that. Jason has more backbone than you think."

"Hmmm." I'm not sure what he means by that.

"Shannon, don't second-guess yourself," he mumbles into my temple, giving it a little kiss that makes me cling harder. "What you did back there in Massachusetts was brave."

"Brave?"

"Yes. You stood up to her. You stopped her. You—and *only* you—gave Marie the first hard 'no' that woman has heard in a very long time."

"I didn't do it alone! You got the helicopter and the jet and called Grace and—"

"I was your operations manager. You were the decision maker. You decided. I just made the logistics line up."

*The first hard 'no.'*

I take three, four, five deep breaths, the humid air making it hard to breathe, the lavender bubble bath aroma soothing and stifling at the same time. Tender and deferential, Declan guides me to the tub, urging me to slip in. I do. He joins me.

Miraculously, the water doesn't overflow.

"Ahhhhhh," we say at the same time, catching each other's

gaze and smiling. My eyes sting, so I rub them, hard, the skin around them so raw it feels like wet tissue paper.

"You did it," he repeats. "You. And I'm proud of you."

"Proud? For making us a media spectacle and leaving the Boston Wedding of the Year in shambles?"

"Yes."

"You're nuts."

"Your mother is nuts. I am unorthodox."

I sniffle-laugh, but his words resonate.

"Shannon, do you remember that very first date we had?"

"Which one? The business dinner date or the picnic date where I nearly pierced your penis with my EpiPen?"

His thighs close in, sloshing a little water over the edge. "Christ. Please don't bring that up."

I throw a handful of bubbles at him. He dunks his head under, then pops back up, a tuft of white foam on the tip of his slicked-back dark hair.

"What about our first date?" I ask. He looks like a hot seal. "I'll concede it *was* an actual date, and not the business dinner we both pretended to share. You brought me a corsage, after all."

We share a smile only two people in love can volley back and forth.

"You were so, so insecure," he says, his voice changing, the register dropping into a deep territory of musing. "Steve had convinced you that nothing inside you was of any value. His need to be the authority in every situation turned you into a vigilant puppy."

I freeze.

"People take the deepest good inside others and use it to meet their own needs. If you're lucky, you find someone who reciprocates. Who potentiates. Like you." He's frowning slightly, so mired in the tangled web of parsing through his point that he doesn't realize it. The tub is huge. I can't just reach across and wipe away the tension from his face.

I also don't want to interrupt him. Some piece of this is resonating within me. I have a lock inside me, and the key is out there, one of a thousand on a big, fat metal circle of keys that Declan holds. For the next six or so decades his job is to pick out a key, try it in my lock, and keep going until the right one fits.

I have no idea what happens when we reach that point.

But I know I hold a corresponding set of keys for his lock, too.

"I was about to tell you that you're stronger than you think, but those aren't the right words." He leans back, resting his head against a small rolled pillow on the tub's edge, his eyes closed, face tipped up to the ceiling. "People say that all the time—*you're stronger than you think*. What they mean is that you have to learn to suck it up. That's not strength. That's being groomed to accept suffering."

His words are like a call to arms.

"You, Shannon, are more *powerful* than you think. Your mother just got a lesson in that. Don't back down now. Don't second-guess. Don't waffle."

My stomach growls.

"Mmmm. Waffles," I say. The joke falls flat. I don't know why I make it.

Yes, I do.

Because what Declan is saying is dangerous.

"I'm not threatened by your power," he says softly.

"What?"

"I'm attracted to it, in fact. You are never more alive than when you harness it."

Oh, God.

"I can't make you use it, or access it. Only you can, honey. But that *no* you just used yesterday—that big, fat *screw you* that you reached inside yourself to find—was mesmerizing in its beauty."

"It—it was?"

He sits up so fast that a small wave crests over the side of the tub, carrying a shelf of white foam onto the floor, soaking the area rug. He's kissing me, and I'm melting into him, our bodies wet and slick and floating and entwined, limbs ending and beginning in a Gordian knot that starts with my mother and ends with a clean, simple cut of the sword of our love.

We show each other our combined power, and I swear, in the distance, I hear the sound of metal against metal, the click of steel against unyielding tumblers as yet another key is tried, and yet another lock remains unopened.

<h1 style="text-align:center">Chapter Nine</h1>

I manage to find a decent outfit and shoes—if by "decent" you mean a Vera Wang dress and Louboutins—among the maze of clothing that the tailor delivered, though Declan's clearly unhappy with my "limited" options.

"I'm sending a stylist up to work with you," he says, calling Grace and muttering a laundry list of issues for her to tackle as he walks around our suite, freshly showered and shaved, his naked body on display for me. He's so much easier on the eyes than the hand-picked interior-decorator-selected original art throughout the room.

I take the opportunity during his twenty-minute call to clean up and check my nine thousand text messages.

*Lunch?* Amanda's text asks. *Andrew says meet us at the private club on the roof.*

Guilt twangs through me like an untuned guitar string. For the past year, Amanda's been my maid of honor, my rock, my stable bestie who helped me through this farce of a wedding, and how do I thank her?

By ditching it all after she nearly drowned at the very wedding I escaped.

*Where are you?* I text back.

*You don't want to know*, she replies instantly.

Huh?

*I'm naked in bed,* she texts.

Oh. She's right.

I *really* don't want to know. We're in new territory now, because she's naked in bed with my almost brother-in-law, who has seen me naked.

And I've seen Amanda naked.

I look at naked Declan, who is the only person in this quad not to have completed a number of naked-viewing transactions.

Let's keep it that way, shall we?

*Lunch in half an hour?* she answers.

*K,* I reply, just as Declan gets off the phone with Grace and starts dressing, morphing from my Declan to the world's Declan.

You ever watch a man go from naked to fully dressed in a business suit? It's performance art. Truly. Declan slides those muscled calves into his black boxer briefs, the soft cotton clinging to toned thighs covered in coiled hair, the color of his skin fading to a soft pale I can almost feel. He eschews a t-shirt under his tailored business shirt, buttoning up but leaving the cuffs alone, for those require his cuff links, which come much later in the process.

I take a seat on the small bench at the base of our California King bed and watch. Forget Cirque du Soleil downstairs.

This is the *real* show here in Vegas.

And it's a command performance for one.

Socks—a funky pattern with accents of hot pink mixed with adobe, which Marcello swears is the latest fashion—then the sound, *oh* the sound of those strong, muscled legs swishing against cashmere woven and tailored for his body alone.

Button. Zip.

And then the belt appears.

It's a classic, simple black leather with an understated silver buckle, but the precision handling and mastery in Declan's capable fingers makes my mouth curve in a secret smile as he finishes. The jacket is next, then out come the links, old heirlooms passed down from his mother's father.

I pick out the tie, a lovely grey that has flecks of adobe.

"That's the one Marcello recommended," Declan says absentmindedly, clearly unaware of my besotted, enraptured observation of what is, to him, a basic set of procedures to enter civil society.

"Then he has good taste." I lick my lips. Can't help it. Watching him dress reminds me of my very first look at him two years ago, when he was Mr. Sex in a Suit, walking into the men's bathroom at the bagel chain store Anterdec owns, and all I could do was caress him with my eyes and undress him in my mind.

I reach out.

He's real now. My fingers walk up the fine weave of his suit jacket, squeezing his arm muscles, finding bone and hard flesh.

And it's mine.

All mine.

"What are you....doing?" he asks, perplexed and intrigued.

"Touching you."

"I see that. I feel *that*," he adds as my stroke goes under the open suit jacket, hand splayed across his ribs, his heat radiating out and warming me. "Why?"

"Because I can."

The low, sexy rumble that comes out of him makes me lean in closer and inhale, smelling aftershave, soap, coffee and the scent of a man I can breathe in for the rest of my life.

"I think you're part man, Shannon."

"Would that turn you on if I were?"

"Nothing could turn me on more than you, as you are, right now." The way he responds to my touch, twisting toward me, sensuously running his hands up and down my spine, his nose in my hair, his lips twitching with a smile....

*Oh.*

"Nothing?" I sigh.

"Not one damn thing."

His kiss makes me regret getting dressed, makes me wish I'd never said yes to this lunch date, makes me spin and grow dizzy in my mind as blood races to all the parts he's touching right now. Maybe we could postpone...

*Bzzzz.*

Or not.

"What the hell?"

Moment transformed. Real life intrudes.

"Grace?" he snaps into the phone. Poor woman. It's not her fault.

I focus on myself, straightening my skirt and running a useless comb through my hair for a moment, trying to fix the mess as Declan barks orders about a variety of media-related wedding crap. Part of me wishes Grace had come to Vegas, but part of me is glad that the long-time executive assistant to the McCormick family is back in Boston holding down the fort.

So to speak.

"What was that about?" I ask as I stand in front of the suite's door, not-so-subtly making it clear we need to go. Andrew and Amanda are waiting for us. I know if we stay here we'll end up naked again.

I also know that if we leave, Mom doesn't automatically know our location, and that is more enticing right now than sex.

Believe it or not.

"Jessica Coffin," he mutters.

If I had any interest in sex a second ago, it is now vanquished.

"What *about* her?"

"She's hashtagging our wedding."

"You're surprised?"

"And talking about us on television."

"Okay, well, there were a lot of cable news vans there."

"National television."

"Huh?" I look at the wall television.

"Don't worry, Shannon. Grace is dealing with it, and—it's complicated," Declan says.

"It's *always* complicated," I grouse, but I grudgingly leave the room with him, teetering on these new heels the tailor brought. As we walk down the hall, I take Dec's arm and work out the kinks in my body, willing joints, tendons, heels and clothing to work together to make me walk in fluid motion, like a graceful swan.

I manage to look like a bull moose on roller skates.

So I'm improving.

"You look so hot in those shoes," he whispers as we wait for the elevator.

"You have a bull moose fetish?"

He lets a few beats pass. "Sometimes I really worry about you, Shannon."

"Hey. You picked me. What does that say about you?"

"That I'm the smartest man in the world." He kisses my temple as the elevator doors open and we glide on.

Like I'm on roller skates, you know?

Exactly like that.

As I rub my sore ankle, the elevator sending us rapidly up to the rooftop, Declan stands within inches of me, ready to dip down and rescue me from my clumsy self.

"I hope our kids have your grace," I grumble.

"And your looks."

"But your eyes. So green," I marvel. The kid conversations are fairly new territory. I love it. A delicious tingle rivets through me like someone's holding a jackhammer of future fun against my skin, injecting it straight into my bloodstream.

Kids.

Kids with Declan.

The elevator doors open into a solarium filled with couples in various stages of fancy lunches. Two years with Declan has made this scene slightly less surprising, but every time we dine out I still have a part of me that marvels at eating in sit-down restaurants where they don't roll the silverware in paper napkins, and where jelly doesn't come in little plastic, foil-topped packets.

The solarium is filled, along the edges, with orchids. Not a few sprinkled here and there. Oh, no.

*Filled* with orchids.

Along the perimeter of the glass-covered room ("room" being an understatement, as it's bigger than my childhood home) is a series of planter boxes, about a foot deep and three feet tall, filled with dirt.

And orchids.

It's like being surrounded by flower labia.

What? It is. Try looking at an orchid without imagining an annual gynecological visit. Go ahead. Try.

The decor is Italian marble. Fountains pumping water 24/7, surrounded by sculptures of half-nude people who look just enough like Matt Bomer and Jennifer Lawrence to make me look twice.

Living with Declan has also taught me to look for subtle corporate influences. Product placement is more widespread than you'd ever imagine.

Like, you know, a coffee bean on top of a car, to advertise a fake coffee shop.

Or something like that.

I spot Amanda and Andrew at a table over by an orchid that would make my friend Josh faint. They are engaging in public displays of affection that result in stoning in a minimum of nine countries across Asia.

"Get a room," Declan growls at them. His words make them break their faces apart, which is refreshing. They haven't fused their flesh just yet, so there's hope.

"We have a room. One we can't use right now, because the cleaning crew is in there," Andrew says with a fake frown, standing and giving his brother a huge hug.

"Only because decontamination takes so long," Declan replies, his face split with a genuine grin.

Andrew just grunts, while I hug Amanda.

All the cross-hugging happens and we sit down. A waiter appears instantly with my favorite bottle of white wine. Declan gives Andrew an arched eyebrow.

"Nice touch," Dec says.

Andrew just shoots him a grin that says, *I win*.

"You called Grace, didn't you?"

The grin falters.

Declan lobs back the grin Andrew lost.

Amanda and I roll our eyes in unison. I didn't know that was possible, but apparently, the collective ego of the two youngest McCormick brothers is so large it shoves everything in the room to the side and forces all objects into the gravitational pull of their orbit.

Including our eyeballs.

"How's married life treating you, Dec?" Andrew asks, just as Declan can't answer, his mouth full of wine.

Amanda shoots me a look that says everything and nothing.

"Oh," Andrew adds. "That's right. You're not married yet. Wonder how that happened?"

"I see why he's CEO. He's direct, fearless, and a bit of a prick," I whisper in Amanda's ear.

She stiffens.

Oops.

"Prick?" she hisses. "He's not a prick! He's a *jerk*," she adds. "He's been a jerk ever since James discovered how trendy your escape has been in the news, and how it's boosting Anterdec's profile."

"Why would Andrew be upset by that?"

She shrugs. "I don't know. Have you ever noticed how competitive they are?"

We look over at Dec and Andrew, who are arguing about whether Montrachet or Scharzhofberger is a better wine.

"Nope. Never noticed," I say faintly. Grasping at anything but the wedding escape as a topic, I notice her earrings. "Oooo, look at those!" A combination of amber topaz, lapis lazuli, and sterling silver catch the sunlight and glitter. I reach over and let the dangling jewelry rest on my fingertips. "Gorgeous."

"Andrew got them for me," she says with a happy smile, reaching over to clasp his hand. "A surprise gift delivered from Tiffany when we woke up this morning. These and my breve latte were the second-best things I woke up to." She squeezes his hand.

Andrew gives Declan the same smile, except on his face it looks smug. Self-satisfied.

Triumphant.

"What did Declan get for you, Shannon?" he asks.

"Get for me?"

Declan's tongue rolls in his cheek so hard it might as well be drilling for oil.

Andrew's eyes light up. "He didn't give you something this morning?"

"Oh, I gave her something this morning," Declan murmurs in my ear.

I bat at him, giggling, reaching for my wine. "I got this outfit. And these shoes," I say.

"Mmmmmm," Andrew says, drinking the rest of his wine and giving Declan a look I don't understand, and definitely don't like.

"James tells us that the public relations department at Anterdec is over the moon about all the positive free press the wedding is getting for the company," I assert.

Declan gives me an appreciative thigh squeeze. Andrew's smile goes sour.

What the hell is going on between the two of them? Is Amanda right? I know Declan was crushed when James picked Andrew as his successor, but he never fought it. He could have created a fuss with the board of directors but chose not to create that kind of divisiveness when James was stepping down because of his prostate cancer diagnosis.

Competition is in Declan's blood, but I'm getting a creepy vibe here, as if they're vying for some title that Amanda and I aren't aware of.

"It's true," Andrew says, clearly reluctant to admit whatever's about to come out of his mouth. If Amanda weren't here to soften him, I'd think he was angry. For brothers who are only two years apart and who work in the same business, the two are so different. Declan's closed off and placid, like a calm sheet of mirror on a lake.

Andrew is all action, with laser focus, and an aloofness that I know masks a boyishness underneath that makes him and Declan spar.

He also has a freakish fear of wasps, generated entirely by his anaphylactic reaction. We both flout death on a regular basis when it comes to spinning the random dial for bee and wasp stings. Andrew takes risk assessment and prevention to a degree that I find intolerable.

Obsessive.

*Bizarre.*

It hits me, though: the wedding. He overcame his deep-seated fear in order to rescue Amanda from drowning. I almost smack my own head in a *Eureka!* moment. Of course.

*Of course* that explains all this weirdness.

Months of wedding preparation made me miss out on so much of my normally layered life. While Amanda and Andrew's developing relationship was on my radar, it wasn't front and center.

Like now.

We're in a new reality, where Declan and I are at the core of a media spectacle, the year-long planning for the thousand-person wedding just got thrown out the window, Andrew is the new CEO of Anterdec and their father is ill, and he threw himself (literally) headfirst into his relationship with Amanda just yesterday, at our wedding.

Good grief.

That was yesterday.

The wine's gone to my head, because the orchid next to Amanda begins to dance.

"Yesterday," I whisper.

"Does she routinely quote Beatles lyrics?" Andrew whispers to Amanda.

"Honey?" Declan doesn't use many terms of endearment in public, so I know I must look a sight. "What's wrong?"

"Yesterday. We fled the wedding *yesterday.*"

"Right."

"It feels like a year. Mom found us this morning. We kicked her out of the room—"

"And us, too," Andrew mutters.

"Because we needed privacy," Declan clarifies, his voice so full of warning that Amanda and I frown at each other in worry.

I look at Amanda's arms, which are covered in a lightweight cotton crewneck shirt, three-quarter sleeves the shade of the wide-open blue sky above us. Angry red welts, swollen and raised, peek out above her wrists.

She looks like Wolverine did a number on her. Surgical tape covers the skin along her other arm.

"Your arm!" I gasp. "Is that from yesterday? In the pool with Chuckles?"

"And Muffin and Spritzy, yeah," Amanda says, wincing. Andrew slings his arm around her shoulders and gives her a side hug, the two of them closing their eyes and sighing together.

"Too much," I whisper. "It's all too much. We've been through a lifetime in twenty-four hours."

Andrew opens his eyes, brown gemstones glittering with a strange mixture of mirth, anger, and protective outrage. "You and Declan sure do know how to make an exit."

Amanda laughs, reaching for the wine and refilling her glass, her stretch making the bandages show even more. I do the math. Somehow, they managed to leave the wedding, get her proper medical attention, fly five and a half hours to Vegas, check into their hotel room, sleep, and find us this morning.

All while managing Momzilla.

It really is too much.

For everyone.

"I'm so sorry," I say, reaching across the table for Amanda's free hand, tears making my vision blur. "You're the ones we should apologize to."

Declan flinches, his chin pulling back and eyes troubled. He gives me a look of compassion tinged with skepticism. "Apologize? To Andrew?"

Ignoring the fact that he's completely leaving Amanda out of this, I respond, "Yes. I know that apologizing in the McCormick family is a form of UN-prohibited torture, but normal people say they're sorry when they've hurt someone, intentionally or unintentionally."

Andrew gives me an appraising look. "She really does study us. Dad said he thought she did, but this proves it."

"Is that true?" Amanda asks him.

"Is what true?"

"McCormicks don't apologize to each other?"

The dual snorts from the men are her answer.

"Well," I announce archly, "I am not a McCormick—yet—and I am going to apologize, deeply, to both Andrew and Amanda," I announce, then chug the rest of my second glass of wine. "I am sorry that by escaping the wedding, we dumped so much of the responsibility off on you."

"Oh," Declan groans, the sound one of relief. "That." He waves his hand toward Andrew. "Right. I'll apologize for that, no problem."

Andrew's eyes narrow. "What did you think Shannon wanted you to apologize for?"

"Doesn't matter." Declan's clipped tones make my antenna go up, too.

"It matters," Andrew argues.

"No."

My eyes dart over to Amanda, who looks at me like, *You're the McCormick men expert. Explain this.*

I shrug and cheer when the waiter interrupts us with salads. Andrew clearly ordered everyone's meal ahead of time. Declan doesn't seem to care about that.

"I'm not sorry for escaping," I add, almost as an afterthought. Declan's hand reaches under the table for mine, clasping it. Aha. That's what he thought I was insisting we say, as if we should apologize for asserting ourselves and reclaiming our wedding.

Oh, no.

*Hell*, no.

"You shouldn't be." Andrew's words come with a healthy dose of laughter as he digs into his salad. "Your mom is nuts."

Declan's grip relaxes and he smiles at his brother.

All is well in McCormick Man Land.

They have a common enemy. And for once, it isn't their dad.

Emotion wells up in me, and not just because the waiter arrives with shrimp cocktail the size of lobster claws. Amanda can sense it, and she reaches for my shoulder, giving me a sisterly touch.

"It's okay, Shannon. You can breathe now. Really. Sure, it's a mess." She chuckles. "When isn't life a mess? But the mess is back there. In Boston. And, really, it's Marie's mess. She made it."

"I can't believe James let her spend $700,000 of Anterdec corporate funds on that wedding," I say.

Andrew starts choking. His phone buzzes at the same time, and the waiter delivers some sort of bacon-wrapped fig thing in front of him as Andrew fights to check his phone.

Declan's stomach growls and he drops my hand. "Sorry. Food first. Affection later." We grin at each other, and Amanda relaxes. This give-and-take between the four of us is casual and comfortable, weirdly familiar and blindingly new. Is this what adult life feels like? Are the four of us about to become a thing, with regular social time spent together and dinners out?

If so, it's an exciting prospect. Dec and Andrew spar and compete, but underneath it all they're each other's best friend. Amanda and I are besties. In this foursome, the getting-to-know-you phase is strongest between me and Andrew, but then again, he's seen me naked. I've seen him drunk.

And we have that whole deadly bee-and-wasp-sting allergy in common.

We have a decent foundation here.

Andrew's call is short but yields this nugget of information:

"PR says the value of all this free press is probably going to be more than the cost of the wedding. *Good Morning America, The Today Show, The View*, and Ellen Degeneres all want you on their shows." He doesn't even bother looking at Declan, zeroing in on me just as I shove a piece of shrimp in my mouth.

"Hmmmm?" He clearly thinks I'm the softer of the two of us, as if appealing to *me* to go on those shows will work.

"No." Declan's answer is firm.

"I wasn't telling *you*." Andrew ignores Declan, eyes on me, charm turned on to the Nth degree.

"Mmmmm mmmm mmmmm hmmm mfff," I try.

I fail.

Amanda just shakes her head and leans in to Andrew. "I think they've had enough. Do they really need to go on major morning news shows and talk about what happened?"

"It's them or Marie."

"They're trying to book *her mother* on those shows?" Declan asks, incredulous.

Andrew surveys the table with hawk eyes that make me realize I consistently underestimate him. "No. They think she's too unstable to book."

"They're right," Declan answers.

I kick him under the table. He reaches down to rub his ankle.

"You know," he says tersely, "it would really be helpful if you wore a sign of some kind to indicate when it's acceptable to refer to Marie as crazy, and when it is not. This is getting old."

"Sorry. Habit."

"Look," Andrew says evenly, "it's basic public relations. Anterdec's getting great passive positive mentions in the traditional press, social media, and on podcasts."

"Podcasts?" I squeak.

"Oh, yeah. One of the wedding guests fed audio of Marie's meltdown as you were leaving, and it's epic," Amanda says.

"One of the wedding guests? The initials wouldn't be JC, would they?"

"Jesus Christ," Declan mutters.

"Was he on the invitation list?" Andrew asks drolly. "I wouldn't be surprised."

"Jessica Coffin," Amanda says in a voice that makes me love her even more. "The Antichrist herself."

Declan stares at Andrew, who suddenly isn't making eye contact with anything not fermented. So many secrets between these two. So many.

Too many.

My Spidey Sense is tingling. The subtext between them runs deep.

*Bzzzzz.*

My phone. My mom. The message:

*We have to talk about this. What are you doing for lunch?*

I look around, grab another giant shrimp, and drown my sorrows in shellfish.

"Marie?" Amanda asks, perking up. She turns her head just as Andrew leans toward her, and her dangling earring catches in his hair. Untangling it, she laughs, the sunlight shining on the gemstones.

I laugh and look at Declan.

Who is stone-faced, staring at her ear.

Then he grabs his phone and types quickly in a series of text messages.

"Did Mom text you, too?"

"What?" He seems distracted.

"My mom," I repeat. "She texted me. Insists we need to talk."

"She's right."

"I know she's right," I murmur as Andrew and Amanda start making out across the table. The shrimp cocktail is just close enough to their suckfacefest that I know I'll be rude if I do a reach-over for another delicious piece, but—

"We do need to talk. Marie needs to apologize to you."

You know that moment in the movies where the record scratches and everyone freezes, because the director has the creative license to make the world stop for dramatic flair?

Yeah. That's not what happens.

Andrew and Amanda start laughing until tears fill Amanda's eyes and she huff-snorts, "Good luck with that."

"Even I'm not *that* delusional," Andrew adds.

There's that word again.

*Delusional.*

Declan takes it all well, a triumphant grin covering his face while I tear into a piece of filet mignon the size of a casino chip, covered in a tower of edible colors and woven pieces of white greenleaf lettuce that look like a group of fiber arts majors at the Rhode Island School of Design spent their entire semester-long internship in the kitchen for this single dish.

I cut it mercilessly with a knife, the Godzilla of culinary design.

Mmmm. Perfection in medium rare form. *Nom nom nom.* Sorry, RISD.

"I don't actually expect Marie to apologize," Dec clarifies. "That's like getting Dad to admit he's wrong."

This time, it's Andrew who laughs until he cries.

The waiter appears, begins to ask about the food, finds four people in various states of apoplexy, and discreetly backs out, leaving a fresh bottle of white wine, which we devour in the next fifteen minutes. By the time the meal is over I am half drunk, stuffed silly, and blissfully happy to be among friends.

Life is good.

Even if we nearly required a SWAT team to escape my own wedding yesterday.

"I thought I'd have a sister-in-law by now," Andrew says after the bottle's been drained and we're smiling at each other.

"You will." Declan's hand caresses the spot between my shoulder blades, making me arch and purr like a cat in a perfect spot of sunshine. "Soon."

"Are you eloping?" I can't tell if Amanda's question holds disappointment or excitement.

"Yes."

"No."

"Uh, oh," Andrew responds to our mixed answers.

"We're still negotiating," Declan says smoothly.

"He *thinks* we're still negotiating." I wink at Andrew.

Bad move.

"Life is nothing but negotiation," Dec answers, his jaw going tight. Whatever loose happiness we had a moment ago turns bleak.

"Right," I say, staying in neutral.

"Nothing is immutable."

"Except for you," I joke.

Just then, the waiter arrives with a cake. Silver sparklers protrude from it, the center covered in frosting that spells out, *I love you.*

He sets it in front of Amanda.

Declan looks like he's going to kill his brother with nothing but a wine cork and a demitasse spoon.

"What's this?"

"A celebration," he says as the waiter lights the sparklers. "To new beginnings. To us."

"To being outdoors at an orchid farm where there are loads of wasps," Declan says under his breath. I jolt.

"That *is* a new beginning, for him, Dec. Please don't do this," I plead as the sparklers light, go out, and Amanda kisses Andrew, shooting me a *sorry* look. I shake my head, making sure she knows it's fine.

And it is. I'm not jealous. The rest of them seem to think I should be, but I'm really not. Andrew's over-the-top gestures are adorable. Amanda's eating it all up. Good for them.

"Don't do *what*?" Declan hisses.

"Get competitive."

"This isn't about competition."

"It isn't? Then what's it about?"

Before he can answer, the waiter has plated the cake and hey...cake.

You know how some men have this thing about breasts because...breasts?

Cake is breasts for women.

*Bzzzz.*

I'm halfway through my piece when I check the message. It's not a text message, actually. Just a notification from an app Declan put on my phone, one that is for Litraeon, informing hotel guests of the day's events.

It turns out today's the first day of a three-day "adult products" trade show being held in the convention center.

I give Declan a hollow look and put down my fork, pushing the plate away.

"What's wrong?" Amanda gasps in alarm, looking at my plate. Failure to finish cake is a full-blown catastrophe in our world.

I hold out my phone with the notification on the screen.

"I don't think we have to worry about my mom for a while."

# Chapter Ten

After *zero* debate, Andrew and Amanda leave lunch to head back to their room, their amorous intentions all over both their faces. Declan, on the other hand, looks about as eager to go find my mother in a sex toy convention hall as he is to have a vasectomy performed by a crack addict with Parkinson's disease.

"Timing is everything," Dec jokes as he reads through his messages on his phone, following behind me just enough to make it clear he's become a phone zombie, eyes tracking my feet so he can stay in line and multitask.

"What's that supposed to mean?"

"Did you know there's a small rodeo convention and the adult products trade show here in the resort at the same time?"

"Yee haw?"

"Ride 'em, cowboy," Dec says as the doors open and we walk slowly through the labyrinth of the resort. We haven't even been here for a day. When you arrive at places by limo, you often miss the actual entrance. I'm spellbound as the elevator doors open and we go into the main common areas of the casino.

This is nothing like any casino I've ever seen on television or in the movies.

To be fair, I don't watch the kind of movies featuring gambling. I'm more of a romantic comedy girl, and my action-thrillers lean more toward natural disaster movies and away from the mob or drug-smuggling features. I can handle tension if it's so unreal I can't imagine it really happening to me.

So this casino puts me in a quandary. It's sumptuous, more Monte Carlo than grungy gambler. Dad used to watch these old '70s and '80s television shows where the casinos were filled with smoke clouds, with people fishing around in cups of coins to shove in slot machines, ladies in muumuus all clustered around that one lever that was going to change their world while some mob boss stole their life savings and granddaughter behind their back.

The casino at Litraeon is about as close to those plots as my mother is to being a Supreme Court Justice.

"Wow," I gasp.

"What?"

"It's just...wow." I slow down, my heels clicking on the marble floor, and as I look up at the Italian style of the hallways, all wide and tan, with beige and burgundy accents, I realize how much I really don't know about the world beyond Boston.

Declan beams with pride. "Pretty great, huh?"

Cigarette smoke tickles my nostrils. "You can smoke *indoors* here? I thought that was illegal."

"In Massachusetts it's illegal. You outlaw it here in Vegas and there would be riots."

Raised platforms with long, thick, velvet curtains dot the casino floor, private enclaves that don't clarify who is allowed to gamble within those hidden spaces, because—I assume—if you're allowed in there, you know. You don't need to ask.

The slot machines dominate, spread far and wide like worker bees in a hive, drones designed to do the heavy lifting to support the larger operation. I imagine this business is like any other: while the largest profit margin comes from high-value, high-cost products, the sheer number of sales made from smaller-level profits on a mass scale means meeting the needs of the many in large quantities is worth it.

Penny slots are example number one. My eye catches a Tarzan-themed machine and I pull away from Declan, wandering toward it.

"What's that?" I ask.

"Penny slots."

"I know, but...why? Why the branding?" As I look around, I see characters from television series' long off the air, from movies that were popular in my teens, and from video games I know my ex-brother-in-law, Todd, used to play for hours.

"Because it draws people in. Once they sit down, they feed their credit card or pre-loaded card into the machine and spend."

A cocktail waitress with mega-cleavage walks by on heels that might as well be knitting needles, smoothly carrying a tray loaded with drinks.

"Are the drinks free?" I know enough about casinos to guess.

"Yep. Get them drinking. Loosen people up. Help them have fun."

My eyes float over to the layered system for the machines. Pennies. Nickels. Quarters. Dollars. Higher value machines with twenty dollar and fifty dollar slots. It's like a flea market, wares spread out in concentric ripples as far as the eye can see, except instead of selling old treasures, Anterdec's resort is selling hope.

"They sit here for hours and just push buttons?" Most of the slot machines don't even have levers.

"Mmm hmmm." Declan seems distracted, eyes darting back to the marbled hallway where we originally were headed. "Is this what you want to do now? Gamble?"

"I thought we were chasing down my mom in the sex toy convention."

"Right."

"Not that I *want* to do it. It's just...." A nagging feeling pulls at me. This open-ended, unresolved tension between me and Mom shouldn't affect me like this. Maybe it's my full stomach. Maybe it's the wine. Maybe it's fatigue and stress from the last twenty-four hours. Whatever this tug inside me is, it isn't going away until I have a long talk with my mother and father.

I don't think I can actually change anything. Mom is Mom. She is going to blame me and Declan for ruining "her" wedding. Between the media circus this wedding escape has triggered and her outrageous behavior, there's no way to put the genie back in the bottle.

That hug this morning was heartfelt.

Like hell I'm apologizing, though.

We spin away from the casino floor, walking to the right, my eyes catching poker tables and, across the slot machines, a room that has a huge sign made of brass on mahogany that says "High Value Room."

"Is that where the big money goes?" I ask.

"Ten thousand just to walk in."

I look back at the penny slots.

More my style.

The hallway widens and changes from Persian rugs to clattering marble, bright lights altering the scenery as I realize we're leaving the casino and entering a mall. A series of high-end, designer-named stores dots the walk, with gelato and coffee shops interspersed.

"An indoor mall? In a casino?"

Declan laughs at my tone of wonder. "Where do you think people want to spend their money after a win? We aim to please."

"You aim to keep them penned in and contained in your little universe so you can mop up their sweet consumer dollars," I scoff.

"Of course," he says with a charming smile. "That's the point of this property, Shannon."

The gelato makes me want to part with some money, for sure, but I'm still full of filet and shrimp and that nagging feeling.

Food will have to wait.

The decor changes even more as we walk up a slight incline, the shops disappearing, the lighting going from artificially bright to a more natural, muted tone as wide glass windows frame the way, leading out to a courtyard dotted with three pools, two hot tubs, and a cabana bar. All of the swimming options are surrounded by giant palm trees and colorful flowers I can't name, because they definitely don't grow back home in cold-climate Massachusetts.

It looks so finished. Polished. Like something out of a soap opera.

An art gallery with works by Picasso, Matisse and Cezanne appears out of nowhere, the walls around it painted in Jackson Pollock style, an Andy Warhol print lighted by LEDs blinking in rapid-fire rhythm. We pass by and a security guard starts to ask us a question, takes a good look at Declan, and steps aside, murmuring, "Mr. McCormick. So good to see you."

Dec just nods.

I'm in awe.

And it's not from the property.

"How do they all know you?"

"I told you."

"But—just like that?"

"Security is paramount in a casino. It's their job to know who the owners are."

"Do they know Andrew and James and Terry?"

"Terry? What does *Terry* have to do with this resort?"

"He's part owner, right?"

"You know Terry doesn't work for Anterdec."

"Right. But he owns stock—"

"No. They wouldn't know Terry from a regular hotel guest. Not unless we notified them he was on the property."

"Has he ever been here?"

"No." I can tell by the way he answers me that Declan's not happy about that fact, either. I drop the topic.

Cordoned-off sections of hallway mark the point where the adult exhibition begins.

"Badge?" the security guard asks. "Or ticket?"

Declan gives him a smile. A muted sound of someone speaking in the guard's ear makes his demeanor change entirely.

"Mr. and Mrs. McCormick!" he says in a low, friendly voice, pulling the velvet-wrapped cord off the metal stand and gesturing for us to go in. "Please. Enjoy yourselves at the trade show." His expression falters as I snicker at his words.

Declan suppresses an eye roll.

Booming music à la Magic Mike XXL pounds through the

doors to the enormous convention hall. Bright lights, a computer-generated laser show from a DJ, flicker in the distance. The closer we get to the ballroom, the louder it gets.

Greeters at the door hand us a goody bag.

"What's this?" Declan asks, holding up a purple shopping tote, the kind you get at grocery stores so you can cut down on plastic bag use.

I look inside the bag and blush-laugh. "It's a collection of marketing promotions swag from some of the companies here. Oh, my."

It's a cornucopia of self-pleasure.

Declan peeks in his and his eyebrows shoot up. "Wow."

Dec isn't a "wow" kind of guy, so....

"That is some swag. I didn't know they put logos on pussy pockets," he marvels.

I frown. "How do you know what one of those looks like?"

His turn to blush-laugh.

My turn for eyebrows to raise.

"Look! There's Marie!" The relief in his voice is palpable, as if my mother's presence is welcomed.

There's a first.

"We'll table this conversation for later," I declare, marching off to talk to my mom.

Except I can't really march in high heels with points made of finely-sharpened pencils. I nearly tip over, but Dec's strong hands catch me at the elbow, guiding me over to Mom.

We stroll past booths devoted to pornography, but with a twist: this isn't just about the visual. It's about devices and products that enhance sexual pleasure. Bacon-flavored lube at the first booth. An iPad attachment that lets you, well...who knew they could attach a vibrator like that?

Sex chairs shaped like gymnastics mats. Drugs for female ejaculation "approved in Europe but currently under FDA consideration." A tantric yoga video series.

And...there is Mom, right in the middle of it all, pink-faced and glowing.

She is among her people.

All she needs is a crown and she'll be set.

As I approach her, she looks up and gives us a grin that makes my stomach flip-flop. Too late to back out now.

"You don't have to actually hash it all out here, Shannon," Declan whispers.

"What?"

"Here," he says again, nodding toward the convention floor. "Just talk to her long enough to schedule a real talk. Get it over with, but don't try to do anything complex while you're in here." He sniffs the air. "I think they're pumping pheromones in through a scenso-rama system."

"A what?"

"It's a trade show convention product. Use aromatherapy to influence buyer behavior."

"That's a thing?"

His mouth twists with a smile, his eyes going dark with lust. "Apparently."

Come to think of it, I am feeling really, well...

"Shannon!" Mom calls out. "Come over here and see all these wonderful toys!"

Libido killer. This time, I manage to march right on over, ignoring my ankles.

"Mom," I hiss, my eyes raking over the unending buffet of sexual devices that are on display like ham-wrapped scallops at a Costco sampler station. "Aren't you mortified to be here?" She's at a table called Edible Incredibles.

They have Maple Bacon lube.

"Says the woman who named her vibrator after a vampire." Mom snorts.

The salesperson, who is a plump, grey-haired woman wearing round spectacles and a saucy grin, looks me up and down. It's like being sexually inventoried by Mrs. Claus. Her name tag reads, "Martha." No kidding.

"Edward Cullen?" she asks.

I nod, my face on fire.

"That trend is *so* 2012," Martha says, grabbing a purple jelly vibrator with what looks like a long string of anal beads and...is that a USB port in it? "As long as you don't name it after your favorite pet, you're fine."

I shudder. "Chuckles the vibrator?" Even Mom has the decency to cringe.

"People are perverted as hell," Martha says, calmly pouring warming gel into a contraption that looks like a Star Wars character's mouth, the opening where a man would slide in his—

"Shannon! There you are!" Daddy appears behind me, hands on my shoulders. "How's the chocolate show going...." His voice trails off as he looks at the item in the salesperson's hand. "Huh. Some merchandising deal. Do people have to pay George Lucas a small fee every time they orgasm while using that thing?"

"DADDY!" I screech.

"You told me this was a *chocolate trade show*," he says to Mom, whose eyes cut over to me as if to say, *Help*.

I look back and say, wordlessly, *You made me wear a tartan thong. You're on your own.*

The salesperson holds up a box longer than my arm, containing a chocolate penis contoured so well it has veins poking out, with white chocolate at the tip simulating, uh....

"Does this count?" she asks.

"That counts!" Mom pipes up, taking it and looking it over like it's from a Parisian chocolatier and worthy of a luxurious once over, handling it like one of the female models showing off a prize on *The Price is Right*. "I'd love to have this in my mouth!" she crows.

Even Martha blushes.

"This," Daddy says emphatically, "is a sex toy trade show."

"Yes," Mom says, giving in, admitting the obvious. It's hard to keep up the ruse when a meter-long dong with the words "Fair Trade Chocolate" is in your hands.

"Why didn't you just tell me the truth, honey?" he asks, pulling Mom into his arms, handing me the giant box. Daddy looks a bit primal right now, auburn curls wild and mussed, and his eyes are tired. We're all exhausted.

Except for Mom, who looks like someone plugged her into

that vibrator using a USB cord attached to a solar panel array the size of Rhode Island.

"I thought you'd be upset."

"Why would I be upset about sex toys? You mystery shop those stores for a living." His voice drops, and his hips shift closer to Mom, who leans in. My stomach clenches and I look wildly round the room to have my gaze anywhere but on them.

Unfortunately, I make eye contact with a man wearing a cowboy hat bigger than the rest of him. He starts to swagger over, his eyes flicking to my hand, then my chest.

I look down. Engagement ring, yes.

Wedding ring, no.

I am in Vegas. I possess a vagina. I have the flushed cheeks that come from arousal or embarrassment (or both). I have no wedding ring on while walking around in a casino in my new black Louboutins that Declan insisted I wear, my Vera Wang dress slit up to my tampon string line.

But most important, I made a lethal error.

I made eye contact with a strange man in a casino.

Warm, wet lips kiss the soft spot under my ear as the cowboy stares at me. I scream from surprise and swing the giant chocolate penis around, whacking what turns out to be Declan with it, bashing his head. The box breaks open and he reaches up with his hands in shock, looking down to find himself cradling half of the enormous chocolate penis, tip up, white chocolate gleaming inches from his mouth.

And this is how I know he is meant for me, because his reaction is simply to grunt and say, "Shame. White chocolate. Ick."

"That's $119.99, miss," Martha says, palm out. "You break the penis, you buy it. Cash or credit?"

"Charge it to the house," Declan says. "McCormick." Martha's eyes flash as she takes us all in, calculating exactly who Declan is.

"What are you kids up to today? Getting married, finally? Don't consummate before the ceremony!" Mom says, Dad trying to look at anything that isn't phallic, and failing.

"Why do you constantly joke about sex?" Declan replies,

mouth twitching with tension. He's inverting the situation, re-asserting control by throwing Mom off guard.

Mom looks shocked, her mouth in a little O, eyebrows clenched. "I never, *ever* joke about sex. I take my sex very seriously."

"She does," Dad agrees.

"Sex is how we make sense of the world," Mom adds, her voice going into a sing-songy lecture, a sound that makes my throat feel like Darth Vader picked me to choke at the conference table. If we stay here, we'll get a twenty-minute discussion about passion and sensuality, nuance and bendy yoga, and I can't handle one more second of this.

"Look, Mom, we need to talk."

"Yes, we do. But not now. I'm busy," she says.

"Then how about dinner? Tomorrow?"

Her eyes light up. "Just you and me, honey?"

Declan squeezes my arm. *It's your call*, that squeeze says. *You're in charge here.*

"How about we make it a foursome?" I say.

"We have videos on that," Martha offers.

"Nice upsell attempt," I tell her through gritted teeth. "But no."

She gives me a nonchalant shrug.

I think my fangs are showing, because she retreats into her phone without another word.

"Eight o'clock. Tomorrow."

"Tomorrow?" Dad says in a low, hurt voice. "Why tomorrow?"

"I need some time, Daddy. I'm so tired." The words are out of my mouth before I realize how true they are. "Can you handle staying here while we sort this all out?"

He has an empty look, but his eyes go soft with understanding. "Sure can, sweetie. Whatever you need."

I give Declan a slightly harried look. *Where?* I mouth.

"We'll get a private table at the members-only club on the twenty-third floor. Choice seats for the nighttime fountain display."

Mom looks like she did the day she confirmed the Farmington Country Club for our wedding.

"Perfect," she says, looking at the broken dong in Declan's hand. "I hope they have good desserts."

Deftly, Declan hands the two halves of the broken monstrosity to my father, who shudders in sympathy at the sight of a broken penis, even if it isn't real. Mom takes the top half and shoves the tip in her mouth, taking a bite.

"Mmmmm, this is so good. Shannon, you need to try this."

"The only penis Shannon needs in her mouth is mine," Declan declares, grabbing my arm. Before I pivot, I see Mom's face flaming in the dim light. Finally.

Finally, someone actually embarrassed her.

Too bad it had to involve embarrassing me, too.

"Did you have to say that?" I hiss. Cowboy looks at Declan, and shakes his head slowly, whistling some country tune as he decides I'm off limits, giving Mom a looksy, making faces of approval until Dad gives him a cold look.

*Get along, little dogie.*

"Yes, I did have to say that," Declan replies.

"Why?"

"Because I can."

"Just because you *can* do something doesn't mean you *should.*"

"I'm taking you out of this sexual device orgy and doing *you.* Upstairs. Now," he whispers.

I pause and look at Declan, realizing I've mistaken his stony demeanor for anger. He's hiding *arousal.* Whoa. My heart hammers in my chest, the sound of the slots behind us and murmurs and shouts a reminder of the social element of waste and outrageous, boundary-blasting behavior.

"I retract my earlier statement." We walk through the crowds, my heels wobbling on the thick carpet that runs in a wide line between marbled tiles. Declan's reassuring hand on my elbow helps. He finds the private double doors and the secret elevator. As he presses the button for our floor, he looks at me, giving a speculative sigh.

"Three-foot chocolate penis?"

"What? That was Mom. Not me."

His voice lowers. "If you could go back in that exhibit hall right now and pick out any item from all the displays, what would you pick?"

Oh. We're going *there*, are we? While sex with Declan is fantastically orgasmic and amazingly tender, rough and ready and ripe as it needs to be when we have it, we've never, um, headed into this territory.

I blush like a bride on her wedding night.

Which is utterly appropriate.

"I wouldn't pick a thing," I admit, his body going slack with released tension. Mischief courses through me as I add, "I'd pick a person."

"You'd *what*? Who? Was it some hot dancer in there? That guy your mom was oiling up with the chocolate mint oil that hooks up to the wristband thing and lets you track his boners with a smartphone app?"

*Blink.*

Declan paid far more attention to that exhibit hall than I've realized.

Setting aside what he's just said—there's an app for that?—I give him a bashful smile. Not sure why I'm suddenly shy, but I am.

"No," I say, reaching for his arm. The wool suit jacket is wrinkled, his white shirt cuff poking out, the hair on his wrist making a web of patterns that is easier to focus on than him. "You. *You* are the only thing in that room I would pick."

A dazzling smile, eyes brimming with lust and love, greets me. A quick tug and I'm in his arms, the tickle of his warm breath making me shiver and break out into a sweat at the same time.

"While that's a lovely sentiment, I've ordered an assortment of, shall we say....tester items. They're being delivered to our room as we speak."

I laugh. "No, you haven't." The elevator arrives and we get on.

"No, I didn't," he admits. "Can't fool you."

"Why would you want to?"

He gives me a look of appraisal, then leans his head against the back of the elevator, letting out a long breath.

"Why, indeed, would I?"

"Especially when it comes to putting something edible in my mouth." Those words ring out nice and loud as the elevator doors open and reveal James McCormick, standing next to Amanda's mom, Pam.

Holding a three-foot chocolate dong.

"Dad!" Declan booms.

"Pam?" I didn't know she followed us to Vegas. She and James take a step away from each other, her arm weighted down by her handbag. Spritzy's face pops out, pink tongue poking between little teeth too cute to cause damage.

Hmmm.

"Hi." James plays it cool and casual. Declan's practically apoplectic, and he grabs the box, turning it so the clear plastic display front is hidden.

"What are you doing?" Pam asks, her voice curious. There's challenge to it. Given the fact that Pam can't talk about tampons without needing smelling salts, this is quite a turn of events.

"Why are you walking around our resort carrying a giant chocolate penis?" Declan asks James, his voice loud enough for Pam to hear.

Sure enough, she goes weak in the knees, her face beet red in a flash, and I have to grab her elbow before poor Spritzy gets dumped on the floor.

"What?" James asks, recoiling. He snatches the box back from Declan's hands and turns it around.

"The Eiffel Tower," the box reads.

"We were across the street at that fake Eiffel Tower restaurant. Pam wanted a souvenir. I was carrying it for her."

"Oh. Not a penis?" Declan asks stupidly.

"Why would I carry my own penis for her?"

Pam's eyelids flutter and she starts to breathe erratically. I take the handbag off her arm and patiently stroke Spritzy's little bow-covered head, because this could be a while. Two

McCormick men talking about penises usually involves more than a minute.

"Would you two cut the peen talk?" I snap before I realize I've said it.

They both wince. "Please don't use the phrase 'cut the peen,' Shannon." James and Declan both fold inward a tiny bit.

"Stop talking about sex or we're going to need an ambulance for poor Pam."

"I thought we were just having a lovely visit and talking about Paris," she says faintly.

"We were." James gives us a dark look, then focuses on me. "You're just like your mother."

"What the hell does that mean?" Declan's protective streak kicks in.

"She can't have a conversation without making it about sex."

Dec opens his mouth to argue, frowns, and turns to me.

"He has a point, honey."

"You're the one who accused him of carrying a phallic piece of chocolate around! Not me!"

"She has a point, Declan," James says.

"Shut up, Dad."

"Hey, now—"

I half-drag poor Pam over to a small bench while Dec and his dad argue. "You okay?" She reaches out for Spritzy, who looks like he's watching tennis, eyes bouncing between Pam and James.

"I think so. Is there really a three-foot piece of chocolate in the shape of a...you know...here at the hotel?"

I nod. "Yeah." She makes me think for a second. "You definitely don't want to go anywhere near the convention center right now. Steer clear."

"Why?"

"There's a sex toy and adult product industry trade show going on."

"They have conventions for those? Like a software convention?"

"Well, there's software..."

I think about the electro-conductive oil and the smartphone

app for boner tracking and decide not to describe it. "What are you doing here? Not that I'm not happy to see you," I add, backpedaling. "But..."

She shrugs. "Your mom insisted I should come along, so I did. It's still Sunday, and I telecommute, so I went home, got my laptop and some clothes, and joined the entourage."

"Entourage?"

"Me, Jason, Marie," she ticks off people on the fingers of her right hand. "James." She blushes.

I say nothing, but I tuck that reaction away for my future gossip-fest with poor Amanda.

"All four of you flew out here?"

"With Andrew and Amanda, yes. Six of us on the 'lesser' corporate jet." Pam laughs. "Those were Andrew's words."

No wonder Andrew and Amanda are so eager to get away from everyone. My flight with Declan involved a private jet with a bedroom. They got to spend their first few hours of reunion at a medical facility and then on a long flight with their parents.

Not the best way to celebrate new love.

"You definitely don't want to join Mom right now," I warn Pam.

"Really?" She's surprised. "Marie keeps saying I need to come check out some big food convention in the ballroom."

"No," Declan jumps in, palm out. "Don't do it." I find his sudden concern for Pam touching.

James frowns, looking at the Eiffel Tower. "You mean the sex convention?"

Pam whips around on him, her face somehow both pale and pink. "You knew about it?"

"Of course. It's my resort. I know about everything." James puffs up like a grey peacock.

Declan clears his throat and flexes his neck and arms. "Technically, Dad, it's my resort."

I cringe, but say it anyhow. "It's *actually* Andrew's. He's CEO."

You ever have two highly-attractive men pissed off at you simultaneously?

Yeah. It's not as much fun as you'd think.

Declan fake-yawns. "I think I need to go to my room now. I need a nap. We've been through a lot."

Nap. Right.

His fake yawn triggers a real one in me. I stretch up, blood flowing into sore, exhausted muscles, my movement catlike and thorough, a little vulnerable. My body doesn't care, though, so I go with it and stretch all the way, not worrying if people watch.

Declan watches, all right. Mad at me or not, he can't help it.

Knowing that is a gift. Being adored isn't a state of being. It's a process, and understanding it in your soul takes time, love, nourishment, and the endless, ongoing attentions of a horny guy who really does make you the center of his world, every day, by choice.

Every day.

The same damn choice.

Thank God.

"A nap sounds great," I agree. He smiles. I really do mean that a nap, with actual spooning and sleeping and no sex, would be fabulous.

James and Pam pick up on our cues immediately, and with cursory hugs and handshakes, Dec and I are relieved to find ourselves headed back to the room.

"Don't you have work to do? Calls to fend off from Southeast Asia? Nine hundred text messages from Grace to manage?"

"No. *You're* what I'm managing now."

"I'm a pretty major project."

"My best work yet. Like any great project, I learn more about myself than I do about you."

"What do you need to learn about yourself?" I ask, yawning halfway through the sentence, sounding like a tired lioness. "You're so grounded. Focused."

He nods contemplatively, biting the corner of his mouth. "Good. My cover's intact. I fooled you."

The elevator dings. We say nothing as we ride up, my arm around his waist, his around my shoulders, the feeling complete.

We enter the suite, walking past new racks of clothing I don't care about. Declan crashes on the bed, eyes closed, on his back, legs hanging off the edge. He kicks off his shoes.

"Be back in a minute," I tell him, going into the bathroom. The Shannon I see in the mirror isn't the same woman I studied yesterday morning.

How can someone change so much in just twenty-four hours?

Five minutes later, I'm done, and come into the main suite ready to—

Uh.

Sleep, apparently.

Because Declan is snoring like crazy, out cold.

A part of me wants to curl up with him. I kick off my heels and start to relax when my phone buzzes.

It's Amanda.

*Coffee?* she texts.

*You two are done already?* I reply.

She just types back "…"

I answer with a question mark.

*Andrew got called away on a ton of wedding media business. You guys have really dumped a lot of work on him,* she replies.

*Sorry :(,* I answer. *Yes to coffee.*

Her answer is a smiley face and an address next door.

My phone buzzes again. It's Mom.

I ignore it.

*Tap tap tap.*

"Can't I get some peace?" I murmur, opening the door to find a uniformed hotel staff member carrying a familiar blue bag from a famous jewelry store.

He hands it to me.

Tiffany & Co.

"What's this?"

The staff person bows and gives me a mysterious smile. "A gift from Mr. McCormick." And with that, the quiet man with the Mediterranean accent disappears, melting into the hallway decor as if he were a Marvel comic superhero.

I open the bag, then the box. I slump against the threshold.

It's a gorgeous silver necklace with an emerald the exact shade of Declan's eyes.

And it's the size of my youngest nephew's fist.

Declan knows I don't like lavish jewelry. The three-carat engagement ring from his mother is hard enough for me to wear. Big rocks snag on *everything*.

I know why he's doing this. What do I do? He saw Amanda's earrings at lunch and assumed he needed to do some grand gesture to—what? Prove his love to me? Show up his brother?

On impulse, I grab my purse and the bag, and sprint down the hallway. The man who delivered the gift jumps slightly when I tap his shoulder, but he's the consummate professional.

"Yes, Mrs. McCormick?"

I shiver.

"Could you kindly return this to Tiffany?" I ask, shoving the box in the bag.

His eyes flicker with deep concern.

"Was there a problem with the item? Should I contact Mr. McCormick and let him take care of the issue?"

"No! No. He's sleeping right now. We've had a rather, um, eventful day and a half."

The man, whose name tag reads Luis, chuckles. He's too well trained and cultivated to say more than that, but the truth is written all over his face.

Of course he knows what the past day and a half has been like for us.

So do two billion other people on earth who've been watching television. Hell, we're a trending story on that stupid right-hand scroll on Facebook. Once you're mentioned there, that's it. You're screwed.

"I just...please. Return it." I give Luis a cultured smile, one I've learned to dish out when I become uncomfortable in Declan's world. Grace suggested this as a strategy a few months ago, and damned if it doesn't work. My usual tactic of using an avalanche of ingratiating, self-effacing words works well in my social world, but not Declan's.

Coolness. Being aloof. Using as few words as possible. Not over-explaining.

That's what works here.

And it is very effective.

"I most certainly will, Mrs. McCormick. I am so sorry it wasn't to your liking." He retreats down a different hallway and I stand before the bank of elevators, wondering if I did the right thing.

That's not really true. I know I did the right thing. I also know that when Declan finds out I returned his gift, we're going to have a fight.

If my goal is to make everyone I love angry with me, then I'm succeeding.

*Bzzzzz.*

*You coming?* Amanda asks in a text.

I push the down button and an elevator opens immediately. It's a sign.

A latte can't hate me.

And can't be returned.

# Chapter Eleven

"What did you do while I was asleep?" Declan asks as I return to our suite. We have a perfect view of the massive fountain downstairs, and the choreographed water show just ended. I'm a bit dazed by it, the jets skyrocketing hundreds of feet into the air, colored lights and opera music piped outside, passersby gathering on walkways and bridges to watch.

"I went next door to the resort over there!" I say, grabbing my amazing coffee and holding it out to him. "It's so awesome! The decor is all sleek lines, with textured walls and ceilings. The variety is spellbinding."

He grunts. It's a sound that says, *I heard you.*

"And the coffee is so much better than the coffee here!" I chirp.

*Now* I have his attention.

"Their casino is spread out in a different formation, so you have to walk past all the patisseries, the baked goods and chocolates on display," I add. "And they have a bunch of sunken tables and really cozy circular couches, all with a great view of the wide-open atmosphere and in welcoming, but trendy, fabrics."

He walks over to me and picks up my latte, taking a sip. His eyebrow goes up.

"Go on," he says, the words slow and deliberate. It's the most focus I've gotten from him all day, and it's exciting to have a real conversation with him. Everything in Vegas is so fake, so ostentatious and over the top that conversations fall into two camps: how to do something wasteful and how to do something even more wasteful.

"I got this mind-blowing coffee at this shop called Grind It Fresh! and a chocolate French macaron that I would marry, if it were legal to wed an almond-flour confection," I joke.

He doesn't smile.

"Amanda and I spent about two hours just hanging out over there, and the place was so relaxing and inviting that I bought lunch in the sushi bar and grabbed another coffee on the way back here." I take my Grind It Fresh! coffee back from him, and hold it up as an example. The logo is a picture of a coffee bean being loaded into a wood chipper, with a starburst coming out of the end.

When our eyes meet, it's like I kicked him in the gut. He's gone green, and—is his upper lip *trembling*?

"What's wrong?" I cry out in alarm. "Are you sick?"

"Maybe," he whimpers, running his fingers through his hair, eyes wild and pained. He has his typical afternoon stubble, but he runs his hand through his hair, peaks of dark standing up straight. The groomed brow hunches down over troubled eyes and a clamminess inhabits his hand as I hold it.

"What did I say? What did I do?" I'm thrown into overdrive at this sudden change in Declan.

"Shannon." My name sounds like the last gasp from a dying man. "Shannon, are you *mystery shopping* the resort next door?"

I freeze.

"What?" Peals of laughter pour out of me, more from relief than humor. "What? No. No, no, of course not. I would never take an assignment from Greg on our honeymoon! I don't even work for him any more!" That's all this is? Whew.

"Not officially, no. But you just read off a laundry list of how my carefully-designed resort doesn't measure up to the place next door." His breathing is erratic and his voice is choked, like he's trying not to cry.

There is genuine hurt in his voice.

This is a side of Declan I've never seen.

"That's not what I—I never meant to compare in a—it's just that the coffee at Grind It Fresh! is so good over there!"

He closes his eyes and groans, like I sucker-punched him in the throat.

Sitting at the end of the bed, Declan drops his head into his hands and takes deep breaths. Do I need to get him a paper bag? Is he hyperventilating? I drop to my knees in front of him and put my hands on his thighs.

"Your coffee here at Litraeon is good. Really. It's *great*."

"Stop lying to me."

"No, I'm—I'm not lying."

I'm *totally* lying.

"You can't get the coffee just right every time. Everyone has moments where they don't perform. It's okay. It happens," I soothe.

"You're acting like my resort's failure to live up to next door is akin to erectile dysfunction."

"I am not!"

I totally am, though. Oops.

But a great cup of coffee is like great sex. Once you've had it, going back to mediocre feels like a punishment.

And it goes down smooth.

"Promise me one thing," he says, grasping my hands. Our eyes meet.

Are those tears in his eyes? Actual tears? Is Declan *crying* because I like the resort next door better than the Anterdec property? I can't really confess that right now, but....

"Anything," I swear.

"Don't go next door again."

My heart seizes. I can't help but look at the cup of coffee. The thought of no more Grind It Fresh! makes me reel.

Noooooooo. Anything but that.

When I look at him, though, I realize I have no choice. I have to be faithful. I can't stray.

Plastering on a fake smile, I nod. "Of course I won't."

"We can make this place better!" he insists, standing up so fast

I fall backwards on my butt. Thank God I'm not clutching my coffee, though, because it would have spilled.

Eyes lingering over the white cup with the beautiful black logo, I realize this is it. My final latte from Grind It Fresh! I won't get another chance like this.

I have to make it last.

A lifetime. This latte is my *Bridges of Madison County*. I'm Meryl Streep and those perfect shots of espresso are Clint Eastwood, never to be seen again after experiencing the throes of ecstasy. Hold on, though. Clint Eastwood? Nooooo. Too old.

Er, Scott Eastwood? Mmmmm, Scott Eastwood in the shower scene in *The Longest Ride*.

Hey. Wait a minute. Someone always dies in a Nicholas Sparks story. I'd better stop there. Then again, if I have to give up Grind It Fresh! forever, it's a kind of death.

The death of caffeine love.

Declan is the Nicholas Sparks of coffee.

"I'll find out who their supplier is and we'll start buying their coffee. And I can have our human resources recruiters snipe their baristas!" The green gill look is gone, replaced by a man with a mission.

A tendril of hope springs up from the dark, scorched earth of my coffee-loving soul.

"You will?" I peep.

"Yes. Anything for you, Shannon."

Anything but letting me walk five hundred feet to buy a twelve-dollar coffee nirvana from the competition, that is.

He smacks his palms on his upper thighs. "There. That's settled. Litraeon will improve. In fact, I am going to give you a new project at Anterdec."

"What's that?"

"Mystery shopping this property. Not you, of course. But let's get a team going. Hire Greg or that competitor, you know. What's their name?"

"Fokused Shoprite. "

"Right. Fokused Shoprite."

"Don't you dare hire Foked!" I say sharply.

He looks stunned. "What? Did you just say—*what*?"

I giggle. Can't help it. Our stupid nickname for our nemesis is about as mature as a twelve-year-old boy, but whatever.

"Why not hire them?" Declan pries.

"Because, because—they're our competitor!"

"*Greg's* competitor," he reminds me. "And besides, we hire the best. Our loyalty is to the product or service that excels. Nothing less."

I stare at my coffee and start to say something.

This is one of those moments, right? A juncture. A fork in the road. I can be right, or we can have harmony. I can speak up, or we can have peace. Whatever I do now doesn't have to set the course for our entire relationship.

But if I point out Declan's hypocrisy, I'm pretty sure it'll trigger a fight I don't really want to deal with right now.

Can I live without great coffee and a better resort experience? Sure.

Marriage involves sacrifice, right? Relationships are built on compromise. Negotiation. Agreement.

I can totally do this.

This will be a breeze.

* * *

I last twelve hours.

I would make the worst CIA agent in the world, because I crack easy. Two shots of espresso in steamed organic whole milk breaks me.

Damn you, Grind It Fresh! I wish I knew how to quit you.

After room service for dinner and a long, slow lovemaking session with Declan that distracts me, sates me, and still leaves me a bundle of jangling nerves about the wedding details left unresolved, I wake up with the sunrise and just stare out over the city, the mountains in the background snow-capped and serene.

*Tap tap tap.*

I stand up from the desk and tiptoe to the suite's main door, glancing at Dec as I walk by. He's so peaceful, his dark hair pressed against his slightly sweaty brow, eyes closed in slumber, his bare chest begging for a lick.

But best of all, he's asleep.

And won't see me coffee-cheat on him.

"I feel like a drug mule," Amanda whispers as she knocks softly on our hotel suite door.

"You are a goddess," I hiss, taking the Latte of Heaven out of the tray she holds with two more cups in it.

She giggles. "This just gave me an excuse to run out and get a breve. I need a break. Parts of me are chafing so badly I think I'll need skin grafts."

"Doesn't Andrew mind?"

"We just add more lube."

"TMI! I meant about your going to the resort next door and getting their coffee at Grind It Fresh!"

Amanda gives me a queer look. "Why would Andrew care where I drink my coffee?"

"Declan made me swear not to buy it from the competitor."

"And you let him? Did you sign some kind of kinky contract letting him dictate your caffeine choices?" As she takes a sip of her short breve, a silver bracelet clinks on her wrist.

"What's that?"

"My new charm bracelet from Tiffany! Isn't it gorgeous?" I see rubies, sapphires, a silver Chihuahua, and, oddly enough, a wasp.

I grin on her behalf. "Yes."

"Didn't Declan get you a necklace?"

"How do you know?" Declan hasn't said a word to me about it.

"The staff here is buzzing like bees about the giant emerald. Andrew told me."

Oh, God.

"I sent it back."

"You *what*?"

"I sent it back. I don't need it."

"Who cares about *need*? It's Tiffany!" Sometimes I think

Amanda and I were switched at birth and she's really Mom's daughter.

Amanda's phone buzzes. "Oops! Gotta go!"

"Thanks for the coffee!" She tosses me a thumbs-up as she walks away. *That* is a bestie.

I close the door ever so softly and tiptoe back into the living room.

To find a naked, angry Declan staring right at me. I jump from anxiety, spilling a few drops of my latte on the thick, patterned rug.

"What's that?" he asks, the question rhetorical. He knows damn well what I'm holding.

I slide the cup around in my palm, as if covering the Grind It Fresh! logo will somehow hide my transgression. "Nothing," I answer.

"You're coffee-cheating on me. You're resort-cheating on me. I can't believe this!" His voice cracks with incredulity. The cafe should rename itself Ashley Madison.

I'm supposed to feel shame, right? Self-loathing and disgust and guilt.

Instead, I drink a long, slow, delightful sip and savor my weak-willed moment, because once you sell your soul to the devil for a good latte, there ain't no going back.

"I am choosing to spend my consumer dollars on a high-quality product, Mr. Let the Market Dictate Winners and Losers." *Sip.*

Wrong answer.

I've seen Declan's face turn red in anger. I've even seen his neck flush and the top of his chest turn a pinkish shade, as if he spent ten minutes too long in the sun.

But watching his, erm, you know, turn the same color as my old Hello Kitty outfit is quite the sight.

"Are you calling Litraeon a loser?"

"No! Of course not." *Sip.*

"You just said that."

"Did not!" *Sip.*

"And by extension, you just called *me* a loser." He puffs out his chest and crosses his arms.

"Honey, I think we're getting ahead of ourselves here." *Gulp.* "We're making more of this than it really is."

"My almost-wife thinks the resort that I practically hand-built in my formative years with Anterdec is inferior to the resort next door."

"You're really getting hysterical, honey. I think we need to just calmly and rationally try to apply reason here." *Sip.*

"Don't you dare accuse me of not being reasonable!" he bellows. "I am perfectly reasonable!"

"Then why can't you apply your own common-sense business practices to what I'm experiencing? Superior product means consumer dollars follow."

He points at me with a crooked finger, eyes narrowed to moss-green triangles, face full of self-righteous fury. "Because you're a traitor."

*Sip.*

He's right.

"And you rejected my necklace."

Oh, no.

I brace myself for what I know is coming. "Declan," I say with a gentle, appreciative sound. "I loved the necklace. You were so sweet for thinking of me. And the emerald matched your eyes."

I can tell it makes a difference that I noticed, even if his next words are cold. "But you returned it regardless." Not just any cold—*liquid-nitrogen* cold.

"It's not...me."

"Why can't it be you? Is the you that you think you are so inflexible?"

"What?" That sounds like a line from a Dr. Seuss book you give to college graduates when you can't think of what else to gift.

"Why can't you let yourself accept what I have to give, Shannon?"

"We've talked about this before." My fingers on my right

hand begin worrying the enormous stone on my left ring finger. My hand feels so weighed down by it. Not by the burden of what it represents—our commitment to spend the rest of our lives together—but by its physical presence. The ring is, literally, heavy.

A weight I hold that is both a physical and a metaphysical reminder that I am about to marry a billionaire and make his life mine.

Forever.

For the rest of our lives, my existence will be defined by him. Sure, he's going to compromise with me and my life choices, and our families—well, we'll have to balance out the varying value systems, rituals, traditions, time obligations, and other issues that every couple experiences when they join and become each other's family.

Billionaires are a whole different story.

"I know we've talked about this before," he answers in a weary tone, shaking me out of my thoughts. "We've talked about it *ad nauseum*. That doesn't mean we've resolved a damn thing."

"What do you want me to do, Dec? Just say yes to everything you want to smother me with?" The words are out and I regret one of them instantly.

"Smother?" he says with a derisive huff.

Yeah, that would be the one.

"I'm sorry." If I rush the apology out fast enough, can I save this conversation? "I really am. That's not what I meant."

"I think that's exactly what you meant. Don't back away from it. Own it."

Is he right? I don't know. I'm so used to acquiescing, because most of the time he *is* right on topics like this. One of the foundations of our relationship is the fact that Declan's so secure, and has such faith that I can overcome my own overly-developed sense of helping others to strike a healthy balance. I'm still not sure I agree with his assessment, but I've gone along with his opinion because so far, every time I follow his viewpoint I feel better about myself.

But what if I'm just replacing my mother with Declan?

Letting people tell me how I should feel gets harder and harder as time passes.

And maybe that intolerance includes Declan.

"Smother." I square my shoulders as I say the word. "You're smothering me."

"With jewelry from Tiffany?"

"And tailored clothing from Italy. And a wedding that costs more than an expensive house in metrowest Boston. And limos and SUVs and helicopters and planes. Restaurant meals that cost more than my first car. You don't live a life that even dips its toe in reality, Declan."

"It's *my* reality."

"Your reality is most people's fantasy."

"But not yours, clearly."

"You are my fantasy. *You.* You're my fantasy man come to life, vibrant and breathing and breathtaking, Declan! I love you. Not your money."

"Is that what this is about? You're worried I think you're after me for my wealth?" Relief washes over him, as if he's figured it all out. "That's it? God, no, Shannon, I know you're not one of those types."

"What types?"

"The Jessica Coffin type."

"She *comes* from money!" I declare, completely blown away by this conversation. We've talked about this before, of course. James wanted me to sign a pre-nup, but Declan shot that down long before the wedding. You can't be engaged to a man with Declan's level of money and not have a long series of discussions, but we're navigating a winding river we've never traveled before.

This isn't about his money.

It's about his lifestyle.

"Right. She comes from a family with connections and a long history of being the equivalent of aristocracy in Boston society, if such a status existed. And yet she's a gold-digger, plain and simple."

He said it. That damn word.

"How can she be a gold-digger when she's already rich?"

"Her gold isn't money. It's status. Prestige. Unearned privilege that she wants to swallow whole, to hoard for herself by virtue of partnering with the perfect husband."

"Sounds more like a merger and acquisition than a marriage."

"That's exactly right."

"How cold."

"How Jessica."

I flash back to that first date, when we went out to dinner and ran into Jessica and my ex, Steve, on a date. The awkward dinner between the four of us, Jessica's compulsive need to insult me through digs and jabs so obvious to me and Declan. Steve, a social climber himself, chose not to see it.

By the end of the night she'd clearly dumped him, anyhow, her eye on catching a bigger fish.

*My* fish.

My soon-to-be-husband fish.

"You're my fish," I mutter under my breath.

"I'm your *what*?" he chuckles.

"My fish."

"You're deflecting."

"Technically, I'm not. I'm thinking about Jessica Coffin and how she tried to steal my fish from me."

He points to himself. "And I am the fish."

"Something like that."

"What kind?"

"What kind of what?"

"Fish. Am I a salmon? A trout? A grouper?"

"You're a lobster, of course."

"Lobsters aren't fish."

"We're speaking in love metaphors."

"It still doesn't make sense."

"*Love* doesn't make sense."

"No shit."

"Declan." The hurt in my voice masks some utterly chaotic emotion that plumes through me like a toxic cloud, a throbbing, pulsing danger that threatens to infiltrate every cell inside me.

Not only has this conversation spiraled into bizarro Mom-topic territory, Declan is still angry. Frustrated. Disappointed.

And I'm the cause of that maelstrom inside him.

Which he hides behind barbs and banter, his stone face intact.

"Why the big emerald?" I ask him, my voice neutral.

"Huh?"

"Why an emerald? Aside from the fact that it matches your eyes?"

"It seemed fitting."

"Because it was bigger than Amanda's earrings? And because those earrings had gemstones like Andrew's eyes?"

Declan's frown tells me he's truly caught off guard, his words sincere. "I didn't think about that when I ordered the necklace. I just wanted something timeless, beautiful, and worthy of your delicate neck."

I melt, blood firing at the words.

"You make me want to give you the world. And when you say no, it's like—" He breaks off his words, turning away from me.

"I have the world." My voice comes out in a shaky sigh. "I have you. I love you. I don't love your money or your power. I don't love your hundred-hour weeks or your press coverage. I love Declan McCormick, the man. Not Declan McCormick, the image. The billionaire. The icon."

His eyes bore through me, as if fusing onto my soul.

"I don't need baubles and designer clothes and stylists and new cars. I'm simple, Declan. I just want more of you."

"You have more of me."

"I want even more." I'm greedy that way.

"And when I give you parts of my life, that *is* how I offer you more of myself."

"You are not the giant green emerald!"

"And rejecting it doesn't make you some kind of better person," he says softly.

"I feel like we're talking in circles," I say, curling up inside, hurt that he doesn't accept my words.

"I feel like I'm spinning my wheels," he replies. If he feels the same way, then maybe...

"We're not really at odds, though, are we?" My look begs him to agree.

"No." He opens his arms and I step into them, pressing my cheek against his chest. Still naked, he stands tall and strong, back straight and his cheek resting against the crown of my head. "Not as long as you stop drinking that damn coffee from the resort next door."

My laugh feels good. "Too bad Anterdec doesn't own Grind It Fresh!" I joke.

His smile spreads across my scalp. "Or a Tesla dealership."

"I'm a cheap date," I remind him. "A good latte is all I need."

"You're all I need." We're trying to find our way across a fault line that has widened during the course of this conversation, tossing tether lines at each other with reasonable certainty the other will catch the weighted end.

Here's the problem with reasonable certainty: a tiny portion of the time, it's not reasonable.

Nor is it certain.

# Chapter Twelve

"All that over a coffee?" Amanda and I are in the fitness center, pretending to work out before lunch. Mom goes to yoga upstairs, some poolside class where she gets to strut her stuff, and I don't want to be anywhere near her right now. Knowing we have dinner tonight at eight p.m., and knowing it'll be a giant mess just makes my avoidance kick in that much harder. By pretending we're using the workout equipment, Amanda and I get a modicum of peace.

And she smuggles me clandestine lattes.

"Right." *Sip*. It's an orgasm in coffee form. Not the kind that makes fireworks explode in your head, though, or that make your hands curl and your fingertips scrape against the wall above the headboard. It's the kind where wave after wave keep coming and coming until you start to wonder if it'll ever end.

Maybe I'm imagining this coffee.

"He blew up like that just because you raved about the resort next door? Seriously?" Amanda takes a sip of her breve and gives a sound of appreciation. We're on treadmills next to each other, set at 3.0 miles per hour, which means we could be lapped by old ladies at the mall with tennis balls on the bottom of their walkers.

"Right. Totally uncharacteristic of Declan. We've been together for two years. I've never seen this side of him." Walking this slow takes effort. Effort requires calories. Which means this latte is actually *workout fuel*.

"He is supercompetitive." She snorts. "Look at him and Andrew."

All I have to do is look at her to get what she means. Amanda's new wardrobe upgrade screams *Andrew hired a stylist for me*. It's a nice mix of tastefully erotic and *Girls Gone Wild*. Never in a bajillion years would Amanda wear this outfit, with a push-up bra that turns her breasts into a reportable FAA obstacle, but she and Andrew are in that early phase of a relationship.

You know. The one where all you can think about is being naked together. Society requires that we cover our erogenous zones in public, so this is the next best thing.

In Man Land.

"Quit staring at my boobs."

"I can't help it. They're so...prominent."

She tugs at the hem of her shirt and *whoops!* There we go. Don't need that helicopter tour of the Grand Canyon that Declan was planning for tomorrow. Just got an eyeful.

"You could sell tickets to that view," I say with some speculation. My treadmill counter ticks over the two-mile mark. We should celebrate with another latte.

"Andrew. It's all his fault. And frankly, yours, too."

"Mine?"

"If you'd just let Declan spoil you a little, Andrew wouldn't feel the need to one-up Declan all the time."

"Huh?"

"They're trying to outshine each other. Declan keeps getting upset that you won't wear the jewelry or the clothes he's buying you. Now he's prowling around Tesla dealers and thinking about getting you a new car."

"WHAT?" Declan's earlier Tesla joke pings in my mind. He *wasn't* joking?

"And you should accept it!"

I give her a speculative look. "Is Andrew buying you a car?"

She shrugs, then brightens. "I don't know. He hates the Turdmobile, so..."

"I don't need these things—necklaces, clothes, fancy cars. Do *you*? Really?"

Her eyes glaze over. I know she's thinking about Andrew naked. "It's nice. I don't know." She shakes her wrist. The charms on the Tiffany bracelet cheer for her. "He likes to give me these things. It brings him joy."

I start to say something snarky, but realize that won't improve matters. I am at a crossroads with Declan and need to fix this. Sarcasm doesn't repair anything.

"Doesn't it make you feel weird accepting all these lavish gifts?"

She peers at me in confusion. "No. I'm not *asking* for them. I've never pressured Andrew to spend money on me. Ever. If he wants to give me these beautiful items as a present, then what's the harm?"

*What's the harm?*

"Don't you feel like it's too much, too soon? I've been with Declan for more than two years and some of the gifts he tries to give me feel too extravagant."

Amanda's eyes tighten, her head shaking slightly, her expression one of intense thought. "If I felt like it made me obligated to him, I suppose it would bother me." Her eyes dart nervously to me. "Is that it?"

"No! No," I protest. "Not at all. Declan's made it really clear that he wants me to have all these beautiful luxuries because he can give them. Not because it ties me to him, or makes me think I owe him."

"Is this about Steve?"

"*Wha?*"

"Are you worried Declan's trying to shape you too much, like Steve did? Worried that he wants you to wear the 'right' clothes, drive the 'right' car, eat the 'right' foods?"

"No." The answer comes so easily, and is crystal clear. For a topic I can't quite wrap my head around, this much is obvious. "I don't get that vibe from him at all. Never have."

Her shoulders relax, and she grabs for her water bottle on the treadmill rack, drinking half before turning back to me with a smile. "Then he just wants to share."

"Share?"

"Share his life with you." A sly smile tickles her lips. "We think of these choices Andrew and Declan make as luxuries, but to them, they're not. A Tesla to Andrew is like buying a cheap Toyota to us. Bringing an Italian designer into your hotel suite to create outfits for you is like one of us going to Ann Taylor at the mall and asking the salesperson for some color-coordination help."

I slow the treadmill down to 2.5 miles per hour and finish off my water, all while contemplating her words.

"Shannon, maybe this is just who Declan is, and he wants you to embrace that. Let him."

"How did you become so wise?"

She jangles her Tiffany charm bracelet. "I don't know. Maybe I'm blowing smoke out my own ass. I just know that Andrew is giving me peeks into his real life, and I'm accepting that. Reveling in it. Besides," she says with a confident laugh, "it's not like I'm marrying the guy anytime soon!"

It's hard to believe that two days ago she was bringing me lattes from Starbucks in the prep room at Farmington Country Club, acting as a filter between me and Mom.

It's even harder to realize she's really with Andrew, and that they're happy, after two years of Andrew being a douche and not letting himself truly fall in love with her.

But you know what's harder?

Realizing that she's right.

Maybe I've gone about this all wrong. Amanda has a great point.

Maybe I need to let Declan spoil me a little.

It can't hurt, right?

* * *

"What are you doing?" Declan asks as he walks into the bathroom, naked, obviously ready to take a shower. I eye the wall of glass, twelve different shower heads all positioned at various angles. If the entire enclosure weren't lined with Italian marble I'd think this was a prison.

I squint, holding the magnifying-glass mirror a few inches from my face, tweezers in hand. "I'm doing my eyebrows."

Reflected in the half-wall-sized mirror, he's a study in artistic perfection. While I am Rubenesque, he's all Greek sculpture, his body suited for display at a national gallery. Declan isn't an enormous, overbuilt gym rat, nor is he a metrosexually-toned man who has a Body By Trainer. He works out regularly and yes, has a staff for that, but the natural grace of muscles stretched over bone that moves through the world as if it owns the space in any given room is part of his mystique.

He sets his neatly-folded underwear on the sink next to my toothbrush and glowers at me.

"Doing your eyebrows?"

"Yes. It's a beauty thing."

"I know what it is, Shannon. Why not go to the spa downstairs?" He frowns again, his eyes buried under a tuft of bedhead hair from last night. Boyishly cute, his look morphs into an expression that makes me pause.

"Spa? No." I don't need the intimidation factor. If I want to be reduced to an ego the size of a fingernail and feel like an awkward middle-schooler out of her league, I'll ask my mother to go shoe shopping with me. I don't need the stress that comes from going to a luxury spa in a place where the breakfast menu includes egg whites with basil-infused *air*.

"Where did you get tweezers? We never packed bags. Did the staff bring those?"

"When I went out with Amanda yesterday, I dashed across the street to a drug store. Got a few things."

His frown deepens. "You're plucking your eyebrows with *drug store* tweezers?"

"Yes."

"While staying in one of the first hotels I created, which possesses a world-class spa I personally designed for optimal marketing purposes and hotel guest satisfaction?"

"Uh…"

Snatching the silver implement out of my hands, he throws it in the trash and stalks out of the bathroom. I retrieve the tweezers from the garbage can and tuck them away in my makeup bag.

He's back in one minute. "Lüq is expecting you downstairs. Now."

"Luke?" He says it in a funny way, like *Lee-ooq*.

"No, Lüq."

"That's what I said. *Luke*. And who is Lüq?"

"The spa manager. Lüq has orders to take care of you."

Terror makes all the hair on my body stand up, especially the southern parts. I know where this is going.

"I hate spas. You know I hate spas."

He leans against the doorjamb with a smug smile. "I know you do. That's why I just called in reinforcements."

"What? You need reinforcements for cucumber skin treatments and hot stone massages?"

His eyebrow goes up. "You *did* read the spa menu."

I shrug. "But at two hundred bucks for a fifty-minute massage, no way."

"That's a bargain."

"That's a *crime*. For five dollars I can get Tyler to heat up rocks in the microwave and put them on my back while Jeffrey walks on my ass and spine in his stocking feet."

*Knock knock knock.*

"Shannon?"

That's my *mother's* voice.

I look at him in horror. "You didn't."

"Reinforcements." His smug smile makes me regret having so much sex with him this morning.

Okay. That's not true. Let's just say I'm angry and leave it at that.

Declan shrugs into the bathrobe in the armoire, then opens the door. Even Mr. Exhibitionist has his limits when it comes to being naked around my mother.

Mom and Amanda are standing there.

Mom walks in, looking as excited as Chris Harrison with a

fresh set of contestants on *The Bachelor.* "We're here to make Shannon learn to relax!"

Right. 'Cause that'll work. *Force* Shannon to enjoy herself.

She reaches for my face and twists it from side to side. "You need a full-face threading. Especially for that chin hair there. A few more of those and you'll have that new lumbersexual look down, honey. If Declan wanted to see growth like that, he'd have married a man."

Amanda mouths, *I'm so sorry.*

My nostrils are flared and my teeth are gritted, so I all I can do is bare my fangs like a dog with rabies. Am I frothing? If not, I should be. In fact, I wish I had rabies. Then they'd have to take me to the emergency room and give me shots to the stomach with super-long needles, which is sounding like Disney World compared to what's coming.

"Let's go get smooth!" Mom crows, linking her arm through mine like we're Dorothy and the Tin Man and off to see the Wizard.

The wonderful wizard of chin hairs.

"Oh, no. No, no, no, no, no." I dig in my heels, physically refusing to let my mom get me out into the hallway. "You are *not* tricking me into a full Brazilian again."

She looks abashed. "That was never a trick! A miscommunication, but not a trick." Right after our first Christmas together, Declan got me, Mom, Carol and Amy a day at one of the Anterdec hotel spas in Boston. Through a series of unmentionable events (involving my unmentionable bits), Mom was in charge of telling my waxer what I wanted, and I was given a Brazilian. You don't get over a "miscommunication" like that quickly.

"I couldn't pee straight for weeks, Mom." I wasn't waxed.

I was *deforested.*

"We have to suffer for our beauty. Pain builds character. And the right waxing reduces that whole Sasquatch thing you've got going down there. I see your father's Polish ancestry coming out in you." She winks at Declan, who just scowls. He wasn't a fan of the all-bald look, but mostly didn't like the fact that I was in so much pain we didn't have sex for a week.

Declan catches my eye over Mom's head. "I already warned Lüq. No worries."

Mom gives him an impressed look. "Lüq? He sounds very sophisticated." Leave it to Mom to confer status on someone based solely on how their name sounds.

"Hu is," Declan answers.

"Who?" Mom asks.

"Lüq."

"You already said that."

"I know, but you asked."

"I just asked who he is."

"Hu."

"What are you talking about?" Mom screeches.

"Lüq is gender nonconforming," Declan says with a sigh he reserves for my mother, and *only* my mother. "We don't use gender-specific pronouns when talking about hu."

"H-u, Marie," Amanda says gently. "It's a way of saying he or she."

"Why not say *it*? Or *they*?" Mom asks.

"Try that," Declan says coldly, "and Lüq will give you a makeover that reminds you of those 1990s photos from Glamour Shots."

Mom's eyes light up. "Promise?"

Amanda drags her away before both Declan and I shove her in the minibar fridge and tape it shut.

"Go," he says. "Get whatever you need. But don't let your mother alienate Lüq."

"Can I get Mom a Brazilian where they wax her tongue out of her mouth? 'Cause that's probably the only way she won't offend him—er, *hu*."

He pretends to consider it. "We could sell that as a popular service to an awful lot of disenchanted sons-in-law. But seriously, Shannon. Go to the spa. That's what it's there for." He shudders. "Not the drug store. Drug stores are good for one thing."

"What's that?"

"Period errands."

We laugh. It feels good. And he's right.

"What about condoms?" I ask.

"What *about* condoms?" Declan's demeanor changes, one eyebrow lifting. The topic of sex makes everything lighten up.

"Drug stores are good for those, too."

"I am so glad we don't need them anymore." I'm on the pill now.

"And soon," he adds softly, "we won't need the pill, either."

"Excuse me?"

"Eventually, I mean." We're sharing one of those looks that make you understand why you're in a committed relationship. "Someday."

"Someday," I agree, my voice faint.

"Right now, though, you're banned from drug stores."

"That means you're running all my period errands, then."

He sighs. "Don't I already?"

I cringe, because yeah. He does. Or his chauffeurs, Gerald and Lance, do.

"Just go to the spa," he orders.

"Fine. But only because you designed it. And I'm coming back with hair."

"I hope so. I don't want you out of commission for a week."

"If I am, it's your fault."

I shut the door on his contemplative face and follow Amanda and Mom down the long hallway. They'd better have good food down in the spa, because as I walk slowly, this is starting to feel like a Star Trek episode where they beam down to a new planet, and I'm wearing a red crew shirt. I need a good final meal.

The hotel is designed intentionally so that you have no choice but to walk through the casino to get to any given point. Architects must have a kind of chaotic evil in their hearts when they design casino-hotels like this. Need to pee? CASINO. Need a latte? CASINO. Need a toothbrush from the twenty-four-hour store? CASINO!

We walk past an awful lot of desperate cowboys who are

bellied-up to the roulette tables, slot machines, blackjack tables and scantily-clad women.

Through the botanical gardens, past the world's largest tequila fountain, and *bam!*—we're in front of a set of greenhouse doors that reek of lavender and verbena.

Which is the universal scent of pampered women.

Steeling myself, I accept my clenched stomach and sweaty palms as trade-offs. By the time I walk out of here, not a stray eyebrow hair will be found, my skin will glow from the inside out, my hair will be layered and powdered and perfectly coiffed, and I'll have smooth, silky legs I can use to run away from my mother.

See? Trade-offs.

Mom walks in there like a boss. A crazy Momzilla menopausal boss who has been at the center of manufactured drama for so long she thinks she's the Maypole and the rest of us are ribbons whose sole purpose in life is to wrap around her.

I'm supposed to be avoiding her for these precious hours before our big dinner tonight. Declan shrewdly conjured up these shenanigans, and now I have to use every tool in my toolbox not to talk to her.

"Hello!" she tootles, smiling brightly. Her purse is new, a buttery beige leather contraption with brass circles in a chain along the front, the handles made of peach macramé that matches her sandals and her eye shadow. "Marie Jacoby here. I'm Mr. McCormick's mother-in-law. Is Mr. Lüq here?"

The cute little pixie wearing six-inch lilac high heels and less cloth than a car shammy looks at Mom in horror. "Mister Lüq? *Non non non.*" The French accent makes me realize we've made a grave mistake.

"*Oui, oui, oui!*" Mom says back, pleased with herself. "*Je m'appelle Marie! Monsieur Lüq, s'il vous plaît.*"

Mom knows about as much French as she needs to cross the border into Quebec and find herself on the road to Montreal for her rare yoga conventions there. She can say "Downward facing dog," "My IT band is too tight and causing pain in that position," and "Please excuse me for passing gas," in French, but that's it.

The spa pixie crinkles her nose like Mom just farted and lit it on fire.

A string of angry French comes back. I hear an intense focus on the word *monsieur*. The pixie looks at Amanda, her eyes going wide.

Pointing a shaking finger, she says, "*Le Faucon!*"

Scrambling for her smartphone, which she must store inside her anus, because there is no way that outfit has pockets, she approaches Amanda with a deferential authority that has Mom's nose out of joint.

"*Le sauveur, mademoiselle.* You are the animal rescuer! Evangi, come here! It is her! The woman who saved the *petit* dog from the hawk! Oh, Lüq will be so happy to meet you!"

And with that, they usher Amanda into a back room that requires the pixie to receive a retina scan, leaving me and Mom in the reception area, a giant bottle of cucumber water burbling in a fountain, a light display sending geysers every minute.

It is a replica of one of the fountains outside.

I hate Las Vegas.

Two minutes pass. I pretend to answer work emails on my phone, but really play a game called Hearthstone. Jeffrey is killing me. The app keeps shouting, "My magic will tear you apart" and it's right. I switch to something easier, staring at red jelly beans and green-striped candy on my screen.

Five. Eight. By nine minutes, Mom looks like she's going to fidget herself off the edge of the world.

"This is outrageous! We need to complain."

I look up from my Candy Crush app. "Huh?" I am in no rush to get any of this spa stuff going. Give me five blue balls in a row and I'm happy.

"This Mr. Lüq can't be allowed to treat you like this, Shannon. You're about to be a billionaire's wife! You need to learn to be a bitch!"

"A *what?*"

"A bitch! Cultivate your inner bitchiness." Mom's hands are

waving all around her front space. I see the Italian. Her maiden name is Scarlotta, after all. She looks like Wolverine conducting the Boston Symphony Orchestra.

I stiffen and bite my lips to hold back the stream of profanity that threatens to overflow like a volcanic eruption.

"You and Dad spent my entire childhood and adolescence telling me I needed to be nice," I finally manage. "And kind. That kindness and being pleasant was the best moral choice." I hold my palm out. Talk to the hand. You want me to be bitchier? How about I start practicing right now?

With you, Mom.

"*Pfft.* Boy, were we wrong!" she backpedals, her eyes rolling. "Those values are great when that kind of social glue is what you need to fit in, but around here it's the opposite. Wealthy people take niceness to be a sign of weakness."

She's blathering on, but there's a kernel of truth in there.

Damn it.

The private spa door flies open, slamming against the wall. A blast of scented air, bamboo and lemongrass and humidity fills the reception area.

"You may see Lüq now," the pixie says. I look at her name tag.

Gagai.

Right.

Mom pretends she's trying to decide whether to go through that open door. "I'm not sure we really should see him," she sniffs. Gagai's eyes go wide, one pupil dilating before my eyes. A thin chain appears to be caught in her long, fake eyelashes.

I can't stop staring, because I'm wrong. It's not a chain caught in her eyelashes.

It's a chain hanging off her *eye*.

"Eeeee!" I squeak, shuddering in horror. "Your eye! We need to get you to a hospital. You've torn...something."

Gagai gives me a look filled with more contempt than Chuckles. "It is the latest fashion."

"Shredding your cornea with metal shavings is fashionable?"

"It is eye art. The eye is the mirror of the soul."

"Your eye looks like a welding project, honey."

Mom looks closely, pulling out a set of reading glasses she bought at Target for $9.99.

Excuse me. *Tar-jey.*

Once they're on her head, she peers, then fishes in her purse and pulls out a second pair, which she puts over the first pair. A satisfied look covers her face as Gagai takes in the entire production.

"Is this a new look?" she asks me. "Two pairs of glasses?"

"Yes," I lie. "In Boston, where we are from."

"My God," Mom hisses. "She's wearing contact lens *jewelry.*" Without pausing, Mom reaches up and tugs on the end of the tiny, whisper-light chain dangling from Gagai's eye.

A string of angry French pours out of the pixie, her heels poking at Mom's shins. Mom looks at me, aghast.

And then sprints through the open spa door to find Lüq.

## Chapter Thirteen

The actual spa is a rainforest.

No. Really.

Someone has taken great care to create a miniature version of the botanical gardens outside. It looks like those pictures of Thailand or Indonesian beaches, with the quaint open-air hut by the green waters, only bamboo rules the day inside this little spa haven. They must pipe in the scent of ocean air.

"A shot?" A different pixie, this one as blonde as the other is dark, offers us little two-ounce glasses filled with green juice, a sprig of lemon and mint on the edge. Her name tag says Elle.

"Thank you," we say in unison. We tip back our drinks and while it's not the best wheatgrass juice I've ever tasted, it will do.

"Urg!" Mom gags, drinking half of hers and setting it down emphatically in a thatch of greenery and dirt. "What the hell was that?"

"Wheatgrass juice," I explain. "It's healthy. Good for your gut."

"I don't give a crap about my gut in Vegas, Shannon. The next one of those better have some vodka in it," she mutters. "Who offers you a shot in *Vegas* that doesn't have alcohol in it? That should be illegal. Now, where is this mysterious Mr. Lüq?"

"Here," says a sonorous voice from behind a thick, wide palm

140

frond. "We are evaluating the stunning Ms. Amanda Warrick." A familiar giggle bubbles up into the air, floating to the skylight.

I look around the giant green leaf to find Amanda in a small, steaming pool, naked except for bikini bottoms, and floating on her back. A thin piece of silk covers her breasts and she has a purple eye mask covering her lids.

Mom starts undressing, peeling off her shoes and socks, reaching up under her skirt to shove her hands, palms in, down her panties.

"What are you doing?"

"Getting out of my Spanx! Look at that natural spring! I hear it's made up of amniotic fluid gathered from untouched populations in places where toxic chemicals aren't found in the breast milk of mothers. Yet."

"Amniotic *what*?"

"Yes," little Elle says. "We only collect the amniotic fluid that the spirit gives naturally, and only from those mothers who give permission during their surges as the spirit bridges from the Motherworld to the Otherworld."

I am never, ever getting pregnant.

"How?" I ask. "Do you use a vacuum cleaner, or a turkey baster?" Mom's hanging on to my arm, balanced on one foot, her shaping underwear like an unbreaded calamari ring around her navel.

"The spirit's rhythms decide when the sacrifice of the sacred wombworld is ready to be—" Elle takes a cleansing yoga breath— "left behind for the sake of the mother's fulfillment."

I look at the spa services menu. Wombwater Restorative Massage: $500 for fifty minutes.

"Do you pay the mothers for their *amniotic fluid*?"

"No, no. Of course not." She seems scandalized by the idea and on the verge of tears. I feel as if I've hurt the feelings of a tiny child in a Pixar film. "It is technically the spirit-child's possession. But we do pay for breast milk and placentas."

*What the hell is a spirit child?* I'm about to ask, when Mom cuts in.

"What do you do in a spa with *breast milk*?" Mom clutches

her bosom as if Elle and Lüq are planning to kidnap her and turn her into a human cow, even though she hasn't lactated since TLC was chasing waterfalls.

Waterfalls *not* made of amniotic fluid.

Elle's smile is so sweet. Her words, not so much.

"First, the chef takes the—"

"Marie? Shannon?" Amanda's voice is soft and happy. Float in enough womb juice and drink some breast milk smoothies and maybe it infuses you with joy.

"Are they disturbing you, dear?" The same sonorous voice. "We can have them removed." A bolt of gauzy fabric floats along my peripheral vision. A shaved head. Thin, long-fingered hands, the nails painted meticulously with Tibetan mandalas. Eyes with thick eyeliner on the top lid, curling up at the ends.

It's like the Dalai Lama and Adele had a middle-aged *hu*.

This must be Lüq.

Mom freezes. "Is that a resort employee threatening to have *you* removed?" She purses her mouth and gives me a recriminating look. "See what I mean? You need to assert yourself here, Shannon. You are about to become the queen bee."

"What?" Did she seriously just refer to her anaphylactic, highly-allergic daughter as a *bee*?

"You're the First Lady of this resort."

"You are making no sense."

"These people work for your man's company. That means, by extension, they work for you."

"I'm a marketing director at that company!"

"Even better. Make them bow before you."

"This isn't a monarchy, Mom."

"Monarchy is underrated," she sniffs.

"I am Lüq," the low, sing-songy voice informs us. "Welcome."

"Amanda?" Pam appears from behind the bamboo forest, dressed in a black and white outfit that makes her look just enough like a panda bear to make me giggle nervously. Spritzy is nowhere to be seen.

A long, deflating sigh comes from Lüq, who gives Elle a sympathetic look and says, "Le schedule is fecked."

That's some Irish-French accent hu has going on there. I peer at hu. Hu's lips twitch.

"Mom?" Amanda calls out to Pam. "You have to try this amniotic-ocean bath. I feel like I'm transported back to another lifetime. Lüq read my lives and says that I was a dog at court in King Louie XIII of France's time, when he attached his little dogs to miniature carriages and had them act like horses."

"What the hell are they putting in that water? Peyote?" Mom whispers to me. Pam's head is cocked to one side as she tries to catch everything Amanda says, while Lüq rushes to Pam, arms outstretched, a beatific smile on hu's face.

"Amanda's mother! So wonderful to meet you," hu says, kissing both of Pam's cheeks with a flourish. When Lüq smiles, it's as if all the suns in the universe have been power-washed, shining brighter than before.

I want Lüq to smile like that at me. Just once.

My new purpose in life is to be the focus of hu's attention. Sometimes in life, you meet a person who has an inner radiance that is so compelling, just being in their presence—not talking, not moving, not doing anything but *being*—is so fulfilling that you'll do anything to spend more time with them.

I'm not talking about romantic love. A barista, a work colleague, that really cool Uber driver, your substitute mailman...we meet personalities so captivating that a sliver of time charges our batteries.

Lüq holds that radiance within.

And I see why the spa is a smashing success.

"I'm Shannon's mother," Mom says, breathless and flushed, obviously under Lüq's spell like me.

"Hmm," is all Lüq says, eyes on Pam. "Your daughter has the heart of a saint."

"Thank you," Mom and Pam say in unison.

"And what spa treatment can we get?" Mom asks, looking around the hot spring like it's a Rainforest Cafe and she's searching for the animals hidden in the trees. "We'd love a massage like the one Amanda's receiving."

"Hmm," is all Lüq says, still not even looking once at Mom.

Mom looks at Pam. Then Lüq. Then Amanda.

By the time she gets to me, her eyes are hard. Determined. Convicted.

I know that look. It's the same expression she had when I came home from eighth grade one day and told her Mr. Humphries, my gym teacher, had announced to everyone that I was sitting out gym because of "female problems." It's the same look she had on her face when some bozo at Tyler's day care tried to tell Carol he had oppositional defiant disorder—at the age of eighteen months—and that he was "disrespectful" for not sitting still for their forty-five minute circle time. Mom had that look on her face the night a very drunk Todd called and chewed Carol out for filing child support papers and threatened to counter-file for full custody of children he hadn't seen in over a year.

It's also the same look she had on her face at my wedding two days ago, when I screamed at her for inviting Jessica Coffin to my wedding.

You know. That topic we've avoided discussing until tonight, at dinner?

Lüq is so busted.

"Do you know who she is?" Mom points to me.

Oh, God.

"Shannon Jacoby," Lüq says softly. "Mr. Declan McCormick's betrothed."

*Betrothed*. The word sounds like *queen* in his strangely mesmerizing accent.

Mom's thrown off by his acknowledgement. "Yes, that's who she is, but do you realize what that means?"

"It means she loves him."

Mom frowns and digs her heels in. She's trying to use power to bully Lüq into giving me attention she feels I "deserve" because of who I sleep with, and it's clear Lüq doesn't buy into those social rules.

"Of course, she loves him!" Mom snaps. "Mr. McCormick is your boss!"

"That seems to be very important to you," Lüq whispers.

Mom's eyes go round.

And Declan is, indeed, my betrothed, but I think I just fell in love with Lüq, too. I wonder if hu has dinner plans for tonight, because if not, I want hu right there as my guest of honor.

"It's—well, it should be important to you!" Mom huffs.

"Is that important to you?"

"Is *what* important to me?"

"That I find the same issues important that *you* find important, dear."

"Well—I—but—but these are universal! You *should* worry about your boss. He's the reason you have a job! And if you want to keep your job, you're nice to the boss's wife."

"What if I don't worry about losing my job?"

"Everyone worries about losing their job!"

"You seem to have a strong need to assume that what applies to you applies to everyone else's internal state." Lüq nods as hu says this, leaning in with concern, touching Mom's shoulder in an act of graceful solidarity, like Oprah comforting a crying refugee who is about to win a car or an elliptical machine and doesn't know it yet.

"Maybe some ocean water infused with amniotic fluid will help," I hiss.

"Ocean water?" Pam replies, Lüq still holding her hand. Lüq has Pam's palm, stroking the thumb joint with hu's index finger, and hu's other hand is on my mother. "Is that why Amanda's so buoyant? Must be the salt water."

"You know," Mom says, giving Pam the side-eye. She's up to something. "The ocean is so salty because of whales."

What?

Pam gives Mom an indulgent look. Lüq tilts hu's head, while Amanda just floats.

"Really?" Pam prompts.

"Yes," Mom gushes. "I read this in a science magazine."

Translation: Mom clicked on someone's Facebook link and

read a half-baked mashup from a website devoted to getting as many views as possible to generate ad money for the owner.

"When whales ejaculate, they produce something like four hundred gallons of sperm!" Mom gushes.

"I'm guessing the female whales don't have to deal with the age-old 'spit or swallow' problem," I mutter.

"But," Mom says pointedly, ignoring me, "most of it doesn't make it into the woman whale."

Okay, now. "Woman whale?"

"Really?" Pam says, obviously aware that my mom is full of utter crap, but playing along for fun. "You mean, women whales don't have vaginas that hold four hundred gallons?"

Mom pauses and puts on her thinking face. "That's a great question! I don't know. How much volume can a whale's vagina hold?"

"This is fascinating," Lüq says. "Gagai! Evangi! Come here! We are in the temple of learning."

We're in the temple of bullshit.

"Well," Pam starts, as if she knows the answer to that scintillating question, "the average whale is about a hundred feet long. Human females are about five feet tall. So, I'd guess the ratio is twenty to one."

Mom does math in her head. "How much does a female vagina hold? In terms of liquid?"

"About six hundred milliliters," Lüq answers instantly.

"That's twenty ounces or so," Pam adds.

"Then," Mom says seriously, as if we're working at Draper Labs and our complex volume calculations are going to help rescue Matt Damon from Mars, "there is no way a woman whale has a vagina that holds four hundred gallons of whale sperm, like I said. And," she adds with a dramatic flourish, her voice rising as Evangi and Gagai gather with Elle, "that is why the ocean is so salty. That buoyancy in the hot spring here at the spa comes from whale sperm."

"Are our clients going to get pregnant with baby whales?" Gagai screams.

Pam and I facepalm simultaneously.

I swear Amanda and I were switched at birth. Seriously.

"No," Mom says, shaking her head as if Gagai were the stupidest person on earth. "Of course not."

"Whew," Gagai says, playing with the chain at the end of her eye jewelry. Pam does a double take and gives me a look. I shrug.

"The amniotic fluid in the spa comes from women who are already pregnant, so it neutralizes the sperm," Mom adds emphatically.

As you can imagine, Mom was of tremendous help when I worked on my AP Biology homework in high school.

"How did you know the volume limit of the average vagina?" Pam asks Lüq as Evangi and Gagai chat eagerly with Mom in a conversation that would make the owner of Snopes.com choose an icepick lobotomy.

"I must know for the vajacials," hu explains.

I suddenly realize that Pam has been discussing vaginas and sperm and has not fainted. Not even a blush. She's conversing as if this isn't a source of embarrassment or anxiety, and I tuck that piece of information away—again—for a future conversation with Amanda.

Who now calls out, "I don't want to get pregnant by a whale. Andrew would be jealous."

What the hell is in that wheatgrass juice shot?

"I am afraid to ask this," I start. I pause. I take two deep breaths as Lüq gives me a closed-mouth smile and waits patiently. Finally, I spit it out.

"What is a vajacial?"

"It is a facial for your vagina."

"That's what I was afraid of."

"Are you always so fearful about new experiences?" Lüq asks.

"Only when they involve having strangers at a spa exfoliate my hoo-haw."

Mom's sex talk antennae pick up the word "hoo-haw" and she comes over to us.

"*Non, non, non!*" Lüq assures me. "We do not exfoliate the sacred rose petals of the garden, the entry gates to the finest lotus flower that is the jewel of your womanhood!"

Lüq should get a time machine, transport himself to 1983, and write for Harlequin.

"Do you use cucumbers, too?" Mom asks.

Lüq's eyes get really wide.

Pam finally blushes.

"The vajacial involves a steam bath for the rose petals—"

"STEAM?" I can't help it. I scream, because my delicate rose petals are about as interested in coming into contact with steam as they were in touching hot wax, which is to say, NOT. I'm more likely to let my mother be my birthing coach one day than I am to let someone steam my va-jay-jay. You steam broccoli. You steam carrots. When you steam rose petals, they curl up and die.

Nope.

Amanda startles in her womb bath and flips over, her thin piece of silk falling off, and now she's topless, bobbing in the water, and it looks like her mouth's open and—

Gag.

She comes up, grasping the silk across her chest, spitting furiously. "I just drank whale sperm!"

"I hear it has plenty of protein," Mom says, trying to be helpful.

"None of this is true! That's not how this works, Mom. That's not how any of this works! The ocean is not salty because of massive amounts of whale ejaculate, and people who get massages in this amniotic ocean water bath aren't protected from pregnancy because of pregnancy hormones in the womb juice!"

"It is the vajacials that protect women from pregnancy, right?" Elle asks sweetly.

"It's basic biology that protects them!" I fume. "Wait." I look at Amanda. "Did you actually have a vajacial?"

Gagai is helping Amanda into a thin bathrobe the color of celery. "Yes," she mutters.

"And did it transport you into a past life where you could see your inner vaginal self?"

"No. But I think my cervix smells like sandalwood now, and I pulled a muscle in my inner thigh from squatting for so long."

"Squatting? You squat?"

"Yeah. Over the steam bath machine."

"This sounds worse than childbirth!" Not that I would know, but...

SPLASH!

Mom has put on some thin, silk outfit like the one Amanda wears, and jumped into the hot spring womb juice. She dips her head under, like a dolphin, and comes up in the swirling clouds of mist that dot the water's surface.

"This feels amazing!"

"But won't she get pregnant?" Elle asks, her lower lip trembling. "She didn't do the vajacial."

Pam slips her arm around my shoulders, a gesture that is less maternal and more in solidarity over the fact that we are actively experiencing the Dunning-Kruger Effect in real time.

"She has already gone through menopause," Pam says seriously, "so she can't get pregnant."

"Whew," Elle says, her hand splayed across collarbones that poke out like doorknobs.

"Your daughter is a hero," Lüq tells Pam as Mom floats on her back in the water, Evangi gliding into the zero-entry pool and holding a flotation pillow under Mom's head. "Have you seen the video on YouTube of her rescue of that poor little puppy?"

"Yes," Pam says as Gagai brings her a cup of something greenish and frothy. Pam eyes it like it might be poison.

"Green tea latte infused with bee pollen and anti-aging RNAs," Gagai explains, as if she ordered a double half-caf skim mocha at Starbucks.

"No ground placenta?" Pam jokes, leaning down for a tentative sip.

"Just one moment. I will add some," Gagai says.

"No, no! I'm fine. Thanks," Pam balks.

"Where's Spritzy?" I ask, not because I care, but because I want to talk about anything but whale sperm and breast milk.

"With James. He took him for a walk and to the pet spa."

"There's a *pet spa* here?"

"I was as surprised as you, Shannon, but..." She makes a face I know well. "He insisted."

"I hope poor Spritzy doesn't get a doggy vajacial," I mutter.

"It doesn't matter," she whispers back. "Spritzy is a boy, so he can't get pregnant from the whale sperm."

I give Pam a fist bump. I freaking *love* Pam.

"Jordan Montelcini is an ass!" Lüq exclaims, anger dissolving across his features like a liquid rubber mask designed by CGI experts.

The *non sequitur* makes Mom startle, just like Amanda moments ago, and flop on her belly in the water, coming up sputtering.

"Ew! You swallowed!" Amanda calls out from her perch across the room, where she's receiving a pedicure from Elle.

"I always swallow!" Mom replies.

"TMI, MOM!"

"I need to sit down," Pam says, going slack against me, her dead weight hard to get over to a chair where I can dump her off so she can handle her case of the vapors.

"What's wrong with Jordan Montelcini?" Mom asks.

"Who is Jordan Montelcini?" me and Pam call out.

"AN ASS!" Amanda and Lüq shout at the same time.

"Darling!" Lüq says, arms opening. Amanda leaps up into the air and glides across into hu's arms. They hug. The universe melts. "I knew we were soulmates in another lifetime. How else would the energy of the cosmos know to bring me to your video, and you to my spa?"

"How did you find the video?" Amanda asks, her voice muffled by hu's muumuu.

"I received a Google Alert for Jordan."

We all frown. Stalking doesn't gel with the whole serenity act Lüq has going here.

"I was a floral designer in my last life."

"Did you learn that from a psychic?"

"No," Lüq says, confused. "My last life. You know. The 2000s. I attended hair and esthetician school in early 2010 and here we are. But Jordan." Hu glowers. "Jordan and Mama Montelcini were my nemeses."

"Floral designers are *that* competitive?" I say with a smile.

Lüq frowns.

The sun dies.

"I do not joke about this," he says, clapping his hands, an action which makes Gagai, Evangi and Elle all bustle out of the room. In the distance, I hear what sounds like an espresso machine and frother working furiously, as Lüq invites us to move to a sunken pit.

1974 drank way too much, did some Angel Dust, and threw up in this depression in the ground, with crazy avocado green, adobe orange, and cigarette-yellow all imprinted with the iconic LOVE work of art, the floor covered in shag carpeting so long it might as well be dreadlocks.

We all sit, and Lüq pulls out a vaping machine. A whiff of vanilla fills the air.

"Do you mind?" hu asks. "I am trying to cut the tobacco, but this...."

We all assure hu it's fine. Evangi, Gagai and Elle return with coffees.

*Actual* coffees. Not tea disguised as coffee, or frothed placenta flavored with chicory and deception.

I sniff mine. It has hints of cinnamon and cherry. "No placenta?" I joke.

"I can get you some," Evangi says, darting for the door.

"No! It's fine." The coffee's not nearly as good as Grind It Fresh!, and Amanda and I share a knowing look, but I keep my mouth shut. Caffeine matters. Origin does not.

I want the scoop on Jordan and *Lüq*.

Mom brought him and his weird little dog into the wedding planning just after Amanda went on a work date with him and saved the tiny Chihuahua from being a hawk's Pu Pu platter. Someone videotaped the rescue, and for whatever reason, Jordan blames Amanda for the little dog being in danger, and considers my mother to be the true rescuer.

What the hell do Lüq and Jordan Montelcini have in common?

"Are you from Boston?" Marie asks hu.

"No. I am a citizen of the world."

Even I roll my eyes at that, and so does Gagai, except when she does it her chains rattle and she sounds like one of the ghosts in *A Christmas Carol*.

"I met Jordan at a rave," Lüq starts, looking at each of us, as if this tidbit were an anchor for the rest of the story.

*What's a rave?* I mouth to Amanda. She shrugs. Hmm. Maybe it's a fast food joint?

"He had this lion's mane of hair, wild and rainbowed, and he looked just like Boy George in his heyday."

Mom and Pam sigh.

*Old people stuff*, Amanda mouths.

I nod.

"Ours was an affair of passion—"

"Hold on. You *dated* Jordan?" Amanda asks with an incredulous squeak.

"Yes."

"But he's straight!"

"How would you know, my dear? And besides, love has no gender." Lüq spreads hu's arms wide, the long arms like wings when draped by hu's muumuu. Hu looks like a butterfly. A bald, aging butterfly with a Grateful Dead complex and tattooed-on eyeliner.

"I went on a date with him after being matched together in an online dating program," Amanda declares, blunt and bold.

Lüq freezes. "Le Hawk has made love with my ex?" Hu's jaw shifts slightly, a tongue rolling in hu's cheek, and Lüq gives Amanda a creepy once-over that is about as thorough as Jeffrey licking clean a pint of ice cream.

"Good for you," Lüq finally says. Amanda is still speechless.

"I didn't sleep with him!"

"Pity. Your loss."

"What? *His* loss! HIS!" Amanda screeches.

"I sense an imbalance in your energy, Le Hawk." Lüq sighs.

"That was me," Mom says. "Sorry." She reddens, and turns to Elle. "What was in that latte?" She stands, makes a very embarrassing sound, and asks, "Where's the bathroom?"

Elle points. "The latte is made with the finest breast milk provided by the—"

Pam, mid-sip, sprays the contents of her mouthful everywhere.

"Le violence!" Lüq cries out. "Is your life force in anguish?"

"I think Marie's bowels are," Amanda mutters as Mom sprints for the facilities.

"There was breast milk in that latte?" Pam asks me, her voice anemic and shaky.

I shrug and whisper, "I'm sure Anterdec would never—"

"Of course," Lüq says. "Research shows that it is a vital source of anti-aging nutrients. I drink it every day."

Amanda gives me a look. "It halts your aging?" The guy is easily in his fifties, so—

"Yes. I am eighty-one years old. Do I look it?"

"You're *eighty-one* and you dated Jordan?" Amanda is still stuck on this, while I'm left wondering if pregnancy and lactation might hold some key to immortality. "Jordan's in his forties!"

"I might have to rethink that whole breast-milk-drinking thing," I mutter. My stomach seizes, rising up in anarchy. Okay. No. I'll take the wrinkles.

"Love knows no age," Lüq sniffs.

"No age. No gender. Love doesn't know shit, does it?" Amanda whispers to me.

"And Jordan Montelcini is a blood-sucking little worm."

"Agreed!" Amanda crows.

"What did he do to you?" I ask Lüq.

"He broke my heart."

I pat Lüq's hand. "It happens to all of us at least once. Sometimes love just isn't enough."

"Ain't," Mom says, returning to the group.

"Ain't what?"

"Sometimes love just ain't enough. If you're going to quote cheesy love songs, get the titles right."

I ignore her.

"Why do you hate him so much? His very existence bothers you?" I ask Lüq.

Lüq gives me hu's compete attention, my eyes falling into hu's. "Do you not understand, child? Only from great love can come such anger. We find ourselves impaled by rage only when we feel betrayed by big love. If we are lucky, we experience so much love that one day—" Hu's voice hitches with emotion and I'm overcome, grabbing the first person I can touch, needing connection.

The hand I squeeze is Mom's.

"—that one day, we burn with hatred like Hades himself, consumed wholly by the power of all that is vile, wishing our former soulmate a pain-filled, loathsome death worthy of a beggar stewed in excrement."

*That* went in an unexpected direction.

"Jordan Montelcini is an ass," Lüq sobs. "But he was *my* ass, and now I have to go through the rest of my life assless."

"Me, too!" Mom wails. "It all just flattens out like a fat pancake after fifty."

"That's not what hu meant, Mom!"

"But it's true! I could bend over and you could use my ass as an end table, honey. I could sell this ass as a level in the tool department at Home Depot."

What's the SKU number for whackadoo?

"It'll happen to you, too, honey. Genetics." She gives Amanda a sympathetic blink. "And you."

"Me?" Amanda squeaks.

"Just look at Pammy," Mom says, shaking her head with pity. Poor Pam reaches around the back of her chair to pat her own ass.

"What about my tushie?" Pam is alarmed.

"It's been more than twenty-five years," Lüq says with a sigh, hu's eyes glassy and unfocused as hu interrupts. Hu is clearly caught in the reverie of the '80s. "His mother made him break up with me, and then that wretched wench destroyed my floral designing career. She wanted Jordan for herself."

Amanda looks like she just licked the top of her Turdmobile.

Lüq claps, switching gears like nothing. "The ladies are here for a relaxing spa day, not a tour of my broken heart's four chambers. You, my dear," Lüq adds, touching my hair, lifting the long strands like they're drugged snakes being readied for medical testing, "need a complete intervention. Top to bottom."

"Bottom?" I gulp.

"Anal bleaching," Mom whispers, then winks. "It's a thing. Guys love it."

I start to dry heave.

"Anal bleaching is *sooooooooo* 2013," Lüq says drolly, making Mom redden and turn to hu in reverence, all ears to learn what this year's trend might be, and how to use it as a form of torture against me.

"Let us start with the top," hu says. "You poor, poor child," hu mutters, pulling me over to a hairstyling command center. "What on earth happened to your hair?"

"I, uh—"

"And these fingernails!" Lüq picks up my index finger on my right hand like he's plucking a leech from a cadaver. "Tartan? What abomination is this?"

Mom slowly slides her hands under her pancake ass.

Gagai picks up Amanda's hand and points.

Lüq's eyes widen and hu gives us all sympathetic looks. "Who is the Scottish monster forcing this crazy pattern on you? You are tartan hostages who need love, sympathy, and a proper fill to recover from the psychic trauma of these hands, which scream desperation and haggis."

Mom doesn't say a word.

I love Lüq.

* * *

Two hours later, I need a break.

When I return to our hotel suite, I mistake it for a high-end boutique and back out slowly. The room is filled with eight racks of women's clothing, forming a corridor behind the sofa. A gold-painted vanity is in front of the left side of clothing, and I see three distinct stacks of shoe boxes on the floor beneath the hanging clothes.

"I'm so sorry! I must have the wrong room!" I call out, hoping I haven't offended the occupant.

"Mrs. McCormick?" The voice is female, with a French accent, but one much more cultured than the spa pixie.

"Um, not yet. This is Shannon, though."

"Mrs. McCormick, I am Evie." A rail-thin replica of Coco Chanel herself, circa 1920, reaches for my hand, warming it between both of hers. Dark hair coiffed in a retro wavy look that frames her face. A suit that is Tiffany Blue, a color I now know. Pale, unlined skin that is timeless. Warm brown eyes. The kind of cultured appearance that could make her thirty or sixty.

"Mr. McCormick leaves his regrets—he is at a business meeting—but he asked me to assist you in finding the wardrobe that best suits your needs."

I'm going to kill him. An image of Hello Kitty in a Georgia O'Keeffe painting slams through my thoughts.

"Declan sent you? You're a professional shopper?"

"I prefer the term *stylist*."

"Oh. Sorry." Great. There's a *vocabulary* for this. It's one thing to have undeclared behavioral expectations when it comes to buying new clothes, but now I don't even have words.

I'm a Fashion Preschooler.

Evie moves like her feet are a hovercraft, her bones in perfect alignment. I am an injured giraffe in comparison. I reach up, wondering what I look like, feeling oily skin and ragged hair. Lüq had me do all the spa treatments first, then let me come up here to grab a book so I could tolerate another three hours in hair-color hell before getting a cut and style and having my makeup done.

"I do know that Lüq is expecting you, Mrs. McCormick, so I will not take much of your time. We need your measurements, your weight, to take a small scraping of your skin, and to pluck some hair samples."

Horror fills me. "Why? So you can clone me?"

She laughs. "*Non*. We can best find colors that enhance your skin tone, the contours of your body, and to allow shadow and light to work for—and not against—you."

"You realize I buy most of my clothes at Savers and the Salvation Army."

She gives me a blank look. "Are those new boutiques? You are from Boston, I know. Perhaps these are local to you?"

"They definitely have an eclectic set of offerings," I reply. "And a diverse clientele."

She reaches for a smartphone and taps on the glass screen with—of course—perfect nails. "I will investigate. Thank you for the information. I am certain we can find you some outfits that are as nice as those you find at Savers and the Salvation Army."

No kidding, lady.

*Bang bang bang.*

Someone pounds on the door, the racket so loud you'd think the hotel was on fire.

"Shannon! Open up! I know you're in there!"

Mom. Surprise.

"If you think sneaking out of Mr. Lüq's spa before you're done is going to work, you've got another think coming. Declan told me to babysit you and make sure you get every single treatment on the spa menu!" she bellows.

"Your mother?" Evie asks, sympathy filling her voice.

I nod.

"And that includes the vajacial!" Mom shrieks.

Evie looks like she's about to faint. No worries about Hello Kitty fashions from her.

I wrench open the door to the suite and grab Mom by the salon drape, yanking so hard she flies face-first into a dressmaker's bust. Mom's getting highlights and lowlights, so her head is covered with foil. She looks like she belongs in Roswell, New Mexico, at an alien encounters convention. A cigarette with a long ash and a story involving anal probes and she'd fit right in.

Actually, now that I think about it, the *only* thing she's missing is the cigarette.

"No one is getting anywhere near my labia with steam or anything else!" I declare. "And that includes Declan," I add in a low voice.

"Saving that for the wedding night?" Mom whispers with a

wink. "Smart girl. Make him hold out until he wants it even more. And a fresh set of lips will really—"

If I pretend she isn't real, she'll go away, right?

Hold on.

She's carrying a coffee.

From my favorite coffee shop next door.

"Where did you get that?" I'm more outraged that she didn't get me a yummy latte than I am by her comments about anal bleaching, which is not happening. Nope.

"Lüq got it for me, Pammy and Amanda."

"What about *me*?"

She lifts one shoulder and imitates his accent. "He said that if you didn't care to stay, why should he get you the divine nectar?"

"I'm here to get a book! To have something to read while I go through all these treatments."

"You always have to be *different*, honey. Lüq has plenty of things to read in the spa."

"They're all pictures of hair styles or magazines in French."

"You took middle-school French. You should be able to read them."

"The pictures make it clear the magazines are all for high-colonic industry workers."

Evie gives a low sound of acceptance. "Everyone has a fetish." Her hand moves in a distinctly French way, the nonchalance so engrained, the lift of one corner of her mouth imperceptible.

Mom looks at her as if finally noticing her and grins nice and wide. She looks like an extra on *Steel Magnolias*. "Yes. Everyone does. Hello. I am Marie. I'm Mr. McCormick's mother-in-law."

"That's how you're introducing yourself now, Mom? Not as 'Shannon's mother', but as 'Declan's mother-in-law'?"

"I've got to use my connections, dear. Declan has more clout here than you."

"Listen to yourself! That's so shallow."

"Oooo, Prada!" Mom says. Clothes are a shiny for her. She's like a magpie. "What's this all about?"

"Declan's forcing me to work with a professional shopper."

"Stylist," Evie hisses.

Mom beams. "Will she get you another outfit like the last shopper? The one who dressed you in that gorgeous Hello Kitty outfit?"

Evie nearly faints again.

"No," I say curtly, offering Evie a glass of sparkling water from her little snack station, which she gulps.

"Mom, I'm coming right back. Promise. Evie's going to take my measurements and I'll be right back in the spa."

"Ooooo!" Mom says, giving Evie an about-face and pouring on the charm. "Can I get measured too? What's Declan buying us?"

"Me. Declan's buying *me* something. Not you."

"How do you know? There are an awful lot of clothes here in an array of sizes."

"Because Declan told me he wanted to do something special. For me. And only me." Territoriality emerges in the strangest way. Evie listens to Mom intently, eyes bright, cheeks pink, as she nods encouragement.

"Your mother is wise," Evie urges. "Let Mr. McCormick do this for you."

"Considering most of your non-work wardrobe comes from second-hand stores, this is a quantum leap for you, honey!"

*Thump.*

We look down.

Evie has finally fainted.

Chapter Fourteen

After experiencing more processing than a Kraft cheese product, I return to our suite with a new hairdo, every pore of my skin exfoliated and moisturized, body hair intact where I want it intact, though the negotiations over that issue rival the Paris Peace Accords and boundary lines.

A note on the bed reads: *Business mtgs still. Sorry. See you @7 for dinner w/ parents. <3*

I check my phone. Same basic text from Declan.

And, to my surprise, one from my dad, left just a few minutes ago.

*Can we talk before dinner, honey?*

I text him back and within five minutes, I'm in a giant bear hug with Dad, embraced between slot machines and a baccarat table.

"Look at you!" he says, his voice hitting three different octaves of marvel. "My little tomboy's all grown up."

I blush. "The stupid spa. Declan and Mom made me." I can't help but be a little pleased, though.

"Declan and your mother joined forces on an issue?" Dad's eyebrow goes up, his mouth down. "That's frightening."

We share a very, *very* understanding laugh.

"What's that?" Dad asks, pointing to the "High Limit" sign in front of a private door.

"I think that's where the really wealthy players go. Baccarat? Declan likes that game."

"Huh. I played that years ago."

"You did? Are you sure? Declan says it's a game for international jet setters."

"What? I don't look like a billionaire playboy?" He mugs for me.

I laugh. "Seriously, though—you know how to play?"

"Just the basics. Before you were born, I worked for three months at the first casino in Connecticut, right after they opened. A temp job. Learned most of these games there." He just nods to himself, his eyes flicking back to the door, then focusing on me.

"Oh, Daddy, thank you for doing this. I need a break."

"From your mother?"

"From everything." I look around the casino in marvel. "Isn't this place amazing? It's so..."

"Awful."

"What?" I laugh, giving him a conspirator's smile. "I know it's a bit much." Dad's not the kind of guy to be negative about pretty much anything. Go with the flow is more his style.

"It's a 'bit much' the same way that I'm 'a little in debt,' honey."

There's that damn topic again. Money. I guess it's natural. We're in Vegas, on a casino floor. For the first time, it occurs to me that it's Monday. And Mom and Dad have been staying here the entire time. I'm assuming Anterdec is comping their rooms, so they don't have to pay for that. What about food, transportation, and all the rest?

Talking about that seems too prickly, especially given Dad's rare frown. I tuck my questions aside for later and pick something safer.

"Declan designed this resort. It was one of his first jobs at Anterdec."

"And he did a fine job. It's just not my style. How about we get out of here and go outside. There's an ice cream shop across the street on the Strip."

"You're remarkably fluent in my language, Dad."

"We're in the land of milkfat and honey, Shannon." He gives me a side hug. "I'd better be, after all these years." We walk through the casino, which starts to feel like it never ends, a repeating pattern of fake Persian carpeting and marble-like wallpaper on the high walls giving the appearance of eternity.

Dad takes a deep breath. "Do they pipe in some kind of money scent?"

I shake my head.

"Focus-group-determined aromatherapy designed to convince people it's safe to keep gambling away."

Horror fills Dad's features just as we reach the main lobby. A twenty-foot ceiling with a skylight the size of an ice-hockey rink is covered with stained glass.

"What? Quit joking."

"I'm serious."

"This place is so fake."

Relief pours through me, and I bump his shoulder, a nudge meant to convey approval. "I know. I can't stand it."

He gives me the side-eye. "Good girl."

We walk down the curved sidewalk that wraps around the enormous fountain outside and reach the main sidewalk. Other than my quick trip to the drug store and my foray next door, I haven't actually walked outside, in daylight, along the Strip. This is the famous Las Vegas, the center of decadence and luxury.

And the first person I encounter on the sidewalk is wearing a billboard on a backpack, the picture flashing a topless woman crouched over the mouth of a man with a one-hundred dollar bill between his teeth.

"GIRLS!" he screams, forcing a small business card in my hand. "Free shuttle to see the girls! Getcha booty on!" Dad gets the same treatment, recoiling and dropping the card.

"Geez," I mutter.

"At least in Boston the street hawkers are more polite," Dad mutters.

"I know!"

"They're just doing their job," Dad adds, his voice changing.

"I remember those days. You'd get a chance at a few bucks to stand on a corner handing out flyers and that helped you make rent."

A woman about Mom's age, wearing a neon pink shirt that says "ALL GIRLS ALL NIGHT" hands me a flyer.

I take it.

Over the course of a single city block, I stop counting the hawkers when I reach twenty. Beggars dot the walk as well, in wheelchairs, sitting on blankets next to dogs wearing bandannas around their necks, and all of them call out to us.

With each encounter, my unease increases. Daddy's expression turns into a scowl.

We reach...an escalator?

Outdoors?

"What's this?"

"Isn't it the damnedest thing? Escalators outside. Must not rain much out here."

"It's desert, Dad."

"It sure isn't New England."

The sky is so clear and blue, with puffs of clouds that run lower than you'd think, as if they just want to try a chance at a slot machine, or to put twenty bucks on red, and if they dip their cotton goodness down low enough, they'll get a shot. Behind the escalator, the Strip rolls on like someone created a Richard Scarry Busy Town, only a very naughty version of it.

The Caesar's Palace sign caps a building so ostentatiously imitating a Greek building, and Linq, across the street, has some sort of wrap spray painting on the entire side of the building, guest room windows and all, advertising a singer who I thought died before I was born.

Maybe cloning has actually happened and the entertainment industry is keeping it a secret.

In order to continue straight down the road, we have to enter a building—which we immediately realize is a mall, replete with a Chanel clothing store, two jewelers, a gelateria and a coffee bar.

That serves Kahlua-spiked lattes.

Where was this place when I was in college?

It's dizzying, though, figuring out how to find our way back to the simple sidewalk outside.

"They make you go through the malls. You have no choice." Dad's observation is so tinged with bitterness I look up in surprise, thinking the voice is some other man.

It's not.

"More consumer value extraction," I surmise.

"More fakery. Is this supposed to be luxury? I don't understand."

We find ourselves at an impasse, realizing we have to go back and to the right to find a walkway that will then lead to an escalator going down.

"Should we just get gelato here?"

Dad's eyes fill with panic. "Here? In this mall? No. I found a better place." He slings an arm around my shoulders. "Let's go over the land bridge and fight our way through the people selling sex on a card."

"On a card?" I laugh.

"On a *credit* card," he says with a sigh.

We walk through a revolving door, onto the land bridge, and face nipples.

Big, uncovered, live nipples.

Painted like a Minion from *Despicable Me*.

"Never saw *that* in the movie theater when I took Jeffrey and Tyler to see that flick," Dad says.

"Please don't say 'flick,'" I beg.

"Wanna picture?" The woman is painted yellow from top(less) to bottom, breasts decorated like a Minion wearing goggles, and she's dressed in a string bikini bottom that is supposed to mimic jeans, but just looks like a blue ribbon chafing device.

"No thanks," Dad says, making eye contact with the woman and smiling.

No, Daddy. No....

Eye contact in environments like this is akin to a war cry. A challenge. A promise.

*A dare.*

She reaches for Dad, bending at the waist, which makes all the men (and two women) standing behind her give an ovation.

"C'mon. Twenty bucks for a sweet pic is all I need. I gotta buy my toddler some diapers," the Minion says in a voice that is just earnest enough to crack wallets open.

Wallets like Dad's.

"How old?" Dad asks.

"Twenty-one," the woman says. "I'm legal."

"I meant your child." His weary smile makes something in me tear, just a tiny bit.

"She's two. Wanna see a picture?"

And right then and there, in the middle of a land bridge on the strip in Las Vegas, Jason Jacoby *oooohs* and *aaaahs* over a half-naked woman's pictures of her little daughter while prying a twenty out of his wallet and giving it to her.

"Can your wife take our pic?" she asks him, giving me a grateful smile.

"Wife? No, no. That's my daughter," he explains with a chuckle.

The woman winks. "Right. That's what you all say."

"EWWWWWWW!" I groan. Her face falls.

"Oh, hell, you're not kidding!" She gives Dad a helpless look, grabbing him, her nipple brushing against his bare forearm. "I'm so sorry."

Dad looks down at the stripe of yellow paint left on his skin.

And turns a furious red so fast I fear he's having a heart attack.

"How about I take a picture of you two?" Daddy says in a low, thick voice.

She grabs me, throwing her arm around my shoulders, jutting her boobs out so the goggles look like a wide-eyed Minion.

"Say cheese, Shannon! Declan's going to love this!" Dad calls out as he takes a series of pics.

Minion Chick grabs a phone from somewhere in her hair and asks Dad, "Could you snap one of us for me to keep?" Her eyes dart from me to Dad, and something feels *off* suddenly. "She's so cute!"

And with that, Dad takes the pic.

She grabs the phone and looks me full in the face. "You're the runaway bride, aren't you?"

Oh, no.

She sprints, Minion eyes like googly-eyes on springs. By the time I can even think to run after her, the crowd has swallowed her up.

"What just happened?" Dad asks, confused and red, tracking her through the revolving doors, just staring. We're in the middle of the land bridge and people begin walking around us, streaming out of the hotel mall.

"I think that picture is about to be all over the internet," I say with a sigh. I look down at the lovely outfit Evie selected for me after she came to. The yellow paint on my side definitely does not go well with royal blue linen.

'What? Why? You're not a celebrity...oh, no." Daddy gets it.

"Yeah."

"Oh, *no*. Shannon, I'm sorry."

"Declan's going to be furious."

"Nah. Men don't care if their women are with other topless women. In fact, your mom kind of likes it when I—"

"STOP!" I shout. "It's bad enough that Mom is inappropriate, but not you too, Dad."

He winces, his nose wrinkling. It's adorable.

"Sorry."

"It's okay."

"No, it's not, but I'll explain it all to Declan," Dad says, deftly changing the subject as we make our way quickly across the land bridge. Two Chewbaccas, one Wonder Woman, and a priest holding a "JESUS SAVES" sign stand at the edge of the bridge.

That's not the opening line of a joke, but it should be.

All these characters in costume mingle with the crowd, hoping to get tourists to cough up a five or a ten (or even a twenty) for a picture. Declan warned me not to go outside—that I'd be "accosted" by unsavory creatures, and he was right.

It's just that I didn't suspect a topless Minion would be my downfall.

We get to a "down" escalator and wend our way through the Caesar's Palace resort, which has an enormous open-air court-yard, like a replica of the Forum, only instead of philosophers applying the Socratic Method to help enlighten the masses, there's a smoothie bar with vodka shots for sale.

Same thing, right?

Dad seems to know the way, leading me to a stoplight that mercifully involves a good old-fashioned crosswalk to get across six lanes of traffic. More cards are shoved our way, advertising strip clubs, nightclub performances, and shows from stars who peaked before I was born.

We make it across the way, a giant pelican on the side of a pirate ship in front of another resort, advertising a singer's chain restaurant, and then—

It's like we've found an oasis of peace in the middle of chaos.

This side street is designed to mimic a middle-America small town, with lampposts that look like gaslights, and old brick facades. The energy is different here, too, like we broke off from a raging river into a tiny trickle of a stream, the transition jarring but welcome.

"What is this?" I ask. A spectacularly huge Ferris wheel presents itself at the end of the long alley, its cars like a ski tram, little bubbles. The alley is lined with gift shops, bars, restaurants, specialty clothing stores, and—

Ice cream.

"I found it this morning when I was walking around. After I shook off the nice young lady who chatted me up. Friendly, but a bit persistent." Dad's face looks troubled. "I asked her for the nearest sweet shop and she kept saying she could give me a 'strawberry shortcake' for an extra fifty. Why would she want a little girl's doll toy? Or did she mean the dessert? Do you know what that means?"

"No." I shudder. "And I don't want to know."

He laughs and points to a restaurant down the alley. "How about a hot dog first?"

My stomach grumbles. Aside from lunch and a latte made for humans without teeth, I haven't had much to eat all day.

"A hot dog and ice cream? It's like we're at a Paw Sox game."

The grin he gives me makes the bridge of my nose tingle with tenderness. "You girls loved going to minor league games."

"I still do, Dad," I say softly. "We need to do that again sometime."

"Jeffrey and Tyler like it," he says, not quite picking up on my emotional storm. "But not like you and Amy always did."

"It's a date. We'll go to a game when we get home."

"Would Declan enjoy going?"

I start to say that Declan would just take us to the Anterdec suite at Fenway Park to catch a major league Red Sox game, but I stop myself.

"I think he would." A brewing conflict inside me pings, as if it's all a mist inside, obscuring a beacon that delivers me to a place where I can find the answer. Declan's world is so different from my family's, as divergent as can be. For Dad, those minor league games were a fun treat, a place to bring us and share experiences he never even had as a kid.

For Declan, going to a baseball game means something qualitatively different. The imprint of how you define that experience —go to a live baseball game—is a different socio-economic language. I can understand that language when it's spoken to me, but ask me to speak back and my tongue ties itself in knots and I stare, mute and anxious, choosing inaction because action is too unbearably confusing.

Dad and I order hot dogs and sodas and have a seat, munching happily until we're done.

"Only one?" I tease, knowing how much he loves them.

He pats his stomach. "Saving room for burnt caramel ice cream."

I raise my eyebrows. "I thought you just found this place this morning?"

He shrugs. "Had to sample it to make sure it was good enough for Marie and you."

"You're such a sacrificer, Dad."

His laughter is love in auditory form.

The ice cream shop is so trendy they have a schedule for

which ice creams are offered on which days. When I order the chocolate mint I'm admonished that I must do a taste test because the flavor is so bold it will pull every hair out of my head by the follicle while blasting the 1812 Overture in my ear.

Or something like that.

The clerk is sweet and peppy, and gives me a description of the various flavors like a sommelier. She's an ice cream steward, and in the end I pick a peanut butter concoction with a cupcake on top, while Dad gets his burnt caramel.

We go outside and find a quiet table under a large umbrella, the shade and ice cream making the mid-day heat bearable.

"How are you?" he asks, just after I've shoved a giant spoonful of gratitude in my mouth.

"Mmmup," I answer.

He acts like he understood that. "No, honey. I mean really. How *are* you? That was quite a stunt you and Declan pulled two days ago." I can't read his eyes. He's gone blank. Not the same way Declan turns into a statue, though.

Daddy's not judging. Just asking. And trying to decide how to respond along the way.

I finish my mouthful of ice cream and realize I'm in safe territory here. I can actually tell the truth.

"I'm a mess."

"I figured."

"I know Mom and I need to have it out," I say with a sigh.

"I'm sorry."

"Yeah."

"No. I mean—I'm *sorry*. I'm sorry for not stepping in sooner and reining her in. She can be...monomaniacal at times."

"Ya think?"

"But she means well."

"A thousand-person wedding with my nemesis as an invited guest and a cat as flower girl doesn't exactly translate into 'means well,' Dad."

He tilts his head and breathes slowly. In Declan, this is a form of control, a calculated gesture designed to make you think he's unflappable. In Dad, it's just how he is.

"Did we ever tell you the story of our wedding?"

"Mom said you guys eloped." A prickly feeling makes my neck tingle. Or maybe it's just sweat. Vegas in July is a miserable sheet of reflective heat.

"Sounds like you don't know the whole story."

"I guess not." Why didn't I pry? Mom's so free with information. She overshares all the time, but as Dad looks like he's fighting with himself to figure out how to say what he needs to say, I run through my memory. Mom's never told a story about their wedding.

"You remember your grandma, Celeste?"

"Sure. We didn't really see her much, but yeah." She died a few years ago from a heart attack.

"Ever wonder why?" He blinks a lot. Declan's told me that's a tell in people, a sign that they're struggling to recall a negative memory, and their brain can't process it fast enough to manage the emotional reaction.

That tingling in my neck spreads.

"Um, I guess?" Some part of this conversation makes me feel like an introverted twelve year old.

"She and Marie had a strained relationship. Your mom spent most of her younger years trying desperately to please her. She was a hard woman." Dad's face goes tight. He stabs the spoon in his ice cream and pushes it away.

"Marie never stopped trying, though. When we met, your mother thought that becoming a famous artist would finally please Celeste. But Celeste only cared about herself. You know she kicked your mom out at seventeen when she remarried and the new husband hit on your mom?"

"What?"

"Like I said—Celeste was a hard woman. She divorced him about two years later. I can't remember his name. Celeste called your mom out of the blue one day, pretending the previous two years had been nothing. Meanwhile, the kindness of friends was the only reason Marie graduated high school. She couch-surfed and finished her senior year a semester early. Then she turned bohemian and lived as a squatter off Congress

Street, long before that neighborhood was trendy. That's when we met."

"I just know you were a vet tech and Mom brought some dog in that had been bit by a rat."

"Yup." He gets a faraway look in his eyes and stares over my shoulder. "You can thank James McCormick for that. Indirectly." Rueful and dreamy, tense and pensive, Dad just sits with his feelings, leaving me to process all of this, knowing that if I interrupt too much the moment will dissolve.

"I knew. I knew the moment I met your mother that I was destined to spend the rest of my life with her. I think she knew, too, but it took a little longer for her to wise up."

I laugh.

He grins. "We got married fast. Part of it was love. Part was necessity. Your mom was living a life that put her in danger, and I wanted her to move in with me. So she insisted I come and meet Celeste."

His face turns to stone.

I jump. He looks so much like Declan.

"Shannon, I have never spent a more uncomfortable ninety minutes in my life than in the presence of that woman. For the next twenty-five years or so, until she died—God rest her black, shriveled soul—every time I saw her I gritted my teeth and tolerated her for Marie's sake, but it took a lot of alcohol afterwards to help shake off the gloom."

The tingling covers my entire body.

"What—what was it about her?"

"Do you ever pick up vibes from people? Not the way your mother talks about it, with crystals and energy auras." He frowns. "More like a tuning fork. Someone whose frequency is off just enough that it begins to clash with normal frequency, until you realize something is very, very *off*."

"Yes," I whisper, sitting up in amazement.

"I don't know how your mother did it. How she came out of a family where she was raised by a woman who had no self."

"No self?"

"The best description for Celeste that I've ever seen came to me a few years ago, in some pop culture magazine. 'Emotional vampire.'" His sad eyes catch mine. "Do you know what that is?"

I nod.

"She couldn't stand for anyone else to be happy. As long as she was happy, it was okay. As long as she was the center of attention, all was well. The moment attention was pulled from her, woe be unto you." Kneading his hands, Dad makes a series of faces that indicate he's caught in that fragile space between past and present, between old events that trigger current emotions.

"That first time I met her, I just wanted to crawl out of my skin. She fawned over me, Shannon. Acted like Marie and me getting together was the greatest thing since sliced bread. She ate up every detail I gave about myself and somehow paired it with some experience of hers. And her story was always just a little bit *more*."

I sigh. "I know the type."

"When we told her Marie and I were engaged, her eyes lit up. Not with happiness. With a kind of frantic panic that I wish I'd understood back then. It would have saved poor Marie a lot of grief."

The tingling pierces my heart.

"What happened?"

"Celeste pretended to be so happy for us. Promised to pay for a big wedding. Insisted we hold it at a grand estate just north of Boston. She and Marie's father came from modest families, and Marie's dad died when she was in third grade in a bad construction accident, but he was union. The union took care of them. Celeste had a good survivor's pension. She volunteered around town and had enough connections to feel important."

"Why do I have a bad feeling about this? Did she make a big scene at the wedding?"

He gets a wry smile on his face, a sickly look that makes the ice cream pool in my stomach like battery acid.

"I wish."

"What did she *do*?"

"She—ah, Jesus, honey, I still can't believe it, more than thirty years later." He lets out a long sigh, scoops out a spoonful of ice cream, and eats it, his mouth moving over the confection, his mind mulling over his next words. "She went all over town with Marie, lavishing her with attention. Marie ate it up. Like a dry sponge that needed water, she just absorbed it. Celeste paraded all over the place, booking this impressive old estate on the North Shore, right on the water. She was dating this guy named Kirby—that was his nickname. His real name was some old Boston family name. Wentworth something. I don't remember. I think I blocked it."

He eats more ice cream.

"She talked it up to all the volunteer organizations she was part of. Whipped herself into a frenzy, and took your poor, puppy-dog mother along for the ride. By the day before the wedding, she'd convinced Marie to let old Kirby walk her down the aisle as her father."

"And then?" I'm dreading what's next.

"Celeste assured us she'd pay for everything. Put down bare-bones deposits on the estate, the caterers, the cake, the dress, the rings—everything. She wanted *fancy*. Keep in mind, I was a vet tech. Your mom had been an artist's assistant, stripping canvas. She quit that job and started working at some health food store when we married, making a few bucks an hour. We were poor. *Scratch* poor. I had about five buddies from the neighborhood and my mom who were planning to come to the wedding. We didn't need all this pomp and circumstance, but Celeste made it sound like she was going to create the Wedding of the Year."

My ice cream sticks in my throat.

"Sound familiar?" His brown eyes, so much like mine, are filled with fury and sadness.

I nod.

"She bailed on us. The night before the wedding, she had a 'heart event." Finger quotes again. "Told all her friends and everyone in her circle—called them all from her hospital bed."

Dad goes quiet, looking at me straight on, holding the gaze until that tingling over my body turns to ice.

"Oh, no."

"She didn't call Marie."

"Oh, Dad."

"All the wedding guests she'd invited showed up to her hospital room, including this guy she'd been dating on and off. In front of all of them, he proposed."

"Huh?"

"Right? So now she's engaged."

"I don't understand."

He holds up a palm. "You will."

"The next morning, we showed up at the fancy estate knowing none of this. Me, Marie, my buddies, and my mom."

"How awful Grandma had a heart attack the night before the wedding! Mom must have been so distraught!"

Dad just stares at me.

Layers of awareness wash over me, until all that's left is abject horror. "She didn't really have a heart attack?"

"A 'heart event.'"

"Whatever—it didn't happen?" I gasp.

"The weird part," he says, ignoring my question, "is that when Marie went to pick up her dress that morning, it wasn't there. They said her mother had come and gotten it for her."

"Huh?"

"We didn't have cell phones then, so we just figured Celeste was being nice. Remember—we didn't know about the heart event, or that Kirby had proposed to her. We thought we were getting married that day."

"Oh, Daddy." My heart hurts.

"We get to the estate, and there's Celeste and Kirby, at the altar with the minister she'd hand-selected. Surrounded by all these people Marie barely knew from Celeste's volunteer work, a few union buddies of Marie's father's from back in the day—and she's wearing—"

"Mom's wedding dress," I choke out.

He nods.

"Celeste comes over, happy as can be, a blushing bride if ever there was one. In front of all those people, she tells Marie how happy she is that Kirby stood by her through her 'heart event' the night before, and that he's her one true love, and the only person she can depend on."

Dad closes his eyes. "Marie's trying to understand what's going on, and she can't stop looking at her own mother in what was supposed to be *Marie's* dress. By the time I put it all together and realized Celeste made it seem like Marie was a cold, callous daughter who hadn't even bothered to go to the hospital the night before, Celeste was screaming at your mother. Kirby was bellowing, and all the guests looked at poor Marie like she was an ungrateful little witch."

I can't keep my mouth from dropping open.

"That's so evil."

"Funny you use that word. Evil." His gaze is penetrating, transforming my dad into someone foreign. "Because that's the word that comes into my mind whenever I think of her."

"What did you do?"

"I stepped in between Celeste and Kirby and defended Marie, of course. I started with logic and reason. That didn't work. Tried to calm them down. That didn't work. Then I resorted to sheer volume."

"You? Dad, you don't really have a 'sheer volume' setting."

"I do when it comes to watching someone I love get mind-fucked by evil."

In that moment I understand exactly what Mom meant by calling Dad a "beta-alpha."

"So," he adds. "I yelled, Kirby nearly punched me, and I carried a sobbing, hysterical Marie away from that damned estate, my mom and buddies in tow, all the guys shouting colorful words you kids find in rap songs today." He gives me a twisted smile. "I think we invented a new vocabulary that day."

My heart slams against my ribs like it's trying to get out, teleport back thirty years, and beat the hell out of my own grandma.

"You eloped?"

"We did. Had the license and waited until that Monday."

I let out a low whistle. "That's insane."

"Oh, that's not the insane part. The truly insane part is that we were stuck with all the wedding debts. Celeste had paid only bare-bones deposits. Put everything in Marie's name."

"WHAT? You paid for that fiasco?"

"In more ways than one."

I sit in stunned silence for a while. We scrape the bottoms of our respective ice cream cups eventually, in thoughtful quiet.

"That's all connected to the way Mom acted throughout this wedding?"

"She wanted the Wedding of the Year her mom promised her."

"That's...weird."

"Yeah. I think it's not so simple, though. Your mom has this need for status, but it comes from wanting to be accepted. Her mother made it damn near impossible for Marie to let me love her."

My face is tipped down and I look up through a frown.

"She couldn't believe she was worthy of everything I wanted to give her."

"Love is so hard, even when it's easy."

"Like parenting." Dad gives me a knowing smile. "Go light on her."

"She expects an apology from *me*."

He waves that away. "All she really wants is a hug and to know she didn't ruin your relationship."

I jolt.

"Why did you keep in touch with Grandma Celeste? We saw her every few years, so...."

"Your mother. Like I said, she couldn't let go. Always needing that mother's love she never had."

"Ouch. Did she ever get it?"

"No. Celeste died and left everything—including all her personal effects—to a local charity."

"Double ouch."

"And left us with the funeral bill. Only this time, I knew how legally to get out from being responsible for that one."

"Jesus!"

"I'm pretty sure he wasn't the person who greeted Celeste after she died, if you know what I mean."

"Mom always talks about missing her mother."

He shrugs, standing. "She does. She misses what she never had."

I know this story is supposed to make me magically forgive my mom's actions regarding my own wedding, but it doesn't. Do I feel compassion? Yes. Heartbroken on her behalf? Sure.

"Vegas," he adds slowly, "reminds me of Celeste. This whole damned city. Nothing but fake luxury designed to impress people who end up footing a bill they can't afford. Except Celeste took it one step further." He shudders. "Maybe that's why I can't stand this place."

"But Mom invited Jessica Coffin to my wedding!" I wail. Shallow. I know. I do have a touch of my grandma in me, after all.

"I understand, honey. She crossed a big line inviting Jessica Coffin. I had no idea she'd done that, or I would have intervened." He shakes his head. "You know what's 'funny'?" Dad uses finger quotes for the word again.

"What?"

"Jessica Coffin. She looks a lot like the old pictures of your grandma. And you can't beat her for a perfect personality match for Celeste."

And with that mic drop, Dad kisses my cheek gently and walks away into the crowd, carefully avoiding the painted ladies reaching out for a kiss.

Especially the Minions.

# Chapter Fifteen

By the time I get back to the room, shower, and change, it's after six, and Declan walks in the door early, looking tired and harried.

"God, I'm starving," he complains, loosening his tie and looking at the clock next to the bed. "Damn." His stomach growls. "At least we're eating fairly soon."

I smile, and he does a double take, feet pointed toward the couch, doing some kind of cha-cha to turn back around and stare at me, full-faced.

"You look amazing."

His eyes take me in, head to toe. He lets out a wolf whistle. "I knew a day at the spa would be worth it. Whatever you tipped them isn't enough."

"They serve *breast milk* lattes in the spa. And offer something called a vajacial." I shudder.

He doesn't even blink. "If that's what it takes to make you look so stunning, I'm fine with it."

I giggle self-consciously. His eyes catch the yellow paint on my dress. His hands circle my waist and pull me to him. "Is the yellow a new fashion feature?" He kisses me on both cheeks, so gentle and soft that his lips feel like rose petals.

Which makes me think of vajacials.

And I go cold.

Dec runs one finger along the yellow stripe on my dress and frowns when he sees it's paint. Questioning eyes meet mine.

"Minion. I was assaulted by a topless Minion outside."

He laughs, lets me go, and walks to the clothing dresser and grabs a box of cashews off the dry minibar.

I've learned something new on this trip. There are wet/cold minibars, and dry minibars. The dry minibars are innocuous-looking set-ups on the bureaus. They look like an array of treats, from chocolate-covered gummy bears to cashews and macadamia nuts to earbuds. Even iPhone chargers.

And for eighty bucks, you, too, can have your own convenient pair of headphones you can get at any Wal-Mart for $4.61.

Declan pops back a handful of cashews that costs more than a latte and looks at me with beleaguered eyes. "Aren't you hungry? Have some."

"I'm fine. I ate with Dad earlier."

"Jason? Nice. Where'd you go?"

"Across the street."

"You went outside? On the Strip? Did you actually *walk*?"

"Yes. I have feet, you know. Sorry to crush the myth that I'm a mermaid." I wiggle one foot for emphasis.

"What did you eat?"

"Hot dogs."

"Why on earth would you go across the street for a *hot dog* when you could order in room service or go to one of the restaurants and have filet and lobster? Or caviar? Or—"

"Because I like hot dogs."

"Why?"

"I'm not justifying what I like to you, Declan. I don't have to validate my choices."

"And neither do I." His voice feels like an icicle tracing my spine.

"Besides, they're *gourmet* hot dogs."

Declan rolls his eyes and does that thing with his breathing where he pretends he's being polite and civil but he's really filling the room with the hot cloud of contempt that he spawns by rubbing two sides of his big, fat ego together to generate a spark.

"No one is making *you* eat a hot dog," I declare, trying to match his understated condescension. I just sound like a whiny twelve year old. Close enough.

"What's going on?" He's asking me, but this isn't a normal interrogation. Some big stakes are on my answer, and I'm deeply uncomfortable with the path this conversation is taking.

"What do you mean?"

"Don't be coy."

"Then be direct!"

"I am."

"Vegas is so *fake*," I blurt out.

We've gone from "You look amazing" to "Don't be coy" in under a minute.

"It's aspirational. Quit being so cynical," he scoffs.

"What do you mean, 'aspirational'?" I know what the industry term means, but I want to hear Declan define this from his own mouth while I stand over here and do a slow burn.

"People come here because they want to think they can achieve this kind of luxury someday. The resorts convey an air of opulence, a potential that you, and you, and yes, *you!* can have this some day. As they walk through resort after resort, past rooms labeled "High Limit Only" and Armani displays with dresses that cost more than they make in a month, they start to feel surrounded by it. Embraced by it."

"Like they're back in the womb, only about to be born rich."

"Yes!" His face relaxes, like he's pleased I finally "get" it.

"That is deceptive." I think about my grandma and Dad's story.

"What?"

"The vast majority of people who come here will never, ever be able to afford a five thousand dollar dress, or a Maserati, or buy a table at the private club behind those guarded doors, because throwing away ten grand on a table and drinks isn't reality, Declan."

"It's the customer's choice, Shannon. We're not making them do anything they don't want to do. We're helping them to aspire."

I snort. "You're manipulating them."

"Welcome to the entire field of marketing, Shannon," he says slowly. "As our Director of Marketing for Anterdec, I should think you of all people would understand that."

"Not *my* kind of marketing!" I'm appalled that he actually thinks this way. A dark snake of fear comes to life in my gut. "My kind of marketing informs. It appeals. When I do campaigns and customer service evaluations and social media pushes, I'm helping people to discover new products and experiences."

"And so is Anterdec's resort. And most of Vegas. The good resorts, at least." I don't ask him to define 'good.' I know how he defines it. More money = better.

"It's not the same!"

"Marketing is about choices, Shannon. When done well, the customer walks away informed, happy, and energized."

How in the hell did we go from *I'm starving* to this argument? Damn.

"They walk out of Vegas broke and hungover!"

"Because they got to choose!" he roars. "Why are you so judgmental?"

"Me!" I'm aghast. "I'm not judgmental!"

"You're saying that the entire design of the Strip and luxury resorts like mine are nothing more than manipulative attempts to remove consumers from their money."

I relax. He gets it. Thank goodness. We can put this conflict behind us. He sees reason.

"Yes."

"And in your mind, those consumers are too stupid to realize they're being manipulated."

Huh?

"You think that this shouldn't be there for them. That they are easily led and don't know what's good for them, and so the businesses that created these entertainment consortiums have done them wrong."

"That's not quite how I would say it, but—"

"Your world, Shannon, involves a mindset that worries me."

Mic drop. Boom. He and Dad should start a tag team.

"What?"

"You want to remove free will from people."

"WHAT?"

"As consumers. You don't want to give customers the choice."

"The choice to get drunk and gamble away all their money and spend it on crap they can't afford?"

"That's up to them! Do they look like they're suffering?"

I falter.

"I'll answer that for you—no. They don't. You're surrounded by hundreds of thousands of people who have come to Vegas to have a fun time and who enjoy themselves because they made an open, free decision to be here and to spend their time and money this way."

I'm speechless.

He tips his head and studies me. "I think I understand you better now."

"What does *that* mean?"

"You won't accept my professional shopper. You don't want jewelry or a nice, new car or any of the other gifts I try to give you." He shakes his head slightly, mouth tight with pensiveness, his hand running through his hair twice, settling at the base of his neck. "I shouldn't really call them gifts. They're just part of life. *My* life."

"How does that pertain to talking about business and resort design?"

"Because you're judging me. These are aspects of my life. You're rejecting my *life*."

He's cold. Closed off. I know what he's doing. For a second, I panic, the feeling exploding in my chest, making me feel like a rat has given birth and all the babies are wriggling around, gnawing their way out.

Then a calmer version of myself kicks in. The part that can actually speak.

"You really think that?"

He holds my gaze, one hand in his trouser pocket, the other

leaning against the small table next to the suite's sofa. "Tell me I'm wrong."

"You're wrong!" I interject, the words fast and true. "I don't reject your gifts." *Or your life.*

"You certainly do."

Fair enough. "Not because I'm rejecting you," I start, trying to explain.

"Then what? What is it?"

"I…I just didn't grow up like this. You did."

"Now we're dragging our childhoods into this?"

"You started it by steering us off topic."

He concedes my point.

"Declan, you've only ever known wealth. It's been a part of your world since you were born. I know your dad's company took off when Terry was a baby and before you were born, but your mom came from money. She worked with James to build Anterdec. You had nannies and fancy vacations, prep schools and tutors, tight expectations you had to live up to. You don't even blink at dropping four figures on a really nice night out. That's an entire mortgage payment for most families."

He just stares. But he's listening.

"I didn't grow up like this. I'm like most people, with money I use as a tool to navigate the world, and my mind in a constant series of negotiations throughout the day about how to allocate my limited resources."

*Tap tap tap.*

I frown at him. "Did you order room service?"

His frown matches mine. "No."

"Delivery!" someone calls out. Dec makes a face of understanding and gives me the side-eye. Wonder what that's about.

He opens the double doors to the suite and two delivery men roll in a seven-foot-tall teddy bear wearing a sweater with my name on it.

I look at him.

"Seriously?"

He shrugs. "Andrew got Amanda a six-foot-tall one, and this one is animatronic, so—"

It begins to *sing*. It sings Katy Perry's "Roar." When the word *fireworks* is in the song, giant silver sparklers light up and a shower of silver foil-covered chocolates shoot out. The damn teddy bear is a creation for nightmares.

"You thought *I*—" my words have to be shouted above the damn singing "—would like this?"

"I thought it would be fun. Those are all milk chocolate, by the way," he adds in an acerbic tone. "No white chocolate."

"You don't do this at home!"

"I—"

Andrew bursts into the room and stares at the monstrosity, his mouth tightening, nostrils flaring, a patented McCormick-man look if I've ever seen one, and trust me, I've see a few thousand of these.

It's the look that says, *Oh, hell. I've been beaten.*

*But I haven't given up.*

"Well played," Andrew concedes as the damn animatronic bear's stomach opens up, like the hatch door on an SUV, slowly rising, and shows a video screen on its belly.

"You got me a gigantic Teletubby?" I groan. This thing looks like Dipsy took steroids.

"A what?" Declan and Andrew seem genuinely confused. I spent most of the late 1990s babysitting toddlers on weekends to make spending money for after-school activities, so I am intimately familiar with that particular breed of kids' television star, the plush little colored stuffed beings with antennas on their heads and television screens embedded in their abs.

The video screen blinks, turns on, and a goat appears on screen.

A goat in an African village, the sun setting on the horizon on-screen.

"Greetings!" says a voice in English, the accent light. "We thank you for your donation of one thousand goats to our foundation. Your contribution will—"

I shut off the video and turn to look at Andrew, who is staring up at the top of the giant teddy bear, as if he's measuring.

Because he is.

"Take your pants down."

"Excuse me?" Declan says, horrified.

"Excuse me?" Andrew echoes, a little too gleefully.

"Measure your penises. Just get it over with. C'mon. The goats are a nice gesture. The teddy bear is going to creep into my subconscious and terrorize me along with Pennywise the clown and those dreams I've started having where Steve Harvey announces I'm Mrs. Declan McCormick and then retracts it."

Declan gives me a *WTF?* look.

*Tap tap tap.*

"That's probably Amanda," Andrew says, going to the door and opening it.

Yep.

"But this competition between the two of you, showering me and Amanda with these ridiculous, over-the-top gifts in an effort to one-up each other is—"

"AWESOME!" she shouts, jumping up and down in front of my teddy bear, giggling and clapping.

When we get home, I am stealing some strands of hair from her brush and DNA-matching her against my mom.

"I'm sorry," Dec says, rubbing my shoulders, willing me to relax into him and lean against his chest. "You're right. I'll take back the goats."

I turn around and give him a playful punch in the breastbone. "Not the goats! We can keep the goats."

"Kinky," Amanda says, eyebrow cocked.

"You want goats?" Andrew asks her. "I can get you goats."

"The goats are for African villages," I explain to her.

"Like the Heifer Project goats?" she asks.

"A foundation like that," Dec says, wrapping his arms around me. I guess we're making up. Fight over. Conflict not resolved, but tabled for further discussion.

Away from the prying eyes of a seven-foot-tall bear.

"I can get you water buffalo," Andrew hisses in her ear. "I can even get you a zebra."

"What are you? A zoo pimp?" I ask.

"Do you mind?" Andrew says, pretending to be offended. "This is a private conversation."

"Your idea of dirty talk is kind of sick," I tell him.

"Get out," Dec says, a pleasant smile on his face, looking pointedly at his brother.

"Why are you guys here?" I ask.

"I saw the bear being delivered and followed it to your room," Andrew admits. He looks at Amanda. "You want a bigger bear?"

She leans in and whispers in his ear. Didn't know a McCormick man's skin could flush that fast.

"Convention hall? Which one?"

Declan names the ballroom where the sex toy trade show's going on.

And they're off.

"Sex?" Declan whispers in my ear just as I say, "Nap?"

He mulls that over. "Nap now, sex later?"

"Deal."

# Chapter Sixteen

"Quit worrying," Declan commands as I fiddle with my earring for the umpteenth time and drink more water. The nap was a waste of time. I couldn't sleep, and Declan spent the entire time answering messages on his phone. We're about to have dinner with my mom and dad, the big meal where we finally talk it all out, and I'm one big nerve jangling like a charm on an Alex and Ani bracelet owned by a four year old on a trampoline.

"I'm not worrying. I am thinking through a delicate situation over and over in an infinite loop of analysis to make sure I don't leave any details to chance."

"Like I said. Quit worrying." He pulls me into his arms, still in a business shirt, cuffs rolled up, eyes tired. He's been working for a few hours, even though we're supposed to be on our "honeymoon." Four different national tourism boards have been lobbying Grace—hard—offering a host of free opportunities for us if we'll honeymoon in their respective nations.

With the paparazzi in tow, of course.

Our kiss is interrupted by my hand reaching up to play with my stupid earring, and the buzzing of my phone. I check the clock. 7:43 p.m.

"Bet that's Mom," I say, pulling out the phone. He lets me go and looks down, reading the glowing screen upside down.

What I see on my text screen fills me with rage.

*Need to postpone dinner. Got free tickets to the Donnie and Marie concert across the street. Love u. Breakfast instead?*

"What does it say? I can't read Mother-in-Lawish upside down," Dec asks.

"They're ditching us for Donnie and Marie!"

"Who? What?"

"My parents are blowing us off for hair and teeth!" I shout, disgusted. Upstaged by a little bit country and a little bit rock and roll.

I'm a little bit *pissed*.

"Donnie and Marie are still *alive*?" Declan muses. "Huh."

I wave my screen in the air between us. "Apparently! And worth more than a special dinner with their daughter so they can clear the air with me!"

"Are you sure 'Donnie' and 'Marie' aren't a euphemism for something?"

We shudder in unison.

"Let's change the subject." He beams. "This is good news! Now we have the entire evening free, and to ourselves."

My stomach growls.

"I see dinner is first on the agenda," Dec says with a smile.

"I shored myself up for tonight. I spent half the day avoiding talking to my mother, even when it came to getting a vajacial, and now—"

"A *what*?"

"I told you about the vajacial earlier, right before you had Smokey the Teletubby delivered to my room."

"I wasn't listening. You were too beautiful." He gives me a grin that he thinks will paper over past sins.

"Never mind." I give him a sour look. "But you really need to have a mystery shopping company come in and evaluate that spa you have downstairs. They have some unconventional practices."

"Let Grace know." He waves the thought away. "What about food? Where do you want to eat tonight?" Declan asks.

My stomach growls again, and I remember the restaurant next door, the one I walked past several times in my free days. You know. When I could get my own lattes at Grind It Fresh!

"I would love to go to a tapas bar," I say, recalling the sleek lines, the grey stools, the bottle-glass backsplash at the bar in the resort next door. Maybe if I can make the tapas bar look like Declan's idea, I can sneak into Grind It Fresh! and get a clandestine latte. Hmmm. This is a sudden plan.

It could work.

"Excuse me?" Declan clears his throat and leans in. "You want to go to a *what*?"

"A tapas bar." I let out a huge sigh. "It's been a long, tense few days, and now that we're off the hook with Mom and Dad for dinner, I could use something to pull me out of my own head and help me relax. You know. Try a new experience. Taste the world a little."

"You could?" Declan's eyes widen with surprise. He leans in further, with a sexy growl in his voice. "You have a place in mind?"

I pull back a bit, a little unnerved by his reaction. Wow. He's really aroused by small plates, huh?

I know the resort next door is expressly forbidden, so I lob the question right back at him. I still can't believe my mom and dad called off dinner, especially for Donnie and Marie.

What's next? Breakfast will be canceled by Wayne Newton?

"Um, not really. No place in mind. You know the town better than I do. How about you pick? I want the absolute *best* tapas bar in town," I reply.

I know from obsessive research that not only is Grind It Fresh! considered the best coffee house in town, so is the tapas bar next door. The word *best* is a dog whistle. Declan has a fine-tuned radar for wanting to give me the best of everything, so I'm stacking the deck.

Which is what you do in Vegas, right?

He struts across the room like a peacock, all buoyant and suddenly a little too happy. Picking up his phone, he taps a few times and murmurs, his conversation muted by his cupped hand over the phone. The conversation ends and he turns to me with a big wide smile, those green eyes glittering like emeralds, a flush to his face and hooded eyes taking me in.

"You." The word comes out in a lustful roll.

"Me, what?"

"I'm the luckiest man in the world." And with that, I'm in his arms, his tongue between my lips, sweeping and searching, the kiss dizzying in its intensity.

Geez. All this over some goat-cheese-stuffed figs and prosciutto-wrapped asparagus?

I'll take it.

The buzzer in the room goes off, indicating our limo is here. Declan groans, his hand up my skirt, fingers digging into my ass. I come up for air.

"Ah, well," he sighs, lips on mine as he talks. "We can always come back and have this later. Let's go have a different kind of fun."

"Right." I lick my lips as he watches me straighten my skirt. "I sure am looking forward to some fine sampling."

I reach into my purse and discover it's a giant mess, filled with a bunch of ones and fives that Amy gave me the other day in exchange for larger bills. She's been waitressing a couple of shifts a week, and needed to make a fast ATM deposit. The smaller bills made too large an envelope to fit in the machine slot. I pull them out and make a neat, orderly stack, which I shove back in my purse.

When I look up, Declan's gawking at me. Mouth open and everything.

"I had no idea," he says, almost gasping. "Why didn't you ever tell me?"

I shrug.

"I've heard about all the great places here in Vegas, especially the ones run by the pros, but I've never been here. Now's our chance!" I explain.

Declan's hand goes in his pocket and he adjusts himself discreetly.

"You seem pretty, uh, excited yourself," I point out as we take the elevator down to the private garage.

"Of course I am!" he replies.

Right. Of course he is. That makes sense. As a high-ranking

man in the hotel and hospitality industry, a person who sets trends rather than copying them, he'd want to make sure he's on the cutting edge of culinary trends. I start to wonder which place he's picked.

Knowing Declan, it'll blow my mind.

We get in the limo and drive through the center of the Strip slowly, pedestrians thick in the streets, drawing out the trip. Sadly, we drive right past the resort next door. No convenient tapas bar for me, one where I can run over to Grind It Fresh! and test how fast I can suck down a clandestine small latte.

First world problems.

Meanwhile, Declan's hand is on my thigh, and he's sliding up, up, *up*, fingertips a little too close to heaven.

"I thought you said that was for later," I whisper. "After we have our fill of something exotic."

He stiffens. "Define 'exotic.'"

I search my brain to think of a tapas menu item that Declan might never have heard of, because *my* idea of exotic and *his* idea of exotic are likely two different things.

"I've heard that Moroccan melon can be really tasty. Some people think that it's better if you lick it before you take a bite."

Why is he looking at me like that?

"Other people prefer a Mexican mocha with a fish flavor on their melons. It's all about individual t-t-tastes," I stammer as Declan peers at me.

"Two years," he huffs.

"Two years what?"

"I've been with you for more than two years and never knew about this adventurous side of you."

"You can make it up to me! Now that you know, think of all the great things we can put in our mouths and savor. If we find something we really like, we can share and go back for more."

He starts coughing uncontrollably.

The limo halts in front of a dark building with blue, glowing LED rope lights around the perimeter. We get out. Geordi, the limo driver, smirks at me.

"Have a lovely evening, ma'am."

"Thank you, Geordi. I'm sure whatever Declan has picked out for me will leave me sated."

The men exchange an inscrutable look as Declan sweeps me toward the door.

The restaurant is smoky, but everywhere allows smoking in Vegas. I need to get used to this. A slow, twisting Euro technobeat fused with jazz pounds through the speakers. There's an enormous stage with tiny lights along the bottom, but no one's on it. We're seated at a large table with a cream-colored leather sofa in a semicircle around it. Two bottles of my favorite white wine are already there.

As Declan scooches in next to me, we center ourselves in the horseshoe-shaped booth. A server rushes over.

Wearing no top.

Okay. That's unexpected.

It's fine. I don't react. I can be sophisticated. Maybe this is a tapas place that emulates the Spanish Riviera beaches. In Europe, women go topless all the time in the sun. No big deal. I avert my eyes and focus on Declan, who is, mercifully, watching me. He pours some wine and the server comes back with a menu, offering it to me.

Forced to make eye contact, I look up and catch a big old view of two nipples pointing up, like *You Are Here* signs. Well, now.

Music volume increases, the song fading, replaced by a deep, intense vibration that builds anticipation. A tapas bar with a show. Unexpected. Then again, this is Vegas, right?

I smile at Declan and widen my eyes, grinning and bringing my wine glass to my mouth.

I look at the menu.

No tapas.

*Huh?*

The stage lights explode with blinding white spotlights, and sparks fly as a show begins. Eight women wearing nothing but little jewels glued to their bare mons and feathered hats come pouring out from backstage, a ninth woman in Middle Eastern dress—which means she's wearing a beaded necklace and a big ruby in her navel—belly dancing her way to a platform that is three feet from my face.

She crouches.

I bury my head in Declan's shoulder.

"What's wrong? She's the closest I could get to..." his voice fades out for a minute and I don't catch what he's saying, because I'm trying to claw my way into his pocket to get away from the naked clam in front of me. "....on short notice. I called ahead to make sure they sent the right one!" he murmurs in my ear, his voice low and shrouded enough by his suit and my hair for me to hear. "Exotic enough for you?"

I look up.

And hello....kitty. Glitter and all.

I open the menu and shove it in front of my face, so close I can't read it. Two inches back and I can make out the words. Appetizers. Entrees. Salads. Desserts. Beverages.

But no tapas.

"See anything you like?" Declan asks, his eyes glued to me. There are nine mostly-naked women up there gyrating and he's looking at *me*.

"No, not really," I say faintly. When I was in college, some friends convinced me to go to Boston and check out this "all male revue," like Chippendale's. Mom is really into male strippers. I'm not. I mean, I'm not a prude. I'll watch porn here and there. I had strippers at my bachelorette party. I don't judge.

But having a real, live, mostly-naked woman in front of my face while I try to eat dinner isn't my idea of fun, especially when it's a surprise.

I chug my wine and stand up. "Excuse me," I say, scooting out the side of the booth.

"What's wrong?" Declan asks, frowning.

"Nothing," I lie. "Just need to use the bathroom." I grab my purse and rush over to the solace of a toilet where I can sit down and not be eye level with a vertical taco.

*OMG HELP*, I text to Amanda.

Please answer. Please answer. Please answer.

*What's wrong?* she texts back.

*Declan brought me to a topless stripper joint for dinner*, I text back.

*WUT?* she replies.

*I know. Help*, I answer.

*How can I help? Rush over with coats to cover the women?* she types, adding a smiley face.

*You suck*, I reply.

*Need more ones and fives? Now that's a topless bar emergency*, she answers. *LOL.*

*I hate you*, I reply. LOL my ass.

"What was he thinking bringing me to a topless bar?" I mutter.

I stop, my entire body flushing.

"Topless bar," I repeat, the words echoing off the steel stall walls.

Oh, no. *No, no, no, no, no.*

"Topless bar," I say again, louder, my breathing growing raspy, hyperventilation a few minutes away.

"Yeah, lady," the bathroom attendant says. "You're in a topless bar. Congratulations for figuring it out. How drunk are you?"

*Bzzzzz.*

I look down at the phone. Amanda has texted back:

*OMG, Andrew's begging me to let us join you*

*WUT?* I type back.

*Declan's texting him and going on about how enlightened you are and how you asked to go to dinner at a topless bar and asked for a Moroccan stripper and now Andrew's pestering—*

I stop reading, shove the phone in my purse, and rush back to the table.

I do not sit down.

The music number halts just as I look at Declan and shout:

"TAPAS BAR! I SAID TAPAS BAR!"

His smile wavers. Hoots and hollers from other tables dot the wall of sound behind me, but I don't really hear because all of the blood in my body has rushed to my face from embarrassment.

"That's right. We're here. You said you liked Moroccan. She was the closest I could get on short notice—"

"T-A-P-A-S. Tapas," I clarify, drawing out the letters as I spell the word. "Tah-pas."

Even in the dimly lit nightclub I can see Declan go pale.

"Oh, God," he mutters, draining his glass of wine and not bothering to refill it. He just starts drinking the rest straight from the bottle. People begin to cheer. Someone throws a casino chip at him. It bounces off his collar and clatters to the floor.

The belly dancer comes over and whispers in my ear. "Hey, honey. Your sweetie bought you special dance from me in one of the back rooms. I'm Amina. Heard you like Moroccan melon." She licks the outer edge of my ear and cups her ample breasts, heaving them up so they're inches in front of my mouth. "And you like to share." She winks.

Declan's jaw drops.

I give him a death scowl. I am also unexpectedly aroused, and the combination of embarrassment and simple biological reactions makes the room spin.

*Bzzzzzz.*

That's his phone.

"If you," I say through gritted teeth, "actually think that I am going to hang out at a topless bar with you, Andrew and Amanda, you're delusional." I look at Amina's rack. "And besides, my boobs are *way* better than hers."

To his great credit, Declan immediately stands up and turns to the dancer, handing her a couple hundreds he's pulled out of his wallet. "There's been an enormous misunderstanding," he says to her, throwing more money on the table and grabbing me so fast I stumble, unable to keep up with him, but somehow I figure a way out.

He bursts through the doors to the street and stands there with such a pitiable look on his face that I burst out laughing, the sound part horror, part hilarity, and part shock.

"You—you thought I wanted you to take me out to dinner at a *topless* bar?"

"That's what you said!" He throws his hands up, flinging

them toward the heavens, as if the God of Pasties will come to his rescue.

"When have I ever asked to go ogle strange, naked women with you as a form of dining entertainment?"

"Never. But there's a first time for everything, and we're in Vegas, and you clearly said 'topless' bar."

"T-A-P-A-S. I said TAPAS!"

"You were going on and on about savoring the exotic, and licking melons, and sharing whatever we both liked—"

"And you thought that suddenly meant I wanted to hang out in a meat show with you? And—" I shudder "—share?"

He stops and goes quiet, looking down at the ground, hands planted on his hips, nodding slowly. Declan looks up, his face half-hidden in the shadows of a street light.

"Well, yeah. It did seem a little too good to be true."

Our phones ring. Simultaneously.

"Don't you dare answer that," I growl as I fish my phone out of my purse.

"You can answer yours, but I can't answer mine?" He ignores me and takes the call. I answer mine.

"What's going on?" Amanda asks, breathless.

"I said TAPAS!" I scream. "T-A-P-A-S!"

"Oh." She almost sounds...disappointed? "Well. I guess we really shouldn't join you, then, if, um, it was all a big misunderstanding."

"Ya think?"

I hear her whispering in the background, then a man's groan of frustration. She comes back to the line and asks, "Just, you know, out of pure curiosity, what's the address you're at?"

*Click.*

Declan ends what is obviously a call with Andrew and gives me a wild look. "I gave the table to Andrew. Texted Geordi. He'll be here any minute. We can go back to our suite and pretend this never happened."

My stomach growls.

"If you think," I say in a menacing voice as I walk slowly toward him like a mother lion going after a hyena eyeing her cubs, "that we can pretend this never happened, you're certifiable."

He winces, his mouth going tight.

I kiss it.

He rears back in shock.

"What?" My kiss muffles the end of the question, his mouth softening fast, responding to the sudden connection. My body is pounding from adrenaline and I wish I had more wine. He tastes like grapes and sweetness, and he's covered in a fine sweat, his scent all male and hot and *what the hell just happened in there?*

"You hired a special dance for me from a woman who can bend like a pipe cleaner with two watermelons attached," I fume, turned on and furious at the same time. I'm not sure whether to slap him or spank him.

Maybe both.

"I'm so sorry." He looks bewildered and confused, contrite and simultaneously really turned on, and it occurs to me that I have the upper hand here. In a big way.

"You should be!" I slap his ass, hard. His hand is on my wrist in a flash, and I'm imprisoned by his grip. He moves me closer to the building and cages me with his arms, his hot, wine-soaked breath sending intermittent chills and heat waves through me.

"That kind of play is private," he murmurs as he drags his lips along my collarbone.

"You were happy to have us ogle topless strippers in public."

"The only body I want to ogle topless is yours, Shannon."

I make a noise that clearly indicates I don't believe him.

"Think back," he whispers, his lips skimming my skin at the hollow of my throat. "Was I drooling over them?"

I can't quite breathe right any more, the chilly night air making my skin ripple with goose bumps, Declan's seductive moves leaving me weak-willed.

"No," I say. He's right. He kept looking at me the entire time. "Why did you watch me watching them?"

"Because I wanted to please you."

"You took me to a nightclub where there were more bare boobies than a La Leche League meeting to please me?"

"I thought you were into it."

I pause. I unpause. "Let me understand this. If I have a sexual...taste, let's say, you want to fulfill it."

"Of course."

"So if I wanted you to whip me—"

"Oh, God, anything but that. Please don't turn me into a billionaire cliché."

"—or wear a chipmunk suit—"

"A what?"

"—or play The Fireman and the Dalmatian—"

"You're veering into sick territory now, Shannon."

"Hiring a belly dancer in a topless bar as a delicacy to meet your perceived notion of my sexual tastes isn't sick?"

He groans. It's the sound of my victory. "I'm never going to live this down, am I?"

"Nope."

"How can I make it up to you?"

"I need to think about it."

"That means you're going to drag this out forever."

He knows me so well, doesn't he?

My stomach growls again. Geordi pulls up in the limo, confusion in his eyes, but he wouldn't dare ask why we only spent fifteen minutes in the nightclub. We pile into the back of the limo and as the driver takes off Declan turns to me, gives me a wicked grin, and folds in half, laughing so hard I fear he'll pass out.

I join him.

It feels great.

"Geordi?" I ask as Declan gasps and belly laughs, chortles and grunts.

"Yes, ma'am?"

"Can you find us a tapas bar? T-A-P-A-S."

He makes a little sound of surprise, as if he suddenly had a flash of insight. "Yes, ma'am," he replies, his voice a little lower. "I certainly will. May I suggest Platos Pequeños?"

I brighten. That's the one next door to Litraeon!

"Is it new? I haven't heard of it," Dec asks, his voice neutral.

"Well rated." He names a celebrity chef.

"Sounds good." And with that, we're on our way.

On our way to coffee nirvana.

I mean, er, a good tapas meal.

As Geordi slows the limo at the light in front of the resort and makes a left turn, Declan lets out a sound of surprise.

"Wait a minute," Declan says with a low, grunting sigh, turning to me with the deliberate, prowling look of a predator. "This is the resort next to Litraeon."

I'm so busted.

"Geordi," he asks evenly, "where is Platos Pequeños?"

Geordi's answer is a simple right turn and a finger point. "Right here, sir."

My beloved crosses his arms over his chest, his body curving away from me on the seat, his shoulders widening as he fills his lungs with air designed to fuel whatever outrage he's feeling.

And it's all pointed at me.

I've lost the self-righteous advantage, haven't I? All it took was one left turn and—

"This was all a scheme to get your hands on that coffee. What the hell is so special about it?" As he asks, his frown deepens.

I open my mouth to explain, but he interrupts.

"Geordi, take us back to our hotel."

"Yes, sir."

"Dec, c'mon."

He's silent, tapping on his phone, and then:

"We're having room service. One of the chefs at Litraeon has been experimenting with tapas. We'll be his taste testers."

"Really?"

"Yes," Declan says with a wolfish grin, shaking his head at me. He looks like he's not sure whether to kiss me or throttle me. "He's confirmed a Moroccan melon dish with fish and Mexican mocha."

Before I can protest, he's kissing me. Whew.

Being busted has its perks.

# Chapter Seventeen

The next morning, I awake in Declan's arms, his naked body pressed against my back. He's breathing slowly, clearly still in some state of slumber, though one part of him most decidedly is *not*. We'd made love with abandon, a joyful enthusiasm triggered as much by the strangely erotic set of missteps between us as by the gradual recovery from the insanity of our almost-wedding back in Boston.

Last night was epic. Bizarre and ripe in all the ways regular life can't be. Our misunderstanding took us both to places we'd never imagined, and left me looking at Declan with new eyes.

He certainly thought I'd changed.

Chaos loves a vacuum.

I throw on a robe and check my phone, finding more than enough messages from old high school friends, some college buddies, a former boss from an internship I had years ago—and they all include attachments of pictures of me.

With a Minion.

A little digging gives me the answer I suspect: the Minion chick sold that picture for five thousand dollars to an unidentified gossip website. A quick look at Jessica Coffin's Twitter feed shows that she posted it ages ago.

Hmmm. Wonder who that "gossip website" is.

Declan will hit the roof when he sees this. Between the

topless/tapas bar fiasco and now a pic of me with a painted, naked woman posing as a Minion, the viral story of the runaway billionaire groom just got more legs.

"Are you kidding me?" he says from the other room, his voice dark and sleepy, a little dangerous. He sleeps with his phone on his nightstand, so I can only guess what he's seeing.

"Shannon?" he calls out. I wonder if this how Mom feels when she's been caught doing something wrong. Except—this isn't my fault. Dad snapped a picture and the woman took off. Preparing my defense, I walk over to the bed and sit on the edge, sighing.

"Did you really send back all those clothes?" He frowns. "Evie sent me an email explaining how sorry she was that she couldn't help you find more than two outfits to your liking."

"Wait. This isn't about the Minion boob picture?"

His eyebrow arches. "The *what?*"

"Never mind."

"What's a Minion boob picture?"

I tell him the story in a rush. He doesn't laugh. He sends Grace a few texts, then turns to me and says, "It's taken care of. PR will handle it. You didn't do anything wrong. Just an opportunist."

"Great," I say, picking up the corded phone by the bed. "Should I call room service for breakfast?"

He gives me a curt nod. I call and within a minute the deed is done.

As I walk away to go shower and dress, I expect him to follow. Shower sex—especially in a suite with so many shower heads—is a Declan delight.

But I shower alone.

As I dress, he jumps in the shower, and while I muddle through my tangled thread of thoughts, the staff delivers breakfast. By the time Dec's out of the shower, toweling his wet, dark hair, I'm drinking coffee, legs crossed in a chair that faces the fountain and the fake Eiffel Tower on the strip.

"Is that one of the outfits Evie helped you with?"

I look down. "No. It's a little from Marcello, and a little from her..." I don't finish my sentence, because some element in his voice makes me pause.

He is angry.

Not this again. As I sit here watching the sun against the brush-covered beige mountains in the distance, the long metropolis before the base of the hills teeming with industry and debauchery in the form of skyscraper casinos and nightclubs, I feel a deep determination. Ever since we arrived here in Vegas, we've been prickly over any issue involving money.

*His* money.

Then again, we can't really talk about *my* money, because that would be a three-second conversation.

His phone is the center of his attention now, as he stands in front of the room service cart, idly picking at a berry bowl and scrolling through messages. "Grand Canyon and solar panels," he mutters. Must be some new business venture Anterdec's involved with.

"We need to figure out what we're doing here," I say. "I feel like I'm living in suspended animation. We got away from the crazy wedding mess back in Massachusetts, and we've been here in Vegas for three days. What's next?" I figure this is safe territory.

"I don't know. Dad's sticking his nose in the resort VP's face constantly and driving her nuts. Your mom and dad dumped us to go watch 1970s entertainers. And you're rejecting me left and right."

"You could have followed me into the shower!" I protest.

"That's not what I meant."

And I know it.

"I'm not rejecting you," I say gently. I don't stand up, instead gazing out at the horizon, my eyes going unfocused as the line between mountain and sky blurs. "I just don't want all this."

"You don't want me?"

"Ha ha."

"That wasn't a joke."

A chill whips through me so fast that I reel, the dissonance too great. "Of course I want you!"

"But not my life."

"What?"

"I try to share my life with you, Shannon."

"You *are* sharing your life," I say calmly, my grounded tone entirely fake. I'm trembling inside. "We live together. We're about to get married."

"And when I try to give you a nice wardrobe, or share a wonderful meal from a new chef, or buy you fine jewelry, you—"

"Don't you understand that every time I look at a designer dress you buy for me, I see a car payment. When you talk about going out to dinner at private clubs, I see a student loan payment. When we take Carol and her boys to Canobie Lake Park and you treat everyone to all the goodies in there, Carol and I secretly feel really strange, because we're used to packing a cooler and eating on the cheap—because just the tickets alone were hard enough for Mom and Dad to manage. And—" I sputter, trying to make up for anything I've said that might offend him—"it's not that I don't appreciate it all. I do. I know it comes from the heart, but I can't unfeel what I feel."

All those words come rushing out of me like a flash flood on a mountain pass, debris rising with the water line, destroying the only path along the way.

He softens, but doesn't back down.

"And don't you see, Shannon, that I am sharing who I am with you when I ask you to enter my world. I *am* designer clothing and private clubs and limos and Teslas and waterfront apartments. I *am* Milton Academy and private tutors and Harvard legacy. I hire people to manage the smaller details of my life because I can. Because I want to. I live like this because it's all I know. You're not the only one who looks at the other's life and has a knee-jerk evaluative reaction to it."

"Huh?"

"Every time we go to your parents' house and Jason's washing the car, I think, 'What a waste of his time. He could be doing something else.' Whenever yet another relative butts into our personal life, I wonder why they devote their psychological energy to someone else like that, when they could be working, or traveling, or just living quietly and entertaining themselves with something other than another person's choices. Conversations around the dinner table about accepting what I consider abusive behavior from bosses get head nods and reinforcement, and in my world—growing up—that would never have happened."

"Because you didn't have a job as a teen?" I feel the sneer before I hear it, and pull back just in time.

I hope.

"No. I did." He tips his head back and forth, thinking. "Internships. I learned to stand up for myself. I learned not to take shit from any boss. Especially my dad."

"Was your ability to remain in your house dependent on that paycheck?"

He pauses, green eyes taking me in. "No."

"That's the difference."

"That's not the *only* difference."

"No. It's not," I concede.

"Shannon, you're entering my life by marrying me. I'm entering yours. I don't reject any part of your family culture—"

"Hah!"

"—except for the intrusiveness by your mother."

"Which *is* our family culture!"

We both marinate in that for a few beats.

"Why, then, is it acceptable for you to reject everything that has shaped me into being the man you love? You're about to become a billionaire's wife. I won't hide my money. I have zero shame about wealth."

"And I do?"

"Yes. I think so."

"Shame? How can I have shame about money that isn't even mine?"

Damn. One eyebrow goes up, a perfect, thick dark arc over that blazing green eye.

"That's it, isn't it? Self-worth again."

"No! Why are you always making any decision of mine that doesn't agree with yours into some kind of psychological problem with my self-worth at the heart of it all?"

"And why does any disagreement on my part always boil down to my being out of touch because I'm wealthy?"

Oh, burn.

My chest aches. The air in the room thickens with a kind of stifling feeling, an almost viscous quality that makes me think my lungs are sticking together. Each breath takes all my effort. Mind, body, soul, volition.

All of it.

"We keep coming back to this for a reason," Declan finally says, his voice tight. A flaring panic fills me, his instant distance like having a knife plunged into my neck. "It's not going away. Maybe this is the real reason you wanted to run away from your mom at the wedding."

That knife in my neck moves to my chest.

"What?" I gasp.

Music begins outside our window, the lulling drift of a classical symphony that quickly evolves into an operatic tune. My ears perk and some bones in my body vibrate and turn toward the sound, instinct strong. I don't give in to impulse, instead watching Declan with open hurt and a simmering resentment that finally boils over.

"We fled that wedding. *We* did. I came to you and told you I couldn't stand it anymore, and—"

"Why couldn't you stand it?"

"Two words: Jessica the Bitch."

He opens his mouth to correct my math, then smartly doesn't.

"Why are you so obsessed with Jessica?"

"Because she's such a bitch!"

"Why?"

"Why is she a bitch? Come on, Declan. Don't do this."

"Don't do what? Try to solve a problem?"

"Try to create one."

"I'm creating *your* shame about *my* money?"

"You're driving us apart if you keep this up."

"Keep *what* up?"

"Pretending that the reason you're giving me all these gifts isn't because you're competing with your brother."

"Andrew is giving you emerald necklaces?"

"Andrew is CEO. Your father hand-picked him. The second he's around, you compete for attention. Taking care of your woman and making sure she looks the part of a billionaire's wife is important for being the one on top. So...."

"You think I want to give you nice things that represent my life because I want to one-up my own brother? That's crazy!"

"I have a seven-foot animatronic teddy bear in our hotel suite that is crazy. Not me."

"Let me get this straight: you think I am giving you gifts and asking you to live a billionaire's lifestyle because I'm competing with my brother."

"And you think I can't handle being given these luxuries because I don't think I deserve them."

We both nod, but I can see his breathing grow harder, his anger bubbling below the surface, ready to emerge. We've had disagreements. We've gone cold with each other and had to thaw, eventually talking problems out.

Never, in more than two years together, have we faced each other from such a distance, as if ready to jump into a foxhole for safety from an unknown weapon.

"You're wrong," he says shortly, words clipped and fast. One hand drags through his thick, dark hair, a nervous fidget if Declan ever had one. "I'm not competing with Andrew by using you as a proxy!"

"Not consciously, no."

"Not one damn bit!" He slams his fist against the bureau, upsetting the dry minibar, hundreds of dollars worth of chocolate-covered gummy bears and iPod headphones flying.

In the face of this kind of anger, I typically freeze. My dad doesn't blow up like this. Dad's anger emerges in a different way. Blood rushes so hard through my ears it sounds like a waterfall in my head, and I unlock my knees, willing myself to take steps toward the door so I can leave. Think. Breathe.

*Be.*

I take two steps, and before I can stop myself, I give him back his anger and more. "Shame? You think I have some misplaced shame around your money? I think you've got it backwards. You're always going on and on about how I need to find my power, how I give my power away to others, and blah blah blah." My face feels like someone napalmed it, and I'm stammering, tears filling my eyes because when I'm flustered, I cry. I shouldn't say any of this. Not one word.

I do anyhow.

"How about *your* power, huh? I think you're the one who has it backwards. It's convenient to think you're the cool, calm, self-controlled, unflappable Declan McCormick, the wunderkind who was poised to take over Anterdec one day. Was. *Was*," I repeat, vicious now. "I think you go on about my power because deep down inside, you can't figure out how to exert your *own*."

His gives me a ragged look so raw that I know I hit the nerve I'm aiming for.

"Quit deflecting your own power issues onto me!" I continue. "You and Andrew compete because you feel like you don't have as much power as you should—so go out and find it! Find your own damn power, Declan, but quit acting like I'm screwed up because I'm having a hard time adjusting to a life that I didn't realize I was signing up for."

My legs unstick, and I storm to the door, opening it.

"Where are you going?" His question is menacing, laden with a threat that says I don't have the right to leave, with that golden authority I admire in him, until moments like this.

"Out. For coffee," I add, turning around. "NEXT DOOR! I'm going to go find my self-worth one damn latte at a time!"

And with that, I slam the door.

With all the power I can muster.

* * *

"I don't understand," Mom says as I sob into a Grind It Fresh! triple breve with cinnamon and ground Madagascar vanilla beans sprinkled on the New Zealand whipped cream top. "You got into a fight because you *don't* want goats to go to African villages?"

I texted Amanda in the elevator, and she came rushing over to Grind It Fresh! to commiserate. Sadly, Mom saw her as she walked past the poker table where Mom's been butchering hands. She followed. Amanda was too worried to notice the tail.

My ability to process anything is hampered by the massive fight I just had with my almost-husband.

"I can't!" I huff, looking at Amanda, who translates my words into Momspeak.

"They got into a fight because Declan is using Shannon as a pawn in his fight for dominance with Andrew."

"Oh. Now I understand. Just say 'it's because they're men,' honey—that's shorthand." Mom takes a drink of her half-caf mocha and sighs. "This coffee is bliss." She gives me an evaluative look. "Does this mean you and Declan broke up? Because if so, I might need to text someone at the networks."

"You're feeding information to the press?"

"James says Anterdec's getting a ton of interest and new financial boosts from all the news about the runaway bride! I knew my plan was genius."

"*Your* plan?" Amanda and I say in unison.

"Well," she falters, going silent. I can only imagine what she's been feeding the press. As long as it's not Minion boobs, we're good.

"He was really angry."

"So were you," Amanda points out. "And rightly so! I think the whole Andrew-Declan one-upmanship contest is getting out of hand. Did I tell you he's taking me on a helicopter tour of the Grand Canyon and afterwards we're going to Mexico to see the solar panels he's donating to schools on coffee farms?"

"Oh, come on!" I groan. "They're competing to see who can be more philanthropic? As if that's the measure of who is the better man? Giving to charity doesn't count if you're doing it to win a contest."

"It's better than the giant jewels they've been giving us."

Mom's eyes narrow to slits. "Giant jewels?"

"Right," I say flatly, drinking more.

"That's not a euphemism for their penises, right?"

"MOM!"

"MARIE!"

"You know," I point out, "*you* weren't originally invited for coffee with us."

"I wasn't invited to Vegas, either," she says, forlorn, her lower lip starting to tremble. Dad's story about Grandma Celeste feels like someone dropped a chunk of concrete on my heart from a Mass Pike overpass.

"Do you understand why Shannon and Declan escaped the wedding, Marie?" Amanda asks, her voice going low, her hand on Mom's free hand on the table.

"Because I invited Jessica Coffin."

"And why did you invite Jessica Coffin?"

"Because she controls the society pages and trends for Boston."

"And why was it important to have the wedding in those—"

I brush my hand against Amanda's knee and give her a look. "I can take it from here," I say.

She blinks rapidly, but recedes. "You sure? You were ready to drown her in whale sperm the other day."

The waitress happens to deliver a new round of lattes and French macarons at that exact moment and gives us a freaked-out look, hurrying off after emptying her tray.

"I'm sure."

Amanda gives me a big hug and whispers, "It'll be fine."

"I know. I'll call you if I need help moving the body."

She looks at Marie and laughs. "No," she says, turning back to me. "I mean with Declan. I've never met two people more perfect for each other, and he loves you like crazy. Andrew says so."

"I think you and Andrew are pretty close in the 'perfect for each other' department."

"We don't have the history you and Dec have. Go talk to him. Work it out."

"We will. I just—I need time. Space."

"I've got this, Amanda," Mom says. "Don't worry. Shannon's got her mommy now and everything's going to be just fine."

*Don't leave me*, I mouth.

As Amanda gives me an apologetic look, her eyes dart over my shoulder and narrow suddenly, telescoping like a big game hunter spotting a target. Amanda's head turns, her hair brushing against her jaw, those big, round brown eyes turning into evaluative slits.

"No. It can't be," she whispers.

"What?" I crane around to look.

"Don't look!"

I twist back around and accidentally dump my latte into Mom's lap.

Mom screams.

"You're drawing attention to us!" Amanda hisses.

"Shannon just burned my cooch!" Mom shouts.

So much for being covert.

The cafe manager rushes over with a wet washcloth, a thousand apologies, and offers to clean everything up and bring us a new round of coffees.

In the meantime, a slim woman in a sleeveless dress the color of a sunflower *click clack*s her way across the floor, her features coming into focus as she nears.

Or, I should say, fokus.

"Kari Whitevelt?" I squeak. She's Amanda's equal at Greg's main mystery-shopping business competitor, Fokused Shoprite.

That's right.

She's Foked.

"What are you doing in Las Vegas?" she grills Amanda, who stands her ground and gives Kari a Cheshire Cat grin.

"We're here on business."

Kari has long, wavy blonde hair and bright, whisky-colored eyes. She has a wide face but sharp bones that stretch nicely when she smiles. I would never in a million years admit this to Amanda, but...I like Kari.

I've worked with Kari.

Because Anterdec hires Fokused for some market testing we do.

Amanda has no idea, and somehow—I need to keep it that way.

With a broken heart and a hoo-haw-injured mother with a drama queen complex.

"My poor vulva," Mom whines as the coffee manager delivers the new drinks, a tray of French macarons in a variety of flavors that are arranged like a double rainbow, and a gift card for $100 for Mom.

"You, too?" the employee, Jonah T. (according to his name tag), commiserates. "Mine breaks all the time."

I look at Jonah speculatively.

"What model do you drive?" he asks Mom. "Mine's an S60."

"Mine is a pink Cadillac," she croons. "Best ride you could ever imagine."

Jonah's perplexed suddenly, and I can't blame the poor guy.

"I thought we were talking about Volvos," he says, backing up and giving me a confused smile.

"One of you is." I give him a head shake that is the universal gesture for *Don't even try to talk to the crazy lady*. Las Vegas resort employees are fluent in Head Shake, and Jonah scampers off.

Meanwhile, Kari and Amanda's prickly conversation has turned to outright suspicion and accusation.

"Are you trying to snipe the wedding chapel accounts?" I hear Kari snap at Amanda.

*What wedding chapel account?* I wonder. Greg doesn't take too many accounts that require extensive travel.

Amanda is trying to freak Kari out, I see, because she replies in a smooth tone. "You know we can't talk about it even if we are, Kari. Client confidentiality."

Kari reddens, and then damn—she notices me.

"Shannon!" Kari is a hugger. By the time she rocks me left and right a few times, I have established that I was a metronome in a previous life. I keep ticking for ten beats or so after she lets go of me.

Amanda's narrow gaze turns me into an injured mother lion with three cubs. I can see her imagining my pelt on her living room floor. "How do you two know each other? Kari didn't start working for Foked until after you left for Anterdec."

Kari reddens at the word *Foked*, but c'mon. They have to know we're *that* juvenile.

"Good thing you left Constipated Value-flop, Shannon. Anterdec is such a great company. And congratulations on your weird wedding fiasco. I wish I had been there, but I was here on assignment and—"

Amanda does, in fact, look constipated right now. I have to give Kari that.

"How do you know each other?" Amanda asks again, drawing out each word.

"The wedding account!" I blurt out. "You know, the one we can't talk about." I over-enunciate those last words, sounding like a preschool teacher with nineteen shots of Novocain in her mouth, and wish this day would just end.

"Shannon?" Mom asks. "Can coffee infect a tattoo? Because last night your dad and I got a little drunk, and now—" She points to her nether regions.

Kari makes a face of disgust.

Saved by Mom.

"It's been charming," Kari says, looking at Mom the way one would watch a rabid raccoon, "but I have to go get married eleven more times in the next three days so I can do my job." She smirks at Amanda. "Have fun!"

And with that, Kari is gone.

Amanda is about to kill me.

"You're hiring Fokused Shoprite, aren't you? You're mystery-shopping-cheating on me."

"Not you, too!" I throw my hands in the air. "I give up." Between fighting with Declan an hour ago, my mother's crotch emergency, and Kari's sudden appearance, I blurt out something that is about as inopportune as you can get.

"Anterdec is buying Greg's company anyhow, so you won't be competing with Foked soon."

See? I'm clearly half Marie.

"WHAT?" Amanda bellows. "Andrew never said a word!"

"It's not like you two were even talking to each other before the wedding." I snort. "And now that you've made up, I'll bet talking about Greg's company isn't top of your list of Things To Do In Vegas."

She gives me a patented Chuckles look.

"It's not final," I continue. "It's why Greg's been so busy. He has a ton of business details and his wife's cancer and..."

My head begins to spin.

"Can we," I beg, "put this topic in the Cone of Silence?"

"Fine," Mom sighs. "I won't talk about my tattoo."

"I wasn't talking to you, Mom," I snap, pleading with Amanda with my eyes. "But yeah—Cone of Silence *for sure* on your crotch tattoo."

"All right," Amanda says reluctantly, "but I can't stay quiet for long."

"I know."

"You kept this from me? And what about my job?"

"If you want to keep it, sleeping with the CEO of your acquisition company might help," I joke.

"Don't tell that to Josh," she growls.

At first, I welcomed this distraction. Drained suddenly of the will to talk or think or argue or do anything other than drink coffee, I slump down into a chair and start to whimper softly to myself.

"Sorry," Amanda says. "You're worse off than I am. You and Declan need to patch things up."

"I know."

"You have to actually talk it out," Amanda says in a hushed voice. "It's time."

"Why do all the feelings have to happen at the same time?"

"Because life doesn't make sense."

"Not fair."

"You're just figuring this out now?"

"I'm a slow learner."

She snorts. "You're anything *but*."

I start to shake. My hands can't wrap quite right around the white paper coffee cup, and the logo blurs before my eyes.

"What have I done?" Declan's back in that hotel room where I left him behind an angrily-slammed door, and all I can feel is a white-hot abyss of pain, a hollow point in an arrow that's stabbed my heart. I did that. I stormed out and left.

I take a sip of my latte.

"It can be undone. You just need to make up with him."

"And with me," Mom says, her lips pressed together, eyes filled with hope.

"Why is exercising my own power so fraught with misunderstandings?" I ask Amanda.

"I think that's called growing up," she says.

"It sucks."

Mom grins. "No kidding. Wait until you're in your forties, like me, and you realize no one's really an adult."

"You're in your fifties, Mom."

"Shhhhhhhh." She looks around, frantic, like someone we know will hear me. I hate to break it to her, but no one she's trying to impress gives a crap, and to a twenty-something person, the difference between someone in their forties and fifties is negligible.

You're all *old*.

"That is the most unnecessary lie in the world, Mom."

"There are plenty that are worse," she counters.

Amanda gives me a hug and whispers, "You can do this."

"I know. I'm just so tired."

Her sympathetic smile is the last image I have before she leaves, because I close my eyes and put my forehead on the back of my hands, resting on the table.

"You used to do that when you were a little girl and overwhelmed."

"I'm a big girl now, and I still do it."

"You must be so tired."

I look up. Mom gives me a close-mouthed smile, her eyes jumping from me, to her cup, to her fingernails.

"Yes."

"Some of that is my fault."

"Some?"

"Not all of it."

"A lot of it, Mom."

"I'm sorry." The expected waterfall of words doesn't come. Mom's simple apology stands on its own, like a messenger sent ahead of the troops.

"I'm so sorry," she says again. Her shaky breath adds to the sincerity. "I can't explain it. I won't even try. Your father had a long talk with me and now I understand better what I did to you and Declan."

"He told me about Grandma Celeste and your wedding, too."

She looks like I slapped her. "He *what*?"

"I'm sorry your mom did that to you."

Tears well up in her eyes, pouring over her lower lids, streaking through her blush.

"I ruined your wedding, just like my mother ruined mine."

"No. Not the same at all."

"I made you come up with that cockamamie scheme to run away from me."

"You did." I have to agree.

She chuckles, wiping the tears with a Grind It Fresh! napkin. I take the opportunity to shove a chocolate macaron in my mouth to stop myself from saying more.

"I suppose," she whispers, "I could give you a bunch of reasons for why I made your wedding into such a production—"

"And invited the person who bullies me most in the world to my own wedding."

She swallows hard, nodding. "And that. But nothing would explain away the pain I've caused you, honey, and so all I can do is ask you to forgive me."

I frown. "Did Daddy put a new microchip in you?"

She gives me a patented Mom look. "You use sarcasm to avoid your feelings."

"No, I use *food* to avoid my feelings. You have me confused with Amy."

She sniffle-cries. "Oh, Shannon."

I lean over and hug her. Mom squeezes tight.

"I don't really have a tattoo," she says, hot breath filling my ear. "I just knew that was Kari Whitevelt from Foked and made a scene to throw her off to help you."

My laughter plumes out of me as if my heart were a sage stick and we're performing a cleansing ritual.

Which we are.

"Excuse me," says a man's voice from behind me. He pulls at the metal-backed chair where Amanda was sitting a few minutes ago. "This seat taken?"

It's Declan.

Mom raises her eyebrows and her eyes roll up to watch him.

"This is the famous Grind It Fresh!," Declan says, eyes darting with a calculated approach, surveying and absorbing, letting no detail go unnoticed.

"Yes."

"Coffee's really that good?"

Except when it feels like a thousand liquid needles in my stomach, like now.

"Yes."

"I suppose I should give this a try." He walks away from me and Mom, my eyes eating up the long lines of his legs. He's dressed casually, in dark jeans and a form-fitting dress shirt in a deep purple. This isn't his normal look. Marcello has left his mark on Declan, and maybe Evie has, too.

I like it. I'd like it more if he didn't feel so remote, so untouchable, right now.

While he's at the counter, probably interrogating the poor barista on P&L sheets and marketing conversion rates, Mom leans toward my ear and says, "You have to make up."

"Of course we'll make up."

"You said some harsh words to him, Shannon."

"So did he!"

"Was he right?"

I drink more of my coffee and borrow a little time.

"Yes," I admit grudgingly. "Only a teeny, tiny bit."

"And do you think you were right?"

"Yes! More than him."

"Uh uh. No, honey. Don't play that game."

"What game?"

"The 'who's more right' game."

"You and Dad *invented* that game, Mom!"

"Learn from my mistakes."

"I would need three lifetimes."

She gives me a long-suffering look that she has no right to give me. If we're casting long-suffering *anything*, I'm the one who should hold that power. Not her.

"Let me play the role of the wise woman for a minute here, Shannon."

"Goody. Pretend play."

She lets out a long sigh. "Go ahead. Get in your digs. I deserve them."

Mom does. She *really* does, so why am I starting to feel bad?

"Okay. I'll stop. Go ahead. Give me your best wise woman advice." I'm sure the next words out of her mouth will involve an order to go have sex with Declan, or to let him buy me fancy jewelry, or to get started on grandchildren.

To my surprise, she says: "Let yourself imagine he's right."

"WHAT?"

"I said 'imagine.' Let yourself *imagine* he's right. That doesn't mean he *is* right."

Before I can lambaste her over this terrible idea, Declan's back with a tray of three coffees, each the perfect order for us. He remembered my favorite and Mom's as well.

We have so many cups of coffee in front of us, we should start a newspaper.

If you close your eyes and flatten your feet against the ground, with your spine straight and your hands splayed on a smooth, sturdy surface, you can take a deep breath and feel how connected you are to all the parts of the world. Think about it. Every item touches every item (unless you're flying). It's all about degrees of separation. As long as I'm in contact with the floor, which touches iron girders, which touch other structural pieces that reach the foundation and the dirt, which goes on to reach the ocean, which carries the current of that touch all the way across the vast seas to another piece of dirt—

You get the picture.

In the space of touching every part of the earth with your seeking heart, you can find yourself more readily.

"Shannon."

His voice seeks, too.

"I'll get going now," Mom says primly, giving me a half-hug that feels like we're in some weird Duggar cult. "I'm so glad we made up." She gives Declan a weird smile. "I would hug you, but my hoo-haw is burning." She walks slowly across the casino floor and disappears into a walkway to our resort.

"Was that code for something?" he asks me. "Her hoo-haw is her—"

"Right."

"I don't want to know."

"No. You don't." Awkward topic aside, the fact that he's talking to me is astounding. Steve and I had a few fights that were bad. Steve gave me the silent treatment for days afterward.

Having Declan talk to me an hour after I slammed a door in his face is surreal.

I feel like I'm in seventh grade again, except now I know what sex feels like and my acne's gone. My skin buzzes with that kind of tension that comes from conflict with another person. You're just not quite right with them, and it's as if the air between you is charged with atoms that can't figure out how to coexist without making you itchy and numb.

I suppose the best way to start is to say:

"I'm sorry." His voice is so sincere it cracks a little.

He beat me to it. "I am, too," I reply. "I shouldn't have slammed the door, either."

He gives me a shy smile. Shy isn't a word I would ever use to describe him. In that little grin, I see his five-year-old self. It's adorable and heartbreaking at the same time.

"At least I knew where to find you once I cooled down."

"I came here to try to talk it out with Amanda, but Mom found us."

He stands. "Should I leave you alone? I thought—"

"No. Please," I beg. "Stay." I don't have the words to explain how his presence is the only way I feel rooted to the earth. Fully. It's the difference between a plant that grows in a container and one that grows in a wildflower field.

I'm *that* different when he's with me, in spirit or in form. With him, I'm connected to every part of the world.

The chair legs scrape against the tiled floor as he resumes his seat, next to me, our knees touching.

We're okay.

It's going to be okay.

"I don't know how to fight with you," he says in a hushed voice. "I'm not good at this."

"And I am?"

"We're both really, really bad at this, aren't we?"

"Of all the things we could be bad at, I'd pick this over any other."

"Can you imagine if we were really bad at sex?" he says in a conspirator's voice, a light joking tone that is meant to knit back the loose threads of the tapestry of our romance.

I close my eyes and giggle. I try to imagine it. "No. I *literally* can't imagine it."

"Me either."

"You know what else I can't imagine being bad at?"

"What?"

"Making up."

His shoulders relax.

"But I don't take back anything I said." My words make him nod slowly, his hands on his knees, eyes cast down as he thinks.

"Me either."

"We're at an impasse, then."

"At least you didn't use the word *standoff*."

I start to shake, my cup of coffee a slight blur as I say, "What are we going to do about this? I can't keep arguing about this. You have your ideas about money. I have mine."

"This has nothing to do with money."

"It doesn't?"

His head shake is imperceptible, but I see it. "No."

"Then what?"

"Power."

"Money is power."

"Yes, but power is power, too. And I think we're both trying to figure out how to exercise it." His hair brushes over a wrinkled brow, the lines creased from tension. "Our relationship is an incubator. A hothouse. A petri dish."

"You're so romantic."

"We're complete beginners at this, Shannon. Both of us. We're trying to figure out the very early stages of how you weave two disparate people together into a single entity that shares a life."

"We've been together for more than two years. I live with you."

"Not the same. The stakes are higher now that we're marrying. We aren't fighting over which toaster to keep, or whether you'll do my laundry. This is about whose emotional reality takes precedence. Whose emotional reactions dictate behaviors. And we're just realizing—both of us," he adds in a rush—"that the relationship we thought we had is more layered than we ever expected."

A chill runs through me. A timbre, a rattle in his throat, the way the words come out so full of sadness—it makes me feel connected to all the emptiness in the world.

This is not a happy feeling.

"What are you saying?" The words come out of my mouth like I'm talking around a mouthful of molasses. The depth of emotion in his voice could go one of two ways.

His eyes move with precision, from left to right in a parabola, finally settling on my hands, which he grabs, both of mine in both of his.

"I'm saying that you take me places I didn't know a heart could go. You feel so well."

"I *feel* well? You're using 'feel' as an action verb? You say that like it's an accomplishment. It's not. It's a curse."

"It's a superpower."

"Stop."

"It is," he insists. "And I forget that you feel differently than I do."

"I am a separate human being," I say with a small smile.

"Not what I mean. You open me up to emotional experiences—an inner life—that I don't realize is there."

I frown.

He looks around. "Like this place. I'll bet you can look at the clerk at the coffee shop for three minutes and tell me her emotional state."

He's right.

"Don't you *feel* people when you walk into a room?"

"That's illegal, Shannon."

"That's not what I meant! I'm talking about walking into a meeting and picking up on the emotional inner worlds of all the faces sitting around the table. Their cues about what they're really thinking and experiencing on the inside."

"That sounds like a form of psychological torture."

"Welcome to my world."

"That's what I mean." His hands are dry and hot, smooth and patient, ready to hold mine for as long as it takes to make me feel fully rooted.

"Declan, I can feel you pull away from me when we're at odds. It's a physical sensation that sends me into a state of being that really is a form of psychological torture. It's brutal and distressing and leaves me feeling like I am clawing for air. Like I'm suffocating from the inside out." I can't stop crying, my breath coming in little spurts, a sudden torrent of emotion piling on, taking over.

He's horrified.

"Jesus, Shannon, I had no idea." His sigh comes out like staccato notes being played against his ribs. "I would never cause you that kind of pain if I knew."

"N-n-now you do."

Those bright green eyes disappear beneath his eyelids, his long black lashes kissing the hollowed space above bone. He reaches for me, then moves his chair over, arm around my shoulders, hand soothing me by rubbing up and down the length of my arm.

"I'm here now," he murmurs. "I'm not going anywhere. We can fight and you can slam doors and I can yell and you can make up a world in your head where you turn me into a big old jerk, but I'll always come back to you and try to talk everything out. I can't not do that, Shannon. Being with you has rewired me."

"Me, too."

"You can't get rid of me. Even if you do resort-cheat on me."

I sniffle-laugh. He grabs me and hugs me so hard. So beautifully hard.

The physical distance between us has been bridged.

Things fell apart.

And now the center does, in fact, hold.

# Chapter Eighteen

A few hours later, after we go back to the suite and I fall asleep in his arms, I awaken to find Declan pacing in the other room, on the phone, murmuring a low, indecipherable string of words. He hangs up, calls Grace, and recites a bunch of numbers and the names of banks.

Must be some big account.

I stretch, my body sore from the unexpected nap, my calves screaming from all the high-heel wearing I've been doing. Rumpled and dazed, I stand in the middle of the suite like a little kid who has woken in the middle of the night and isn't quite sure what to do to get back to bed.

"Hey, sleepy," Dec says, tapping his phone's screen and tucking it in his jacket pocket. He pulls me into his arms just as someone knocks on the door.

We put two feet between us and I give him a look that says, *You didn't.*

After that fight, the last thing I need is a giant teddy bear, or jewelry, or a rare meerkat, or whatever Andrew's lavishing on Amanda.

The door opens. It's a staff member holding a tray with two coffees in it. That's it.

And they're from Grind It Fresh!

Declan tips the delivery person and hands it to me with a flourish.

"Not quite Tiffany, but…"

It's the best apology I've ever received.

"You're right," he says as we take our respective drinks. "This *is* the best damn coffee I've ever had in a shop."

"Too bad they don't have any Grind It Fresh! stores back in Boston," I say in a mournful tone.

"You've got a point." He drinks and closes his eyes, savoring.

"See? Orgasm in a cup."

His eyes drift to my breasts. "D cup? DD cup?" he speculates.

I punch him. "I'm serious. I would trade Chuckles for a Grind It Fresh! in the Seaport District."

"That can be arranged," he says with a wink.

As I laugh, he walks across the room, stops, then swings around.

"Here." Declan hands me a piece of paper with his handwriting already on it. I'm surprised. I don't think I've seen him physically write more than little domestic notes and birthday cards to me.

Grace writes everything for him.

"Your handwriting is so neat! Like an architect's!" I gush. It literally looks like Frank Lloyd Wright himself filled out this…application for a marriage license?

"I know. I was bored in school and learned to write like that. It was a coping mechanism." He smiles and points to the paper. "Can you finish that up so we can go to the license bureau?"

"The what?" I stare dumbly at the page. It's a marriage license application for Nevada.

"We need to have a license if we're going to get married, Shannon. The one from Massachusetts won't transfer easily. This is a quick fix."

So we're really doing this. We're getting married in Vegas. I sit down on the settee at the end of the giant California King bed in our suite and clench the end of the paper.

"I thought you wanted this?"

"I do, but…" We've been here for *I-don't-know-how-many*

days now, running into Mom and Dad, James, Pam and Amanda and Andrew at odd intervals, an uneasy equilibrium in place. Mom stopped asking when we were getting married as soon as she discovered the adult products trade show, and Dad keeps disappearing for long stretches of time, probably hiding in his hotel room and watching a twenty-four-hour sports channel between meals.

Amanda and Andrew are obviously grabbing every chance they can get to chafe parts of her I don't need to know about, and James and Pam are a mystery. They've become buddies, and I'm starting to wonder if Amanda's fears about becoming the woman in some stepbrother romance book aren't real.

I distract myself by looping through all that because I can't quite bring myself to look up and meet Declan's eye. The hotel pen is right there, on the desk behind him. Telekinesis would be a great superpower to have right now, but lacking that, I stand, pick it up, and complete the form.

He smiles. Not nervous or worried, Declan's removing an obstacle. I'm sure that in his mind, marrying in Vegas is just a checkbox. Not that he doesn't love me. Of course he does. He wouldn't put up with my mother if he didn't. But the actual ceremony itself is just a transaction. A legal transfer of our relationship from one that is based on respect and love and mutual trust to a codified, licensed agreement that becomes part of the public record forever.

That's how he views it.

I don't know how I feel, but when it becomes hard to fight the tears that want to take over my throat, I know I have to say something.

"Um, is this really how we're doing it?"

His back is to me, encased in a perfectly-tailored suit. Some staff member brought him an array of clothing and it's all been here, the washables neatly washed and folded, crisply-pressed business shirts hanging in the armoire, suits in the closet, all his size and bespoke. As my words sink in, he straightens up, like an animal at a watering hole that hears something worth its attention.

Declan's eyes are wide and open, soft and accepting, when he turns around. He bends on one knee to be at eye level with me. The gesture reminds me of his proposal at the Museum of Modern Art in New York.

That moment feels like lifetimes ago.

"Isn't this what you want?" Stillness lingers in the air between us, a welcome change from the chaos that has driven me forward through a life I didn't choose, the Boston Wedding of the Year a tidal wave I never decided to ride. It was thrust on me. In the questioning quiet between us, right now, I can really take him in. He's so handsome, the skin around his eyes full of expression, the green irises reflecting back a querulous me. His body heat warms the chill that invades as I navigate new territory.

"Dec, I don't—I don't know." Salty regret fills my mouth, making it nearly impossible to untangle all the feelings and thoughts inside me. I don't want to hurt him. I don't want to say the wrong words, but it feels like every part of my life involving expressing myself is a gear with teeth that don't fit in with the other gears that keep the machine working.

"You don't know...whether you want to marry me?" His eyes dart to the three-carat ring on my hand, to the half-crumpled Nevada marriage license application in my hand, and then to my lap.

I drop the paper and cup his jaw in my hands. "No, no, I do. I do. I want to say those words more than anything in the world, Dec." His mouth tightens, eyes going blurry, and I realize we both have too much emotion stored inside us to be able to handle it all.

There's a point where your emotional resilience can be stretched so thin that even an overabundance of love isn't enough.

And that is when you know that the outside world needs to be put in check.

I take a deep breath. He joins me. His arms slide around my neck as he comes up and in, holding me in an awkward embrace, a movement of impulse that lacks his usual grace. We're all arms and elbows, knees and breasts, the grating sensation of a pen in his shirt pocket scratching my neck, his cufflink catching in a lock of my hair, but as my own palms spread across the fine cashmere of his suit jacket and my hitched sob dissolves into the little sanctuary our bodies create, I know it'll be fine.

Better than fine.

"Thank God," he says. "I was worried you were calling it all off."

"I want to call off the bloodhounds. Not the marriage."

He laughs through his nose, then sniffs. I pull back and look at him. He's not quite crying, but emotion has overwhelmed him, his fiercely blank poker face completely disassembled by love.

Love for *me*.

"What do we do?" I ask, my fingers tender along his jaw, worrying a tiny scar.

"That's up to you."

"No, Dec. It's up to us. What would you do? If I weren't a factor."

His full-throated laugh is contagious as I realize how ridiculous that sounds. "Considering I can't marry myself, honey, I don't think I can even begin to give you an answer to that question."

"You know what I mean."

Scratching his face, then rubbing his chin like he does when he's sorting through a complex issue, he finally seems to give up and make a half shrug. "I'd run off and get married at a little wedding chapel here in the hotel. Alone. Just the two of us."

"No Mom and Dad? No James?"

"You asked what I'd do. That's the answer."

"It wouldn't bother you? In the future, when you look back on our anniversary, to remember the day without your loved ones there?"

"My loved one would be there. The only one who will be there with me through the end of my life."

"Oh!"

"I do love my dad." That's the first time I've ever heard Declan say *that*. We're in very vulnerable places now. "And I love Andrew and Terry, but I love you so, so much more, Shannon. You're my real life." He grips my arms harder, as if increasing the pressure will make me understand him better. Will make his words truer.

Will make his declaration more real.

"I have these circles. They're concentric. I'm at the center, but you're right next to me. Then there's Dad, Andrew and Terry. Grace is right on the edge there, too. After that, there's your family. Beyond that, a handful of friends. Then there's everyone else. Business colleagues, old classmates, people on the street, employees....and they're not quite real."

"You sound like a sociopath." I smile when I say it.

"No...not quite." He frowns. "Maybe when it comes to business, but I can compartmentalize. I can't do that with you, though. I can't just put you in a box where I pull you out and deal with you and then tuck you back away. You are at the core of my life with me. You bleed into every part of who I am and you are going to shape the man I become for the rest of my life."

Now he actually *does* have tears.

"We have spent the better part of a year letting all those outer circles drive us away from our inner core. You and me. When we marry, I view it like a fusion. We're fusing our lives together. For nearly a year our families have worked on fusing themselves together through the wedding planning, but we let them take off with the pageantry of the wedding itself and forgot that at the heart of this big celebration, there's a couple. *Us.* A couple who are going to have a marriage that lasts five or six decades. We let one little day become more important than the rest of our lives."

He's right. Oh, how my heart lifts at his words, his emotional unraveling like being caught in a maze and having someone give you an aerial map so you can find your way through to freedom.

Gazing over my shoulder, deep in thought, he adds, almost absentmindedly, "We did it to ourselves. Blaming Marie is a convenient outlet, but it's our fault."

"How about we reclaim that day?" I say. "Run off alone. Get married with just the two of us. Not even Andrew and Amanda there."

"You're sure?"

I nod. "You're right. We made the marriage less important than the wedding. We let Mom and James take over and turn us into pieces on a chessboard. We forgot our own power."

His smile is radiant. As he bends to pick up the marriage license application, I drop to the ground and kiss him, hard, interrupting him. The press of our mouths and the warm invitation to be with him whenever the need arises closes some circle inside me that has hung open and empty, all its energy drained by not being finished.

For the next minute we are nothing but caresses and kisses, the rasp of stubble on skin, the feel of fingers threading in hair and seeking the warm asylum of a lover's embrace, a partner's welcome, a friend's ever-present hello. We are more than two when we cleave, or so religion says, and in this pinpoint in the long, eternal flow of time, I fuse with Declan McCormick and become more to him than any piece of paper can ever declare.

The edge of my engagement ring scrapes along the back of his neck as I play with the thick waves, our mouths saying *I'm sorry* in the way only a kiss can confer. As the kiss deepens, his warm mouth reluctant to pull back and give even an inch between us, it's as if the frayed threads of our souls are weaving together to form a patchwork quilt to warm the heart.

We're warm and comfortable, enveloped in whatever our sequence of touch, sight, taste, and sound generates for that layering Declan mentioned earlier.

Our inner lives have to merge for our love to flourish.

Undressed in what feels like wisps of time stolen from breath and worry, we're under the covers and luxuriating in the sheer joy of having access to so much of each other. As my hand caresses his chest, the hard, molded lines of his ribs, the small hills of his abs and the delightful strength of his back, I marvel at how he's both familiar and new.

He's given me more of himself.

And it didn't cost a penny.

"I've never met anyone like you, Shannon," he murmurs

against my neck as his hands bring me to places where blood runs wild, the anarchy of pleasure destroying all the rules.

"You say that all the time." My voice hitches at the end as he breaks a rule again and again and again and *oh*—

"I mean it. There's only one of you in the world. The universe. The multiverse, if you believe in quantum physics. And of all the worlds and millennia in which beings have existed, I'm so lucky to find you."

"Declan?"

"Mmmm?" My own hands decide to do a little chaotic good in Declanland.

"Shut up and make love to me."

"God, I love you."

"I love you, too."

And then we stop talking.

* * *

In the quiet that always descends after making love, a spiritual cloud that hangs over us like a protector, watching and guarding, my throat tightens, an emotion so visceral I can only experience it in the fiber of my flesh, in the clench of muscle, in the open pores and the closed eyes.

"I love you so much," I whisper. He stirs beneath the sheets, reaching for more of me, making us connect as much of our bodies as possible without having him inside me.

"I know."

"I can't do this without you," I add, my throat filling with a sadness that tastes like regret.

"Can't do what?"

"Live. I mean, I can. If something happened to you, I'd—" A sob cuts off my words.

"Shhhhh. Shhhhhhh, honey," he soothes, his voice filled with concern and consternation. "Where's this coming from?"

"I—I—I just think about how hollow I felt when we fought. And how, for a few minutes, I wondered if you didn't want me any more."

"Never. I could never *not* want you, Shannon."

"But it felt like that. And even just a few minutes of feeling so separate from you made me want to die. Not in an active way. Passively, like I just wouldn't want to exist in a world without you in it. You're my anchor. You've become part of me. I can't handle the thought of that part being ripped out."

"You tore me apart, too, you know."

"I did?"

"I don't show emotion the way you do, but I feel it just as deeply. Spending so much time fighting over our differences made me feel so distinct from you, so separate. All of our relationship has been focused on what we have in common, which is so much. Arguing about money seemed trivial in the beginning, but then the issue grew and grew, and soon if felt so much bigger than the two of us combined. And I couldn't find a way out." He sighs. "I can always find my way out of a problem. But not this one."

"Because it wasn't a problem. It was just life."

"Maybe."

"Sometimes the structure of life works against us."

"What do you mean?"

"I come from a family with limited resources. You don't. We have patterns ingrained in us, and emotional realities imprinted on us by our parents. It's not your fault that I'm the way I am. And it's not my fault that you're the way you are. These institutions—family, financial management—clash sometimes. It makes the people who are part of those systems clash."

Declan sits up, propping his back and neck up with pillows, and watches me as I talk. "You're saying the structure of those institutions and systems is what's in conflict, and not you and me?"

"Exactly."

"That sounds like cultural economics."

"Maybe."

"You are so hot when you play the social science professor." His smile goes impish.

"I'm trying to have a serious discussion about what's happened to us this week."

Declan's head disappears under the covers. Seconds later, I learn where his tongue is.

"And so am I," he says between my gasps. "So am I."

*Tap tap tap.*

His palm splays against my belly, pinning me in place. "Don't answer that," he says, his voice muffled.

"Why? Is it a nine-foot koala bear that vomits dollar bills?"

"No." Pause. "Why? Did Andrew give one of those to Amanda?"

*Tap tap tap.*

"Please," Mom's voice carries through the door. "Please, Shannon. Please be there. I'm trying to find your father."

I sit up, Declan crawling out from under the covers and looking at me with concern.

"He's disappeared," she calls out. "I can't find Jason anywhere."

# Chapter Nineteen

Oddly enough, it is James who figures out where Dad went.

After throwing on whatever mismatched designer clothes we could find, Dec and I race out the door with Mom, riding the elevators to the security office, where Declan and the head of security, a tall, gaunt man named Jed, scan video footage using facial recognition software to spot him.

"You spy on people when they stay here?" I say loudly, a bit outraged.

The head of security glares at me.

"Do you have legal permission to *do* that?"

Now *Declan* glares at me.

"Do you want to find your father or not?"

I sigh.

A fast scan shows nothing.

"When did you see him last?" the head of security asks Mom.

"Not since breakfast."

His eyes grow angry. "He isn't missing, then. That's what? Eight hours?"

"He's not answering his cell phone, and my husband doesn't *do* this."

Declan and Jed share a grimace.

"What?" I ask.

"When people gamble and lose, they tend to disappear."

"Forever?"

"No, no," Declan backtracks. "More like they go and try to find enough money to hide their loss."

"We don't *have* enough money for Jason to gamble."

I wince. "Actually, Mom, you do. My wedding fund."

"He wouldn't!"

Dec and Jed just look away.

"People behave in really aberrant ways when they have a big loss."

"Wouldn't he be on-camera if he did?"

"Maybe he gambled at a different resort."

A numb fear grips me and I clench Declan's forearm, hard. "Dad doesn't disappear, Declan. If he lost a bunch of money, he'd come back shame-faced to Mom and just tell her. I'm worried."

"Does he have any medical conditions?" Jed asks Mom.

"Nothing life-threatening," she says with a head shake. "Just some acid reflux and an intolerance for red peppers. Don't go anywhere near the man after he's eaten them."

Jed puts up his hand. "Got it."

"Jason could use his ass as a bioterrorism weapon if a government provided him with enough red peppers."

"GOT IT."

James strolls in, commanding and authoritative, his grey hair conferring immediate power. "What's wrong?"

"Jason's missing," Mom sobs. "He's not answering his phone and he never came back this morning from going out for coffee."

"But I saw him downstairs earlier. Near the fountain, outside. A group of us were talking about the resort and investments. He started ranting about how fake Vegas is. I agreed heartily—and told him the fakery paid for Shannon and Declan's wedding."

"Oh, no," I groan.

"I meant it as a joke, but he didn't take it well. Turned red, muttered something and stormed off." James shrugs with one shoulder.

"When was this?" Mom asks.

"Around ten this morning."

"Oh, Jason," she says with a long sigh. "Where are you?"

"Does he have any haunts?" Jed asks.

"A hot dog place and ice cream store across the street?" I offer.

"What about Louie's Stiff One?"

"Is Louie a friend of yours with a penis problem?" Mom asks.

"That's the name of a casino we own," Declan explains. His phone buzzes in his pocket. His eyes cut to me, then to the phone, as he answers.

"Is it Dad?" I ask.

He shakes his head, covers the phone, and dips out of the small video security equipment room.

Jed, James and Mom huddle around, speculating where Dad might be. I hear Declan saying a string of numbers and talking about capital, leverage, private ownership, and a bunch of other business *blah blah blah*.

A tiny flutter begins in my chest, like a butterfly drowning in a rain puddle.

Where is Dad?

Jed's suddenly on his phone, his voice tight. He's all military, his voice flat like a Midwesterner, the tone of the general in a techno-thriller who takes command and fixes all the crap the wild cowboys mess up.

Mom gives me a helpless look.

Jed says, "Security confirmed he's at Stiffy's."

Me, James and Mom give him a round of looks.

Jed reddens, but doesn't flinch. "Louie's Stiff One. He's there."

"I knew it," James crows.

Declan finishes on the phone and comes back in, extremely pleased with himself.

"What's going on?" I ask, glad there's good news somewhere.

"Oh, you know. Business," he says breezily, eyes raking over my mom, James and Jed. "You find him?"

"As I predicted," James explains. "Louie's Stiff One."

"Why?"

"Why what?"

"Why would he go there?"

"Dad is more of a hot-dogs-and-ice-cream kind of guy. Louie's sounds like it's more hot dog than filet mignon."

"More like Spam in a can," Declan says in a voice tinged with disgust.

"That would be my Jason," Mom says with a relieved smile. "Let's go find him."

"Why?" James asks.

"Why? Because I'm worried about him," Mom explains.

"He's a grown man. If he wants some privacy, give it to him." James makes a sound of disgust.

Mom's eyes narrow. "What, exactly, is this Stiffy's? A strip joint?"

Declan, Jed and James all start laughing.

"It's about as far from a strip joint as any place in Vegas can be," James says with a chortle, his condescension clear. Is he...protecting my dad? Siding with him on some issue I don't understand?

"Then why are you trying to stop me from seeing him?" Mom protests.

"I'm not stopping you." James gives Mom a gimlet eye. "I just find your way of treating him like he's on a leash to be a bit much."

"Since when did my relationship with Jason become any of your business?"

James points to me. "Since she sprayed me like a dog while your husband attacked me for allegedly having an affair with you."

"Which you would have been lucky to have," Mom counters.

James is nonplussed.

Mom turns to Declan and says, "Can we please go to Stiffy's?"

We walk down into the cavernous private garage, James driven in a separate car, while Dec, Mom and I climb into an SUV limo. The first two minutes of the ride are full of tense silence, which ends with Mom opening her mouth.

"When are you two actually getting married?"

She had to bring it up again, didn't she?

Dec gives me a micro-look so swift I almost don't see it, eyes darting to Mom, face going slack. "When we're ready."

"You're already more than ready."

"When we decide, Mom. Not you. Besides," I add with a little too much glee, "we're trying to find the right Liberace impersonator."

Mom's face goes sour. Carol was right. Hah! Mom doesn't take the bait, though.

"Are you eloping?" Her voice is soft, turned up at the end, the question a cold squall on the surface of my heart.

"Maybe," Dec and I say at the same time, then share closed-mouth smiles.

"Will you let me and Jason be there?" She blinks hard, holding her hands in her lap and twisting them, worry about Dad etched on her face.

"We don't know." Declan answers for me. It's the same response I would have given.

Because it's true.

"I would understand if you just ran off," she says as she inhales, the words so airy I almost can't hear them. "I would."

Dec starts to answer, looks at me, stops, and crosses his legs, face impassive.

"Good," I reply.

And the rest of the drive to Stiffy's is quiet, but not calm.

* * *

You ever wonder what sour beer would look like if it took human form?

*I* don't have to wonder any longer.

If Corrine and Agnes, from Mom's yoga classes, came to Vegas, Louie's Stiff One would be their place. As Declan and I walk in, I do a double take. At his other resort, we're about the same age as most of the guests.

Here, we could be everyone's *grandchild*.

"Don't you dare steal my slot machine, Helen!" an old woman croaks, standing by, holding on to a tennis-ball-covered

237

walker. As she moves one lurch at a time away from her spot, she calls back, "I'm going to start wearing diapers just so I won't have to deal with this shit."

This is *so* not Litraeon.

"How did Anterdec acquire this place?" I ask James, who looks around the casino like he's starring in the corporate version of the *Hoarders* television show.

"Bankruptcy and buyouts and, hell, I don't even remember." He scrubs his chin with his palm. "We can't sell the damn thing. No one wants it."

I spot Dad easily, because he's the only man in the room with red hair.

Hair, period.

He's at a baccarat table, a pile of chips in front of him, and two empty drink glasses. He's slumped in his chair, a small crowd around him, one man wearing an oxygen tank and—

"Is that man *smoking*?" I gasp.

"Sure. It's allowed. We've been over this," Declan says with a weary sigh.

"While wearing a nasal cannula and having oxygen pumped in him?"

Dec grimaces, then gives the room a calculated look. "I wonder how well-insured we are on this place."

I hip check him and he shuts up.

"We have baccarat here?" James sniffs.

"What's wrong with that?" I ask.

"It's generally associated with finer establishments," Declan explains.

"Even the games have a condescending hierarchy?" I say with a snort. James and Dec stay silent.

"Seven hundred dollars! I'm up seven hundred," Dad says, looking up at me. "Oh, my honey. My little Shannon found me. C'mon, Shannon. Pull up a chair. Have a beer. This is the real Las Vegas. No one's fake here!"

"Except for my teeth," some old dude says with a rheumy laugh.

I see why Dad is here. It's more his speed.

Dad does a double take when he sees James. Curiously enough, Mom hides. I can tell she's doing it on purpose, watching Dad from behind a row of slot machines.

"James!" Dad booms. "It's James McCormick, the self-made billionaire from Southie. Hey, guys—this is your owner!"

"I ain't no pet. No one owns me," Rheumy says.

Dad cackles.

How many beers has he had?

"James! I'm up seven hundred bucks. A thousand more winning streaks like this and I can pay my debt to you."

Genuine bewilderment fills James' face. "Debt?"

"Pay for my daughter's wedding."

The two give each other the most uncomfortable looks I've ever seen on grown men's faces. Some part of my heart starts shrieking, and if pain were a scent, it would smell like burning ego. Like missed opportunities.

Like regret.

"No." James' single word is like a thick, brittle stick being cracked over someone's knee. "That's not how this works, Jason."

"Oh," Dad says, dragging out the word with bluster, his arms stretching over the backs of the chairs of the men on either side of him, men who give Dad arched eyebrows with expressions that say, *You gonna let him talk to you like that?*

"Well, Mr. James McCormick, why don't you tell me how this all works." His words are slurred, and I wonder not only how *much* he's been drinking, but for how *long*.

James' mouth goes tight. Declan just watches my dad with a neutral expression.

"Really. How does Vegas work? How does wealth work? Because I sure as hell don't know anything about that," Dad continues, giving the men around him a collegial smile, all of them with bitter, twisted lips in various states of scorn, remembrance, or wrapped around a beer-bottle neck.

"Daddy," I say softly. All of the men jerk slightly, looking at me with hardened expressions.

*Be quiet, little girl.*

I can hear them, even if all I do is imagine them.

"You're changing, Shannon." Dad's voice goes loud, then soft, like he's talking around a curve. "You're entering a world that is as familiar to me as Mars. About as safe to breathe in, too. For the past few days I've marinated in all this money—fake money—and I'm crawling out of my skin."

James and Declan share a look.

And then Declan's attention turns exclusively to me.

"I can't spend five grand on tartan ribbon," Dad chokes out, his voice low and sad. "I just sat in your casino, James, and watched some guy lose fifty grand, his entire life savings. Saw another guy win fifteen grand and blow it all in one of those mall stores. He shot his wad on a dress, some purses, and shoes for his wife. Said it was his one and only chance."

A tiny, pained sigh comes out of Mom. I'm the only one close enough to her to hear it.

"I gave my girls the best I could, but I'll be damned if it was even one iota of this." He spreads his arms around the room, his face crumpling slightly. "Not, uh—not this. Not Louie's. But you know."

I try to think of something to say and glance back at Mom. She's dumbfounded, staring at Dad, her lips slightly parted.

"I look around this town, this destination city where people from all over the world come to vacation and play, to gamble and be entertained, to get shit-faced and revel and unwind and become part of something bigger than themselves while they're here, and all I see is my own failure," Dad says, that last word spat out like a growl.

Tears choke me, Declan's hand on my hip as I let a small sob escape. Declan was right, earlier, about blending our inner lives, and how our outer lives have to be woven together, too. It never —not once—occurred to me that marrying Declan meant asking my mom and dad to adjust to a new reality that would force them to confront deep questions about themselves, too.

I don't want to *adult* anymore. Adulting is too hard.

A small, high gasp behind me makes me turn. Daddy can't see her, but Mom is behind a small curtain that covers the booth parallel to us. She's moved closer.

"Failure?" I finally ask, putting my hand on Dad's forearm, completely confused. "Why would you ever feel like a failure, Dad?"

He looks down at the neck of his beer, avoiding my eyes. Something tells me to keep touching him, to maintain the connection, though. His bravado is fading, and as it drains out of him I see his authenticity coming back in.

"I've worked hard my whole life, kiddo. Was born in New York. Moved to Boston as a little kid. Lived with him in Southie." He juts his chin toward James, who nods slightly in acknowledgment. "We didn't know each other back then, but he gets it. He knows. When you're born into poverty there's a kind of grinding feeling that's always a part of you. It never goes away."

James closes his eyes and swallows, once. Declan's eyes are riveted on his father.

"I finished high school. That's better than either of my parents. Did a few years of community college and met Marie that way, at the veterinary clinic where I worked. That's it. My greatest financial success came the day we scraped together a down payment and managed to buy our house. Five more years of payments and it's really ours," he says, chest puffed with pride.

He deflates, his arm sweeping out in a gesture that makes it clear he's not pointing to Louie's Stiff One.

"But *this*? I can't give you this. I can't give *anyone* this. When you kids were little we wanted Marie home with you. A vacation? Hell, no. That meant I wouldn't get paid for the time I took off. Stay in a hotel? I think the first time any of you girls got that was when you went on a school trip. We could finally manage weekends camping if I stacked my days off just right." He looks at me. "About when you hit high school. Carol was out of the house by then."

"Daddy, none of that makes you a failure," I choke out.

I hear a sound of agony behind me, a sob being smothered. Mom's wet eyes meet mine and I am helpless, caught between two parents filled with an aching pain I can't fix.

"I know that," Dad says, clearing his throat with a rumbling sound like rocks in a clothes dryer. "And when I'm back home, puttering in the garage, mowing the lawn, going to work, or babysitting Jeffrey and Tyler, none of this—he gestures again—"is real. Coming here makes it real. Your wedding made it real. Seeing all these people with more money than me, giving all these luxuries I could never provide for my woman and my girls, well, Shannon, it eats a man up."

Mom catches my eye and puts a long, manicured finger to her lips. Mascara lines, wet with tears, run down her lower lids. She looks like a sad clown.

"Daddy—"

He drinks the rest of his beer and looks around the table. His new friends are looking at their own beers with sad-sack faces. James is holding a plastic cup with ice cubes and a thin drizzle of amber-colored liquid in the bottom, staring off into space. Declan is a stone wall, his face showing nothing about the tornado of emotions that I know is whirling inside him.

Meanwhile, my mother is falling apart behind me, little pieces of her littering the dirty carpet like heart confetti.

"No." James' voice cuts through the melancholy. His soft eyes fall on my father, who rears back slightly at the baritone timbre of his nemesis's voice. "No, Jason. You are anything but a failure."

Mom pinches off a sound of shock, her chest rising and falling rapidly, hand over her mouth now, as if she's physically holding back her impulse to speak. Dad's face lifts, like the sun rising over the ocean, slow and deliberate until he's looking straight at James.

"Says the billionaire," he replies, an unrecognizably bitter tone in his voice, making me recoil. That's not my dad.

His words ring out in the now-somber cluster of tables around us, people watching with a bemused curiosity, a cocktail waitress delivering a fresh round of American beer to a group of slot machine players behind us. A gust of wind from people coming in through the main doors blows a billowing cloud of cigarette smoke our way, the taste in my mouth making me cringe.

The cacophony of hope is the soundtrack to this face-off, the electronic dings a kind of reinforcement as players feed money into a slot, push a hope button and watch a disappointment display, convinced that they can beat those random odds if they just get luck on their side.

A decidedly pissed-off female voice declares, "Says a man who is lucky, ambitious, a financial success—and a failure in his own way, too, Jason."

James's eyes narrow as he searches for my mother.

At that, Mom steps out of the shadows, Daddy's sad eyes widening slightly then rolling down with a humiliated tightness. He clearly wishes she hadn't heard what he just said, and the defeated sigh that comes from his dropping shoulders makes me convert my touch on his arm into a desperate hug.

As I pull away, Mom steps forward, a few feet from Daddy, looking down. Tears openly pour down her face. She doesn't make the effort to wipe them away. Shaking, she opens her mouth, her voice tremoring like buckling asphalt.

"If I didn't love you so much, Jason, I would slap you right now." Her fingers twitch, and her right hand curls into a ball. "Might even punch you."

Her voice is trembling from fury.

"How dare you," she says. "How dare you call yourself a failure?"

"I—"

She shakes her head slowly, not even bothering to make him talk to the hand. "I won't hear it. You are shredding me, Jason, with this failure nonsense. I've been your wife for more than thirty years. I have borne you three wonderful children. We've suffered through two miscarriages together. I've searched for change in the couch to buy another jar of peanut butter and a loaf of bread to stretch through to the next paycheck, and I sat next to you at a conference table at the credit union when we signed the paperwork to buy our house, with eleven dollars left to make it through half the month."

The table goes to a hush.

"You worked two, sometimes three jobs while the girls were young so I could stay at home. I watched you make broken cars work with nothing but your hands, your wonderful brain, some duct tape and magic. I've seen you fall asleep at dance recitals from being awake for twenty hours straight, and I've watched you sit patiently through your third nail polish color at a princess tea party surrounded by Carol, Shannon and Amy."

Dad's mouth hardens. Mom's trembles.

"I've been able to whisper my darkest fears to you in the inky night when I think you're asleep and it's safe to be scared, and your warm hand always reaches out to grab mine."

I am openly crying. I think James has something caught in his eye, because he's rubbing it pretty hard. Declan grabs my hand and squeezes it, tight.

"You have been to so many soccer games and school plays and concerts and recitals—and the ones you missed really hurt you. I've watched you coach a T-ball game and hop in the car to go work an extra shift, then come right back in the morning to help with church youth group. You lend money to people who need it, have gotten really screwed a few times over the years—and you still always want to give people another chance."

Mom's makeup is in streaks down her face right now, and she's holding Dad's hands. His eyes are so wide a ring of white is around his irises, and he looks like he's barely holding it together.

"I don't know what your definition of success is," she says, looking over Dad's shoulder to James, then Declan, "but by my standards, Jason is a god-damned emotional billionaire." She tugs on his hand. He takes one step toward her, and she looks back at Dad. "And I'm taking you to our nice hotel room, where I'm going to spend as long as it takes with you until you really feel your success all the way in the marrow of your bones." She turns away from us and they take a few steps, Dad pocketing his chips first.

I swear she adds, "You fool."

Dad doesn't look back at us, but as they reach the main doors, the bright desert sun shining behind them and making the wide rectangle of the door's threshold feel like a blinding imprint, I see him clasp her to him tightly, their kiss like something out of a 1940s glamour movie.

Even I say, "awwwwww," and I'm supposed to be grossed out by them.

James lets out a sigh, like he's nostalgic, then winces. Declan and I give him the side-eye, but I think for completely different reasons.

Mom turns back to us and shouts:

"If it wasn't clear, when I said 'spend as long as it takes,' I meant I'm taking Jason back to the hotel room and we're going to have sex until he can't remember that the word *failure* exists."

*All* the men over fifty in the casino sigh, including James. Again.

Dad gives us a thumbs-up and they leave, Mom's hand splayed across my father's ass.

"Your mother," James says with a sigh, the words hanging loose like one of Tyler's baby teeth, not quite ready to let go.

"My mother what?" I ask as Rheumy moves to the seat next to me and offers his half-consumed beer. When I decline, he pats his shirt pocket and mouths the word *maryjane*.

Or maybe he says, *Marry me?* It's hard to tell. The guy has three teeth left, and either phrase is likely.

"Your mother is one of a kind," James declares.

"I'll drink to that," Declan says.

Old Rheumy offers up his beer. Declan declines.

"Maryjane?" he offers, pulling out a fat joint the size of my ring finger.

At least that mystery's been cleared up.

"No, thanks," Declan demurs, helping me stand. "I appreciate the offer, though."

"It's free and clean," Rheumy swears. "Got me a medical card in California and this is some prime weed."

"I'm sure it is," James assures him. "But, um…"

I jump in for the rescue, leaning over and tapping Rheumy on the arm. "The Illuminati are watching them. If the feds ever take them into custody and they have weed in their piss test, they're toast."

Rheumy's eyes go wide. "No shit?"

"No kidding."

"I knew it was all real," he mutters, shaking his head slowly, giving Declan and James a sad, sympathetic look.

I nod toward the door and the three of us escape.

"What the hell was that about?" Declan says with a low whistle.

"That was a young woman thinking on her feet," James replies, his face pensive as he walks fast toward the waiting limo, Geordi at the door. "You Jacoby women are a formidable force."

"We have our moments," I say, holding my head high, my sophistication infinite.

Until I trip over the outstretched leg of a beggar carrying a sign that says "WILL EAT PUSSY FOR CASINO CHIPS" and fall right into his lap.

"My prayers have been answered!" the guy hisses in my ear. "It's raining women!"

Geordi rushes over to pull the guy away, while Dec and James extract me quickly, not looking back. My knee's ripped to shreds, blood blooming like a rose through the torn pantyhose, and I feel like my elbow banged into a steel door. They funnel me into the back of the limo and shut the door, locks activated instantly.

"Your knee," Declan says, reaching for a bucket of ice. James hands him a perfectly pressed handkerchief and in seconds, I have an ice pack on my bloody joint, leg stretched over Declan's lap, James in front of us, frowning out the window.

I shouldn't look back. Declan even tries to shield me from the tinted window. I can't help myself. I know I shouldn't.

But I do.

When I fell, my scarf must have unraveled and landed on the beggar. He's currently, uh, using it as a sex toy.

Let's leave the description right there.

Because what happens in Vegas—stays in Vegas.

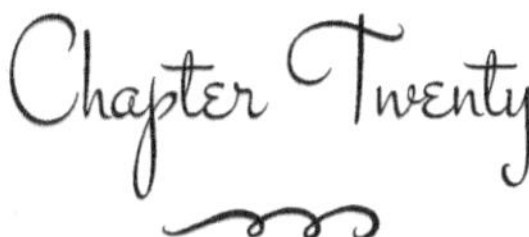

# Chapter Twenty

When you don't have a thousand guests, when you're not bringing in forty-one bagpipers, and you don't use a floral designer who has more flowers than the garden at Versailles in your wedding, the actual ceremony is so simple.

And the emotions are still the same.

All the big resorts in Vegas have their own private wedding chapel on-site. In the movies and on television, you see people going to some twenty-four-hour quickie wedding place, getting married by an Elvis impersonator. Those places exist, but what you don't hear about are the more sedate, calm chapels where couples can just tie the knot in peace, then go up an elevator and screw like bunnies afterward.

As husband and wife.

Or wife and wife, or husband and husband.

Early this morning we made the trek to the Regional Justice Center in downtown Las Vegas, and they issued us a shiny Nevada license. Once we're married here in the resort chapel, the officials will file the license and in a few weeks we'll get a copy.

It'll be legal in a few minutes.

I'll finally be Mrs. McCormick in the eyes of the law.

A leisurely walk through the convention center section of the resort reveals the chapel, tucked away behind bright white doors, a little oasis of peace in the go-go-go atmosphere of the casino and malls.

The chapel is simple and stately, with pews that look like we could fit as many as fifty guests. Dark, polished oak contrasts with bright white trim and a soaring ceiling, support beams cutting through visually, the altar like the bow of a boat, the windows facing the elaborate gardens in the courtyard.

Tasteful flower arrangements dot the end of each pew and cover the altar, which isn't religious. It's ornamental, meant to be a symbol, a holding place for the wedding party.

The color scheme is generic yet complementary, sedate and yet welcoming.

It's simple.

It's quiet.

And there are no tauntaun cats acting as flower girl.

We have the license. Declan's arranged for an officiate. Andrew and Amanda have agreed to be witnesses.

At 3:13 p.m., too many days after our original wedding date, we assemble, rings and hearts and all, and get ready to make what is true in our souls a legal record as well.

"Are you sure this is fine?" Declan asks for the third time, giving me pause. He generally asks a question once and takes the answer at face value.

"I said 'yes' twice. Why do you keep asking?"

"Because you look like you're about to throw up, cry, and punch someone at the same time."

"That's just my Resting Bitch Face look."

His eyes soften, compassion radiating out to me. "Shannon." The way he says my name makes me melt. "You don't have a Resting Bitch Face face."

I try.

"You just look like you're nauseated."

I try again.

"You look like a Vermeer painting."

I give up.

"You don't look so calm, cool, collected, and like you have the pulse of a corpse yourself, mister."

"I knew I picked you for your complimentary nature."

"Flattery will get you nowhere." I'm right, though—he *is* nervous. What's going on? As I start to ask, Amanda and Andrew arrive. Andrew's wearing a lovely Armani suit without a tie, and Amanda's dressed in Dior with high heels that carry the signature Louboutin red sole.

Las Vegas loves when people are in the red.

"Ready?" Amanda asks, giving me an extra-long hug.

"More than ready. You're sure Mom and Dad don't know?"

"Your mom was offered the opportunity to emcee a male strip-a-thon at the trade show convention for the adult sex toys."

"What?"

"Which happens to be right now." Amanda waggles her eyebrows. "I made a few calls."

"What kind of people do you know that you can call to accomplish that?" I ask.

Andrew frowns and looks at Amanda. "Yeah. What kind of people do you know?"

"You're the one who paid me to mystery shop the O spa," she says, patting his cheek.

He sighs heavily, turns to me, gives me a hug that smells like limes and cardamom and soap, and a big, dazzling smile. Andrew looks around the room and declares, "Not a shred of tartan in sight!" then grabs Declan for a manly hug.

We all laugh.

Nervously.

James appears, a bit winded, his eyes settling on Amanda as he walks across the room, regal in his fine, dark wool suit, his hair a shock of grey against the collar.

"I have Marie firmly in hand," he assures her.

"What did you do?" Declan's voice is filled with a delicious mirth.

"I tried to offer her a position as the emcee for a 'battle' between two different male dance revues," James explains.

*Strippers*, I mouth to Amanda, who giggles.

"But she said she and Jason are renewing their wedding vows."

Declan, me and Amanda stare at him, mute.

"What? Where?" I peep.

"They didn't say. She told me they want to be alone, and they'd be back later today."

Any worries about not inviting Mom just went out the window. A wellspring of emotion rises in me, because it was one thing when I wanted to choose whether she attended.

It's quite another to have that choice removed.

Amanda and I share raised eyebrows. "She's up to something," we whisper to each other.

James looks at Amanda with concern. "Your mother is in her room with Spritzy, resting. She said something about a flare?"

Amanda's expression changes, matching James'. "I'll check on her later." She pulls back slightly, processing James' tight worry. "Thanks."

He nods and looks at Declan.

"May I have a word?" James asks, pulling him aside. Dec's been nervous, touching something in his inside breast pocket, little sighs and toe taps unusual for him. Maybe it's nerves, but there's something else. The two huddle, heads together, one dark, one the color of ashes in a fireplace. In twenty years, Declan will be more ash than coal. In twenty years, I'll be thicker and greying, with skin that wrinkles and fine lines from smiling so much that my love folds in on itself. So will Declan, his face marked by time spent being thoroughly, utterly, madly adored.

And I get to watch it all happen in real time, day by day.

What an honor.

Mild surprise covers Declan's face, shifting into a look of deeper contemplation as whatever James says hits him emotionally. People who don't know him like I do wouldn't catch the difference, but I do, antenna picking up signals and musing about their significance.

James says something more, his arm going around Dec's shoulder, their eyes catching in an intense look. Declan's face changes, eyes widening, throat working hard as he struggles to control his emotions.

A hug follows. A long one, full of promise and love, with

James closing his eyes and holding on to Declan like he's savoring every second of this connection with his son.

The first in many years.

As they pull out of the hug, their faces are close, a sign of camaraderie and the tearing down of walls erected when Declan was just graduating high school. Maybe this crazy mess does have a purpose in the end. Perhaps my mother's maniacal obsession with offering the perfect wedding has yielded a perfect result.

James walks down the long path between the pews, Andrew giving Declan a puzzled look, the officiant beginning to herd us for the ceremony. I watch Declan, knowing that some major emotional event just took place before my eyes, and that he's still experiencing it in the moment.

Being given the gift of time with this man is a cosmic blessing.

As James reaches the main doors leading to the large walkway outside near the ballrooms, Declan suddenly shouts, "Dad! Wait!" Holding one finger up to James, Dec turns to me and says in a rush, "Can he stay? Please?"

*Please?* Did Declan really just say that?

"Of course he can," I whisper, my eyes full of tears, my empathy off the charts for whatever just passed between them. I can feel Declan's full heart.

Declan waves to James, then leans over to me and whispers, "He told me that if Mom could have handpicked someone for me, she would have chosen you. And he asked me to forgive him for—" Dec's chest begins to shake. The rest of him is stoic, but the body leaks emotion. It has to come out somehow, somewhere.

If you're lucky, it pours out in words and deeds.

Otherwise, it's on a mission, and like water flowing downhill, uses the laws of physics without mercy.

"What do you need, son?" James asks. Andrew's watching every second, his eyes blinking rapidly, and there's hope in him. I can tell he's holding his breath, so I breathe for him. I breathe and I breathe, as I hear Declan say one word that carries the antidote to more than a decade of pain:

"Stay."

"Stay? For the ceremony?" James looks at me and I nod.

"Yes. Please. I want you here," Declan confesses.

James' eyes shine under the glow of the lights, and if he were a slightly different man, he'd let those tears spill over. Even *his* body leaks.

But it does not overflow.

"Of course, Declan. Of course." He beams. Andrew starts breathing again.

And I'd like to think that somewhere, Elena McCormick is watching all of this. Sadly, the laws of physics apply to her, too. She's here in spirit, but not body.

James reaches for my left hand, Elena's ring shining in the sunlight that pours through the windows. "She's here." The look he gives me is stark and stripped to bone. Did he read my mind?

Or maybe he just read my heart.

James opens his arms wide. I have to take the first step, and the embrace is sweet and fatherly, open and informal.

As he lets me go, he whispers, "Take good care of him."

"I will."

"I know." He kisses my cheek and steps back, motioning for Declan to stand next to me, as it should be.

And so the ceremony begins with me in tears. I don't hear most of the words, my eyes reading each person's intentions, my body and mouth moving as needed to act or speak based on nonverbal observation, a mimicry of expectations based on anticipation. I don't need to hear the introductory words, the platitudes, the codification of sentences designed to lend stability to a tradition that stretches back millennia.

This I know: he is mine. I am his. For better, for worse, for billionaire, for Turdmobile.

For Toilet Girl and Hot Guy, there's only one choice:

Forever.

Andrew flanks Declan on his right, and Amanda's to my left, holding a tissue discreetly. I don't reach for it, instead letting my emotions pour out of me like that waterfall, not caring. This is my wedding. My ceremony. My show—mine and Declan's—and if crying like this is what happens when I realize I have so much love in my life that it truly overflows, then so be it.

I cry because the excess of love should be shared and spread, dissolved and displayed, made public so that it can be taken and absorbed where it is needed most.

"Do you—" The officiant says the words and Declan's eyes become all that exists in the world, two green circles of life where my true self resides, my heart tucked under his, my stardust buried in his marrow, my spirit rejoicing at the touch of his hand against my finger. The ring he procured this morning at Tiffany fits just right, a simple band designed for a simple purpose:

A claim.

We claim each other. As he says *I do* and I say *I do,* we do. We *are.* We kiss, we hug, we rejoice, and we laugh.

Oh, how we laugh. I'll hear the echo of that warm, rich baritone in my last moments in this lifetime, as my consciousness fades into whatever comes next, and I will smile wherever I am, for this lifetime is ours.

"I now pronounce you Mr. and Mrs. Declan McCormick," the officiant says, a genuine smile turning his face to hills and richness, the flat, polite look of a man whose business it is to pin down love on paper gone, swept away by the force of our bliss.

"You did it!" Amanda squeals, hugging me until I stumble, while Andrew embraces Dec.

My husband.

I close my eyes and imagine Mom and Dad, wherever they are, renewing what they needed to escape to more than thirty years ago. Their wedding was fraught with disappointment, but never their marriage.

Never their connection.

Never their love.

We reach for each other, and in the space between us I find lifetimes.

.

# Chapter Twenty-One

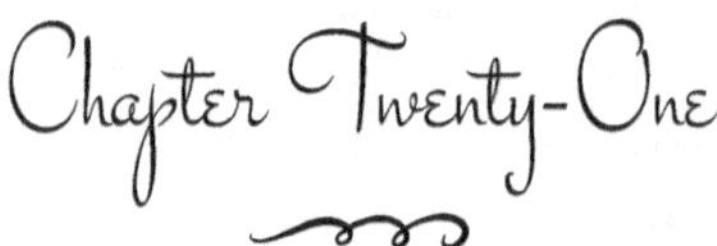

We're in the lobby of Litraeon, just after the wedding ceremony, and Declan insisted on coming through here to look at some new fountain. Made Andrew follow us, which means Amanda's coming, too.

"Why in the hell do you need me to look at a fountain?" Andrew asks, his hand running through his dark waves, the gesture similar to Declan's. "We're headed over to a private fitting for Amanda."

"They put diamonds on diaphragms now?" I ask.

Amanda snorts. Andrew rolls his eyes.

"I'm not going to give that the answer it deserves because today is your wedding day and I'm supposed to be nice to you," he replies, but he's smiling.

"Speaking of gifts, though..." Declan's voice is so full of triumph it makes Andrew's hands curl into fists. As my husband —*husband!*—reaches into his jacket pocket and pulls out an envelope, Andrew watches with great suspicion.

"Here. Your wedding present," Dec says to me, eyes darting to Andrew, who smirks.

"I thought you were paying off my student loans," I whisper to him.

"Done. This is a little something else. And before you even try—no. You can't return it."

I open the envelope, which is made of a heavy linen paper that feels expensive. When I unfold the thick packet of papers inside, I find the name of a law firm in the upper left-hand corner, with what looks like nineteen lawyers listed beneath the address.

"Dear Mr. McCormick," the letter begins. The first paragraph is legalese, something about the final sale of all private shares of a company. Majority ownership. Minority ownership. Transfers.

I see the three best words on the planet other than *I love you* and *Ben & Jerry.*

*Grind It Fresh!*

Declan pulls his coat away from his waist and buttons a button, taking in a deep, satisfied breath as my eyes race over the paperwork.

"Does this say what I think it says?" I gasp as I realize what my sweet, new husband has done.

"What do you think it says, Shannon?"

"You—you—!" I look up in amazement, my chin dipping down to read, then back up as I look at him. "You bought me *Grind It Fresh!?*"

His face splits into a dazzling grin.

"What the hell is Grind It Fresh!?" Andrew asks, his brows turned down.

Amanda grabs me in a hug and we jump up and down, squealing.

"Your husband bought you a coffee shop!" Amanda crows. "Oh, my God!"

I can see Andrew giving Declan a dirty look.

As we bounce and shriek, it starts to sink in. The man bought me a *store*. My wedding present to him was a case of his favorite wine and a private tour of the vineyard.

I *owe* him.

I peel away from Amanda and give him a kiss. He's clammy and happy, but clearly unnerved quite suddenly.

"What's wrong?" I ask him.

"I didn't buy you a store."

Oh, no. Have I misunderstood? Did I just make a huge social blunder? "You didn't?"

"I bought you a *chain*. Grind It Fresh! has nineteen stores in California and Nevada. You're forty-nine percent owner. Pick your job title, honey. The only job that's taken is CEO."

And with that, he unbuttons his coat, reaches into his jacket pocket, and hands Andrew an envelope. A very, very slim envelope.

"What's this?" Andrew asks as he takes it. "My wedding present? You buy me a Dunkin' Donuts? Because that would be a dream come true," he adds in an acid tone.

"Not quite."

Andrew slips his finger under the envelope flap, tearing it open, and pulls the single piece of paper out. Just as he begins reading, I realize what it is.

CEO. Declan said CEO—

"You're *resigning* from Anterdec?" Andrew thunders. "You can't do that!"

"Just did."

"But—"

Declan whirls around and grabs me, his hands shaking. "You told me to find my power. I am. You get your favorite coffee place —which, by the way, has an amazing financial profile—I become CEO, and we grow our own national chain together. Grind It Fresh! is like buying Starbucks in the mid-1970s. We're going to do great things with this, Shannon."

"Dec—I—you bought me an entire *company*?" I squeak.

"Better than a seven-foot animatronic teddy bear, I hope."

I grab him in a hug and nearly topple us to the ground.

"What if I want to be CEO?" I joke. I am truly teasing. No way am I ready for that.

"Wait! Slow the hell down!" Andrew demands. "I'm losing *her*, too? She's one of our best employees!"

"But you're acquiring *me*," Amanda says with a sour look. "When were you going to tell me you're *buying* my boss's company?"

Andrew's perplexed anger shifts into a contrite look. "I swear I was going to—after, uh, you know…"

"After what? All the sex slows down?"

Andrew gives Declan a *help me out, bro* look.

Dec just shrugs and kisses me. Joy radiates from him, tension banished by the sheer act of exerting his will.

"Does Dad know?" Andrew interrupts, his tone clear. It's a threat, not an actual question.

"Not yet."

"He's going to explode."

"That's his problem."

"Jesus, Dec, you're serious?" Andrew's voice actually cracks.

"Yes." Declan kisses me between his replies. "You win, Andrew."

"I win *what?*"

"You're CEO of Anterdec. You win."

Andrew looks wildly at the three of us, eyes bouncing from Amanda to me to Declan. "But *you're* winning!"

"I found a way we both win."

"How am I winning if I lose two of my best employees?"

"And I beat you in the gift department."

Amanda looks at me and whispers, "He totally did."

"You want your own company now?" Andrew asks Amanda.

"I want Shannon's job at Anterdec," she says smoothly, tucking herself under his arm. "How about that? Imagine working together every day. I could even attend private meetings in your office."

"There might be a silver lining here," he mutters.

"But not your office *closet*," she clarifies.

Just as I'm about to say more, I hear my name shouted from near the main doors.

We turn and look to find a burst of familiar faces.

"Look at the fountains outside, Auntie Shannon! Did you see them!" Jeffrey's so excited he's jumping up and down like a human jackhammer. Tyler's face is buried in a 3DS we gave him for Christmas, his go-to when he's overstimulated and there's just too much going on. I grab him and force him to hug me, getting a smile and a "Level 38! Achievement Unlocked!" shout in response.

"What are you doing here?" I gasp, glancing at Declan, who flashes his eyes at me and gives Carol a conspirator's grin as she joins us, enveloping me in a big-sister hug that I really, really need right now.

"Ask him," she says, pointing to Declan. "He arranged for all of us to come to the wedding."

My heart buries itself in my knees.

"What? The wedding?" I look at Declan, helpless and hopeless. How can I possibly explain?

"We already got married," he says bluntly. "Just now."

Well, he took care of that awkward moment, didn't he?

"I know," she says kindly, rubbing my shoulder with a familiarity that should make me relax but instead, makes me cry. "As long as the Elvis impersonator who married you two didn't try to get you to give him a blow job for fifty bucks in the back room, you had a better wedding than I did."

"How did you spend your fifty bucks?" Josh asks Carol, appearing behind her, carrying a small plastic case that holds a large martini glass on its side. It looks like a pet carrier, but that's not right, is it?

"What's that?" I peer in through the cage door and get a Hiss of the Damned from its inhabitant. It's the sound of all the forces of evil being called forth for the ultimate challenge, to destroy and reign over us mere mortals.

I think there's a *meow* for dinner in there, too.

Josh sets the case down, opens the door, and extracts a very pissed-off Chuckles from the pet carrier. He's wearing a Cone of Shame and has the look of a beast who is determined to pee in every single slot machine if it's the last thing on earth he manages.

"Chuckles! What happened?" I gasp. As if Chuckles would answer. That's impossible, of course.

Because he's clearly giving me the silent treatment.

"After that whole fiasco with falling in the pool and getting caught in the leashes and Chuckles' flower girl outfit," Josh explains, his voice going low and confused, eyes searching for my mother, "he needed minor surgery. The cone is so he doesn't lick his, you know..."

"So he doesn't lick his tethticleth, Auntie Shannon," Jeffrey adds. "You should never, ever lick tethticleth."

Josh turns a bright shade of pink and cocks one eyebrow at that statement. I give him a look that says, *Not the time for witty banter.*

"Right," Josh says, simultaneously answering both me and Jeffrey.

I give Jeffrey the hairy eyeball. "Your lisp isn't *that* pronounced any more."

He grins. "I know. It's just that testicles sounds even funnier when you say it with a lisp."

As Jeffrey walks away, Josh leans in and says, "Your nephew scares me a little. What ten year old is that self-aware?"

"Declan says he's going to either become the highest-paid hedge fund manager in the world or the head of Anonymous."

"That kid might damn well manage both," Josh mutters.

I'm surrounded by everyone now, Josh explaining that Greg didn't join them, as he's holding down the fort back home, Jeffrey and Tyler begging Carol for ice cream, and out of the corner of my eye I see Declan talking to Terry, who must have arrived with this fresh wave of East-Coasters.

Guilt infuses me.

My wedding party, family and friends followed me here.

And I got married without them.

Mom appears, beaming from ear to ear. "I arranged to get them all out here for your wedding." She winks, the gesture big and fake. "I knew you wanted privacy, so I told James that your father and I were going to renew our vows."

"You didn't?"

She shakes her head. "Jason stayed here while I went and got Carol and the boys and Josh. Terry asked to join us. Hamish has some endorsement opportunity in New York for that company, you know..."

"Jockey for Men? Coca-Cola? Pepsi? Nike?" She shakes her head at all of them.

"No! Fresh Balls."

I snort.

"And Amy's stuck at work and can't make it, but she'll try to get here tomorrow."

"What? No. Really?"

Mom shrugs. "It's some crisis with a client. She said she already saw you run away from one wedding, so she doesn't need to see you do it out here, too."

I glower at Mom.

"Where's Jason?" Mom asks. I shrug. She wanders off in search of him.

"Let me see the ring!" Carol shouts, diving for my hand. "You know Jeffrey still has the original ones?"

"I do, Auntie Shannon." He frowns. "Wait. That's for you to say. I do."

I offer up my hand for inspection. The simple platinum bands Declan bought make me smile, mine pushed up against his mother's engagement ring. Catching my eye, Dec holds up his left hand, pointing to the ring for Carol's edification.

"Nice," she says with a nod.

"What am I supposed to do with these, then?" Jeffrey asks, pulling a long Star Wars lanyard from his front pocket, our Boston wedding ceremony rings dangling from the metal curl at the end. "Are they mine now?"

"No," Carol says sharply.

Jeffrey ignores her. "Because I was watching that show, *Pawn Wars*, with Grandpa, and he said pawn shops are a great place to get money for expensive things people don't want any more."

"What's *Pawn Wars*?" a deep voice asks, Terry appearing behind Carol, making her jump.

"A show about pawn shops! It's really cool," Jeffrey gushes. A perfect ten-year-old-boy answer. Not one to be distracted from an opportunity to make money, he pivots his attention away from a confused Terry and returns to me. "What are you going to do with these?" he asks as he hands me the original rings.

I take them gently from Jeffrey and slip them into my purse. "We'll think of something," I assure him.

"Ice cream?" Tyler asks, snuggling up to Carol's hip.

A familiar tense look crosses her face. All single mothers on limited incomes wear this look with more frequency than they'd like. Expectations Management 101: how many times can she say "yes" to something the kids want that involves spending money? And how to prioritize on a limited budget?

Declan appears, leaning in to Carol and whispering in her ear. She jolts, reddens, and her eyes water. She gives Declan an incredulous look, her expression making her look so much like Mom when she was younger that I'm choked up.

"Seriously?" she asks him, her voice so quiet I almost don't hear it.

He nods and gives her a small smile, a dawning in his eyes that I can't pin down.

Carol grabs Declan in an enormous hug and I hear her say, "You're sure?"

He nods against her shoulder.

What on earth did he say to her?

She reaches down to tousle Tyler's dirty-blond hair and looks at Jeffrey. "Yes to ice cream."

"Yay!" Tyler calls out. "Yes to ice cream."

"Except here it's called gelato," I explain. Setting expectations with Tyler is critical.

He looks at me intently. "I want ice cream."

"Gelato *is* ice cream," I explain. "It's ice cream with a different name."

Declan tilts his head and starts to open his mouth to object. I know they're not the same. He knows they're not the same. All the adults know it, but to Tyler, the difference isn't important.

Avoiding a meltdown is.

"Right," Declan says with a slow sigh. "And gelato is even better than ice cream."

"Better?" Tyler's face lights up.

My turn to argue. "Actually, it's not," I murmur in Dec's ear. "Too sweet. Not creamy enough. The mouthfeel is totally different and—"

He's kissing me before I can continue with my analysis of sugary treats I shouldn't shovel into my mouth anyway.

"EWWWWWWWW!" Tyler and Jeffrey say in unison as they watch us.

"Yuck," Jeffrey adds, turning away. "Can I get a double cone, Mom? I deserve one after seeing that."

"Sure," she says as Declan ends the kiss. They walk off, Carol practically skipping.

"What did you say to her?" I ask, breathless.

"Told her Anterdec's covering everything. To charge whatever they want to the room."

I'm agog. "It's one thing to do that for my mom and dad, but...are you sure?"

"Dad says Anterdec's turning a profit off our 'manufactured fiasco'—his words, not mine." Dec holds his hands up as if fending off a protest he expects from me. "Everything's on the house for your family."

"And besides," he says, pausing. He's struggling inside, and finally continues, "the look on her face. I couldn't—I realized what was going on, and I wanted her to not worry. To treat Jeffrey and Tyler to whatever they want."

Are his eyes...shining? Mine tingle with emotion, my nose filling, and just as I'm about to reply, Jed rushes over, says something in Declan's ear, and he sprints away.

"Where are you going?" I shout.

Heads turn at the sound of my voice, but he doesn't stop, so I follow Declan, running as best as I can in heels.

And there isn't even a clown chasing me.

He slows just before the very same "High Limit" room my father asked me about the first day we were here, and as Declan parts a curtain, we walk past a table, to another curtain, where yet another baccarat table is placed. My dad is standing at the table, poker-faced, arms crossed over his chest. A bald, intimidating guy wearing an earbud stands behind him, grabbing Declan's attention with a brow raise and the slightest hint of motion.

Dec nods.

"What are you doing?" I'm huffing, struggling to breathe.

"When a bet gets this high, sometimes they clue in the higher-ups. Jed came over and gave me the courtesy of letting me know Jason's betting a high-five-figure amount."

I *know* I heard that wrong.

"Daddy doesn't *have* high five figures."

"He does now." Declan nudges his head toward the table. "He's got about eighty grand there, with odds 9 to 1 as he bets on a tie."

"English, please."

"Your father is betting eighty thousand dollars on a 9 to 1 bet. If he loses, all eighty grand is gone. If he wins, the resort pays him seven hundred and twenty thousand dollars or so." Dec glances at the dealer, who gives him a courteous nod. Or a sly signal.

"WHAT?" Mom screams, appearing behind us. "Is this what you were doing while I was getting everyone from the airport?"

So much for keeping this secret. Dad is stone-faced, ignoring all of us.

"Where in the hell did Jason get eighty THOUSAND dollars?" she hisses.

Declan recoils from her. "I have no idea."

"I gambled my way up," Dad says from across the table. His eyes meet mine. "I took your seventeen-thousand-dollar wedding fund, honey, and just kept playing hands."

"And now it's up to eighty?" Dec lets out a low whistle. "Good work."

"Thanks."

"JASON!" Mom shouts, her voice a sob. "That's a huge amount of money! Take it off that number right now!"

He ignores her.

"Marie," Declan tries to explain. "It's not a bet on a number. It's—"

Mom tries to get closer to the table. All Declan has to do is glance at two guys who look like they starred in *Breaking Bad* and they close in, forming a wall of muscle between Mom and the table.

"You can't do this!" she cries out.

"Watch us, lady." Whoever said that smirks. The twist of his lip makes my mouth go dry with fear.

"Declan, you have to stop him," I plead, my legs aching as I try to stand, squished in the growing crowd around the table.

"Why?"

"Because he can't jeopardize that kind of money! Eighty thousand dollars will pay off my parents' house! It's a huge amount, and he can't lose it."

"Sure he can."

"No, he can't!"

"He can, Shannon. It's likely. The odds are way worse than 9 to 1."

"But if he loses it..." I lean against him, all hope of rationality gone.

"If he loses it, it'll be of his own free will, a man making a decision to risk it all on the tiniest chance he can make it big. I'm not about to short circuit that."

"How does this work?" I ask in a blind panic.

"He's betting on a tie. That means he's betting that his cards and the dealer's cards will be a tie. The same number." He starts to explain more but gets a look from the dealer that makes him shut up.

I cannot believe that my father is standing in the High Limit room at Litraeon, betting eighty thousand dollars on a game that is about to induce a heart attack in me.

The dealer deals two cards to Dad and all the other players, and two cards to himself. Other players are stationed on either side of Dad, who is number six at the table—the table is full, with fourteen people playing. I don't know much about baccarat, but I know this: Dad's probably the only one betting on a tie.

The cards begin to be revealed. Anyone with a hand that is over nine points is out. Anyone with a hand at nine points wins. No one has nine points.

Dad has a five of diamonds and a three of clubs.

The dealer shows his cards.

A pair of red fours.

The table goes *nuts*.

"Hot damn!" yells one of the players. "The crazy dude got it right!" He walks over to Dad and rubs his head for good luck.

Dad's shoulders sag with relief, his chest puffing up with pride. James is next to me, muttering expletives under his breath, while Declan claps and nods with approval. People are quietly cheering for Dad, clapping him on the back, and the game at the table closer to the main casino breaks, people wandering in to see what's just happened.

"He just took the house for more than seven hundred thou and you're *clapping*?" James admonishes Declan.

"He found his power, Dad."

James frowns, while Mom rushes over to my father and hugs him, jumping up and down like she's being shocked when she touches the ground.

"SEVEN HUNDRED THOUSAND DOLLARS!" Mom screams, hugging and kissing Dad.

Declan weaves his way around the table and shakes Dad's hand. Dad's staring at the stack of chips just as James pushes through and stands next to him, flanked by two guards.

"Actually," the dealer says with a big grin, "you keep your eighty-grand bet, so it's closer to eight hundred thousand."

Mom's eyes explode.

"Congratulations, Jason. That was quite some run," James says. They pump hands and Dad blinks, over and over. People around us are rubbing his shoulder, making supportive comments, and a ton of phones point our way, snapping pictures as the guards try to stop them.

Dad just stands in a daze.

"We're rich!" Mom says, starting to hyperventilate.

The next few seconds tick by in an unreal set of still images. Dad looks down at his hand, clasped in James' own, then up at me. His face is slack, serious and intense. His eyes move to take in Declan, his body not following his own gaze. He looks at the chips. The table. The vested table worker. The hands again.

I see him fighting to breathe normally, how he isn't really there, and if this agony stretches on for three more seconds I'm going to shatter the dissonance with a scream.

Dad saves me.

He looks at James, then points to the chips, which the table worker is counting.

"Those are for you."

James frowns.

"What?"

Dad shoves the stack of chips, upsetting the neat piles, all toward James.

"Take it."

"WHAT?" Mom screams. "JASON! ARE YOU ILL?"

"I was," he says slowly, his smile glorious. "But now I feel so much better." He looks at James and holds out his hand for another shake. James returns the gesture.

"What's this?" he asks.

"Payment," Dad says. "I'm paying for my daughter's wedding."

"But the free publicity more than covers it," James assures him.

"No. Not the same." Dad's eyes bore into James' own. "Street code. I owe you. Debt is now paid."

A long few seconds go by, James holding Dad's gaze.

"*That's* how this all works," Dad adds with a clench of his jaw.

"THAT IS NOT HOW ANY OF THIS WORKS, JASON!"

There's a Wifezilla version of Mom's voice. Who knew?

James and Dad stare at each other, their chests rising and falling with each breath, the skin under their eyes tight with tension and study. Each is trying to read the other, and it's anyone's call who will win.

An imperceptible nod from James ends the standoff. "You sure?" He's alluding to the chips.

"Sure as anything I know."

"I AM NOT SURE! I AM NOT!" Mom screams.

James looks at the pile of chips, and I watch it all in slow motion. He separates them, the eighty-grand original bet in a pile of its own.

He takes the rest and gives my dad the eighty.

Dad scowls. Mom makes a series of moans that make her sound like a professional mourner at an Italian funeral.

"NOOOOOOOOOOOOOOOO," she finally wails.

Jed appears suddenly with two more beefy security guards. "Need help, Mrs. McCormick?" he asks me.

James startles at the sound of my new title, his eyes widening, then watering just slightly. He's in a zone of ultra-focus, unreadable and unreachable within seconds, his attention entirely on my dad.

Whose face relaxes as he offers his hand to James.

The two pump furiously, sly grins spreading across their faces.

"Deal."

When James motions for one of the guards to start taking the larger stack of chips, Mom lets out a bloodcurdling scream aimed at James that includes the words "seven," "mine," "crazy," and "you were such a bad kisser."

Dad walks over to her, his pockets bulging with chips from his win, slings Mom over his shoulder, and marches out of the casino like a caveman.

To the sound of raucous, enthusiastic applause from a bunch of strangers who have no idea what he's doing.

And a bunch of loved ones who do.

* * *

It's our true honeymoon night. Finally. We left the gaggle of friends and family downstairs, Chuckles safely managed by the pet concierge (yes, it's a real job), our bodies burning to join together what our hearts combined today.

"I am sleeping with someone's wife," Declan says, his toe lifting up out of the thick layers of bubbles in the bath, teasing my shoulder.

"You're sleeping with *your* wife."

"You're the first wife I've ever made love to."

"And I'll be your last."

"You'd better be." Haunted eyes meet mine, and the implications of what he's saying make me half-mad with sorrow.

"Amanda says there are new allergy approaches to the anaphylactic risk," I whisper, putting words to the emotions flowing between us like currents. In any other setting, with any other man, I wouldn't talk like this.

But Declan isn't any other man.

"Good. But I don't want to talk about that."

"Me neither." I smile, holding my wet left hand up for the bathroom glow to highlight. "Married. We're married."

"Finally."

"I can't believe my father gambled away my wedding fund, turned it into eight hundred thousand, and gave most of it to your father."

"That's one hell of a dowry," Declan says, deadpan. Then: "Ow! You poked me in the thigh with your foot!"

"You deserved that."

"Watch the balls! Jesus, Shannon. We need those. For later." I know he means for sex, but I also know he's hinting at the future, a time when we'll actively try for children, and the pregnant promise of the rest of our lives together fills me with a warmth the water can't match.

A low, tired laugh makes my chest ripple the hot water. "My mother has a new target now. I was worried she'd never forgive me for escaping the wedding, but now she'll *really* never forgive Dad for handing all that money to James."

"She will."

"How can you be so sure?"

Declan's eyes are closed, his body relaxed again in the water, the white foam covering his chest just under his pecs. "Because they love each other so much."

"Does that mean you forgive me for resort-cheating on you?"

"I do."

I'm skeptical. "You sure?"

"It's not cheating if we own the place."

For that he gets a face full of foam.

And in return, I get a big, soapy kiss.

Ten minutes later, we dry off and crawl into bed, the curtains open, sheers closed, the city lights glowing through the thin, shimmery fabric like stardust illuminated by the dying light of a thousand stars from long before the earth began.

He reaches for my left hand, fingers worrying the thin wedding band. "We're really married," he says, his voice strong, his breath hot against my shoulder.

I find his matching band, hard and cool against the warm skin, light hair encircling the ring. "Yes. It only took two tries to get here." The rustle of skin against soft, Egyptian cotton sheets that feel like silk prickles my ears.

"It took forever. At least, that's what it feels like sometimes. I wish I'd met you sooner." He kisses my neck, his nose brushing against my earlobe, his fingers still tracing my ring as we snuggle between the sheets.

"I wish we'd met sooner, too." He's familiar and new. My husband—and just Declan. We're some kind of different right now, and the change is just enough to make this all unspeakably real, as if every experience I've had before now was just practice for *this*.

"Think of all the years we've wasted," he says, pausing his kisses. We're in no rush. I'm pretty much a sure thing.

You know. For the next sixty years or so.

"You bought me a company."

"Too much?" He's on his side, facing me, his profile in shadow, eyes bright.

"If the only reason you did it was to beat Andrew at his own game, then well played, Declan. Very well played." My hip brushes against his, and as I tuck my legs in, thighs brushing against thighs, my smooth calves finding just the right place to rest between his, the tickle of his body hair makes me smile.

"I did it for you. And me, too. I told you to stop letting people take your power away from you. Turns out I was really talking to myself."

"Is that what you want to do now, Mr. McCormick?" I flatten my palm against his chest, tickling a nipple with my thumb, the tiny point of attention a pleasant bump along the road that leads down to even bigger encounters. "Talk?"

"I—" His voice hitches, and he clears his throat, a sensual sigh emerging in the resulting seconds that tick between talking and what my hand decides to do to my husband.

Flipped on my back by strong, corded arms that know how to say so many words without uttering a sound, Declan's naked body covers mine, parts hard and muscled, some sections peppered with coarse hair, others blissfully smooth and determined to elicit a response from my prone, pinned form. His kiss is neither tender nor rough, but instead a pressing engagement that tells me it's time to descend into a world under the covers, where we make this marriage truly official.

The good old-fashioned way.

After more than two years of making love with each other, you would think this would be routine. Pleasant and passionate, yes, but also a bit too known. A bit too tame. A sequence of moves and touches, mouths and fingers, a joining that is scripted to maximize pleasure, but that comes from a place where the unexpected gives way to the predictable.

But no.

Each time his mouth touches my breast, I shiver like it's the first time. Every sigh, every moan, is a fresh sound. The gravelly sound of his groan sets off new neurons in my brain, a lightning-fast signal speeding through my brain, traveling through my blood to my heart.

The path of love doesn't always make sense, but like the laws of physics, it doesn't care.

We're so serious, Declan taking my face in his hands, the light notes of a symphony rolling out of speakers somewhere in the suite, a low, contemporary sound of music that fills the air with a mood designed to highlight this newness. Never before have we made love for the first time as husband and wife.

And we never will again.

I kiss him, rising up to meet his mouth, the tender taste of him making my mouth tingle. Every breath sounds harsh and soft against my ear. The drag of his lips against my jaw and neck is a world unto itself.

"Shannon," he whispers into the mingling of our breath, mouths so close we become one taste. I sigh, the long exhale a release of the past, my body letting go of uncertainty and fear, and as I breathe in his breath, I feel that grounding I have spent my entire adult life seeking.

Bloom where you're planted, they say. Tonight we do just that, in each other.

"Declan," I gasp, his name tickling my mouth, which soon meets his lips as his hands touch me in gentle and slow ways, fingers lighting my skin with love that masquerades itself as passion. The cold slide of my wedding and engagement bands against his inner arm leads to the metal absorbing the heat from his blood that pumps to the surface, the exchange of warmth from his heart to my ring a transfer that leaps from organism to object, turning physics on its head.

Turning love into a physical transfer, from his body to mine.

My hands ride up from his hips to the tight band of muscle at the base of his ribs, counting one, two, three...and losing count as he enters me, my gasp against his mouth making him quicken, our bodies connected in the most spiritual of ways.

"Mrs. McCormick," he whispers, the words punctuated by a delightful sigh, then a groan that tightens into a raw sounds that I am privileged to witness, for I am the only person who will hear them.

*Ever.*

"I am," I murmur back, the words replaced by emotion that jumps from skin to skin, dancing across the electricity that friction and love so deliciously create.

In the part of my soul that only Declan has glimpsed, but not yet touched, I hear the distinct sound of steel on steel, feel the scrape of yet another key sliding into a lock, sense the tingling hope that *this* is the one, a prayer which resides, ever present, in the ever-searching fingers of the holder of the key ring.

*Click.*

With great love, the tumblers release, the key holder's hand shaking in exaltation as love turns, turns, turns and releases, Declan's soul unlocking my own, reuniting what was once whole but has spent lifetimes seeking reunion.

Our eyes meet and our bodies fall away as he presses into me, affixing me in place, planting himself in the fertile ground of *us*.

We dissolve.

We merge.

We join.

*And they shall become one flesh.*

# Chapter Twenty-Two

"She's not answering her phone."

"Neither is he."

"We can't leave without saying good-bye."

"And I don't want to leave without grinding it in a little more with Andrew." Declan takes a sip of the latte he had delivered earlier and laughs, a loose sound of joy and victory. "*Grind* it in. Get it? And you're right. This coffee is the *best* I've ever tasted."

I groan. Now that he owns the damn company, *of course* it's the World's Greatest Coffee. Declan's never met a superlative that could be applied to his own business that he didn't love.

In this case, it's true.

We've been up, showered, dressed and packed for the past half hour, already late for a flight to Hawaii, but when you fly in a private corporate jet, the pilot waits for you. We decided on Hawaii and Japan for our honeymoon, but I don't want to leave without my good-byes. We'd like to get Amanda and Andrew in first, because I don't know what we're going to find with Mom and Dad and the seven-hundred-thousand-dollar-giveaway fiasco.

"I'm worried, Dec. Amanda was supposed to meet me for coffee. She's not answering. What's their room number?"

Instead of answering, he walks to the phone and dials. I hear the phone ring and ring and ring, until he puts the receiver in the cradle.

"Nothing. They're not answering." He shrugs. "Maybe they're out?"

"They partied long after we went to bed. Didn't you get the crazy texts? Amanda's became increasingly less readable until finally they looked like Chuckles was typing for her. And that was an *improvement*. I can't imagine they went anywhere this morning."

"Maybe we should give them some peace." He frowns. "Though I'm surprised I haven't heard from Andrew."

"But I want to see her! She's my bestie!"

Declan's sigh could warm the arctic. "Fine." He picks up his smartphone and taps, then looks at me. "Let's meet Jed at their door."

"Their door?" I ask stupidly.

"If something's wrong, he can open the door and we can check on them." A chill runs through me, taking all the loveliness of last night with it. Declan can tell, lacing his fingers through mine, his thumb rubbing the back of my hand.

"I'm sure they're fine. Probably just drunk and passed out."

"Both of them? Andrew's not the type to ignore his phone for this long, either. I know from Amanda. She feels like it's his other girlfriend."

Declan's laugh makes something in me unclench. "Mistress Siri?"

"Something like that."

*Bzzzz.*

"Is it Andrew? Amanda?" I leap up and practically rip the phone from Declan's hands. He just holds it up in the air, like a guy with a lighter at a concert.

*Tap tap tap.*

"It's Jed," the voice behind the door says.

Declan gives me a withering look and opens the door. Jed stands there, tense like a Secret Service agent, his Bluetooth earpiece yammering in tinny intervals.

We leave our suite and walk to the elevator in silence, wending our way through the enormous resort to Andrew's private room. He and Amanda didn't even bother with the pretense of giving her a separate room.

*Tap tap tap.*

Nothing.

Jed tries again. *Tap tap tap.*

Nothing.

"Mr. McCormick?" Jed says in *sotto voce* against the door.

Nothing.

Jed and Declan share a look, and Dec nods.

"Go ahead. Enter the room. I'll take full responsibility."

Using a special keycard on a cord, Jed waves it in front of the electronic door reader, and the lock opens. Dec slowly inches the door in, me behind him, Jed tastefully waiting in the hall, but at the ready should we need him.

The first sign that something's wrong is the scent. Dear God, did they paint the walls with alcohol in here?

"Ugh," Declan grunts, covering his face with his palm, breathing through his mouth. "What the hell did they do—move the tequila fountain from downstairs in here?"

"Andrew's the CEO. Who knows?" We walk about eight feet into the suite, the bathroom door on the left, the living room directly ahead, bedroom door closed, on the right.

While the living room isn't exactly clean, and is littered with alcohol bottles, half-full glasses of mixed drinks, and what looks like Amanda's infamous Cheeto-marshmallow treat crumbs, no one's dead in here.

I hope.

*Tap tap tap.*

Declan knocks on the bedroom door. No answer.

He pulls out his phone and texts someone.

*Bzzzz.*

We can hear the phone buzz behind the bedroom door.

My eyes fly wide open. So do Declan's. The buzzing is loud. Why isn't Andrew answering?

Panic fills my chest. "Open the door!" I urge. "Amanda!" I start knocking.

"You sure?" Dec's hand goes to the doorknob, but he pauses. "He could be naked."

"So what?"

Declan makes a face. "I don't want you to see my brother's junk."

"They could be hurt or in danger, and you're worried about whether I see Andrew's *penis*?"

He shrugs. He doesn't move.

*Men.*

I shove past him, open the door, and halt.

Two lumps—clearly bodies—are under the covers of the enormous bed. A pair of men's underwear hangs from the ceiling fan, which whirrs slowly, the motor whining because in addition to that pair of underwear, there is a giant soap-on-a-rope dangling from another blade.

In the shape of a marijuana leaf that is at least twelve inches wide.

The floor is covered in a mixture of clothing, shoes, Cheetos, Star Wars action figures, empty alcohol bottles, a pet carrier, and—

"Is that pile of clothes moving?" Declan asks with alarm.

A translucent plastic thing shakes its way out from under a silver disco top, a fabric I vaguely recall Amanda wearing yesterday evening.

"Meow."

Chuckles' face pokes out from a plastic Cone of Shame, his *meow* pointed at Declan.

Written in purple Sharpie, on the side of the cone, are the words:

WILL SLEEP WITH PUSSY FOR FOOD

"Chuckles!" I gasp, but Declan beats me to it, bending down to pick up my poor cat, who is wearing...lipstick? And someone has attached hundreds of fake whiskers to the outer edge of the cone, making it look like the mouth of a hookworm.

"What the hell happened in here?" Dec barks.

Andrew's head pops up from the foot of the bed, his neck and shoulders bare. "WHAT THE FUCK?" he bellows, which causes Chuckles to hiss and claw at Declan, who drops my cat right on the other lump in the bed.

Chuckles's back arches up and he hisses again.

"AIIIIIIEEEEE!" screams the lump from under the covers. I'd know that scream anywhere. It's Amanda.

"Thank God you're okay," I shout over her piercing screams.

"Claws! Claws!" she gasps. "I've had enough cat claws. Get him off me." Her bare arms reach out from under the sheet, still bandaged from her animal encounter a few days ago. I wince in sympathy.

Declan has the presence of mind to reach down and pluck Chuckles off the covers and hand him over to me, but we see why Amanda screamed: Chuckles' claws are out, deeply embedded in the duvet. I assume they went through the thin sheet that is the only cover Amanda has. Andrew reaches over to hold her in his arms, and sunlight catches something on his left hand.

I'm not the only one who notices.

"Is that a *ring*?" Dec asks, dropping Chuckles like a hot potato and taking a step forward over the thick layers of clothing and crap on the floor. He grabs Andrew's left hand and stares at it, transfixed, like those cartoon characters whose eyes turn into spirals.

Andrew's hair is standing up on end, and Amanda's hair looks like it went through a salad spinner coated with yogurt. I can't see her hands, which are under the covers, but a creepy-crawly feeling begins in the pit of my stomach.

I lurch toward her and my foot—my beautiful, Charlotte Olympia-covered foot—lands on something soft that says, "Oof."

Clothing doesn't *talk*.

I look down to find two eyes peeking out around a thick terrycloth robe that is littered with chocolate boxes from the chocolatier in the resort's mall. When I say littered, I mean *littered*. There must be no fewer than fifty such boxes. How many French macarons and bacon-lavender-infused plaid chocolates did these people eat?

"Shannon," the clothing pile groans.

"JOSH?" I gasp.

He sits up, thankfully clothed, wearing the same outfit I remember from last night.

"AIIIIIIEEEEEE!" Amanda screams again, holding her left hand away from her body like it's a poisonous snake about to bite her.

Her hand is *shiny*.

And there it is.

A ring.

"WHAT DID YOU TWO DO?" Declan bellows, the sound a sonic boom.

Josh does a weird jazz-hands thing and squeals, "Oh, my God, it's contagious!"

He's wearing a ring on *his* left ring finger.

Amanda faints.

Chuckles sniffs around what appears to be Andrew's shoe, stops himself, and looks over my shoulder. I follow his gaze. Behind me is a six-foot-tall stuffed teddy bear.

My cat's face breaks out into a look I know.

It's the look Mom gets when she watches *Sons of Anarchy*.

Pandemonium breaks out as Declan gets right in Andrew's face, shouting all sorts of profanity I've only read on Urban Dictionary but didn't know people actually used in real life. Andrew's patting Amanda's face and looking around the room like he's woken up in the middle of a hurricane, and meanwhile the giant soap pot leaf and men's undies on the ceiling fan go *whee-whee-whee* like a soundtrack of the damned.

And Chuckles is claiming his territory one pee-soaked piece of fake fur at a time, starting with the giant stuffed animal's head. Once his bladder empties, he climbs down the monstrosity, shredding the teddy's face, and rubs against my calves. I pick him up and he purrs.

In the middle of it all, a blitz of multicolored neon hair shoots up from the other side of the bed, where we can't see the floor, and it crouches, warrior-style, holding a can of pepper spray in one hand and a baseball bat in the other. A dark brown baseball bat.

No. Wait.

That's a three-foot-long chocolate penis that looks awfully familiar. I open my mouth to tell him that is pretty much the least effective weapon for self-defense *ever*, when I'm interrupted.

"Geordi?" Josh shouts.

"Geordi?" Dec and I say in unison. What the hell is our chauffeur doing here?

Geordi drops the chocolate dildo, abandons the pepper spray, and rushes over to Josh, cradling his face. "Oh, my God! It wasn't a dream. You're still here."

The owner of the men's underwear on the ceiling fan becomes evident. Geordi's wearing a button-down men's dress shirt and socks.

And nothing else.

Josh, being a gentleman, grabs the duvet and covers Geordi, who reaches up to clasp Josh's shoulder and freezes.

"What is that?" he says in a tone of disgust, pointing to his left ring finger.

Amanda comes to and looks around, palms on either side of her head. "Stop playing the tuba," she whines.

"No one is playing the tuba," Declan snaps. He gives the entire room a glare worthy of James.

"Amanda," I say gently, letting Chuckles down so he can—I don't know—go find some pussy to sleep with. "What happened?"

"Who the hell is she married to?" Andrew groans as Amanda jumps away from him, almost letting one boob show. She pins her head in place with her hands and looks at him.

"Who am I married to? What? What kind of question is that?"

"There are three men in here with wedding rings on!" Andrew shouts back.

"That's riiiiiiigggght," Josh says, drawing out the word, wiggling his hand with a grin. He gives Andrew a saucy look. "And the Supreme Court declared last year that I can marry anyone I want, too."

Andrew already looks like hell warmed over, but that comment drains the *hell* from his blood.

I look at Amanda, then Andrew, then Geordi, my eyes slow and steady, my breathing controlled and strong. Finally, I settle on Andrew, and just as I'm about to speak, Declan beats me to it.

"Little bro, the more important question is: who the hell are *you* married to?"

:)

# Shannon and Declan are husband and wife! But what about Amanda and Andrew?

What's next for Amanda and Andrew as they figure out what happened? Will Shannon and Declan finally get their honeymoon?

**We skipped right over the whole fiancée thing and went straight from girlfriend to wife.**

At least, I think that's what happened. I woke up after my brother's Vegas wedding reception with my luscious girlfriend in bed with me. We're both wearing wedding rings.

So is her coworker, Josh.

And our Vegas chauffeur, Geordi.

Who the hell am I married to?

Unraveling this mystery will be as difficult as figuring out why Amanda and I are having panic attacks over the thought of being husband and wife.

Or, whoever we're actually married to.

Oh, ^%$#.

It's true that what happens in Vegas stays in Vegas, with one exception:

If she's my wife, we'll make it work.

If she's not?

I'll make it happen.

You can read *Shopping for a CEO's Fiancée,* the next in the Shopping series, now! Keep flipping for a sneak peek at Chapter One!

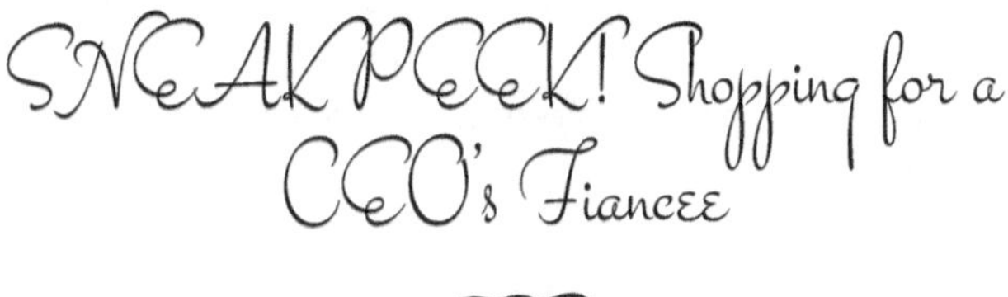


## Chapter One

Waking up naked with your face between your girlfriend's legs is the *best* way to start your morning in Vegas.

With your brother screaming at you from the other side of the covers? Not so much.

Amanda's thighs make great pillows that muffle out my brother bellowing, "What the hell happened in here?" His outrage makes the mattress vibrate, like those beds in seedy motels on television shows. In a pinch, Declan's yell is worth a quarter. Maybe fifty cents.

I sit up and scream back, "WHAT THE FUCK?"

Because that is a perfect example of executive mastery and grace under pressure.

It's the morning after my brother's wedding. I am in my hotel suite here at Litraeon, the Las Vegas Strip resort owned by my company, Anterdec. My girlfriend, Amanda, is with me. We're both naked. We should be alone.

We're *not*.

That needs to be rectified.

My head fills with metal shavings masquerading as lightning bolts that run through my veins. I flop back, eyes closed.

The world needs to stop spinning. Now.

I reach for Amanda. Her soft, creamy skin anchors me to the world. She's mine again. Mine. All mine. She moans, the sound unrecognizable. It's nothing like the little gasp I elicit during intimate moments. She sounds like Gloria Steinem at a Ted Cruz rally.

If I ignore Declan, he'll go away. Maybe this is a nightmare.

"ANDREW!"

Nope.

I lift my arm to rub my eyes and ask Declan why the hell he's barging in on Amanda and me. Who keyed him into my suite? Someone on our security team is getting fired. Besides, it's the first day of his honeymoon. Doesn't he have something better to do right now?

Something deep in my core stirs, a discontent that is both familiar and exasperating.

I start to rub my eyes in a weak attempt to wake up and—

Wait. What's that weight on my left hand?

And when the hell did Declan start to look so much like my dad? My vision clears and there's Dec, standing next to Shannon, who is watching Amanda with an intensity I've only seen in one other woman, ever.

Jessica Coffin.

"Is that a wedding ring on your left hand?" Declan shouts, like I'm Gollum and he's Sauron. What ring? What the hell is he talking about?

I check my hands. Right hand clear. Left hand—

Uh, oh. How did *that* get there?

Amanda screams. My sister-in-law's cat, Chuckles, is on the bed. He's wearing a veterinarian's surgical cone with the words "WILL SLEEP WITH PUSSY FOR FOOD" written in Sharpie.

The handwriting is familiar.

*Too* familiar.

Chuckles claws Amanda, yielding a wild shriek from both. Declan gets the cat off her and she sits up and—

She's Gollum, too. Yep.

My precious has the Ring.

Amanda starts saying something about a tuba, and then her friend Josh pops up from the floor. He looks like a really whiny ninja with no body fat. He's fully dressed, fastidiously so.

I clear my throat and start to stand, ready to resume control over this mess. The stirring inside me has taken more breaths and awakens, assessing, observing. Time to exert authority over these people. The cacophony is too much. I can't take it. They need to do exactly what I tell them, which means *leave*.

I stand.

I'm naked. Damn.

Unlike my brother, I don't believe in parading my junk for the world to see. Only people with something to prove need to do that.

You know. Like guys who aren't CEOs of Fortune 500 companies.

I clutch the covers. My stomach twists. I feel like a victim in a Dexter episode, except there's been a mistake. Amanda's pinning her head in place with her palms, and a weird ringing fills my head. Josh has his hand in the air, a strange glare of sunlight on—

Oh, shit. A ring.

What the hell *happened* last night?

Rainbows explode all over the other side of the bed. Rainbows and chocolate penises. A chocolate penis the size of a baseball bat is in the hands of a guy wearing a tie-dyed shirt and a head made of rainbow hair.

This is all a dream, right? The rainbow is wearing a wedding ring, but no underwear, and a sudden, cold clarity hits me as I look around the room.

I have a wedding ring.

Amanda has a wedding ring.

Josh has a wedding ring.

Rainbow chocolate-dong-holding dude has a wedding ring.

One of the hallmarks of my moving up the ranks so quickly at Anterdec has been my split-second decision-making ability, and my willingness to take business risks that scare the hell out of anyone else. Puzzle pieces fall in place in seconds when I observe, analyze and act. No wishy-washy wondering.

Intuition kicks in. Judgment is based on the gut. Decisions rest on data points and an ambiguous collection of—

Hold on. Sunlight passes over Amanda's left hand.

"Who the hell is *she* married to?" I ask Declan, pointing at Amanda. Her skin is so luscious in this morning light. A lovely, healthy glow that reminds me of sunsets on the ocean.

Then I narrow my eyes and realize her breasts are orange.

Day-glo orange. The nipples are paler than the rest, like eyes.

Shannon's damn cat pees all over the really nice giant teddy bear I bought Amanda, prances over, and leaps into Declan's arms. I want to ask how my brother trained the cat to do that, but Amanda's screaming in my ear.

"Who am *I* married to? What? What kind of question is that?" she snaps. I liked her better when she moaned like Rachel Maddow interviewing the Zodiac Killer at a presidential primary.

"There are three men in here with wedding rings on!" I shout back. Only one of us should be her husband, of course. *Me*.

I pause. Why did I think that? I don't want to marry Amanda. Not yet, at least.

Not *yet*. Not...what? What am I thinking?

"That's riiiiiiigggght," Josh says. "And the Supreme Court declared last year that I can marry anyone I want, too." He wiggles his eyebrows at me like I'm a dessert buffet. "You could be my hubby!"

Guys have hit on me before. It's cool. Signals get crossed.

But hold on, here.

Josh is not my type.

If I had a guy type, I mean.

Oh, hell.

Declan's voice cuts through it all. "Little bro, the more important question is: who the hell are *you* married to?"

My brother has this way of looking at me that combines disgust, amusement, determination and just enough abuse to make me jump off the bed, nakedness be damned, and tackle him around the waist.

And right into the giant teddy bear.

"Ooooo! Cat pee! Cat pee!" Shannon squeals.

"Cat fight! Cat fight!" Josh shouts, clapping. "My bet's on my hubby, Andrew!"

"I am not your husband!" I shout, my cheek against Declan's belt.

"You don't knoooooow that," Josh calls back.

"Why is Andrew's mouth orange?" someone asks.

"I'm *Shannon's* husband, you dumbass!" Dec grunts. "Speaking of which—hey! Shannon! Get a spray bottle!" Dec calls out.

"Why? Just wrestle him off you. He's drunk and in pain. You can take him," she replies.

Shannon has a hidden dark side.

"I don't know where to put my hands!" Dec confesses. "His junk is everywhere!"

"That—*grunt*—is because—*grunt*—my junk is so big —*grunt*," I groan.

"YOU BOYS STOP RIGHT NOW."

As if this couldn't get any worse. Just did.

That's my dad.

We ignore him.

Like hell I'm giving up.

"You are such a little shit," Declan hisses, as he tries to fight me without actually touching my bare skin.

I am winning.

And then Dad shouts to Shannon, she tosses something at him, and I hear:

"This is remarkably satisfying, Shannon! You're on to something," he says with a tone of admiration, as I get a face full of water mist. Declan lets go.

"For the record," I say, wiping my cheeks, "you let go first. I win."

"Dad sprayed us like dogs!"

I rush him again, but he stops me with arms of steel.

Mine, however, are titanium. We lock grips and wait, poised.

"Andrew James McCormick, you just blew off a two-hour meeting with the Sultan of Al-Massi. The damage control on this is incalculable. I didn't build this company just so you could tear it down because you were on a bender in Vegas!" Dad roars, his body tense and immobile, but his voice carefully calculated to intimidate.

That doesn't work on me, though. It makes me let go of Declan, who casually hands me something from the floor to cover my groin. It's brown and plush but it makes me respectable.

*Ish.*

"I'll fix it," I snap.

Amanda gives me an odd look, then goes back to fighting her inner tubas.

"No time." Dad turns to Declan and looks him over. Dec is dressed in a bespoke suit from a tailor I discovered and referred him to. "Your brother, unlike you, looks professional enough for a meeting with the Sultan."

"Or a Moroccan stripper," Shannon whispers in a weirdly bitter tone that makes Declan's eyebrow arch.

Declan's demeanor changes instantly, his stance uncomfortable. Shannon averts her eyes and the two look like teenagers at a dance in *Napoleon Dynamite*, trying to figure out how to fit in.

"How," Josh asks, peering intently at my crotch, "did you turn your love pole into a Wookiee?"

"Love pole?" The entire room says the phrase in unison, and in the *exact* tone I'm thinking.

I look down. Dec handed me a Chewbacca stuffed toy as my junk cover.

"Maybe he just wants a little Chewie down there," Rainbow dude notes, as he starts to back out of the room, taking Josh with him. Self-preservation is a strong instinct.

Rainbow dude finally covers himself. I hold one finger up to Dad, like I'm pausing him.

Dad doesn't handle being paused well.

"Well," Josh says slowly, giving Rainbow dude, who I realize is one of the chauffeurs (George? Geoff?) a series of nervous looks. "We snuck back in to find Geordi's pants sometime after three a.m., I think."

Geordi. That's right.

"And my dong." Geordi holds up the item in question. The chocolate is starting to melt in his hand.

"So you didn't sleep in the room all night? You weren't, er...." Shannon grimaces, looking at Dec, who gets an *aha!* expression on his face.

"This wasn't a foursome?" Dec asks bluntly.

"What a ridiculous question!" Dad shouts, exploding on the spot.

"Oh, no!" Josh squeals, flailing his hands. "No, no, no! I don't sleep with—" He breaks off the sentence and looks at me, biting his lower lip, eyes filled with the kind of panic usually reserved for contestants on *Hell's Kitchen* who move a basil leaf counterclockwise as Gordon Ramsay's coming over.

"You don't sleep with...what?" I ask.

"I don't sleep with *women*!" He points at Amanda like she's wearing a scarlet letter on her chest.

A scarlet W.

"And I don't sleep with gay guys!" Amanda moans back.

"Aside from that hook-up our freshman year," Shannon whispers.

"You pinkie promised never to talk about him!" Amanda hisses.

Declan and Dad start hooting.

"Trust me," Josh says in an acid tone. "The only two people in this room who had sex last night were you and Amanda." He looks down with a forlorn look.

Declan thumbs toward Shannon. "Actually, we did, too."

Josh's turn for a raised eyebrow. "In this room? Kinky."

Declan shuts him up with a glare. Josh and Geordi wisely leave.

"Now that we've gone into more detail about my sons' sex lives than an IRS audit, could we please get back to the fact that the CEO of the company I built from scratch is currently wearing a Star Wars action figure as a penis cozy and can't perform his job!"

You can guess who said that.

"Technically," I correct him, looking down, "this isn't a Star Wars action figure. That would be far too small to cover my—"

"Are you really arguing with the semantics about a stuffed Chewbacca toy?" Dad snaps.

"Declan can't take that meeting with the Sultan, Dad," I grind out, trying to take the heat off me.

"Why not? You're here, Dec. Delay the honeymoon by a few hours." Dad's hand does the familiar dismissal gesture. "The jet can wait."

"No, Dad," I explain, trying to catch Declan's eye. He won't give it to me.

"Andrew, you smell like a distillery and—" he sniffs the air. "And oddly enough, cat urine. You're standing in a disgusting room filled with people who are staring at your naked body while you use Disney merchandise in a decidedly unconventional manner. You're hardly in any position to argue with me over whether Declan is a better fit for representing Anterdec in a high-level meeting for a multi-*billion* dollar deal."

I try. Declan has a chance to cough it up on his own. Instinct makes me pause. Or maybe that's nausea, roiling in my gut. What the hell did I drink last night? Normally, I can hold my own with liquor. I go up to the line, and even cross it by a single, regrettable drink, but I don't do what I've clearly done to my body.

Mustering clarity, I give Declan a hard look. Silence.

Huh.

Looks like he isn't going to step up, after all.

"Declan resigned from Anterdec last night, Dad. He bought a coffee chain for Shannon and he's declared himself the CEO of the new company. He can't represent Anterdec because he doesn't work for us anymore."

Declan flinches at the word *us*.

If I had any muscles to spare, I would, too. It sounds really awful coming out of my mouth, and a part of me wishes I could take it back.

But not a big part.

Declan clears his throat and does the unexpected. He reaches into his breast pocket and pulls out another resignation letter. I had to lead the way. Big brother follows.

Does this really have to happen *now*?

Dad looks at me with disgust, then turns his attention to Declan, brow turned down, the lower half of his face blank. He starts reading the letter just as Amanda's mother, Pam, appears behind him, stepping gingerly through the mess on the floor, her eyes catching mine, briefly stopping at the beast I'm pressing over my groin to hide my...beast.

Her teacup Chihuahua, Spritzy, jumps out of her little handbag and sniffs the area around the giant teddy bear. Then he lifts his leg and does what any self-respecting male would do.

Claims his territory.

"You *resigned*?" Dad's words scream in my head, echoing off the walls of my skull like—

Like a tuba. Amanda's got a point.

Dec squares his shoulders and faces Dad, and now I smile.

Achievement unlocked: deflection complete.

"Yes." Declan's voice is forceful. He won't take crap from Dad. Shannon moves closer, her fingers wrapping around Declan's elbow, and for the first time in my life, I think Declan has a shot at truly taking on Dad. In a game of tennis, this would be *Point*.

"You can't resign!"

"Just did."

"I won't allow it."

Oh, big mistake. Big mistake, Dad. When we were kids, the worst phrase you could utter to Declan was "You can't."

"Allow?" Declan's across the room in a flash, right in Dad's face, making Pam take a step back. Spritzy rushes across the room, collar jangling like he's Quasimodo the serial killer, destroying me and Amanda with that gong of a collar.

"That's right." Dad won't back down.

"I do not need your permission to buy my own company and to resign from yours."

I flinch at the word *yours*.

*Set.*

When my mother died, I woke up in the hospital to a life that was someone else's. Nothing made sense. Dad was angry, Declan was shut down, and Terry was off at college. He came back for the funeral and disappeared again. Mom was gone.

One arena made sense, though: business. Joining Dad in running Anterdec was the only way to get his attention.

And now Dec is leaving.

Sharing Dad's attention is one thing. Being the top dog and edging Dec out just slightly is enough.

Having the full fire hose of James McCormick's expectations aimed at your face is more than enough.

I have a beast inside me. No, not the flesh stick between my legs.

This creature has no name. It thrives on control and vigilance. It needs to know all. Complete control is not its goal. Oddly enough, it defers at times. Rare times.

*Very* rare moments.

This is not one of them.

"ENOUGH!" I bellow, dropping the Chewbacca pillow, because why not? I have nothing to lose.

I bend down and find the first piece of clothing that will cover my body. It's the pink robe I bought Amanda when we arrived. The one with lace at the breasts. I'm not picky. I'm not one of those guys whose masculinity is threatened by feminine attire.

Not that I have a history with that. It's just that pink lace is an upgrade from Peter Mayhew.

True to form, Dad doesn't budge, Declan shifts his weight to one hip and thinks he can give me a blank, intimidating look and that will work, and the rest of the interlopers actually do move toward the doorway.

Amanda starts to crawl out of bed.

"Not you. *Them.*"

"But I need to pee. And quit staring at my breasts. You always stare at my breasts."

"That's because they're luscious."

"Oh, brother," Dad and Dec say at the same time, finally moving toward the door.

"So firm and supple," I continue.

Declan glares. Pam looks like she's starting to faint. Dad grabs her arm and escorts her out of the bedroom.

Ordering them out of the room doesn't work, but talking about Amanda's naked body does? Fine. I take a deep breath and ignore the nine-member funk band in my head and start to talk about my favorite subject.

She looks down and screams bloody murder.

"I look like a human Cheeto!"

And then she faints.

"OUT!" I shout.

They listen to me. People do. I have a voice that makes it clear that not following my command is not an option.

Though I'm guessing that the Chewbacca crotch had something do with their exit.

I join Amanda under the covers and pass out.

*Match*.

**Read the rest of Shopping for a CEO's Fiancee *wherever you find books.***

# Other Books by Julia Kent

Suggested Reading Order

Shopping for a Billionaire
Shopping for a Billionaire's Fiancée
Shopping for a CEO
Shopping for a Billionaire's Wife
Shopping for a CEO's Fiancée
Shopping for an Heir
Shopping for a Billionaire's Honeymoon
Shopping for a CEO's Wife
Shopping for a Billionaire's Baby
Shopping for a CEO's Honeymoon
Shopping for a Baby's First Christmas
Shopping for a CEO's Baby
Shopping for a Yankee Swap

Shopping for a Turkey
Shopping for a Highlander

Never Plan a Billionaire's Wedding

Love You Wrong
Love You Right
Love You Again
Love You More
Love You Now
Love You Fiancee

Little Miss Perfect
Fluffy
Perky
Feisty
Hasty
Tasty

Random Acts of Crazy
Random Acts of Trust
Random Acts of Fantasy
Random Acts of Hope
Randomly Acts of Yes
Random Acts of Love
Random Acts of LA
Random Acts of Christmas
Random Acts of Vegas
Random Acts of New Year
Random Acts of Baby

In Your Dreams
Her Billionaires
It's Complicated
Completely Complicated
It's Always Complicated
Eternally Complicated

Maliciously Obedient
Suspiciously Obedient
Deliciously Obedient
Christmasly Obedient

Our Options Have Changed (with Elisa Reed)

Thank You For Holding (with Elisa Reed)

# About the Author

SIGN UP FOR MY NEWSLETTER ->
EEPURL.COM/UXB4R


*New York Times* and *USA Today* bestselling author Julia Kent writes romantic comedy with an edge. Since 2013, she has sold more than 2.5 million books, with 5 *New York Times* bestsellers and more than 23 appearances on the *USA Today* bestseller list. Her books have been translated into French and German, with more languages coming.

From billionaires to BBWs to new adult rock stars, Julia finds a sensual, goofy joy in every contemporary romance she writes. Unlike Shannon from Shopping for a Billionaire, she did not meet her husband after dropping her phone in a men's room toilet (and he isn't a billionaire).

She lives in New England with her husband and three kids in a household where only she has the gene necessary to change toilet paper rolls.

She loves to hear from her readers by email at jkentauthor@gmail.com, on Twitter @jkentauthor, on Facebook at https://www.facebook.com/jkentauthor . Visit her at http://jkentauthor.com

# Join My Substack!

What the heck is a Substack, you ask? It's like a blog/newsletter/podcast, all rolled into one.

You don't just get an email from me saying "Hey, buy my books!"

Instead, you get a richer, more fun experience, with posts/newsletters that are designed to be savored over a long stretch in a comfortable chair, sipping your beverage of choice while you laugh, imagine, and stay entertained.

You can read one (or more) of my posts here, and sign up on the spot to get my "Julia Kent's Writing Cabin" delivered to you at least once a week.

https://juliakent.substack.com

Many posts include an audio conversation between me and my husband, Clark. We talk about my books, ideas about romance, and so much more. Sometimes we're even funny! ;)

I'm having so much fun reliving into topics ranging from wedding romance to one-night stands to cover design to food insecurity and volunteering. Designed to be a free-flowing place for ideas, my little online writing cabin invites you to come on in, take a seat by the fire, and chat with me and other readers in the comments.

Or just read. It's all up to you.

<3